PRAISE FOR *MY THO*

Cast in the form of a diary written by Thomas Jefferson's wife, Martha, Grimes's first novel chronicles the years from their courtship in 1770 to her death in 1782. Atmospheric and richly detailed, with exact accounts of such contemporary activities as leaching lye and boiling soap, the novel captures the personalities of two extraordinary people and the tumult of the Revolutionary War that consumed their lives. We view the conflict through the prism of Martha's sharply perceptive mind; the maneuvers of the era's famous men—George Washington, Patrick Henry, and Benedict Arnold—form a well-integrated backdrop to her story.

The novel also traces Martha's evolution from a self-indulgent Southern belle to an outspoken young mother with radical social views; conversations with her slave Betty on the explosive subjects of emancipation and miscegenation are revealing of the complex relationship between white and black Americans in the 18th century. Thomas Jefferson's steady rise as a lawyer, lawmaker, and statesman takes second place here to his role as husband, father, and lover, so shattered by his young wife's death that he never remarried. The moving tale succeeds both as a gripping historical saga and a powerful love story.

—*Publisher's Weekly*

My Thomas a literary tour de force

Roberta Grimes's first major novel is a marvel, a historical novel whose detail, scope and depth seem much greater than the book's slightly more than 300 pages. *My Thomas* captures the complicated nature and depth of Thomas Jefferson's wife, Martha, who died just ten years after the couple were married and whom Jefferson mourned the rest of his life.

The novel is presented as Martha's own journal of her life with Thomas, and the hand of the author is neither seen nor felt anywhere in the book. The reader is totally immersed in Martha's life, in the person she must have been.

Grimes's mastery of the tone of life in late 18th century Virginia is complete. Her characters live, breathe, and speak with such truth and realism that the reader is drawn unconsciously into the complicated and fascinating lives of Martha and Thomas.

Not since Michael Shaara's Pulitzer Prize-winning novel of the battle of Gettysburg, *Killer Angels*, have I read such a fine historical novel.

—Daniel L. Mallock, *The Patriot Ledger*, Quincy, MA

I loved it… The greatest compliment I can pay this novel is to say I was furious when it ended. I wanted much, much more of Martha, I was so beguiled by her. I have no doubt at all this novel will be an enormous success—after all, how rare is it to find a novel so quiet and yet startling, so dignified and yet passionate, so sincere and so deductive.

—Margaret Forster, author of *Lady's Maid*

Roberta Grimes is a highly intelligent and richly gifted writer. Those with a curiosity about the American past will read *My Thomas* with delight and urge it upon their friends.

—Alf J. Mapp, Jr., author of *Thomas Jefferson: Passionate Pilgrim*

Such a different, interesting and insightful look at the family life of Thomas Jefferson. Martha was truly the love of his life yet I think there were times that in her short life she doubted that. She never failed to support him and stood by his decisions even if she did not agree. Definitely an historical novel "must read."

—Charleysangel, Amazon.com

I don't know how much of this book is factual, but it was very romantic and endearing, exciting with all the moves during the war, sad with all the children Martha lost, and had interesting dynamics between Martha and the slaves. I really enjoyed it. A great read!

—C. Lane, Amazon.com

An excellent book about the life of one of the most elusive of the presidents' wives. I would definitely recommend it for anyone interested in learning more about Thomas Jefferson, and also for anyone who is interested in the presidents' lives and their families.

—Zann A. Gibson, Amazon.com

Loved the book! So well written. I learned so much about that period of history, from the extremely vivid descriptions.

—Rebecca K. Isley, Amazon.com

LETTER

⁓ FROM ⁓

MONEY

❧By the Author❧

FICTION:

My Thomas

Rich and Famous

Letter from Freedom

Letter from Money

Letter from Wonder

NONFICTION:

The Fun of Dying – Find Out What Really Happens Next!

The Fun of Staying in Touch

The Fun of Growing Forever (2017)

THE LETTERS FROM LOVE SERIES

LETTER

⋈ FROM ⋈

MONEY

ROBERTA GRIMES

Published by Wheatmark®
1760 East River Road, Suite 145
Tucson, Arizona 85718 U.S.A.
www.wheatmark.com

ISBN: 978-1-62787-054-2 (paperback)
ISBN: 978-1-62787-055-9 (ebook)
LCCN: 2013952361

Rev201401

This story is lovingly dedicated to all those who struggled and sacrificed to pass down to us their American dream, and to our grandchildren, for whom it is our legacy.

⊰ The Letters from Love Series ⊱

Letters from Love is a collection of independent novels that together tell the tale of three generations of a wealthy American family. Although *Letter from Freedom* comes first in time, these novels can be read in any order. For example, you might begin with either *Letter from Money* or *Letter from Wonder*, both of which are set in this century, and then read *Letter from Freedom* as their backstory. How ever you choose to read them, thank you for joining me in this adventure!

⫷ 1 ⫸

The season of little leaves was so far advanced that Liz had been feeling a thrilling in the trees as she passed them, roiling cascades of energy that felt to her like a soft sizzle. It was lovely, although sometimes it did trouble her to realize that plants everywhere must be giving off perceptible energies this way, and only on this tiny island were human minds developed enough to notice.

Her climb through the woods was becoming steeper. The opening onto the windmill hill was ahead. Then Liz was stepping from the forest path directly onto sheep-cropped grass that giggled softly in the sunlight. There before her was the big umbrella tree that Jack used to call their "bed with a view," and the sight of it made her breath catch. When he was a boy, their son had slept on a pallet beside his parents' bed whenever his father was on this island, so Liz and Jack had spent many private afternoons beneath that tree.

Liz walked up its little hillock to stand beneath their special tree, at the tallest spot on this island's southern tip, and shaded her eyes against the sea's overwhelming glittering. She was trying to spot the ships that she had been told were approaching the harbor. When Jack had first begun spending time here, back when their son was barely two, he had hired what Liz thought of as a mercenary navy to patrol the waters around this island in order to avoid having to bring ashore the disruptive nuisance of security staff. And apparently, even after years away, Jack still cared enough about protecting his family and also protecting this pure island culture that his mercenary navy was there to this day. For two ships to have been allowed to come past the patrols and approach the harbor now was an event so unusual that a friend living in the village of Darakan, at the island's southern tip, had sent his daughter running inland to let Liz know about those ships.

And there they were.

A gunship was out beyond the Darakan promontory, looking flat black against the ocean's glittering, heading for the harbor just below the village. But what was horrifying was what was behind the gunship. Jack's yacht had been white and stately and lovely, as sweet to behold as the man himself, but there behind the gunship was a considerably smaller and racy-looking black-hulled yacht. And the fact that a yacht so different from Jack's was being allowed to approach the harbor, and maybe the fact that it was black besides, made Liz know for certain that this was the message that her husband had long ago promised to send. She would never be able to remarry here unless it was known that he had died, and Jack was careful in all that he did. He wasn't going to leave her with that trailing end.

Liz dropped to the grass where she and Jack had sat and talked and laughed and made love and felt so united that they used to say that now they finally understood the Atlantican creation story, and they were indeed a single person split so they could have the joy of reuniting. Thinking of that, Liz clapped her fingers to her mouth. She was trembling but, oddly enough, not crying. What would have seemed impossible when she first got up this morning was seeming now to have been inevitable. Of course Jack had died. He had had a heart attack on this island at the age of only thirty-eight, and his father's first heart attack had been fatal at the age of fifty-five. Liz would have to figure out how old Jack must be, time being such an elusive thing here, but surely a great deal of time had passed. And now Jack had died. He was never coming back.

———◆———

This little island in the South Atlantic, less than twenty miles from south to north and roughly eight miles wide, was populated by fewer than five thousand people who now were uniformly tall and brown, but whose ancestors from all over the world had been shipwrecked here over thousands of years. Listening to their island's oral history recounted in dozens of children's stories, Jack and Liz used to marvel at the fact that what had been millennia of bloody warfare had led to a way of life so joyous that this island's culture had been stable for what was now going on five hundred years.

Liz had first arrived here as a teacher for the children of Jack's island staff. Having grown up in a clumsy poverty that had made her always an outsider, she had come here at the end of her twenties because when you have nothing in your life, even taking a dead-end job at the edge of the world seems like something. And Liz had been cynically reckless enough, fearless enough and smart enough to interest a man so wealthy that the odd piece of work she had been at the time had seemed to him to be a refreshing change.

Liz had always known it couldn't last forever. Jack Richardson was already famous as the richest American under the age of forty, on the cover of *Time* when he was twenty-six, and seldom out of the news thereafter until eventually the fun of being famous wore off, and by his mid-forties he was routinely suing anyone who dared to publish his name. Jack was still unmarried in his mid-thirties when Liz began to work for him, but eventually he was going to marry. For that he would want someone prettier than Liz, someone used to being rich, someone much more suitable. So, feeling certain that whatever they had together couldn't last for long, Liz had broken up with Jack repeatedly. How many times had that happened? Three times? Four? Her need to protect herself from being hurt had made her ditch this man she adored whenever she suspected she was soon to be ditched. That he had calmly accepted such treatment and always come back to try again still astonished Liz, as she thought about it. A man who so carefully controlled every other aspect of his life had graciously allowed her to control their relationship.

After the first time Liz broke up with Jack, he abandoned her here. He thought he was leaving her with his staff so she could have the clean break that she seemed to want, but without him here she felt more secure in moving to one of the native villages. Neither time nor distance mattered on Atlantica, but Jack had been the sort of man who liked to time things, and he had told Liz that Morakan was exactly one hour's walk north of Darakan. Samitkan was another three hours beyond Morakan. So Liz had glumly trekked out to Morakan on that long-ago dismal morning when the man she had been trying not to fall in love with had unexpectedly left without her. And she had been living in Morakan ever since.

It was during those early months long ago that Liz first became entranced with this place. Atlanticans had stumbled upon the fact that when people have perfect freedom of mind, they can develop such spiritual unity that they have no need for governments. No need for ownership or money or laws. No aspect of civilization is necessary.

And what was most extraordinary to Liz was the way that living as Atlanticans lived allowed people to develop hitherto unsuspected mental powers, as if living in any other way put shackles upon the human mind. People here became aware of plant and animal energies, and especially aware of other people's emotions, so living as Atlanticans lived produced an extraordinary deep-seated joy. Liz had long thought of it as "the Now," this pleasure you felt here in simply existing, and it was continuously astonish-ing to her. It surprised no one else, since these people couldn't conceive of living any other way. Liz knew her mind-sensitivity was less than theirs. She was feral, while all the others here were wild. And her son had grown up as wild as they were, deeply and joyously free from all the bonds that would have been forced upon him if he had grown up in the United States.

Liz refused to give in to crying now. There was no point. She and Jack had tried so hard to make their life together work, and then they had resolutely made what had felt at the time to be their best decisions, so of course living rich was going to kill him and he was going to die too young and there never could have been a different outcome. Liz was feeling their umbrella tree's old familiar energies the way most people felt individual trees, as if perhaps her body were the tree itself. But Jack had never managed to feel plant-energies with any consistency. He was never here for long enough to develop much mind-sensitivity at all, and then he would be right back in the States, and whatever progress he had made here would be gone.

One of the peculiarities of this island was the fact that time passed differently here. That highly pleasurable Now seemed somehow to suspend time in people's minds, so there was not the daily awareness of its passage that people felt in civilization. People here had no concept of time, no verb tenses, no linguistic way to transform the blissful Now into anything linear. Children grew up, true, and people aged, but somehow you didn't notice that here. This morning, Liz was seeing that as a trap. She hadn't noticed the passage of time, but years had gone by since she had last seen her husband. Years had been stolen. Hadn't they been stolen? If you don't even notice the passing years, then have you really lived them at all?

As she had walked their path up toward Jack's "bed with a view," Liz had been trying to figure out how many of what she was calling earth-years had gone by since she was last here with him. She could measure time most easily in the fact that Jack had kept track of Relandela's age, and he had told her their son was twelve years old on that last awful day that Jack ever spent with them. Twelve. And now Relandela was married and a father.

Liz and Jack had learned early on that his wealth intimidated her. She saw being wealthy as a complicated dance that she couldn't even learn how to fake; she wasn't pretty, and a man so rich could afford and surely deserved much better. Jack had found her attitude so mystifying that after a brief, early time when he thought it had something to do with him and therefore it might be something he could fix, he just accepted it as part of the package he had bought when he fell in love with Liz. And it told you a lot about the man that for year after patient year thereafter, he respected her need not to see him as wealthy. He used to arrive in Morakan already dressed in the homespun woolen tunic and pants that the people here wore. He would stay with his family for a couple of Atlantican seasons, living exactly as these people lived, and let his hair and beard grow wild, so by the time he was ready to leave he would be adorably scruffy. Jack was never rich when he was here. And seeing how easily he could shed his wealth and go native, Liz had long cherished the hope that eventually he would be able to stay here. If he could just get into it enough, and perhaps develop his mind enough, he would see how little consolation there was in having money in that desolate world where money was even necessary. Without it, he had the chance to live in a place where people had the infinite wealth of never having heard of money.

The buildings of Steve's old Farm were right below the cliff that was a little to the south of where Liz was sitting. Having seen what personal freedom could do, Jack's childhood friend Steve Symington had long ago conducted an experiment in freedom using thirty-odd hippies and hangers-on. Steve had meant well, but he never had thought through the fact that just removing all constraints without grounding people in spiritual unity would leave them rudderless. So Steve's Farm had ended badly, with the men there turning on the natives in a way that had sealed in these folks' minds the certainty that the people of the rest of the earth were in every way inferior to the people of this little world. Surely the Farm's buildings would still be down there. Liz was glad that from where she sat, she couldn't see them.

Farther out on the promontory beyond Steve's Farm was Darakan, a village of a thousand people that looked from here like just a few roofs floating in a sea of branches. The harbor would be there beyond the village. When Jack was still coming here, he had used an Argentine company to maintain a manmade channel through the outer reef to the pilings where he moored his yacht. That he came and went in a yacht that was nearly three-hundred feet in length and required a crew of forty people had been something that never had mattered to Liz, although she later understood that perhaps it should have mattered.

Sunlight shimmered fiercely on an expanse of ocean so vast that from where Liz sat it seemed not even to meet the horizon, but the ocean eventually became the sky. There used to be a couple of dozen windmills maybe twenty feet tall on the sloping part of the cliff to Liz's right, but most of them were broken now. A few still clacketed slowly. Until the communications tower had been taken out by a storm, it had been important to maintain the windmills so Liz and Jack could stay in touch. Otherwise, electricity was useless here. And while he was here, Jack also had seemed to see electricity as useless. For a long time, there appeared to be a kind of switch in his mind that would let him come and go easily, so he lived with Liz and their son each spring and fall in a place so far beyond civilization that he had taken to calling it post-civilization. A place where human life finally worked. But then he would be able to step back on his yacht and spend each winter and summer in what he had been willing to admit was a civilization that really didn't work at all.

That gunship was slowly beginning to emerge from the shadow of the Darakan promontory, so close to the village that the nasty mind-energies of the men it carried must be troubling the villagers.

Liz and Jack had had such fun together! It wasn't only the friendly people and the healthy lifestyle that had made their lives together so perfect, but also it was the fact that everything that happened to them here was more or less funny. Jack used to say he never really laughed except when he was with Liz. One year they even wrote a book together. What was it called? *Strange Dogs and Their Masters.* That was it. It was a book about fixing failing businesses that was based on notes Jack had been keeping, and over a year's time when Relandela was tiny, he had dictated it to Liz in clipped sentences that she wrote out in more creative longhand.

Because everything they did together was more or less funny, their book had ended up humorous, too, and it had been a bestseller in fourteen languages. That someone so famous for being wealthy had finally been willing to tell some secrets would likely have dictated that it would sell well. But Jack had been sure that its success was due to what he called its "Lizzie voice," full of what read like a hard-won sense that life was so tough that our only rational approach to it was basic silliness. Even the cover was silly, with a ceramic Cerberus whose three heads displaying three different moods were arguing with one another. The title was above the dog, and below it was "Jack Richardson as told to Elizabeth Lyons beneath a tree" as the authors. It had surprised Liz to find her name there at all, and astonished her that their names were in equally large letters, with the rest of that foolishness in small script. Jack had told her at the time that there was a lot of curiosity about who this woman was, and he had variously answered questions about her by saying that she was his secretary, then that she was his business partner or his lover, and then finally—when he was tired of being asked—that she was his secret wife on a secret island where she was raising their secret family. The truth was the only answer no one believed.

≒ 2 ⋩

Jack never learned to speak Atlantican, so Relandela started out bilingual. Whenever Jack was here, he and his son would spend a lot of time together, logging or working in the forge or fishing or otherwise following the Atlantican custom of doing just whatever they felt like doing. Liz would be going about her day and come upon them reading side by side in the childhouse, propped on sheepskins and chuckling together over some little-boy joke. Or, later, helping to re-roof a building, with Relandela sorting wooden shakes and handing them to Jack, and then Jack handing those shakes up to roofers, so tall that he didn't need a ladder. Or earnestly play-arguing, which was something they both loved to do, when one or the other would take a position on something trivial—why sea water was salty, or why the horns of Atlantican sheep varied so much in shape—and they would earnestly, creatively debate it.

So that had been their family life for a decade. Relandela grew up in Morakan perfectly free, a fact that for a long time had made Jack happy. He used to say that his son was growing up to look so much like him that if he were in the United States he wouldn't be able to live a little-boy life because of the kidnap risk. There came to be a rhythm to their year, with Jack here every spring and fall, but away from them every summer and winter and communicating with them almost daily. A kindly Atlantican named Desedala had long ago been trained to run Jack's communications equipment, and apparently he enjoyed the job so much that he had happily done it for years, until the storm that finally took down the tower. Jack and Liz were a husband and wife who were precisely attuned to one another, but preferred to live opposing lifestyles. Surely that must happen to other people? And probably no other couple had managed to solve the problem so neatly.

It all worked well for more than a decade, but then in the spring of the year when Relandela was twelve, it no longer worked at all. Their son was six feet tall by then, still shorter than his father at six-foot-eight, but rapidly acquiring the build of a man. Liz herself was just over six feet tall, with blond braids to her waist that were already graying. Jack's hair was dark-brown with considerable red, a color Liz thought of as mahogany, and their son had inherited his mother's blond hair with a coppery tinge that came from his father.

Liz recalled watching them walk across the bridge on the morning of that final day, as they headed for the Darakan trail to go and ready Jack's yacht for his departure. Jack didn't want his American crew to interfere with the Atlanticans' lives, so he would require them to live aboard his yacht for the couple of months that he would be here. Relandela never had liked those foreigners. He found the mind-energies of Americans to be so stressed, so aggressive and fearful that he would come back to Liz from his visits to Jack's yacht mildly irritated by them and complaining. But still, he always wanted to go and help his father prepare his yacht. Liz thought that the fact that Jack was about to leave him again made especially precious to Relandela those final few days when they were still together.

On that last day, Jack came looking for Liz as she was heading down the river street, after having spent the morning giving lessons in the pottery shop. Over time, she had taught herself to be a good potter, and by now she was making graceful bowls and pitchers to replace the wooden bowls and squat iron pitchers that people here had long used in their homes. Atlanticans had an aversion to anything that was easily breakable; but well-fired pottery that was thick enough was turning out to be pretty tough, so now lots of people were eager to learn how to shape it and glaze it and fire it as Liz could. Jack came striding back across the bridge, looking around, and he spotted her. He called, "Have you seen Rex, honey?" "Rex" was what he called Relandela.

Liz stepped out of the cheery group coming down to have their dinner, saying, "What's wrong, darling? Is something wrong?" But then as he approached her and she was able to feel the chaotic stress of his mind-energy, she blurted, "Jack! What's wrong? Tell me!"

She could see from his face how upset he was, but even more than that, she could feel it.

Jack caught her hand without saying anything and led her resolutely up the street to the house they shared opposite the pottery shop. Married people didn't live together here, but Jack insisted on living with Liz, so they shared a larger but still one-room house. He directed her inside and closed the door as he said, "Rex just told me to go to hell."

"He didn't say that. Tell me what he really said."

Jack's jaw was set. He was pacing, and now he looked at her sharply. His eyes were his most arresting feature, large and wide-set under heavy lashes, the color of a pale sea-mist. Even now, when he was angry, his eyes were soft and kindly. Sometimes Liz would have to remind him that no matter how annoyed he tried to sound, his gentle eyes always gave him away. As he looked at her now, he said, "It's time to come home. He needs to go to school. He thinks he's an Atlantican!"

Liz was never going back to the States, and the thought of inflicting America's culture on their child was inconceivable to her. She murmured, "What did he say, darling?"

"This has been coming on for a year. He doesn't understand my life. I never said anything. I didn't want to upset you. But he asks me why I keep leaving—"

"I know. He's been asking me, too." Liz moved to sit down on the bed, hands folded. Now that she knew what this was, she could deal with it.

"Whatever you told him wasn't helpful, honey. My only child just told me if I leave him today, he's no longer my son."

Liz winced internally. But she said, "He's just sad. I'll fix it."

"I can't do this anymore! I spend three months traveling or living here, then three months at home trying to manage my affairs so I can turn around and come right back. It's insane! My life is a mess, and it's getting worse. I've tried, honey. You know I've tried, but it's too complicated now. I can't do it anymore. I need you to come home."

"But this is our home! We don't need money. Please stay with us, darling—"

"I answered his questions honestly. I told him I've got to get back for a closing. So he asked me what a closing is. I tried to tell him. So then he asked me what a business is. Honey, he doesn't have a concept of money! Money? Do you know how insane that is? He's the heir to a fortune in the billions, and he doesn't even know what money. . . ."

Jack stopped talking when he noticed Liz's face. She was sitting there looking up at him. She looked away. Had he said "billions"? With a "B"?

"I'm sorry. It slipped out. You're making my life impossible!"

"That's more than millions, right?"

Jack came and drew her up into his arms and held her while she digested what he had just said. For all the many years that Jack Richardson had been the beating heart of her life, Liz had felt that she was fighting his wealth as her rival for his very soul. But she always had thought of him as a millionaire. Millions would be a lot. But now it was billions?

He said into her hair, "I'm sorry, honey. I'm really sorry. I've tried, but my life is too complicated for me to keep living it part-time. I want you and Rex to come back with me now."

"Millions was bad enough," she mumbled into his woolen tunic. Her eyes were stupidly filling. All she wanted was her husband to be here with her forever, never leaving her again. Even if it were millions, she always had known that his giving up his money for her was unlikely. But if she had all along been fighting not millions, but billions, then there never had been any chance.

"Oh honey, don't cry! It doesn't matter—" Then he said wryly, "You would be surprised to know the percentage of the population that would consider the fact that it's billions and not millions to be actually good news."

But Liz was really crying now. She was crying for Jack, that he never could possibly free himself from so much money; and for Relandela's impending loss again of the father that he so adored; and for herself. She might have beaten millions, but not billions. There was something about his inadvertent revelation that day that made her give in, without realizing it was happening until later. She gave up that day. She accepted the fact that whatever little bit in the future he might be willing to give her was going to be all that she ever could have of him.

So she cried off and on for hours that day. Jack held her, eventually lying down with her and holding her and letting her cry. By midafternoon Relandela was there, still angry with his father but frightened, too. Liz could feel his fear, which was so unaccustomed an emotion for him that she sat up and held him for awhile then, still crying. That whole afternoon was a blur of tears. But Jack really had to leave that day. It turned out that he had not one closing, but three, and two of them were having issues that he was going to need to work out in person. So eventually he stood and held his wife and rocked her in his arms and told her he loved her, and then he left them and walked alone to the harbor.

Liz realized long after the fact that at about the same time that she gave up, Jack apparently gave up as well. He sent his regular notes for awhile, but that was the winter of the great wind-and-ice storm that took down five windmills and crumpled the communications tower. Once the tower was down, his notes stopped coming. So then Liz began to count the seasons, making charcoal marks side by side on the top of their table against the wall. She stopped at twenty. Twenty seasons was two years in this place where people kept track of the cycles of the trees and the times for planting and growing and harvest by naming ten seasons. Not having seen or heard from Jack in two years, Liz understood that he had felt forced to make his choice. After the communications tower was gone, they never heard from him again.

———◆———

That yacht offshore had been stationary for awhile. Perhaps it wasn't going to risk the old channel through the reef. And now it seemed to Liz as she shaded her eyes that they might have put a rowboat down off that yacht. The sun had moved to stand directly overhead, shining hot through the lace of infant leaves. She stood. Once she was out from under their tree, the grass beneath her feet was lightly bubbly with the joy of its being in full sunlight.

To avoid having to see the buildings of Steve's Farm, Liz set off walking directly to the east. The slope was gentler there, anyway. She passed through the forest of windmills that looked even more pathetic up-close, their gray paint flaking and their wooden supports beginning to rot out at the joints. But they would be old now, too. They had been built in the year before Liz arrived, and now Relandela was in his early twenties. Had she really been here for twenty whole years? But that would mean that she was in her fifties. And Jack could be as much as sixty years old, an old man, gray and balding now, when the last time she had seen him he had been in his virile latter forties and only barely graying at the temples.

Jack had suffered a heart attack when he was only thirty-eight, but fortunately it had happened here, and the Atlanticans' powerful connection to the unity of all things had saved his life. Some twenty years later, and having lived for so long in the rich American culture that had nearly killed him in his thirties, Liz could readily imagine that he must have had a second heart attack. She had just lost her mother, and now apparently she had lost the great love of her life as well.

Liz's mother had died of what was apparently pneumonia at the start of the season of greening twigs. She had been dead for less than two earth-months. So she would have been here for twenty years as well, lured away from Brooklyn and all her friends by a soft-spoken man with a fancy yacht who carried her halfway around the world because that man loved her daughter, and the daughter missed her mother. Myra hadn't meant to do more than visit. She hadn't planned to spend two decades here, and she certainly had never intended to die here. But Jack had also brought Liz's two orphaned nieces, so all Myra's grandchildren were growing up here; and then she even had found love here. And that insidious Atlantican illusion that time wasn't passing had likely kept her from noticing that her life was going by.

No one had realized that Myra was dying. She had, as usual, been scurrying about, devoting her life to caring for four disabled boys who lived on litters. She had a respiratory illness that seemed to be worsening, and still she had insisted on going out in the cold and rain from house to house until she was too weak to do that anymore. Liz had scavenged in the Farm's old clinic and found some long-expired penicillin, the only antibiotics left on an island whose people mistrusted foreign drugs. Here fevers were treated with teas and sweats, and since Atlanticans knew that human minds are eternal and they interacted easily with their dead, there wasn't the panic here to preserve each life that people felt in the civilized world.

That old penicillin had seemed to be working. Myra was getting better, they thought. Her fevers had lessened. She was conscious and beginning to talk. Liz and Lucky, Myra's wonderful husband, had been taking turns holding her propped in their laps so she could breathe more easily. They had been softly talking, even joking a little, when Liz had heard and felt her mother take a long breath, then let it out slowly. And then that frail body sagged in her arms, so light that it seemed to have no weight, and there was a sense as if every vessel in it closed up, never to open again.

By the time Liz found a way down the cliff to the harbor road, she was running tears. The guilt she felt about her mother was tremendous, but pointless. Yes, of course she wished now that she had insisted that anti-biotics be included on the list of things that the supply freighter would unobtrusively leave on the longest dock toward the end of every summer. She should have insisted! But nobody here ever insisted on anything, so for Liz to have done that would have felt unseemly. Every decision here was made by a consensus of nearly five thousand people, and usually all they could agree to order would be scrap iron, nails, tools and clay, scratch corn for the chickens, maybe twine, and probably thread and needles for their treadle sewing machines. Each order would be left in a leather pouch that was nailed to the end of the longest dock, to be con-veniently filled for them whenever the freighter returned the following summer.

And now, oh my God, Jack was dead as well! Jack and Myra, the only two people besides Relandela and her two lost babies that Liz had ever deeply loved, had both died, and she had been helpless to prevent either death. She even felt, in a way, that she had caused both deaths. What had Jack's life been like without her? She actually hoped he had found another love, but she knew him too well to believe that was likely. His problem was trust. He had trouble trusting women, and since his mother had sexually abused him, perhaps that wasn't so surprising.

———•———

There were hundreds of people milling on the little hillside above the harbor, watching as a rowboat made its deliberate way down the channel toward the longest dock. As Liz stood at the top of the hill above the harbor, flooded and swamped by memories, her beloved friend Jude came and slipped his arm around her waist and said, "I am reminded now of how painful it is to be near the beardless ones."

That looked like Ted in the rowboat. A crewman was rowing with his back to them, but seated facing him was what looked like Jack's old friend and longtime personal lawyer sitting primly in that old stiff way of his, knees tight together. Jack wasn't with him. Liz hadn't needed confirmation, but there in that rowboat was her confirmation that the great love of her life had died. Well, but at least he had died still loving her, for him to have sent Ted all this way.

Liz had never grieved Jack's loss because she was seeing it only in retrospect. She had long been used to sometimes being without him, and this had felt like just a longer separation: living here suspended in the perfect Now had kept her from noticing how much time was passing. But as Ted climbed the ladder out of the rowboat and began to walk up the longest dock, Liz could see that he was stooped a bit, and his hair was gray above a higher forehead. His face was softly sagged and ashen. Oh, how many years had passed!

People here seldom cried past toddlerhood, when they first gained a sense of how precious they were and how perfect was the Now in which they had their being. Not even children cried, so for Liz to be suddenly wailing and shrieking made people rush and stumble away from her in horror. She could feel the buzzing distress of their minds as Jude grabbed her. She barely heard him whispering. She blubbered, "He died, and nobody sang him away! How could he have known where to go?"

All Liz could think was that she hadn't been there for him, hadn't held his hand as he was dying, hadn't made sure that the last thing he heard was how much she would forever love him. And then she hadn't sung to him as Atlanticans always sang to their dead, to help them make it safely to the blissful village. But did the United States even have a blissful village? She had to make sure that he was all right!

Jude moved them to sit side-by-side on a sightseeing bench that was still there beside the old road. He hugged her and whispered to her, pointlessly. She couldn't hear anything but her own lamentations. Then she vaguely heard Ted calling her name from somewhere down the hill. Here, English was a reading language. Liz hadn't heard it spoken in years, but the sound of Ted's old tentative voice that made her think of Jack in a bearable way made her stop crying as abruptly as she had started.

Liz stood up and watched Ted climbing the hill, all out of breath and with elbows akimbo. The harsh energies of his mind were clanging almost visibly on the air, so people were falling away as he approached. Liz had always thought of Ted as Jack's evil alter ego, because whenever Jack had something unpleasant to do to another human being he would send Ted to do it. And the funny part was that Ted was a mouse. He just was one of the very few people on all the earth that Jack thought he could trust.

"Oh. Good. Liz. Hi," Ted called, out of breath, as he spotted her. He stopped at the top of the hill, bent double with his hands braced on his thighs as he gulped air. "It's hot here," he said as he straightened. "I forgot. Are you Jude? I hardly recognized you. Hello. Good to see you." He reached and shook Jude's hand. Liz could feel her friend laughing internally at this foolish intrusion of American stuffiness in a place where minds were so densely connected that no formalities between people were needed.

Ted drew a long breath and said, "Can we talk privately, Liz?"

"There's no need."

"We've got to—"

Liz was able to put her arms around Ted and hug him, but she stepped back quickly.

"Please don't say it. I can't bear to hear it. But thank you for coming. He's kept his last promise."

Ted gave Liz a startled look. He swiped at his sweaty brow with his shirtsleeve. He was wearing the same dark pants and dress shirt that he used to wear on Jack's yacht long ago, but now minus the vest and tie. He ran the fingers of one hand back through his hair in his same old way, and he stepped and turned and sat down on the bench and patted the spot beside him. Liz sat down, but not close to him. Being so near the clanging tension of his mind was beginning to make her feel disoriented.

Ted glanced around. He said to Liz under his breath, "Look, I do aggression badly. I've got to take Rex. Don't make it hard. Please."

"What?"

"We've been attacked. It's not safe here now. You can come, too. Your whole family can come."

"What? There's a war?" Liz was straining to think clearly.

"Remember the World Trade Center towers? Last month they took them both down. Flew planes into them. Terrorists." Ted was still breathing unevenly. He sighed a catch-up breath and added, "Jack wants Rex where he can protect him."

What, Jack? You mean, he's not dead?

"Is he all right?"

"Is who all right? Jack?" Ted paused in his face-wiping and looked at Liz. She could feel his little rush of anger as he grumped, "You wrecked his life, and now you wonder how he is?" Ted's fingers were in his hair again.

"We don't need to leave. We're fine. We've always got warships out there protecting us."

"Do you see that gunboat?" Ted lifted his head and looked at it as he added, "Aboard that ship are a thousand Argentine mercenaries. Rex is coming with me." He added wearily, "Please don't make this hard."

Liz had just been deep in grief, but now abruptly not only was Jack not dead, but he was trying to steal their son away and wreck his life. She was struggling to catch up with herself.

Ted said conversationally, "I never understood why he put up with you for all those years. He could have had anyone. He picked you. Why?"

"Is he really all right?"

"No, he is not all right. He's sixty-one years old. *Forbes* says he's worth nineteen billion dollars, and now he has nobody to leave it to but a kid who has never been off this island. Would you be all right with that?"

"He's how old? What year is it?"

"Two thousand one."

Liz sank into that reality. She had come here in April of 1976, just before the American Bicentennial celebration. A quarter of a century had passed while she had lived here suspended in a blissful Now. So she would be, what? Fifty-five? Good grief! And Myra had died at seventy-eight. As gloriously happy as Liz had been, this island had taken so much of her life of which she now would never have awareness. What had happened during all those years? Only bliss? And could that have been enough?

Ted was looking at Liz. She had to say something. She sputtered, "But he's not a kid! He has a wife and baby. And he . . . the whole reason Jack stopped coming here was they couldn't get along."

Of course, that wasn't true at all. Rex and his father had been intensely close, and it was only Jack's attachment to his wealth that had destroyed his relationship with his family. But Liz wouldn't say that. It was none of Ted's business.

Ted said patiently, "We can't protect Rex here anymore. He has to come with me. He can bring whoever he wants."

"You think it's really not safe here?" Liz asked as she gazed at that warship out beyond the reef, like a wart on a beautiful face.

Really, Jack? Mercenaries?

"It's never been safe here. The world is too small. The only reason you've been left alone is he pays off everybody. But the older he gets, the more he wants his heir, or what was any of it for?"

"Relandela has no idea what money is!" But even as Liz said it, her mind was turning. She realized only in that moment that Ted was right. Their precious little world wasn't safe, since whenever Jack died his naval protection of this island was going to die with him. It wasn't so much a military attack that she and Jack had long been fearing, but it was more the intrusion of well-meaning fools who could corrupt and destroy what the two of them had come to see as this extraordinary experiment in what it means to be human. And if the home he loved really were at risk, then Relandela would want the chance to protect it.

⇥ 3 ⇤

Myra was trying to lift her great-grandson. Her arms kept passing right through the baby, but still she kept trying, so everyone in the childhouse was laughing at her antics. Relandela's family lived in Samitkan, a full morning's walk away from where Myra had lived in Morakan, and she never had managed to make that walk during the whole twenty seasons of his baby's life. But she had died as the season of greening twigs was beginning, and wonderfully, she was visiting him now.

Relandela's distress was troubling his wife. For the whole day he had been sitting cross-legged on the childhouse sheepskins beside Gaprelagh the beautiful, working a spindle and basking in the gentle strength of her right there beside him. His mind was fed by the melody of her voice, the sweet interplay with her mind's energies, the calm certainty of her very being. He needed her now, with the clanging energies of the beardless ones permeating even the childhouse since first light this morning, all of a sudden, overwhelming him, mind-energies that he knew his Gaprelagh could selectively ignore. Relandela was trying the techniques that she had taught him, but he could neither ignore nor even reduce these emanations of the beardless ones. By now he was feeling near to panic with his need to get away from this clanging metallic vibration that felt like blades in his mind and put a bitter taste in his mouth.

Kitten was so fascinated by his shimmery phantom friend that he was giggling, watching her, toddling with her as she moved, reaching to try to touch her. Their son had a real name, but his eyes were so large and round and pale that from his birth he had been called by a name that Relandela suspected he might wear through life. The woman who had died old but now looked young seemed to be singing a song that Kitten was hearing. Relandela couldn't hear it. His mind was so exquisitely fixed upon the comfort of feeling Gaprelagh beside him.

Little Kitten's skin was nicely darkening. His hair was curly and nearly black. As a boy, Relandela used to throw his yellow braids behind his shoulders to avoid seeing them. Sometimes he tied them together behind his back, and there even had been a time in his childhood when he rubbed dirt into his hair so he could look more normal. He had learned to accept the odd way he looked, but he was very glad that his son was free of it.

Travelers from the other place had not set foot on land since Relandela was a baby, but instead they lived sorry lives on ships that wistfully still circled the world. The common word for them, "beardless," was an insult that seemed to Relandela to nicely fit men with minds so aggressively weak and stressed and fearful. He had been feeling the emanations of their minds now and then for his whole life, this metallic coarseness on the air that felt like blades. But never had it been so strong.

Then he realized that his mother was nearby.

"Litzlagh is approaching, beloved," Gaprelagh said to him softly. "She is as distraught as you are. You might walk with her among the trees."

Relandela laid a hand on Gaprelagh's shoulder and leaned to touch Kitten and stood up into that awful, clanging energy. He stepped carefully over legs and laps and babies playing on the floor, and from the child-house's open doorway he saw his mother coming through the archway that ended the long trail up from Morakan to Samitkan.

Relandela had grown up in Morakan, but he and Gaprelagh had moved out to Samitkan at the northern end soon after their marriage. Relandela had felt safer in Samitkan, which was the only village of the three that was far enough from every shore that within its walls you almost never felt the mind-energies of the beardless ones who wistfully still circled the world. But apparently, that would no longer be the case. Now there would be no part of the world still free of them.

Relandela's mother had about her an air of soft sadness like an ancient scar. She was married to a man who had disappeared without dying, which seemed to be reason enough for her sadness. Relandela had long ago made peace with his father in his mind, accepting the fact that the man he had adored had loved him so little that when Relandela had begged him not to leave again, he had left here anyway and never come back. Relandela had made peace, but peace would be something forever denied to his mother now because her husband's having disappeared without dying meant that she never could remarry.

Now Liz was weary from walking, she was hungry, and she was frightened. Feeling all of that so strongly distressed Relandela even more. He stepped down off the threshold-stone as she approached him. Despite his discomfort in being so close to the discordant energies of her mind, he hugged her to give her a little of his strength. He said with forced cheeriness, "Your mother is playing with the baby! Come in and see her."

"You know I am unable to see shimmers. But that is exactly how she would choose to spend forever. I am so glad!"

Gaprelagh had been right about the trees. It was deep in the season of little leaves, and this was the time when the bright-green vibrations of the trees were gloriously at their height. People would walk the forest trails to enjoy this exultant thrilling of the trees. Relandela started to take his mother's hand so they could head for the western break in the wall and enter the old-growth forest, but Liz said, "No! No walking. We must talk right now."

The stridence of the way she was feeling was nearly unbearable for him.

As Relandela followed Liz down the slope to where tumbled blocks made a place to sit, he complained, "But you should be less troubled than I am! Are you not of the other place yourself? Now we are feeling them even in the childhouse. I accept your opinion that there is no harm from them, but they are troubling our peace. Do you not consider that harmful?"

On the long slope beside the Samitkan childhouse were tumbled remnants of the ancient wall lying scattered like mossy children's blocks. Relandela sat down there on one of the stones. Liz sat down facing him, a little too close. Immediately she slipped into formal speaking. Relandela composed himself to hear her. Apparently there was a decision to be made.

"My beloved child, I let you believe that the other place is small and harmless and an object of laughter. It seems not to matter what you think, for you are always safe in your father's arms. He is powerful. He lets nothing harm you. But now I understand that I am wrong for your whole life to keep you here. Now I realize that no one else but you can help him to keep our world safe."

Relandela had been expecting her to make some proposal about how to reduce these annoying disruptions from the beardless ones. So now, what was this? He said, "I do not understand you. I have no father now."

"That is my fault as well. For my whole life I cause tragedies because I cannot see where events are leading. Your destiny is there with him, beloved. It is my task to help you understand this."

Relandela was feeling such distress from her mind that he leaned and touched her hand where it rested in her lap and said, "Please eat and rest, dear one."

"No! I must make you see. . . ." She stood. She stepped away and turned to him and said, "The other place is not small! The other place is so much bigger than our little world that our world is a drop and the other place is the ocean. Can you hear what I am saying? This precious drop of world is at the mercy of that ocean. Your father is our protector, but your father is an old man now. Upon his death that ocean swamps us."

What she was saying made no sense to him. His people's world was under the protection of forces so powerful that nothing could harm it.

"Relandela! Are you hearing my words?"

"The sielrah is the world. No ocean can swamp it."

The sielrah was the unity of all things. How could anything harm that?

"But the Teacher tells us there is an outer darkness! And that other place is his outer darkness. This tiny drop of world is his candle. When you are the only one who can protect it, how can you refuse to do that?"

The fierceness of her concentrated mind was battering his own. She sat down and took his hands and looked into his eyes and said earnestly, "There is a power of the other place that is not unity. It is discord! But the only power that performs in that place is discord. Your father has it in abundance, and it is his intention to pass his power to you so you can continue to protect our world. Because you love your people enough to join your father in the other place, our world is safe for another generation."

Now Relandela was hearing her. And she believed what she was saying. He could feel no uncertainty at all from a woman whose mind was often vague and fluttery. He opened his mouth, then closed it. He could see that she was waiting for his counterargument, but he could think of nothing to say.

"You must go quickly! While he keeps his body, he is able to teach you how to use his power. Without his body, he cannot help you. In that place, the dead abandon the living."

———— •·•• ————

If only Relandela were still a child, this could have been so much easier. A child might have been carried off bodily, if all else failed. His mind would have been malleable. But Relandela was about twenty-four now, a husband

and a recent father. He was just at that stage of his life when it was impossible for anyone to make him believe anything that he had not independently thought through and decided upon. Liz knew he would eventually soften past this omnipotent flush of early manhood, but it would take time. And they had no time.

By the next morning, Liz had eaten and rested and walked the dozen or so miles back to Darakan, the village beside the harbor, having spent enough time with Relandela to believe that she had convinced him to go with Ted. His task now was to explain it to his wife.

Liz's walk the whole length of this island and back had given her plenty of time to think. Until yesterday, it hadn't entered her mind that she might ever want to leave this place, but she had been playing with the thought of leaving ever since she first saw that black-hulled yacht. Even while she thought the yacht must mean Jack's death, and even before she knew that Relandela would be going, her first seeing that yacht had felt to her like awakening from a wonderful dream. She was astonished to realize how much time had passed, and Jack hadn't been here for more than a decade, so clearly he had moved on with his life. And now her mother had died of something that antibiotics could have cured, just as Jack's friend Steve Symington had died of an infected leg fracture long before. Liz didn't want anyone ever again to die here for a lack of antibiotics. She wanted to reestablish communications, in case they ever had a real emergency. Now that she fully understood that Jack was no longer involved with this place beyond what he would see as the chump-change of paying for its mercenary naval protection and sending a little scrap iron once a year, Liz knew that she had to take control.

Oddly, the fact that Jack was alive might be a complication. Even the thought of going back to his hemisphere was making Liz feel soft and fluttery, as if no time had passed at all, as if they were going to be once again falling joyously into one another's arms. But Liz understood from his long silence that Jack had moved on. It was time for her to move on as well.

Liz came to wish as she walked for hours, enjoying the exultant thrilling of the trees, that she and Jack had discussed their alternatives before he gave up on her altogether. While once she had found the thought of living with wealth impossible to contemplate, she did think that she had come to trust him enough by the time he made the decision to ditch her that if only they had talked about it, she and their son likely would have gone back with him. She had grown a lot by then. Perhaps he never knew that.

Liz was thinking that now she preferred not even to see Jack at all, but of course she was going to have to see him. The two of them shared a son and grandson. She was trying to reconstruct in her mind the details of living in the United States, and her first thought was that she was going to need money. She was determined to live off waiting tables rather than take Jack's charity, but then it occurred to her that Relandela would have money—or rather, Rex. She had to start thinking of him as Rex. He would have money. Perhaps he could hire her. Liz had been recklessly strong long ago, before she had met the great love of her life, when something about being in love with Jack Richardson had made her turn fragile and self-protective. Now that love was over. He had moved on, and it was time for her to again be strong.

There was nothing happening down in the harbor, so Liz moved on to Darakan, where breakfast was ending and people were leaving their great-house and heading up the streets toward their workshops. As Liz passed through the ancient gateway in the wall, she thought that the people seemed oddly stressed; then a little past the gateway she also could feel that humming beardless busyness coming from one particular house. She followed it and found Ted standing just inside the doorway, gazing toward the middle distance while he ranted into the palm of his hand. But what was making that peculiar vibration? Ted was muttering into his hand,

"... if you've got to make the deadline, then I can't make the closing. I won't be back for at least two—No! Listen to me. Tell Butler we're done. If he wants the party. . . ."

Liz's friend Jude was sitting on a bed against a wall of that little one-room house in the dusky haze that was usual in Darakan's buildings because the village was full of trees. Ted seemed to be really annoyed with his hand.

"... he gets it done now, or we move on. No! He's got enough on his mind."

"Why is he angry with his hand?" Liz said to Jude as she sat down beside him. She was suppressing a giggle at the thought that Jack and Ted had been wasting their lives on this drivel for, what? More than thirty years?

Jude said, "His hand holds a clamshell that makes words."

"... all right then, . . ." Ted was saying.

Liz said to Jude, "Why does it feel as if the air is fuzzy?"

"I believe it is the maker of words. It uses energies rather than wires." He inserted that one English word. "But how can it be so small?"

"... No, I'll call him," Ted was saying more pleasantly. "Okay then. Tell him the end of November works for us."

Liz could see now that Ted held a dark-red clamshell thing in his hand. As he clapped it shut, he said to Liz, "Where's Rex?"

Ted looked ridiculous in a homespun woolen tunic and pants, his hair and skin and clothes the same color, his bare cheeks making him seem pathetic. Liz said in English, "I think he's going to go, but he's wild. He won't be able to take—what is that thing? Turn it off."

"I can't—"

"Then he won't come near you! Off!"

As Ted was irritably switching off his phone and tossing it onto the table, bringing an instant extinction of its fuzzy energy, Liz stood and pulled out a chair and sat down at the table. She was saying, "I need paper and something to write with. This? Thanks. He's a day behind me. We've got work to do." Apparently ballpoint pens hadn't changed. She went on, speaking to Jude in English, "We'll strip out a room on the yacht for him?"

"Not just the furniture. Down to the studs. And give him three or four rooms while you're at it. As far from the wires as possible."

"Away from wires." Liz was writing. "Good point. Then hang sheep-skins, maybe? Bring in some furniture?"

Liz could feel Ted's irritation rising. When she glanced up at him, he said, "That's my own yacht! You're not taking it apart."

"It's going to be hard enough to persuade him to go aboard in the first place. It's still a two-week trip? He won't survive two weeks."

"Tranquilizers might help," Jude offered. "Do you have something, Ted? They put me on a pill. I wish I knew what it was."

"Ask Jack about that," Liz said to Ted, writing. "The only reason I think this can work is he got Jude through it. Have him look at what they did for Jude, will you?"

When Jude had been a teenager so enraged by Steve Symington's Farm that he had become a nuisance, he had been transported from here to the States and had lived with Jack for seven years. For a time, he had been so completely American that even a quarter-century later he still spoke English without an accent. Jude was saying, "He'll need food, too. They fed me hot dogs. All I did was throw up."

"Great point. Bring a few weeks' worth of food. Maybe make him stew here so they can heat it up?" She said to Ted, "Do you have refrigerator space?" But Ted's irritation kept stabbing into her mind. She added, "Stop thinking! Everything you think is nasty. Think of nothing but flowers and birdies, Ted."

"Send enough clothes so he won't have to switch to polyester right away," Jude suggested.

When Liz and Jude had last been in the States, polyester double-knits and blends had been in fashion. But maybe that wasn't the case anymore because Ted blurted, "Polyester?"

"Or what do they wear now? Space suits?" Liz said, smiling.

Ted said irritably, "How many are coming?"

"He and his wife and baby. And me, I think," Liz said as she considered her food list. It was going to be hard enough to help even one young family make this transition, so how could she cope with trying to do it for Relandela's two cousins and their husbands and five children? Anyway, with Relandela helping Jack, this island should be safe for another generation.

Then Liz could feel that Relandela was already nearby. Jude was standing and heading for the door. Ted whispered, "My God!" and Liz looked up and saw reflected in Ted's face what she had known from her first sight of her newborn baby lying bundled in the crook of her arm: Relandela was the image of his father. He was ducking to come through the doorway as Jack always did, a polite little stoop. Jack was just over six-foot-eight, and Relandela seemed to be a bit shorter, but still he was the tallest man on this island. His body was more like her own, Liz thought. But he had his father's pale blue eyes, with some trick of the way they were widely set that made them seem unusually large and round. He had his father's mouth, full lips that smiled easily. He had Jack's nose, although perhaps the general shape of his face was more like her own. Still, despite the braids and woolens, what Ted was unexpectedly seeing before him was Jack forty years ago. And he was stunned.

Liz could feel coming from Relandela's mind a strange vibration that kept her frozen in her chair. He was calm. Too calm. He was resolute. He had made his decision, and he was at peace with it. She said in their language, "Can you be in this house with us, dear heart? Or would you rather be outside?"

Relandela was feeling Ted's mind, taking his measure. He lifted his chin on a long breath, which was another of his many habits that reminded Liz of Jack. She realized as she looked at their son that one of the reasons she had missed Jack less had likely been the fact that Relandela was so like him.

"I going," Relandela said to Ted in English. "Now. I going," he repeated when Ted said nothing.

"They must prepare that ship for you," Liz told him in Atlantican.

"Speaking Yinglitz," he said to her calmly.

"Where is Gaprelagh?"

Relandela looked at Liz. He said in their language, "The beardless ones slaughter her infant twin in the face of his parents. Before their face! When I see her with our son in her arms, I cannot tell her where I am going. Her mother agrees to tell her that my remnant is discovered beneath the cliff of wooden birds. Your mother agrees to tell her that I am happy in the blissful village. My beloved finds a new husband. I do not do to her what your husband does to you."

When the men of Steve's Farm had subjugated the villages, they had shot Gaprelagh's two-year-old twin to show Morakan what a gun could do. And Atlanticans called that windmill hill the cliff of wooden birds. Relandela was faking his own death. Liz stared at her son, dumbstruck at the immensity of what he was saying.

"You've got to speak English!" Ted said, clueless.

"I going," Relandela said to Ted, man-to-man. He gestured toward the door, suggesting that Ted might go first. To Liz he said in English, "I laying my life for friends."

Oh no. Before he got there, Liz would have to make sure Relandela realized that the Teacher was not just a treasured ancestor who had taught his people how to live the sielrah.

Ted was stuffing papers into a briefcase and grabbing up his phone from the table and looking around with a frenetic urgency that brought back to Liz what it had felt like to live there. She sighed and stood up. Relandela took her hand, and she followed him out the door.

⇥ 4 ⇤

It was over underage beers consumed illegally in their prep school room that Jack and his friend Steve Symington were inspired to name this island Atlantica. They never in later years could decide who it was that first thought up the name, but always afterward it seemed to them that no other name could have been so right. Steve's family had more or less owned this island ever since his great-great-great-grandfather had felt inspired to escape the American Civil War by moving to the Empire of Brazil. While in Brazil to scout for land enough for all the families that were going with him, the Colonel (as they always referred to him) had gotten word of this faraway island and purchased it from the Emperor himself. Jack and Steve liked to imagine the two of them sitting lazily on a Brazilian veranda, getting drunk together as they gazed out over thousands of acres of cotton and slaves, and slyly ripping one another off because the Emperor knew that the island was useless and the Colonel knew that the price was dirt-cheap.

Family stories had it that the Colonel went on to establish a colony of slaveholding families on Atlantica. Steve and Jack never found any evidence that such a colony existed, though, so they came to think that story was folklore. Atlantica was far from shipping lanes, so you didn't find it randomly. It was occupied, tiny, mostly vertical, and fundamentally not worth much.

Steve's father was the one who developed a modern interest in Atlantica. Having found the old deeds, he rented a steamer and managed to find it in the 1930's. As he reared his family, this island became their almost-annual vacation spot, and Steve's best friend often came along.

"Jack and Steve grew up close as brothers, but eventually they went in different directions. Jack learned to build the beardless power, but Steve tried to improve the lives of our people. Then when Steve died, Jack bought this island from his family so he could continue to care for us. A few years later he was hiring a teacher for the children of his employees here, and that was how your parents met, darling."

Liz was telling the story as simply as she could, using English because Relandela insisted on English, and trying to help him begin to understand that the island he had always believed was the center of the solid world was actually just a tiny bit of it. They sat together aboard Ted's yacht on a narrow Atlantican bed, while around them Jude supervised the crew in removing drapes and carpeting. Liz knew that Rex often found her mind's vibrations troubling, but he was glad now to sit so close to her that their thighs touched and he was holding her hand. She could feel from him the same calm resolve that had so surprised her when he appeared that morning. With it, though, was a rising emotional fragility that made her want to hold him in her arms. He was so young! He was barely out of childhood, and now unexpectedly she was giving him the burden of leaving behind everything he knew and venturing forth to save his world.

"Your father couldn't speak our language, so he gave you an English name. Do you remember it?"

"Righ."

"Rex. Without the click. Try again, baby."

"Rek?"

Relandela had come to hate that name, but now here he was, practicing saying it. Liz slipped her arm around her little boy's waist, feeling freshly

34

amazed at the grown-up bulk of him. "There's a village at your father's house," she said as Ted appeared in the doorway. She said to Ted, "Is the village still there?"

"No. And I told you not to take this room apart!"

"Tell him to rebuild the village. Think puppies and bunnies, Ted."

Ted said more pleasantly, "Rex? Is there anything you need?"

Ted was suffering a rising rage unlike anything Liz had felt before, as if furious anger were smothered in feathers so it puffed out a little around the edges. It felt ugly and duplicitous. She found it troubling, but Relandela's mind was so much more sensitive that it was beginning to upset him very much. She stood, saying, "I'll be right back, sweetie. Jude will tell you some of the nicest things about the other place."

Liz had one mental template for yacht décor, but Ted's yacht was very different from Jack's. Rather than rich colors and soft lights and crystal, Ted's was wood paneling and neutral carpeting and still-lifes and silk plants and flowers. She hustled him down a narrow hallway and into a sunny salon that seemed to have retractable walls, so even though they were still indoors, on three sides the stern was open to breezes like an Atlantican building. Very nice.

Ted was plain angry by the time Liz stopped hustling him. "You are not in charge here!" he shouted.

"No. Jack is."

Her calmness seemed to confound him. Perhaps he had thought they were here to have it out.

He said, "I think you should just leave and let me deal with him."

"You have no idea how to deal with him. If he's stuck with you, he won't survive the trip."

"I'm not doing anything!" Now Ted sounded flustered. That weird suppressed anger was rising again.

"He can read your mind. Or no, what he can read is your emotions, and that's even worse than reading your mind. To be around you feels awful! And I don't know how to fix it," she added, turning away, thinking.

"It's you! You're fussing and upsetting him. And look at him! He could be Jack's twin! What right did you have to separate them?"

Liz said thoughtfully, "Maybe you can just stay away from him?"

"For the whole two weeks? He'll be fine. Look, you tell Jack what you want. I don't get it. I don't want to get it."

Ted pulled his clamshell from his pants pocket and flipped it open and listened to it, then punched some buttons before listening again and trying to hand it to her. But Liz was cringing from that phone. It wasn't so much that she still loved Jack; it was more as if they were a single being, and all the places where they had pulled apart were still raw and bleeding. After, what? Eleven years? Twelve? How could she still feel as if he left just yesterday?

Ted was saying into his phone, "I'm sorry, son. I don't think she wants to talk. Butler's still pushing. I sent you an email."

"What?" Then Ted covered his phone with his hand and said to Liz, "Are you coming with us?"

No! No, she wasn't going. If this was how it felt to be as close to Jack as an open phone line, there was no way she was going to get closer. She shook her head grimly.

"Just Rex, I guess. We're planning to leave tonight."

There was a longer pause. That really was Jack. Ted had been calling him "son" since college. And Jack called Ted "kid." Liz used to think that was cute.

She extended her hand for the phone, feeling shaky. She glanced at Ted as he gestured to show her which end of the thing went where. Holding it at a little distance from her face to avoid some of the fuzzy energy of it, Liz said softly, "Hello? Please don't talk. Rex is coming to you willingly, but he's scared. He's going to be worse than Jude." She took a breath, then added, "Please build him a village where he can feel safe. Familiar food and clothing. Please give him time." She paused again. She started to say, "Please take care of him," but before the words were out she had to toss the phone to Ted. She folded into a nearby chair, wracked by physically painful sobs that she tried to suffer soundlessly. What kind of terrible love was this, that just the thought of Jack after all this time should make her fall apart this way?

Ted was saying, "She's okay. Just a mother."

"Tell him to grow a beard!"

"Oh. She says to grow a beard." Ted paused, then said, "Sure. Call you later, son," and he clapped the clamshell shut.

Liz stopped crying as suddenly as she had started. She stood, feeling shaky. Ted was looking at her, not angry anymore, but instead with a chilly and calculated feel to his mind. Relandela had told her that the mind-energies of the beardless ones in the ships offshore felt like metal to him, and that seemed to describe Ted.

As Liz hurried back to Relandela, she could feel how shaky his mind had become, so the stark way he looked was not surprising. Jude had his arm around Relandela's shoulders. He was saying something eager about how happy the grass had been in a park he had once visited.

Wait—maybe Jude could go with him? Jude had been a much-loved surrogate father to Relandela through all his growing-up, and Jude had spent seven years in the States. Of course!

"Jude, you've been there. You could take him to Jack and spend a little time—?"

"No."

"But he really—"

"No-o-o-o." Then Jude said to Relandela, "You'll be fine. Just get there. Jack's not like the others."

Liz's eyes met Relandela's unexpectedly. He said with surprising softness, "You coming, memelagh."

He really said that. This boy so dignified almost from birth that he seldom had used the word as a baby, this boy who had called her Litzlagh from childhood, looked at Liz now and called her "mommy." She rushed to sit at his unoccupied side and slipped her arms around his waist. What could they do? He was trembling now. He said, "You coming other place. I doing this. So you."

"Oh, but—"

His eyes slid beneath his father's long lashes. Up close, he resembled Jack even more. He said, "Is ocean swamping world. You nah saving candle?"

You sly dog, she thought.

"But they want to leave tonight! There's no time—"

"Teralagh knowing she nah seeing you dark light dark, they finding two at cliff of wood wings."

Teralagh was Gaprelagh's mother. Liz blurted, "What? You've already worked this out? You planned it? But I haven't said goodbye!"

Relandela's tension was easing a bit.

"Goodbye nah helping them. More good we die." Then he added, "You seeing Teralagh, is only me at cliff of wood wings."

Here was her beautiful, brilliant child sounding like a fool in a foreign language. Liz thought about the struggle ahead of him to understand even basic things. Clocks. Laws. Ownership. Money. Money! Even spending seven years in the States, Jude never grasped the concept of money! Liz had been living for twenty-five years in a Now so perfect that at this point even she was having trouble making sense of clocks and money, but she had lived with those concepts for thirty years. He was right. He needed her.

So she shifted her mind back to toughing this out. Staying here felt easier and safer, but being strong was always a choice. She didn't even have to see Jack, and he likely wouldn't want to see her, anyway. She could take Relandela there and stay with him long enough to get him settled in, and arrange for the medical supplies and communications equipment that they needed here, and come home. Or not. She could work that out later.

Liz sighed and stood and drew Jude to his feet and hugged him. He said, "Give the old boy our love."

"Help our family get over this. Please!"

Liz thought of how her nieces loved Relandela, how his wife and many friends adored him, how devastating his loss would be to them. Yet he was right. This was best. If they were only dead, there would be no need to tell people things that would forever trouble their peace.

Liz could feel Ted's mind approaching them. He appeared in the doorway, fingers in his hair, saying grumpily, "Jack called back. He's nervous about doing this alone."

She said, "I know. Tell him I'm coming."

———◆———

Because Rex found being inside Ted's yacht unbearable for reasons that he couldn't really articulate, within a day he and Liz were living camped on the forward deck in a nest of sheepskins and unvarnished teak lounges. He was used to doing lots of walking and very little sitting down, so while Liz would lounge, he would pace and listen and keep asking questions, looking thoughtful, rarely nodding. What she was telling him made as little sense to him as if she were trying to help him envision an elephant by describing it in random square inches.

"I don't know why it's sixty minutes and not fifty minutes or a hundred minutes," she was telling him as she sat with her feet up and watched him as he watched what was likely a whale breaching off to starboard.

"Can any number minute? So why caring?"

"Well, um, they think if they put numbers on the minutes they can get more done."

"More what they doing?"

His English was improving. He had spoken it for the first decade of his life, and of course he still had the words in his mind because what the Teacher said was written in English. Still, going from Atlantican to English was hard because English was linear and required activity while Atlantican had no verb tenses and assumed stasis.

"I seeing ship. There!"

"I think we're in a shipping channel. They, um—I think that's a tanker," she said, shielding her eyes and squinting to see where he was pointing. But now here were three more things—shipping, channel, tanker—that she winced to think he might ask her about. Each could require half an hour of nested explanations of each word used, until finally he would nod and accept whatever picture her words had painted in his mind. She assumed that most of what he was learning from her was nonsense. This was just English practice.

He glanced at her with smug satisfaction and said, "Shipping! Is say '-ing' there!"

Most Atlanticans learning English got past the fact that they couldn't grasp the concept of verb tenses by simply adding "-ing" to verbs. Liz was concentrating on getting Rex to drop his "-ings," but he was fighting that. She said patiently, "My love, may we cut your hair now?" He said nothing until she added, "They say we'll reach your father's house this afternoon."

Rex turned from gazing at the sea and looked at her and said, "Is cutting—Is cut."

Liz had borrowed scissors days ago, when she first got Rex to accept the idea that his braids should be cut. He had never seen scissors, but his mind barely rippled as he tried to make sense of what was in her hand. Perhaps at this point, nothing was surprising him. He turned his back, looking out at the sea, and she reached up to cut one braid as close to its base as she could. She wasn't sure how much tidying-up he was going to allow her afterward.

He said "Throw," as he felt the braid release.

His hair was a beautiful thick, deep blond that had a reddish tinge in most lights. Even braided, it hung nearly to his waist. Liz said, "May I save it, baby?"

"Throw. Is hrastinit."

"Hrastinit" was a universal word for anything that made life more complicated. The more he was learning about the other place, the more he was using it in every other sentence.

"Please. Let's give it to the children." He glanced at her. "There's a disease in the other place that takes children's hair. They can use your hair to help the children."

He thought and nodded once and said, "For children." He was reaching to explore the place where his braid had been as she started on the other one.

"They're building a village for us," she said chattily as she cut. "They say it's really nice!"

———◆———

Liz had been meeting with Ted almost daily as the village was built and Jack had questions. At first the men had assumed that she was going to get past her telephone phobia, but eventually Jack began to write to her. Ted would send a crewman to fetch her. She would read Jack's letter, give Ted her quick answers, then hurry back to Rex.

Jack's first letter to Liz was an unexpected shock. She entered Ted's study off that open-air lounge, and he stood from his desk and handed her a Larkin International envelope. She sank onto a chair, looking at it in both hands. Then she said, "No," and tried to hand it back. During most of their long relationship, a lot of what Liz had had of Jack had been his cryptic transmitted notes in these envelopes. No more notes. No more envelopes. She was starting to stand, but Ted took back the envelope and pulled out the note and unfolded it and handed it to her. Well, okay. She was being silly. She guessed she could read a piece of paper.

Dear Liz:

I know you hate me. Please forgive me. I couldn't be there. You know I tried.

Thank you for bringing him. I will take care of him.

We are building him Morakan North. It even has a greathouse. Jude got better in about a year. I won't rush our boy. I promise you.

Liz looked at Ted and said, "Did you read this? Now he thinks freedom is a disease?"

Should we re-seed when we take off the grass? Will he mind if we cook his food in our kitchen? When do you think he can wear regular clothes?

She said to Ted, "Please tell him I'm not angry. I don't hate him. We tried for a long time. He tried as hard as I did. We tried." Ted was passing her a pen. She said, "No. Either tell him what I'm saying, or—nothing. I'm done."

Liz was standing as she spoke. She dropped the letter, and for a couple of days she ignored Ted's summonses. Eventually he came for her himself, and just his close presence was so disruptive to Rex's mind that Liz understood that she had to go back to making those almost-daily visits to Ted's study.

⚜ 5 ⚜

About a week later, Ted summoned Liz on what he told her was the afternoon of November 1st. She was feeling better about Ted now. She had met him when she first met Jack, and then she hadn't seen him once as a quarter of a century passed. But it had been Ted's willingness to stand in for Jack that had made Jack's spending time on Atlantica even possible, so Liz was grateful to him. Every time she saw Ted now, she was on the verge of asking him whether Jack had a girlfriend, or whether perhaps he had remarried, but she really didn't want to know. The more she thought about it, the more she realized that of course he must have someone else by now. He was the sort of man who needed the soft support of a woman close to him.

Ted was a skinny, awkward man who seemed to have a need to actively think about doing the most basic things, like taking a step or even turning his head, and certainly forming the simplest sentence. Ted's mind at rest gave off a fluttery energy that was unlike anything Liz had felt before, like a small bird in a smaller cage. As she entered his study on the first day of November, she could feel something more, though. He was upset. He was frightened. She took her usual sheet of paper from his hand and sat down. Before she looked at it, she said, "Is something wrong?"

He was rocking in his desk chair as Jack used to do, but while Jack did it peacefully, Ted seemed to be trying to work off agitation. He said, not looking at her, "My father died in a bar fight. My mother worked herself to death scrubbing floors. I managed to get a scholarship to Dartmouth, and I met this big eccentric kid who used to cover his windows with masking tape. Did you know that? He thought people were spying on him. Jack's family was so rich, he used to come and go in a gray limousine with a liveried chauffeur. A chauffeur! Back then? We're talking the sixties." Ted paused, but he kept on rocking. Liz thought his talking about this might be helping.

"He told me he'd put me through law school and hire me. I think he liked me because I didn't ask questions about his family's money. Some of the others were suck-ups." Ted glanced at Liz. He stopped rocking and said, "I'm sorry. Go ahead. Read your letter."

"It can wait. Please go on."

"So I went to work for him. I had nothing. That was thirty-five years ago. Today I own a hundred-and-twenty-four-foot yacht, and I have a net worth over eighty million dollars."

"Oh good," Liz said to encourage him.

"Jack didn't get married, so I didn't get married. He thought it made sense to hire these brainless fools to pretend to be secretaries and, you know, sleep with them. I did that, too. He kept giving me little pieces of deals. And then my money started making money." Ted paused in his speech and stopped rocking. He was gazing at the ceiling. He said, "I met Linda in 1972. I always had lived with Jack, you know. He had a big house. Just made things easier. But then I fell in love. Jack thought it was funny. 'You're in love, kid? How can you know?' But I knew." Ted swiveled to face Liz. He added, "It wasn't until Jack met you that he understood how it hits you. Love. He thought he could control it with you. Did you know that? He hires them for sex and you for love, and everything is under control."

Yes, Liz knew that.

"Then I guess you gave him an ultimatum. He started almost living out there. I moved out of Sea Haven and got married. I have one child. I married too late." Ted was back to rocking again. "Her name is Catherine. She went to Dartmouth, too." He began to smile a bit at the thought of her. "She's the most beautiful person you ever met in your life! If all you're going to have is one, my girl's the one."

"Please tell me what's wrong. Is she okay?"

"She graduated last May. Jack hired her, of course. She's planning to get her M.B.A." He drew a breath. "Jack is building a native village for Rex. You know that." Another pause. "This morning he told me he wants to move her into that village so Rex can have a companion. A *companion!*" He spit that word out.

"Oh! But you can always say no."

Ted looked at Liz then, and in his eyes even more than in the chaotic vibration of his mind she could see his impossible choice.

"He means well. Everything he does! He has not a mean or selfish bone in his body."

No mean bones. Liz agreed with that. But, selfish? It seemed to her that Jack's whole life was selfish.

"He's been talking for years about how we have to get the kids together. Rex is growing up out there, Jack never sees him, but it's like his kid is on a shelf. Whenever he's ready, he can reach out and get him and he and I can be sharing grandchildren."

Yep, that sounded like Jack, Liz thought. And it explained a lot.

"I know he means well," Ted was telling the ceiling. "He wants to make my daughter a billionaire's wife. Sounds like the biggest favor, doesn't it? But she already has a boyfriend. And she has a life. And I've met Jack's son now. No offense, but he's a wild man." Ted paused, then added, "Literally."

"So you told him no."

"That's the point. I can't tell him no. I have never in my life said no to him. I tried this morning. I said, 'I think she likes living in the city.' 'I think she's kind of settled on Frank'—who also works for Jack, by the way. He said, 'Okay, we'll leave it up to her.' So while I've spent the morning trying to come up with a way to tell him no, he had a talk with her."

"And she said . . . ?"

"Yes. She couldn't say no to him, either."

"So I'll say it for you," Liz said, thinking. "Do you have a pen?"

He paused for so long that she almost asked him for a pen a second time.

"I don't think she's a virgin. It's not that. It's more that I want her to have her own life! I look back now, and I see I've been living Jack's life. Living my own wasn't good enough."

"A pen?"

"I don't want you in the middle. Forget I said anything."

"If it helps, Rex is married. You know they take that a lot more seriously out there than we do." Liz paused, feeling just a bit stunned by the fact that she already had shifted mentally back to being an American, even while this yacht was still underway. But then she remembered that Rex had killed himself off. Would he still consider himself to be married?

Ted seemed quieter now. He said, "Tell me about your son."

Liz felt herself beginning to smile. "Everything your Catherine is, my Relandela—my Rex is. He's the brightest, wisest, strongest, most selfless person you ever could meet. That's why Jack stopped going to Atlantica. By the time Rex was maybe ten, he was seeing right through him. Jack was too sheltered. He couldn't take that."

"So either way it's bad," Ted said reflectively. "Either he's a wild man and she's disgusted but she can't say no to Jack, or he's a saint and she falls in love and he breaks her heart. There's no good news in this."

Ted's yacht had such a deep draft that it had to lie half a mile offshore and wait for Jack to send a launch. Liz and Rex stood at the railing beside what had been their traveling home and tried to make out what they could of Sea Haven in the hazy distance. From here it looked like an interruption in what was an otherwise busy shoreline, a house much larger than all the others with a lawn around it of enormous size and woodlands on either side.

Liz had been hearing about Sea Haven ever since she first met Jack, and she had nurtured so many aversions to it that just the thought that she was looking at it now was breeding in her a rising panic. She had spent her life on Atlantica cultivating phobias about wealth and certainties about her own inability to function in Jack's world of wealth, and now she was seeing how foolish that had been. Every one of those fears that had for so long felt self-protective was landing on her like a pile of bricks. She had fought so hard not to see Jack as wealthy, and now of course all that had been for nothing. She had convinced herself that the only way she could have this man who had for so long been the center of her life was when he was shorn of his wealth, shorn of the outside world, shorn of everything except himself. But her thinking that way had been so stupid! In refusing to grapple with the complexities of the life that he was actually living, she had been constructing a future trap for herself. And now that future had arrived.

It always had been so thrilling when Jack would arrive back in Morakan. They would know the day, so Liz and Relandela would watch that hillside all morning. Usually it would be around noontime when he would appear, walking over the hill. They both would run across the bridge, and then Jack would be hurrying when he saw them. The three of them would fall together into the long grass at some point on the hill, hugging and laughing, with Jack and Liz then kissing and needing to hold one another, feeling whole again and at peace, while their little boy chattered to his father. The joy of it had been so intense and overwhelming that a remnant of that feeling seemed to be hanging around them even now. They were about to see him again.

Liz said to Rex, "He's going to be so glad to see you, sweetie."

"I laying life saving candle."

Liz glanced up at him. His jaw was set, his eyes were calm, his mind was fixed and intent. As they had traveled north, his conviction had grown.

"Then you're going to have to befriend him. Please love him! He's a very good man. His power is a curse, but we need it now. Please, sweetie. Give him a chance."

Ted was approaching them along the deck railing. With their trip nearly over, his former rigid distance from Rex had broken down. He came to stand near Liz and said, "The launch is on its way. Jack asks when and where you want to meet him. Should he be in the village? He says it's up to you."

That was not what Liz had been envisioning, although now that she thought about it, she had no idea what she had been envisioning.

"Rex has never seen a house like that. Okay. Tell him we'll meet him in the village."

As the launch approached a narrow dock, they were able to get a better view of the house at the top of a long, broad lawn. The face toward the water looked to Liz like red brick and white stone and slate-blue glass more or less in a colonial style, but so overblown on a four-story building that had to be at least two-hundred feet long besides wings extending on either side that whatever colonial features it had were purely decorative. Improbably, though, it looked lightweight and pretty. Liz said to Ted, standing beside her on the launch, "Did they build that all at once?"

"Thirty thousand square feet with the office. In the sixties, Jack was in a building phase."

Even before the launch hit the dock, the vibrations of this place were troubling Rex's mind. Liz couldn't really feel them herself. She thought

Jack's home was beautiful, the enormous house, the formal gardens. In all the years she had been hearing about Sea Haven, she never had imagined it would be so beautiful.

The dock had been built to hit the side of the launch precisely, so they could walk off it easily. Liz slipped her hand into Rex's as they started up the dock.

"Are you okay, sweetie?"

"I laying life."

"Please, baby . . . !"

They stepped onto a pebbled path off the end of the dock. Rex was becoming ever more distressed, almost as if his mind were being singed and the edges were beginning to fray. Liz murmured, "Are you able to bear this?"

"Yes." But now she could see his pain in his face. After a moment he said with reluctant anguish, "Is grass! Why hurting grass? Is tree!" He slapped the bark of a tree with his palm as they passed it.

"Is it chemicals?" Liz murmured to Ted on her other side. She was feeling the stress around her now, too, but bearably. What troubled her more was the fluttery feeling of panic coming from Rex's mind.

Ted said, "Jude thought it was chemicals, but most of what we do now is organic. They've taken everything out where the village is. See if that feels better to him."

⤙ 6 ⤚

Rex had not thought much about what the other place would be like. He must do this, and he had assumed that he would have the strength to do what must be done. But he never could have imagined this! To his eyes, it looked normal. Smaller trees. A strange stone mountain that Liz had told him was his father's house. But all of it was buzzing and clanging and shrieking with nasty energy, and there was no way to control it, no way to make it stop. Liz was holding his hand now and talking to him, but he wasn't listening. Some of the worst vibrations seemed to be coming from the plants, but that made no sense. He was feeling plants as strongly as if they were beardless ones in pain.

As they passed through a stand of little trees, Rex glimpsed beyond it a circle of houses golden with new wood. He lifted his chin. Before any of this had begun, he had been learning to protect his mind as Gaprelagh the beautiful could protect hers, by withdrawing it into a well of peace within her. She was able to do that naturally. She had been teaching him how to do it, too, and he was trying to do it now. Beyond the trees, the clanging ache was less.

Then Rex was feeling people's minds. He recognized Jack immediately, a kind of expansive, gentle energy that was so much the same that it made Rex feel like a boy again. His father had done so much to hurt him! And had done so much to hurt his mother, which made Rex think of Liz and realize that he could no longer feel her nearby.

When Jack spotted Rex there was a flash in his mind so strong that feeling the energy of it made Rex stop walking. But Jack was running. He grabbed Rex, hugging him, rocking him in his arms, talking rapidly into his ear, giving off an overriding joy that seemed to smother even whatever beardless energy had to be coming from his mind. Rex's first thought was that Liz had been right, and Jack was not after all a bad man. His second, overwhelming thought was that his father loved him. No need to earn that. Done.

Jack stepped back and looked at Rex, grinning, laying both hands on his shoulders. He was examining Rex's face with such intrusive interest that Rex looked away and eased out from under those hands. Jack reached to tousle Rex's hair as he always had done long ago and said, "I love you, son. God, it's good to see you! Hey, come meet someone."

Rex was opening his mind to better feel for Jack's mind, surprised that there was so much less of the beardless stench about him. Rex and his friends used to try to break down that awful, clanging metallic mind-energy, and they thought it was mainly aggression and fear. Jack had little of that. Rex was relieved to think that this was not going to be as hard as it could have been.

Jack's friend was small and very young. He introduced them. "Honey, this is Rex. Rex, this is Cathy. She's going to be living here with you."

Rex had assumed that just he and Liz would be living here. Why also this one? Cathy had a sweet and velvety feel to her mind. Well-loved children had that feel, as did some of the oldest ones. It impressed Rex to find it in a young woman. She didn't feel very beardless to him, and on closer look she wasn't far from his age. Her hair was nearly black. Her eyes were brown. If Jack were trying to choose a woman for him, Rex thought that he had chosen well.

Jack said pleasantly, "How was your trip? I hear you wanted to be outdoors?"

"Fixing grass."

Hearing him speak startled and sobered Jack. He said to the woman under his breath, "He didn't grow up with English." To Rex he said, "You're going to want to learn it better, son. We'll get you tutors."

Rex looked Jack full in the eyes and said, "You hurting grass, you hurting the sielrah!"

Jack said, sounding meeker, "Do you know where your mother is?"

Ted didn't want to have to see his daughter in native woolens in Jack's little village, so before they entered that final copse of trees he turned back down the path toward the dock. That felt like Liz's signal to do the same. She wasn't ready to see Jack now. The decades-long bond between them was still so central to her life that she wasn't yet ready to face the likelihood that while she still had it, he had moved beyond it. Besides, just landing here seemed to have put her immediately deep into his world, a place she had fought hard never to be, and she found that sobering. If this were a contest, he already had won it.

As they walked, she said to Ted, whose mind seemed fluttery, "It's going to be fine. We'll find a way to, um, get her out of there gracefully."

"She told me this morning she broke up with Frank." Ted paused as he freshly considered this news. "What gets me is Jack always wins! I used to love that. His wins were my wins. He doesn't even seem to know how he does it. I've seen him take some impossible deal and push a little here and pay a little there and outmaneuver people until he had checkmate, and then not even pause to gloat. Just on to the next one. Do you know why he chose my Catherine?" Ted went on angrily. Liz glanced at him. "He needed someone from his safe little world. Rex needs a girl, and hey, here's Ted's daughter!"

"I am so sorry."

"And it's checkmate, because she wants to be there. Why go off and try to make it on your own, if just getting close to the Richardsons does it? And don't I know how that feels," Ted added bitterly. "You know, I've been thinking about this. I think the reason he fell so hard for you was he couldn't buy you. But now of course he's bought you, too."

"No he hasn't!"

Ted glanced at her and said, "You're here, aren't you?"

Liz thought about that. Jack's coin had been the happiness of her son and the safety of the island she loved, but yup, she had to admit Ted was right.

Liz was waving Ted off on the launch and thinking about taking a walk in the formal gardens that took up most of the lower end of the lawn above the ocean wall. But then someone came running, calling her name. "Are you Mrs. Lyons? Mrs. Lyons, right? Mr. Richardson wants you. Come with me, please."

So she followed a man in a dark-green jumpsuit up through the worst of that negative energy that even she was feeling now, and through the trees and toward the raw-wood buildings. What Ted had just said about Jack's having bought her was ringing in her mind so strongly that she had to take it apart and try to figure out how she should feel about it. If she were about to see the great love of her life after so many years apart, then at least she wanted to react in a way that wasn't going to have her regretting things later.

As Liz reached the buildings, she ducked away from the man she had been following and slipped out of sight behind a little house. She peeked carefully around it. The three of them were sitting cross-legged on sheep-skins in front of their mini-greathouse in an early twilight that lent to the scene a rosy glow. The men seemed to be arguing the way they had loved to argue when Rex was a boy, just mind-jousting, no emotions attached.

Liz had been expecting Jack to look ancient, but he didn't even look much older. He looked quieter, a little bit smaller, but the last time she had seen him he had been island-fit, and now he was city-soft.

Liz realized that on some level she had been seeing this trip as a business proposition. Give Jack his heir, give Rex the power to protect their island for another generation, get medications and communications in place for Atlantica, then dust her hands together and move on. But seeing Jack again made her realize that, far from waning, her love for him seemed to have mellowed and strengthened, revealing further highlights and additional deep notes.

Yet her rush of joy at the sight of him felt buried in a wave of overwhelming shyness. She couldn't bear to go near him now. He looked so much like her same old Jack! But now that she was here, she understood that he really wasn't her Jack at all. He had never been hers. He had always belonged here. And she had seen herself in a mirror lately.

Jack was gesturing in the waning light, and sure enough, a servant appeared. Jack spoke briefly to the man in a white jumpsuit bending over him, and the man then hurried off down the path toward the ocean, likely looking for Liz. Good grief. Jack was sitting on Atlantican sheepskins before an Atlantican greathouse in Atlantican clothing talking with their Atlantican son, and still he had to be surrounded by staff on the odd chance that he might need something?

What Jack really seemed to most enjoy was playing at life in controllable ways. Even his having for so long had a distant family that he could visit had been playing at family life, hadn't it? He had never been there for the real crises, the childhood fevers, the time when Relandela fell out of a tree and broke his arm. Liz's nieces, Flower and Rain, had briefly ended up in this house as young children, and he had happily done the whole daddy thing with them, buying them ponies and taking them to the zoo and watching *Sesame Street* with them. Of course, Liz had learned later that their trip to the zoo was after hours and *Sesame Street* had been watched in his office, but still.

Liz could at any moment have stepped out of the shadows and joined them. Jack was glancing around, perhaps looking for her. But now that she had seen his house, had seen how he looked and the way he lived and the leaden fact that the man she had so desperately loved for so many years was so wealthy that she was completely outclassed, Liz didn't want to make him have to see her. Of course he had moved on with his life! Eventually he had wanted his son, but he hadn't asked for Liz. She had tagged along. And now that she had seen him, she was anxious to spare herself the humiliation of having him ever see her. She couldn't bear to have him treat her politely. She wanted to spare him the inconvenience of even having to deal with her at all.

Without planning it, Liz was slipping among the trees and heading east away from the house. At first she was determined to go home to Atlantica even if she had to swim, but as she thought about the fact that she was dead there now, it occurred to her that what might be good would be for her to become dead here as well. She had seen that Rex was settling in nicely. She hadn't been close enough to feel his mind, but just his posture and the look on his face had told her that he was enjoying his father. Whatever more he might need from Liz, Jack could pay someone else to do. Better.

There was a strange euphoria in the thought of staging another death for herself. Her notion was to get down to the beach and leave something there—her sash, she was thinking—then follow the beach east until she found a road where she could hitchhike. She enjoyed imagining them bringing him her sash, him rushing to see where they had found it, calling the police, scouring the beach. She would be far away by then, maybe making it all the way to Maine, where she could change her name and possibly waitress in one of those seaside lobster places. The only trip she ever had taken with Bradford Lyons, her despicable first husband, had been to Maine. She had enjoyed being there.

It was becoming dark so quickly that being sure about direction by the light was difficult. Liz was feeling with her toes through ponyskin moccasins, testing the ground so carefully that by the time she was glimpsing what looked like the glint of moonlight on the ocean through trees, she thought it had been awhile since she had even broken a twig. Then she distinctly felt that nasty beardless mind-energy. Close. She froze and strained to listen. She didn't dare move. She was hearing stealthy footfalls now, pausing every step or two. She was trying to hold her breath, but then she barely gasped and someone feet away from her growled, "Halt!" He grabbed her by an arm and threw her down. She shrieked. He said coldly, "Who are you? What are you doing here?" A harsh light was flashing in her face.

"I'm a guest," Liz whispered, squinting. She was too frightened to speak louder.

Then he was pulling her to stand. She saw glints where moonlight hit metal and heard the clink of metal fittings. My God, he was armed! He began to push her through the dark woods impersonally, neither roughly nor gently. Apparently his job was to pick up human debris, and now here was more. He gathered two more guards along the way who had to be told the story of her capture as all of them followed her on her trek through the woods, fighting brush and dodging branches.

Then eventually the woods thinned, and with relief Liz was looking at Jack's enormous house. The grounds were gracefully lit with low smudges of light here and there, with sparkling lights along the paths and along what likely was a driveway. The walk seemed to take forever, but eventually they were approaching a black wrought-iron fence and a lit gatehouse beside tall, closed gates. A man in brown sat behind a desk in the gatehouse. Beyond him were dozens of small television sets in a grid, all flickering, but most showing blackness. Liz's guards pushed her inside. The fellow at the desk seemed to be glaring at her with one eye while he studied her Atlantican woolen pants and tunic with the other.

"Name, please?"

"Elizabeth Lyons."

"See some ID?"

ID? Sure. In my back pocket.

Liz said, "Is this Jack Richardson's house?" and the guards exchanged glances. The one at the desk pressed a button on his shirt lapel and began to talk. Liz had discovered on Ted's yacht that electronics had changed a lot in twenty-five years.

Then she heard the word "stalker." She heard her name. After a long pause she heard, "Yes, sir. Right away."

What Liz had come to think of as her personal detail herded her more respectfully down the driveway toward the house. Even in darkness it looked airy and beautiful, tastefully lit enough to show its shape, and with a few bright windows. Before they had made it halfway down the driveway, the front door opened and Jack stepped out. He started walking quickly, then he hopped into a half-run and caught Liz in his arms. He said, "Are you all right? What happened to you?" and he sounded so exactly like the same old Jack that she was hugging him tight and burrowing into him. He pried her off, murmuring, and he managed to walk her down the driveway while she kept trying to grab him and hug him again.

Liz was grateful that the enormous foyer was dimly lit for nighttime. Not only did that make its gaudiness more bearable, but it was kinder to her fifty-five-year-old face. Jack closed the door behind them and stood and looked at her. She lifted her eyes to his, and he smiled his old soft private smile, his smile that said that what was happening now was funny or touching or surprising to him in a way that only Liz would understand. He drew her into his arms then and kissed her exactly as he always had kissed her, one hand moving back under her hair and the other at the small of her back, stroking her against him while his mouth worked on hers so wonderfully that she whimpered. He broke the kiss and held her with his cheek against her hair and said, "Welcome home, honey."

Liz had to know where this was going. She drew back a little and looked up at him, and then she stepped back, but gently. She said, "Jack? You wanted Rex here? You don't have to see me, you know. It's okay."

He was standing there looking at her. Close up, he did seem somewhat older, his skin a little looser, his eyelids heavier. More gray in his hair. But still, he looked so much the same, and the energies of his mind were so much the same. When he didn't at first say anything, she had to purse her lips and look away. Then he said, "What's it been? Ten years? I should ask you the same question. Do you want to see me?"

She looked at him. Just the beyond-amazement sudden sight of him after so much time apart brought all of it right back to her, their perfect connection of yin and yang so tightly wound that each time they had managed to be together for awhile you would have thought it was impossible for them ever to be apart again. But it never had worked for long, and the reason was money. That was the only disgusting reason. Hearing him ask the question so frankly made her ask it of herself. Did she really want to start this again?

He was looking away from her now. His face was grim.

"You'll never know how much you hurt me, Liz. I'm still not really over it. I guess I don't take rejection well."

"You don't take anything well! This is such a tragedy! If you didn't have this stupid money thing, we could be so happy."

"'Money thing'? What 'money thing'?"

"You without money are the loveliest man. Kind and smart and funny and real. With money you're selfish and spoiled. And lazy! You must have put on thirty pounds." Then she added, "Give Ted back his daughter."

He brightened at that. "Did you meet her? Isn't she sweet? Rex really likes her." Then a new thought occurred to him. He said, "Is this really your first time inside a single-family house?"

Liz had grown up in a ratty apartment building. That whole building wasn't as big as this house. One of their running jokes in the first joy of their falling in love had been the fact that he owned this enormous house, but she had never been inside a separate house of any size. It had been a lot funnier at the time. But this was not at all the way she wanted their first meeting to go. They were falling back into stupid patterns that stemmed from their contentious beginnings. She said, "Do you still consider us married?"

"Yes. Do you?"

They had been native-married on Atlantica. Liz was relieved to hear that still mattered to him. But on the other hand, what could he have said? No?

"I'll come back tomorrow. We've got to talk. Where is that village from here?"

Jack said automatically, "I've got meetings until two. Will two work?"

"Good grief. Tell you what. I'll come to this door at some random time of day tomorrow. If you open the door, we'll talk. If somebody else opens the door I'll go back to the village."

Liz moved to the front door, meaning to sweep out gracefully, but there seemed to be a whole row of locks built into so much decoration that she couldn't find a doorknob. Jack reached from behind her and touched a lever and the door opened, apparently on its own. It was the size of maybe four normal doors.

Liz turned to him on the step. He bent and kissed her lightly on the lips and said, "To the right, past the gazebo and the aspen grove. I'd walk you there, but for now Rex seems to want me just in bearable doses."

"One more thing. We need Bibles. Ted says you can get them with the Teacher's words in red. Get that kind."

Jack looked as confounded as if she had requested unicorns. "What—?"

Liz reached and touched a finger to his lips and said, "While I teach him about you, I'll teach you about him."

In spite of herself, she could feel their old yin and yang of connection making its circle. Was he feeling it, too? Did he even want it? She thought she was strong enough now to deal with whatever this was going to be, but it would be so much easier if she didn't still feel that at their core they were so densely connected that they were essentially one being. Even now. A dozen years apart had been an eye-blink of time. She said gently, "I love you. I hope you'll want to spend time with me tomorrow. But if nineteen billion dollars still doesn't seem to be enough, I'll understand."

⇒ 7 ⇐

From the seaward terrace there was such a spectacular view of the eastern end of Long Island Sound glittering in the morning sunlight that Liz was stunned and overcome by it. She could see a few small white cabin boats here and there—maybe fishing, she thought, shading her eyes—but otherwise there was nothing but the same kind of endless ocean view that you could see from the windmill hill on Atlantica. This familiar yet extraordinary view gave her the sense that, unexpectedly and profoundly, she was home.

A housemaid in a black dress with a white apron had answered the front door and led Liz through an enormous library and out to this terrace, where there was a table under an awning set for two. But Liz had needed to come right to the edge of the terrace to better see that amazing expanse of ocean. Jack came out while she was studying it. She heard him call from behind her, "What does this remind you of?"

She turned. There he was, standing by the table that likely had been set so they could share whatever meal would be appropriate whenever she got here. He was wearing what he used to wear on his yacht twenty-five years ago, dark pants and a dress shirt and tie with a cashmere sweater. Liz grabbed for the back of a chair. But no, she could do this. Being strong was a choice. As she approached him, he said, "I know it's too cold to eat out here, but before we go in I want you to see this. What does it make you think of?"

Did he say cold? Liz wasn't cold, but she realized that this November wind would feel cold to someone living in civilization. She had become so used to basically living outdoors that she was experiencing cold more as Atlanticans did, and that thought pleased her. She said, "Please get a coat. I'm still allergic to opulence."

The appropriate meal turned out to be a late breakfast. They were sipping coffee and lightly alcoholic orange juice and eating mixed fruit much richer in flavor and color than she remembered it, and eating omelets and excellent whole-grain toast that he told her had been baked right here. Liz could taste that he had remembered to order her meal to be made without salt. He was telling her that he had chosen this site to replicate the Atlantican cliff with the view where he would later put his windmills.

"Steve and I used to love it up there. I told him when I grew up, I was going to find another place like that and live there. He thought there was no place else so beautiful, but this comes close."

Jack had been studying Liz's face between bites, looking at her so closely that she had to keep looking away. Now he said, "I thought when I saw you last night I ought to suggest you have a few things done." He took another bite of omelet. "I don't know whether you've thought about it." A sip of coffee. Then he said, "That was what I thought last night. But as I get used to looking at you, I think maybe this is the way you always were supposed to look." Another bite. He studied her face as he chewed. He added, "You weren't pretty before, but you've grown into your face."

Liz glanced at him repeatedly, watching him use his hands, noticing details of his hairline and the way his ear was set and the way his lips moved and the way his eyes slid under lashes still long and dark and the way his beard was darker than the hair on his head, and his mustache was even darker. She didn't talk. When she was talking, he wouldn't be talking, and she was trying to fill all those years when she had been without the sound of his voice.

He said then, "When you and Rex kicked me out, I didn't realize you meant it to be permanent. But then you shut the system down." Jack added wryly, "I got the message."

"There was a storm, darling. It took down the tower."

He looked at Liz. He set down his fork, looking at her.

"Are you saying you didn't mean to cut me off? It wasn't deliberate?"

"Of course not! Then you never—"

He stood up. "I thought you and Rex were telling me to go to hell! It was only a storm? Why didn't you let me know?"

"You never came back. I thought—"

"We sent that supply ship every year. Every year I checked. There never was a message. Christ, Liz, every month they sent a cutter in to make a sweep around the island. Did anybody try to flag it down? No! And I know that. I checked. Every damn month. I checked."

He was pacing now, intermittently glaring at Liz, looking furious. She watched him, feeling stunned. Feeling horrified. She said softly, "I thought you gave up on me. You said it was too hard—"

"You gave up on me!" he shouted. She tried to shrink smaller in her chair. "It's billions! Oh no!" he said in a simpering little mocking voice. She had never heard him do that. "So I gave you what the hell you wanted. You don't want me? Fine. You and Rex! Both of you! I gave you everything that mattered to me, and you never could be bothered to let me know it was only a goddamn storm?"

Liz had never heard him swear, although Jude used to say Jack could swear like a sailor. Her eyes were filling. None of this had ever occurred to her. She said very softly, "I love you. I'm sorry."

He said, not looking at her, pacing, "I was amazed when Ted said you were coming. Hell, I was amazed when you let Rex come! Twelve years, it's been? I thought I'd see you last night, and nothing. Then I saw you. Not nothing. So I thought this morning we could put a bow around it. But now I find out it was only a storm? You were just so goddamn sure I was too fucking rich to want you. I finally dropped you. You were right all along. That's what it was? That's all it was? Damn it, Liz, how could you do that? And not just to me! How could you do it to yourself?"

Liz stood up. Then she was running, grabbing him, hugging him, sobbing. But he wasn't hugging her back. After a pause, his arms were around her, but lightly. He was saying close to her ear, "I would have done anything for you. Anything. I thought giving you up was the only thing you wanted from me. I was even willing to give you that."

"Oh darling, I'm so sorry!"

He was right, though. She was scrambling now mentally, trying to come up with some sort of loophole, but he was right. She had always been so sure that a man so rich never could want little Lizzie Brandt who grew up in Bed-Sty and was clumsy and socially ridiculous. She always had been so sure he was going to ditch her eventually that she had ditched him first. Repeatedly. And it never once had occurred to her that Jack's not coming back might have been anything but his final ditch decision. He was right. And she had to admit that he also was right that his having left her there with Rex but still sending the supply ships, still protecting their island, would have been the only thing she might have wanted from him that his money could buy . . . if she had wanted it. But it was the last thing she had wanted.

He was genuinely hugging her now, and saying into her hair something he used to say repeatedly, every time she dumped him but he took her back, and whenever it struck him yet again that his having fallen in love with her seemed to be a well-targeted punishment for every previous sin of his life: "You're proof there really is a God, Liz. We've got proof. We'd better alert the *Times*."

She looked up at him then with tears on her cheeks. He really was completely the same old Jack, they still saw everything exactly the same, and this was hitting him the way it was hitting her. What a relief it was to know that he hadn't ditched her, after all. And she hadn't ditched him. And how funny this was! No one else but the two of them would have gone from his rage and her tears to immediate laughter, but their eyes met. Then they were laughing so hard that they couldn't stand up, so he edged them closer to a big green sofa and they fell onto it, hugging and laughing. As they started to get past it and he was sitting up, wiping his eyes with his fingers, trying to compose himself, he said, "It's not as funny as you think," but then he was laughing again.

Liz was trying to compose herself, too, and was startled to realize as she looked around that there were people there now, six of them, eight, all appearing to be wringing their hands with concern from a respectful distance. She said, "Oh no! It's the men in white coats!" But it was white jumpsuits, actually. Four men in white jumpsuits, two maids in black dresses with white aprons, two men in black tie. One of these came forward now and handed Jack a handkerchief. Jack said to them generally, "We're fine." To Liz he said, "I never laugh like that. They think I've lost it." Then, "I'm fine," he said more crisply, and they dispersed. The maids began to clear away breakfast.

Liz said, "I'm so sorry! But why didn't you know I was being an idiot and send someone to check with me?"

Jack was sitting up now, looking thoughtful.

"I took it hard. I thought you meant it this time. For Rex's sake. You were being a mother. The things he said were terrible! So Ted knew a big shrink in the city. When I told him you were so insecure you kept breaking up with me so I couldn't do it first, he convinced me it was time to let you be. We were taking my life apart by then and trying to fix it. The last thing I needed was more rejection."

Liz slipped her hand into Jack's, but he sat back and drew her in cuddled close beside him with his arm around her. From where they sat, far back on the terrace, they could see just that endless ocean view and only a couple of small white boats. Whatever this was going to be, Liz was finding that the opulence around her seemed to matter nothing at all beside the fact that she was again in her husband's arms.

"You let people fish there?"

"Fishing? No. That's security."

"The guys in white, too?"

"No. Security is brown. Grounds-keeping is green. Serving is white."

"Good grief," she said softly.

"Staff is in uniform, and we control the uniforms. It's a safety measure."

Liz sighed and said, "Being rich is certainly complicated."

"More than you know," he murmured, kissing her hair.

"So, um, but at least you don't need a shrink now."

"No, I do. You're not my big problem. Milly is. But it's going to bend his mind when I tell him about your latest maneuver. And it turned out funny. He'll never believe that!"

"Milly? Your mother?"

"Apparently every problem I've ever had in my life stems from sexual abuse. Every one of them! I should have been a shrink. What an easy job that is."

"Not enough billions," Liz said at once.

Jack drew back a little and looked at her. He said, "Does everything look funny to you? I think that's what I missed most of all." He stroked her head down onto his shoulder as he went on, "I always thought it started when I was almost thirteen. On Christmas Eve. My mother began an affair with me to get back at my father. Weird, but I've been dealing with it. But it turns out it started when I was small. And it was really bad. We're working it through. I'm supposed to learn to hate her now. But how do you hate your own mother? She was such a sad little lonely person. She loved my father, but he only stayed with her so he could manage her money. She was so miserable. She had no friends. I was all she had. How do you pull hatred out of that?"

"Don't hate her. Forgive her."

"I can't. I've got to reject my abuser. Apparently that's how people get better." He paused, then added, "I'm working on that now. My shrink—his name is Chuck—he comes twice a week. And it's been twelve years now? Amazing."

"Do you forgive me?"

He didn't immediately say anything. Liz began to shrink internally. Then he said, sounding chilly, "If any other woman had put me through the hell you put me through because she was too stupid to try to get a message to me, she'd be in a car right now. I wouldn't have her in my life, and it wouldn't matter whose mother she was." Liz was shrinking further as he went on, "But I'm thinking now it was mostly my fault. I should have known you'd never cut me off. But I was so broken up when you shut me down that I started right away with Chuck, and immediately he was into the sexual abuse. Finding out she was doing things when I was so young kind of rocked me. For awhile, he was coming here every day."

"Maybe I shouldn't have come back? Maybe—"

Jack glanced down at her then in close-focus, nestled cozily as she was with her head on his shoulder. He said, "I haven't laughed like that in twelve years. You took that insanity and made it funny? But I need to know what you intend. I can't take another little-Lizzie rejection. I'm sitting here freezing my butt off now because you refuse to step inside my house?"

"I don't—no, I can go inside. I'm just being silly."

"The problem is that you're not used to money and I'm not used to being without money, so we're star-crossed." Jack had turned a little now, and he was sitting back enough so he could look at her face as she lay against his arm. She found herself able to look at him, even though he still looked so much the same. Her love for him was such at this point that if he were to reject her as she thought he might be about to reject her, she would die of it. And death would be a relief.

"I just want you to be happy! And you can do so much better than me, darling."

"No, I can't do better, and you of all people should know that."

"But I—"

"Prettier? I don't trust pretty. Smarter? There is nobody smarter. I have never known anyone else whose mind connected so completely with mine. What just happened back there? We realized we'd wasted twelve years of our lives because of absolute, complete stupidity, and that struck us both as funny? Have you any idea how profound that is? With anyone else, I'd still be fuming. With you here, I just feel whole and at peace. Whatever happened then, it doesn't matter now. How could you think I could do better?"

Liz was watching his face, and she could feel his mind a little. It felt soft and calm. She said quietly, realizing as she said it that her courage in saying this felt surprising, "I want to stay with you forever, darling, but I couldn't survive if I trusted you and you rejected me. So, um, if there's just maybe, you know, one chance in a million you're ever going to reject me in a million years, then it's okay. No hard feelings. But if it's never going to happen, and you know for sure it's never going to happen—"

He didn't wait for her to finish, but he drew her closer and rocked her against him and said, "Deal. Done. Now you can never reject me, either."

⪥ 8 ⪤

Wandering back toward the village holding hands with Jack felt more natural to Liz than anything else that she had ever done in her life. She was hearing details about how he had accumulated all the land for his estate, buying houses through straw purchasers for most of the sixties until he got the last few holdouts to complete almost two hundred acres of land that included fourteen hundred feet of beach. Yesterday all she could have thought would have been how expensive it must have been to buy all those homes just to knock them down, and where had all the families gone? But today it was just an interesting set of facts about their beautiful home. It seemed to Liz that it might be the beginning of a normal life. She and Jack had never had a normal life.

During the nearly four hours that they had just spent together, breakfasting and casually touring the house and then sharing sandwiches at a twenty-seat table in an ornate pillared dining room, Liz had reached what felt like an equilibrium in her mind about her husband. She was seeing now that fundamentally she had been wrong and he had been right, and it had been mostly her own insecurities that had kept souring their relationship. Jack was not his money. He had money; he was tall; he had a crooked front tooth. None of that affected who he was. He had shown her most of his house, talking about the objects it held but not caring about them beyond an impersonal appreciation for their beauty. He didn't seem to see them as part of him, and now Liz found that she didn't, either. There was a lot of gilding in that house. He told her he liked it not for the opulence of it, but because it lent a sparkle to rooms and it better set off wall colors. So then the gold leaf became another fact about him. He was no longer all about the gold leaf.

Even his mother's clocks and eggs! Liz realized as they entered the drawing room that the whole room had become such a central phobia that she likely would have refused to make this trip if she had known she was going to have to see it. But it was just a pretty anteroom off the gigantic three-story library around which the central part of the house was built. It had rose damask on the walls and ocean views and lots of gold leaf, even on the ceiling. It was full of dainty French chairs and tables and an amazingly beautiful gilded settee on impossibly delicate legs that faced a small carved marble fireplace surrounded on either side by glass shelves that held Milly's vermeil clocks and Faberge eggs.

Those little clocks were amazing. In Liz's mind, they had loomed as grandfather clocks too big to stand on any shelf, but in fact they were just ten richly ornate gold-and-silver nature-themed clocks that were not much bigger than alarm clocks. They alternated on their shelves with eight gem-encrusted eggs.

Jack told her, "We think the clocks are worth more than the eggs. There are sixty-nine original Faberge eggs, but there were fewer than thirty of these clocks ever made. They were a fad in the Russian Court around 1880, but then the eggs came along."

Liz was studying a clock that reminded her of home, tiny silver and gold horses like Atlantican ponies on what could have been a pale-gold Atlantican hill.

"You can touch it, honey. Go ahead."

"What are they worth?" she asked, barely grazing one of the horses with a finger.

"Who knows? We can't even insure them. To insure them you've got to show them to appraisers and say where they are." He added, "You spooked the security staff when you used my name. Nobody is supposed to know who lives here." Then he went on to say, "Everything will be appraised when I die. All of it goes to the Smithsonian. The Jonathan and Millicent Richardson Collection."

Liz looked up at Jack quickly. They had talked a lot about his parents, his frustrated love for both of them and their twisted and blighted love for one another. He always laid the blame for the destruction of his childhood on the fact that his mother couldn't risk another pregnancy, so his Catholic father kept mistresses because neither birth control nor divorce was an option.

Liz said, "Does this feel as if you're getting back at them?"

"No. But I get to write their history, and this is the history I am willing to write." Then his breath caught. He swallowed and added, "This is what she would have wanted. It's all that I can give her now. The Smithsonian will get the contents of this house and my penthouse. Eventually there will be a building or a wing with their names on it—"

Liz said, "Take that, Dad!" and Jack barely smiled.

"We've told the Smithsonian they can sell my things to fund the wing, but everything my parents owned they've got to keep in perpetuity. Of course, they don't know who they're dealing with now. Eventually they will know."

Liz was watching Jack's face as he finished this speech. That he could talk so calmly about his own death and the tidying-up details that would follow it was a new fact about him. Still, she had seen on Atlantica that despite his surface emotional fragility he had a strong and peaceful core.

She long had wondered what he would have been like if his mother had not so outrageously messed with him.

And there was something else she had wondered about, a piece of his history she wanted to know. Atlanticans never would dream of asking such a personal question, but Liz was shedding her Atlantican identity a little more with every step. Studying Milly's clocks and eggs, she said, "So, did Steve know about you and Milly?"

He glanced at her and said, "What do you think?"

"He knew."

"At Andover they seemed to put the richest boys together. I used to think that was disgusting, but now I realize it was a kindness to all of us. His family was so old-money, they made the Rockefellers look *nouveau riche.* We were assigned as roommates our freshman year, but I'd have chosen him from all the earth. He got me. Nobody else but you ever has."

Jack had picked up and was examining one of the eggs. When he didn't continue his story, Liz said, "So you told him?"

Jack gave her a pointed glance, then went back to examining the egg, testing some of the gem settings with a fingernail.

"I didn't have to tell him. He said later I'd come back from weekends so devastated that it would take him the whole next week to put me back together. All he could think to do was keep me away from her. You know me, honey. Do you honestly think I would have been eager to spend summer after summer roughing it on Atlantica in the middle of winter if it hadn't been a way to get so far from her that I could think of her as just my mother for awhile?"

"I'm so sorry, darling."

"I wish you had known Steve. He was a little like your mother, trying to right every wrong. It's hard to believe she's dead! She seemed like a force of nature. But Steve was like that, living for other people. And money really meant nothing to him. His father was into genealogy, and eventually he discovered that a lot of the original family money came from two slave traders. When Steve learned that, he wanted to spend his whole inheritance on the Atlantican natives. He and I always assumed they were descended from slaves removed from South Carolina, but then he brought in researchers to try to prove the island's connection to slavery. He learned that the Atlanticans are mostly African, but they long predate the Civil War."

Jack set down the egg and reached for Liz's hand to move on as he added, "Of course, it was very like Steve to be spending his inheritance on them, with never a thought for himself. They had no antibiotics on the island because the Atlanticans had rejected antibiotics, so his infected leg killed him hours before help could arrive."

And a lack of fresh antibiotics had killed Myra, too. Liz was already seeing how much more useful she could be to Atlantica from here than from there. As she and Jack started to climb an enormous staircase that curved up to the second floor, she said, trying to sound casual, "If you consider us married, why do you still refer to me as Mrs. Lyons?"

"Probably for the same reason I've never put my name on anything else I own. Whatever reason that is." Then he said, "Chuck the shrink says I started trying to disappear in childhood so my mother couldn't find me. In so many ways he is full of it! I think it's more that I'm private by nature. I was very young when I lost my parents, and I trusted the wrong people in the beginning. I let them talk me into developing this public image as a playboy rich kid. It's taken me years to undo all that damage. Now I so seldom go anywhere that if people think of me at all, they assume I must have become so eccentric that I have long hair and fingernails and wear empty tissue-boxes on my feet."

Liz smiled up at him as they reached the top of the stairs, tickled by that image.

"The only way to get around the library is the walkways along the bookshelves. That's a design flaw. But I don't need thirty bedrooms, so

73

we've just closed off the second and third floors of the west wing." As they began to meander down a furnished hallway as wide as a room, he said, "Do you want to be Mrs. Richardson? I don't know what more it would get you. Do you have a secret urge to be a socialite?"

"No. But I think we should get married again here. I mean, if you want to."

Jack paused at a doorway. Standing there and looking in, he said thoughtfully, "This is my suite." He wasn't leading her inside. "Chuck the shrink has all sorts of theories about my sex life that are off the wall, but one that's true is I would undo all that with Milly if I could. I told him a lot about you. He developed a theory that you're my pure replacement for Milly. He thought that was why I was willing to have someone I loved living so far away that I couldn't sleep with her, but I could keep her safe."

"It's the face, right? I need plastic surgery?"

"You don't need plastic surgery. You look more beautiful to me now than you did when you were younger. I mean that." Jack stepped away from the door to his suite and started to lead Liz back toward the stairs as he added, "Please lose the braids, though."

Her feet weren't budging. Jack stopped then and looked at her. He was holding her hand out at arm's length as she stubbornly pulled back. He said, "Honey, I think I need to start us over. He yanked out so much mess in my head and spread it around and made me look at it. When you rejected me—"

"It was a storm!"

"Rejection is independent of the weather."

"How do you think I felt? It was pretty clear during all those years that you chose all this crappy money over me! How do you think that felt?"

Liz was sure he was about to drop her hand because technically they were having a fight, so she squeezed his more tightly.

"Money matters to me less than you think." He drew a breath and looked away and added, "Chuck thought you had rejected me. He wanted me to move on and start dating. But it turns out there is only one you."

Her indignation withered. She stepped and slipped her arms around his waist and laid her cheek against his cashmere sweater. He hugged her and tipped up his chin so he could rest it on the top of her head as he used to do long ago. After a moment his cheek was against her hair. He said, "Give me a little time."

———— • ————

There was so much going on in Rex's mind that Liz could feel his agitation as they passed the first little new-wood house and entered the circle of village buildings. He was sitting cross-legged on the sheepskins in front of the greathouse with a Bible open in his lap, beautifully clean and containing all its pages. Before they were quite past that first house, he was calling, "Litz! Having Teacher in red!"

Otis Miller had been the clergyman on Steve Symington's 1962 missionary team. By the time Liz first met him, fifteen years later, Otis had so completely joined the Atlanticans that despite the fact that he was short and blond rather than properly tall and dark, they considered him to be one of them. When Liz had had trouble understanding what the sielrah was and why the miracles she was witnessing should not be freaking her out completely, Otis had introduced her to the Teacher. He insisted to her that the Teacher hadn't come to start a religion at all, but rather he had come to teach people how to have the same relationship to spirit and to one another that Atlanticans had developed on their own. Others had then overheard their conversations and gradually joined their Gospel studies, and for a time studying the words of the Teacher and using them to refine their work with energies had been a big thing in the villages. A confused but delighted Otis, already an old man, had continued to conduct his Gospel classes until he moved on to the blissful village. The five or six

Bibles they had started with had disintegrated in people's hands, so by now there was at most some part of a single Bible left in each of the three village childhouses. The pages of the Gospels had been underlined, finger-stained, torn and frayed and separated from their crumbling bindings, so a lot of the Teacher's words were available now just from other people's memories.

Liz knew that she had started all this, and she briefly worried that she was corrupting a pure native culture with a modern religion, but there seemed to be no theology attached to the Teacher's words as Otis used them. And Otis was right: his explanation of the workings of the Atlanticans' sielrah in light of what the Teacher had said about the Holy Spirit had given Liz some semblance of peace.

Rex had been very young when all of this was going on, so it was only when his father never came back that he turned to the Teacher. Twelve-year-old Rex, not understanding nor wanting to understand why Jack wouldn't live on Atlantica all the time, had built up such a head of rage as his father was preparing to say another goodbye that he had told him that since he preferred the other place to his family, he should stay there and never come back.

So Jack didn't come back. As the seasons passed, and he never returned and the season of leaves falling again came and went, the boy's anger at his father and fury at himself became such a torment to Liz while she herself was also dealing with the loss of her husband that all she could do was read to him what the Teacher had said about forgiveness. Her overgrown son, more than six feet tall but still a needy little boy, had gone from curling miserably on the sheepskins for hours sometimes, intermittently crying, to beginning to listen, to eventually starting to talk with Liz about the Teacher's words. For a time, what was left of the Morakan Bible was seldom out of his hands. Liz thought then that the Teacher had saved her son's life. And as he grew into manhood, the Teacher's wisdom seemed in a way to replace for him the guidance of the father he should have had. So for Rex to now have his own Bible, a Bible tightly bound and clean and with the words of the Teacher in red to boot, had him gleefully flipping through the pages. But for Liz, the Teacher's greatest gift was what happened next.

Jack said, "We're calling in soil people, son. We'll find out what's bothering the grass and trees over there." And Rex looked up with an open face and smiled at the father who had abandoned him.

"Is like pain. Like—" his eyes shifted beneath his lashes as he searched for words "—like hurt from run? Leg?"

"They'll figure it out," Jack said cheerfully. "Is the Bible all right? They brought just two, but we can get as many as you like."

"More is hrastinit." Rex went back to exploring his new book.

Jack said in an aside to Liz, "You think my whole life is hrastinit, don't you?"

Rex said then, still reading, "Litz? Myra saying okay people's world. Nah sad."

"My mother? You saw my mother?"

"I asking she watch my family."

"What does she look like to you?"

"Young. Like Kethy."

"Where is Cathy?" Jack asked.

"She sleeping," Rex said with a gesture of his head at the houses behind him.

"But do you really see Myra? Is she solid?"

"Some solid. Vibrate higher." Rex added, "She saying Gaprelagh marry."

Liz gasped. She dropped to the sheepskins next to him and slipped her arms around his shoulders and said, "Oh darling, I'm sorry! So soon?"

"Nah soon. I dying some many day ago."

Liz could feel from his mind still the calm certainty with which he had started this journey, but with it a fluttering. She hugged him hard around his shoulders from behind with her head against his. Of everything that ever had happened, all the pain for as far back as she could remember, the fact that her child now had to see the love of his life marry someone else felt like the worst thing, and was made worse somehow by the grace with which he was accepting it. Now he said, as she was thinking it, "Laying life for friends."

Jack was calling to Liz from the doorway of one of the houses. When she ignored him, he called more loudly, "Honey! Come help her."

Liz stood up, sniffling, and left Rex with the Atlantican gesture of her hand on his shoulder. Jack stood aside, and she entered one of the little houses and glimpsed Ted's daughter lying on a cot in the dim light with her knees drawn up and her hands beneath her cheek. Liz turned once she was inside and said to Jack in a loud whisper, "His wife's remarrying! And he's got my mother watching out for her, so for the rest of his life he's going to be hearing about her life with someone else."

"I'll send people to get her. Why didn't you bring her?" Jack was ducking at the door to see Liz from outside. His whisper was so loud that Rex likely could hear it.

Liz flagged his volume down with an exaggerated wince and a pointed glance toward their son. She whispered fiercely, "He won't take her from her life. He thinks it's bad enough he has to be here. He loves her so much! I think everything he's doing now is for her."

As Liz was emphasizing the drama of that with a steady look into Jack's eyes, she heard a whimper from behind her. She turned. Cathy was staring at them with wide eyes in a tear-stained face. Liz dropped to the sheepskins beside her, saying, "I'm sorry. What's wrong? Are you all right?"

Ted's daughter had from the first reminded Liz of the wealthiest girls at Smith. Liz had attended Smith College on scholarship, but had never fit in or really made friends because nearly all of the girls there had grown up either middle-class comfortable or wealthy enough that they had seemed to come from a different dimension. The wealthiest ones had been snobby, true, but there also had been about them a sense that they knew their having been born at the top of life's ladder made their positions precarious. Maybe they weren't after all quite who they were trying to seem to be, and they were hoping you wouldn't notice.

Cathy said softly, "I'm sorry. I've really tried. Tell Mr. Richardson I've really tried!" Just her mention of Jack's name seemed to bring more tears. She swiped at them with her hand from under her cheek.

Liz settled herself cross-legged as close to Cathy's face as she could comfortably get. As she was determining how best to begin this conversation, she noticed that Cathy's eyes were fixed on the doorway. She called over her shoulder, "Let me talk to her, sweetheart." She knew Jack had gone when Cathy's eyes came back to hers.

Given his long, narrow face and close-set eyes and the funny way his ears turned outward at the top, Ted had a surprisingly beautiful daughter. She was small, perhaps five-foot-four, and slim as a teenager. Her face was a perfect oval, her nose fine and delicate, her eyes almond-shaped and gracefully set. As Liz looked at her, she realized what a beauty Ted's wife had to be.

"Honey, what's wrong?"

"Is he really Mr. Richardson's son?"

"Yes. You can see that by looking at him, can't you? I know he seems unusual—"

"But I'm afraid of him. I'm sorry. Please don't tell Mr. Richardson I said that!"

"Oh sweetie, don't worry. It's just between us. But why does he frighten you?"

"He talks crazy. He can't speak English. Okay, I knew that would be the case, but he's so big. He's like a Neanderthal! I'm sorry! And he talks about how things 'feel', and—and—and—he talks to people who aren't there? He says his grandmother's there, and he's talking to the air as if she really is there. And—and—and—now he's a Jesus freak?"

Liz sighed and said, "Okay, one point at a time. First, Rex is the gentlest and kindest person who ever walked the earth. He'd never hurt you. Second, he's brilliant, and soon he'll be speaking English as if he went to Oxford, so give him time. Third, where Rex grew up, people live differently than we do here, so we've got to teach him about our culture. He can learn it, but it's in his nature to question everything. And—what number is this? Fourth or fifth, where he grew up, people develop more sensitivity to a lot of things than we have here. That's nothing weird about them at all, but it tells us there is apparently something wrong with us. Can you see that? He'll lose most of that sensitivity just by living here. I hope not all of it. Sixth, he really is talking to my mother, who's a lovely person and won't hurt you, either. And where the Bible is concerned, he's not a Jesus freak in the usual sense. He's an admirer of someone who came long ago to teach us how to live. There's nothing freaky about that, is there?"

"My father is Mr. Richardson's best friend. I don't want to let either of them down!" She sniffled. "My father would disown me if I upset Mr. Richardson." Just the thought of that made her shudder a little.

"You won't upset him. They tell me you like to ride horses, right? Well, ah, think of Rex as a thoroughbred that's top of the line or whatever you'd call it, but he's just green right now. Mr. Richardson has hired you to teach him to wear a saddle and be happy about it. That sounds like a good challenge, doesn't it?"

⇥ 9 ⇤

Liz had expected to spend the next day having her American makeover, but Jack didn't come for her until she was finishing her midday stew with Rex and Cathy in the greathouse. Jack appeared in the doorway and caught her eye. Liz had been listening as plucky Cathy tried to explain Christianity to someone who had no notion of what a religion would be, nor why anyone would want one, and who moreover was personally invested in his own understanding of the Teacher's role. He was doing to Cathy what he had done to Liz on Ted's yacht all day every day, asking to have each new concept defined, and then each concept used in that explanation defined, and so on backward through sometimes three or four levels of explanations. He seemed to be able to hold a diagram of the whole discussion in his mind, so he could systematically close each nested level as he came to understand the sub-concepts. But Liz had frequently become lost, and she could see that Cathy was having the same problem.

The most basic notions had them tied up in knots. The concept of a powerful separate God shocked and befuddled someone who had grown up with the understanding that anything that wielded that sort of separate power would be a massive disruption of the sielrah. And, perhaps foolishly, Liz had given him to understand that the sielrah was essentially the same as the Christian God. So that made God into anti-God? A logical impossibility. And the idea of sin was incomprehensible to someone who couldn't see why imposing any sort of restriction on others was not a far worse crime against the unity of all things than whatever infraction the restriction was intended to correct. So if rules were worse than whatever they were meant to correct, then that made what Cathy was describing to him as "sin" actually preferable.

As she listened, Liz again rued the fact that Rex was so bright and so ardently straight. He insisted that things make sense from his perspective, and since his perspective was Atlantican, almost nothing about America made sense to him. Most things didn't even rise to the level of being hrastinit, but rather they sounded to him like the lazy half-thinking of children who had not yet learned to carry reasoning through to sound conclusions.

As Liz stepped out and took Jack's hand, she said, "We've kept Rex's braids. We'd like to give our hair to help kids with cancer, although maybe there's no cancer anymore?"

After all their talking yesterday, Liz was feeling so comfortable with Jack now, so used again to being close to him, that it really felt to her as if there never had been any time lost between them. Already she seemed to have managed to entirely distinguish him from the trappings of his wealth, to see him purely as the husband of her heart, although she had to admit that this new equilibrium was feeling a little shaky. She was holding tight to his promise not to ditch her, and thinking that for the rest they would have to figure it out as they went along.

They were crossing the open space within the circle of little buildings as Jack said tightly, "Honey, I have to be frank with you, and I need you not to do a Liz. This is hard enough as it is."

Liz stopped walking and looked at him. That had been a term of Jude's, and she realized now that obviously Jude and Jack had chuckled together about her foibles. She said, "I would find it easier not to do a Liz if I were not suddenly realizing that you and Jude both think I'm a joke," and she stalked off ahead of him.

He hurried and caught her hand and edged her away from the house and down toward the ocean as he said, "I'm sorry. Cancel that." Then he said, sounding formal, "My love, I must make a confession that I know will upset you. I ask you please to understand that it upsets me as well. You should see it only as confirmation that you are the true love of my life. Was that better?"

"Who is she?"

He hesitated, then said, "It doesn't matter." He went on, "Not long after I started seeing Shrinky Chuck, I lost my desire to give orgasms to airheads. It happened overnight. One day it was a normal part of my life, and the next day I was disgusted that I had ever touched a woman I didn't love."

From the moment she first learned of his existence, Liz had been referring to Jack's analyst as "Shrinky Chuck." She was trying to help him get past what seemed to have become too deep a dependency on the man. Now apparently Jack was referring to his analyst as "Shrinky Chuck" as well.

And, yes, Liz long had known that her husband was dallying with his secretaries. They even had talked about it, sitting side by side beneath their tree and gazing at the South Atlantic. She had said something like, "Please, darling, thinking about it upsets me."

He had glanced at her, plucked a stalk of grass and stuck it between his teeth, and said mildly, "My wife insists on living here. My businesses are half a world away." Then he had added, "Perhaps you just shouldn't think about it."

The fact that he was the only man on earth who had an actual aversion to intercourse had made it possible for Liz eventually to rationalize it into something less than cheating. It was more like a hobby. She didn't think about it.

Jack went on, "Chuck was thrilled. He'd been telling me the reason I did it in the first place was because I was still trying to please my mother.

It never occurred to him it was just easier. But when I got sick of it, he thought it would be healthy if I did a little dating." Liz glanced at him. He wouldn't meet her eyes. He said, "A team comes here from Larkin twice a week, and there was a woman added to it that summer who seemed to see me as more than money. We hit it off, I guess."

Larkin International was Jack's primary holding company. Liz wanted to blurt that she already knew the story and shut up, but she also felt the need to hear every word of this. He went on, "I lived in that house for three months without women. Then I finally invited her to dinner. Pretty soon she was coming to dinner every night. She wasn't you, honey, but she thought of me more as a person than a wallet, and she had a decent education. She wouldn't push if I pushed. That was too bad. I think that's what got me from the day we met, the way you had no hesitation about playing with my head and telling me off."

They were approaching the formal garden above the sea wall. There were lovely wrought-iron benches here and there, facing the sea. As they sat down on one of the benches, neither cuddled close together nor very far apart, Jack said, "It was spring by then. I hadn't seen you the previous fall, and now I should have been back there with you. After a year, I was starting to realize that maybe you were never going to turn the communication system back on." He drew a breath and added, "So I let her move in."

Liz murmured, "I am so sorry," looking numbly at the steel-gray ocean.

Jack went on, "She knew Ted had gone down there to try to get Rex. She was upset even knowing I had a son I'd never told her about, so I didn't get around to mentioning you. And anyway, I was convinced until I saw you again that you hated me now. And maybe I hated you."

Liz had to murmur, "Did you marry her?"

"Of course not. She's the woman in my life, but you're my wife. For years I thought you were about to turn the system back on. Send a message. Something. I was getting reports from the security team down there, and every month I'd read their report and sit for awhile and feel as if you were right there with me."

Liz swallowed. She murmured, "Thank you for the ships, darling. It helped a lot. Sometimes I'd go up and sit beneath our tree and watch them go by on the horizon. It felt good to know you still cared enough about us to protect us."

Jack slipped closer and put his arm around her as he said gently, "It comforted me, too. I came to think it was the only thing you would ever again in our lives let me do for you, but it was something. And you were always safe. I couldn't have let you stay there otherwise."

"Will you please keep on protecting Atlantica? Even if we're here now?"

"If you like." She looked up at his face. He said tightly, "I don't know how much time we have. They'll call me if she leaves the office."

"What?"

"They're negotiating with her now." He shifted his feet restlessly, looking away.

"When did you tell her about me?"

"Last night. It wasn't until after you and I spent a day together that I had my head straight enough to tell her. I sent her to D.C. for a couple of days so she wouldn't be here when you arrived. She came back last night loaded for bear. She knew something was up." He added, "The hard part is I love her, honey. I love her. She's been what amounts to my wife for the past ten years. Even the name. I let her call herself Mrs. Richardson, which was stupid. But I love her, and she wanted to get married, but how could I marry her? I watched my parents stay married while they put each other through hell, and I thought, at least you and I weren't doing that! Clarice loves all that social garbage I hate, so she's become a big New York socialite. She tells people I'm too busy to come to this or that party, but maybe next time. We give away a lot of money in the name of Clarice Prescott Richardson—" then he startled, having said her name after all.

"But of course, there is no such person. I've come to like it. I've got a social presence without having to do anything."

Oh my God. Jack had found a suitable wife after all. He had one now. Liz heard herself mumbling, feeling appalled to be saying this and trying not to finish the sentence even as it was leaving her mouth, "If you'd rather be with her, I'll understand."

Jack cuddled Liz and said, sounding lighter, "I knew that was what you'd say. She's up there doing a Louise, and you're telling me you just want me to be happy." He kissed the top of her head against his shoulder.

Louise had been Jack's first wife. He had married her on the rebound from one of the first times Liz had broken up with him in order to spare herself the pain of his inevitably breaking up with her, so the fact that his first marriage had turned out badly had always more or less weighed on Liz's conscience. And now this. Louise had been cultured and beautiful, surely a much more suitable wife, but what Liz was learning today was that apparently she herself was no judge of anyone's suitability to be his wife.

Liz said, "Darling, you know, the reason I've always hated how rich you are was the way it put a space between us. I'm trying to get past that now. So, I'm poor! I'll move—" The clamshell in his pocket started to ring. Surprisingly, he ignored it. She went on, "I'll move into your house. I'll pretend to be rich. I'll . . . ." Her voice was stumbling as she watched discomfiture growing in his face. She could hardly feel his mind-energies anymore, and it amazed her to realize how fast that was happening. But what little she could feel of his emotional turmoil made her say, "Are you okay?"

"Honey, I wasn't going to tell you this, but you make me think maybe I should say it." He looked away, then back at her. "Please don't let it matter. Don't do the stupid socialite thing!"

"I couldn't be social if I wanted to. You should have seen me at Smith. A bunch of debutantes and a horse. I mean, they all had horses, but—"

"You're not poor." He drew her closer to him and took her free hand for additional closeness and said, "Another reason I couldn't go right back to you was that about two years after you shut me down—"

"It was a storm!" Liz blurted. Then she took her hand back so she could cover her mouth.

"—I had a second heart attack. They said I needed a triple bypass. I was laid up for a year." He paused thoughtfully. "Clarice helped me through it." He went on, "Before I had the surgery, I started to get my affairs in order. What a job! It continues to this day. But as part of that first emergency planning, we established a trust for you. We funded it with ten million dollars in Treasuries, I think. Or maybe it was more. I'm sure it's worth a lot more today."

The clamshell had stopped ringing. Now it started again. Cuddled close to him, wanting to support him and ease his mind, Liz tried to think through what he was saying. Then she said, "What's a trust?"

Improbably, amazingly, wonderfully, Jack laughed. He threw back his head and laughed. He cuddled her and tickled her a little and whispered, "That's my girl!" into her hair. Jostled into giggling a little, too, Liz tried to think of another way to frame her question. But then she thought she probably ought to quit while she seemed to be ahead.

Jack retrieved and answered his clamshell as it started ringing yet again. "Ted?" Jack listened for a moment, then said, "Give her fifty. Use Switzerland."

"I don't care that it's only been ten years!"

"Come on, kid, don't be ridiculous. What does this have to do with you?"

He sighed as he listened. Then he said, "Fine. Go ahead. But get the deal done by six so she's past it and happy. I'll go over then and give her a hug."

When Liz and Jack went back to check on the kids, they found them huddled over Rex's Bible on a table in their greathouse. Liz peeked quickly and drew back before they spotted her. Jack ducked to peek as well. As he took Liz's hand and they started back out of the village, he said, "How did he become a religious nut down there? How was that even possible?"

"Do you remember Otis the Elevator? That's what Trevor called him?"

Trevor had been the physician member of Steve's 1962 missionary team. Sour-tempered by nature, Trevor had been furious at the way Otis had moved out to Samitkan at the far end of the island and left Trevor and his wife to do what Trevor saw as most of the work in supporting Steve's Atlantican mission. Trevor took to calling him Otis the Elevator when Otis insisted that he didn't need to be a missionary anymore because now he was sure he was going to heaven.

"He was a little tubby guy, wasn't he? He only came up to maybe my waist?"

"That's him. Well, you know the way Shrinky Chuck helped you get over me? When you were gone so long because you married Louise, Otis the Elevator helped me get over the fact that I could never get over you." Liz glanced up at Jack and was rewarded with a glance and a small smile. She went on, "I had trouble dealing with the fact that Jude was supposed to be dead but he survived, and then the same thing happened to you when you had your first heart attack. The Atlantican prayer circles? When you don't believe in God in the first place, watching God save people you love can hit you strangely."

"How is Jude?"

"He's fine. He's a grandfather."

Jack seemed to be leading her toward the terrace so they could sit and talk and enjoy the view, but those negotiations in the office would likely soon be over, and the last thing Liz wanted was an encounter with Clarice Prescott Richardson.

"Let's go somewhere else, darling. This could get awkward."

Jack flipped open his clamshell, hit a button with his thumb, said, "I'm on the east terrace," hit another button, and flipped it shut again.

"What, they don't know where you are every minute?"

"They do roughly. But I'm pretty free here."

Liz glanced at him as they sat down together on another of those big green sofas. His face was grim. When Liz caught his eye, he said, "This feels like one more betrayal. Two days ago we were happily married and she loved me. Now today she's demanding money and threatening to sue me. For what? The way she used my name was all her idea!"

"I'm sorry, sweetheart."

Liz was trying not to suffer any emotional reaction at all to Jack's talking about Clarice as his wife. She knew he needed her support now, and not the further stress of her being annoyed with him for having gone on with his life without her. He had begged her so often to come back here and live with him in this beautiful place. That she had forced him to take up with another woman who now was causing him pain had been yet another of little Lizzie's screw-ups. Jack glanced at Liz, then slipped his arm around her, and she cuddled in close to him. He said, "Tell me about Otis the Elevator. Wasn't he the one you said looked like Alfred E. Neuman?"

"He did! Didn't you think he did? Missing tooth and all?"

"I'm not sure I know who Alfred E. Neuman is."

"You need to get out more!" Then she said, "You gave up your pipe?"

"The second heart attack did it. They said I was inhaling. Tell me about the Bible thing. It's a great distraction for him now, but it's starting to creep me out."

Given the stress of Jack's day, Liz didn't want to trouble him further. She thought for a minute, then said gently, "Rex was sad when you didn't come back. What helped him were the Teacher's words on forgiveness. And he . . ."

She stopped talking when the clamshell in Jack's pocket began to ring. He checked his watch as he answered it.

"Hi kid."

"That's fine. Fifty's fine. Thanks for doing this on such short notice. I didn't tell her until last night, and then—"

His voice tightened as he said, "Are you serious?"

"No, I don't blame you. No."

"Then don't tell me. She did sign?"

"It doesn't matter."

"Thanks, kid. No, I'm fine."

Jack hit a button with his thumb, closed the phone, and slipped it into his pocket.

Liz glanced at him. His mouth was pursed; then he chewed his lip. He seemed to be fighting an impulse to cry. He pulled Liz into his lap and held her so tightly with his cheek against her head that her neck was cramping and other parts of her body began to scream in protest, but she tried not to move because now his whole body was wracked by nearly soundless sobs. And then he was keening softly, a man more than six and a half feet tall making infant sounds so unbearable to hear that Liz lifted up out of his arms enough to cradle his face with her hands and kiss it all over as he went on crying.

Then Liz realized with a start that the black-tie man who gave out handkerchiefs was standing there behind the sofa with no expression on his face. When Liz looked at him, he handed her a handkerchief, barely nodded, and walked away. What, that was his job? He stood around all day watching the boss live his life on the odd chance that he might need a handkerchief? Liz blotted Jack's face with the handkerchief, stroked his hair, told him she loved him, and all the while she sat there in his lap thinking that every bit of his pain was her fault. As he began to compose himself, she said, "Darling, I love you. I love you. I swear I'll never betray you."

He took the handkerchief from her, looked at it, then wiped his eyes. He said half-angrily, "If people can turn on you like that, did they ever love you at all? How can you tell who loves you and who just wants to use you? Is there even such a thing as love that's independent of self-interest?" He looked at Liz then, grimly. "What if I did something to you like what she says I did to her? Something outrageous? Unforgivable? Would you still love me then?"

"Um, you mean like maybe abandoning me on a rock in the middle of the ocean for twelve years and then sending a thousand Argentine mercenaries to steal my only living child? Something like that?"

His face softened as he looked at her. He said, "Yes, something like that. Okay. Good hypothetical example. Suppose I did something unforgivable like that to you. Would you still love me then?"

Liz was giving him a little smirk.

He murmured, "Was that really how it felt to you? That I'd abandoned you?"

"Do you want the truth? It felt as if I forced you to make a choice, so you chose all this over me. But I had no idea! If you're used to living with even a handkerchief-man, then how—"

"A valet," he said patiently. "Clay is my valet." He eased her off his lap to sit beside him as he added, "The mercenaries were all Ted's idea. He told you it was nine-eleven, but it was really Cathy's graduation that made me know I had to try to get Rex. Here she was, graduating from college, and he was even older than she was. Ted was so scared to be down there by himself that he had mercenaries at both ends of the island, just in case."

Jack was smiling a little now, too. He shifted his weight, and she cuddled in closer to him. He said, "I'm about to make some decisions for Rex that are going to affect the rest of his life. They have to be made now, but he's not ready to make them. My legal team prefers that he not be my child, so you're his only relative. I have to ask you to trust me, honey. I'll explain what we're doing, and if you like you can talk with my lawyers. But

I want him to know in later years that you were involved in making these decisions."

Liz sat up quickly and looked at Jack. "Good lord, what's wrong now?"

"First decision. Where was he born? It will probably be Argentina, but we're still working it out with the Argentine government. It would be good if you were willing to specify no father. Now, second decision. Where is he going to establish citizenship? Not here. They've been trying to talk me into renouncing my own citizenship, but I'm not ready to do that yet. If Rex is a citizen elsewhere, maybe I'll never have to do it. We're in talks now with Switzerland and Singapore."

"But why can't he live here?"

"He mostly can. He just won't be a citizen. My team was delighted to hear I have a foreign-born son! We've spent the past forty years trying to get everything we could offshore, and if Rex is a citizen of a freer country and what he owns has never had a U.S. nexus, then he can start to build what no tyrant can take from him."

Liz was feeling ever more overwhelmed and distressed as Jack was talking. When he paused, she said, "So you want our son to be the fatherless bastard of a loose woman? That's what you're saying?"

"No, that's not what I'm saying. We can make up a father's name for his birth certificate. Would you rather do that?"

"I'd rather have a birth certificate with your name on it!"

"That makes it harder for him to have a clean paper trail for financial purposes. My assets—"

"You know what? Screw your assets. Pardon my Singaporean. I realize all of this is basically a game for you. I get that. But you and I have a son who is going to be the great joy of your life, and I want you to acknowledge that you're his father!"

Jack nodded once and said, "Opinion noted. We'll see what we can work out."

⫷ 10 ⫸

Rex's grandmother appeared to him as the darkness was beginning to pale and he was practicing the technique for ignoring painful energies that he had learned from his wife so he might sleep a little more. This big body-shaped pillow full of feathers had an unpleasant energy that he guessed came from the pain of the birds, but he needed the illusion of sleeping with his beloved in his arms. He had said to Cathy only, "Miss holding my wife for sleep," and the next day she had kindly brought him this pillow.

The feel of being in a tiny village that was nearly devoid of people was becoming less distressing to Rex. A normal village would hold a density of human mind-vibrations in a constant current that was always with you, no matter what you were doing. You were part of that glorious net of energies, so just relaxing into it and holding your wife warm against your body with your face in her hair and hearing her soft breathing could produce such a wonderful sleep! But the human mind-energies here were tinged with the aggressions and fears of the beardless ones, and they had no constancy. Rex had thought at first that the people in this other place simply must share their own vibration that was different from the vibration of the people of the world from which he came. He was coming now to suspect, however, that each of these people might be almost a vibration unique to himself.

Only the thought that might conceivably be true horrified him, to think that they must live their lives in an isolation impossible for him to imagine.

Rex's grandmother had been coming to him often in the daytime. The fact that Cathy was unable to see Myra's shimmer when it was plainly right in front of her had at first confounded Rex, but now he was coming to suspect that the mental isolation of the beardless ones might cut them off from the dead as well as from the living. Rex could feel Myra coming now, at a time when Gaprelagh the beautiful's mind-shielding technique was starting to work. He mumbled in Atlantican, "Those of us still in bodies must have our rest." There was no need to speak aloud. The dead spoke by thought, but to speak by thought he would have to focus his mind, and then he would be awake again.

You do well here.

"I sleep," he mumbled in English.

I help Gaprelagh know that you are happy in the blissful village. She worries because she does not feel your thoughts nor see your shimmer. I tell her that you love her, but the blissful world is vast and you are exploring it all. That thought pleases her.

Myra's words brought his beloved clearly to mind, the peaceful depth of her that fed his life as surely as a body is fed. "Thank you," Rex mumbled, still groping for sleep.

You are so much the husband of her heart that she feels still united with you, dear one. But she accepts her new husband now. She enters his bed. Now you also can move on with your life.

Rex went from drowsily hugging his pillow to standing and flinging it against the wall. He said fiercely in his mind, *I cannot move on! My life is for her!*

He looked at Myra, shimmering and flickering like candlelight in the darkness. She always chose to appear to him as a pale young girl in beardless clothing; he could recognize her only by the feel of her mind.

94

You are young, beloved. You must have a wife.

I have a wife! he shouted by thought. *That I free her to take another husband changes nothing for me! She is my eternal wife!*

But beloved, for you to be alone is disruptive to the unity of minds.

There is no unity of minds in this place, foolish one! He cruelly added, *You are beardless yourself. Do you forget that?*

Myra had always had a basic silliness that now seemed to make it hard for her to fully grasp the change in her condition. She tried to hug Rex. He could feel her busy energy passing through him as her hug came up empty. "Go away!" he said to her aloud. "Does it comfort me to have you tell me that she is united with her new husband? Have you no thought for me?" He picked up his body-pillow and threw it through the shimmer. He couldn't sleep now, so he slipped into his shoes and tied on his sash and stormed out into the darkness. And at once there were beardless ones nearby. Whenever Rex fled to the comfort of the woods, there would be these tentative, fearful beings following him at a distance, not talking, and not even answering if he called to them. Liz had told him they were harmless and he should just ignore them, but who could ignore them? And how was it that they never slept?

Rex had spent his childhood exploring an island of hills that were covered in ancient trees so huge that two men couldn't touch hands around the trunks of many of the larger ones. The forest floor was almost devoid of growth; the woodland paths were in a blue half-light. But this bit of woods with metal barriers around the far side of it contained shrunken trees, any one of which he could hug by himself with some arm-length left over. There always was patchy sky above him and brushy growth at his feet. Still, it was woods. Rex had begun to study these woods, first confirming the astonishing fact that not one tree that he could find was of any normal kind. He could find no soup-bark trees here. No tooth-twig trees. No softwood trees for making baskets. No trees of the fragrant wood that people would have in their houses for the lovely smell of it, nor even the basic furniture trees that had the finest-grained wood for carving. With no normal trees to be found, Rex had been planning to study the new kinds of trees that were here. He had asked for and received a knife that was similar to a killing knife that you would use to dispatch a sheep, but longer of blade, and with a leather cover made to hook on your sash so you could have both hands free.

The darkness was paling enough for Rex to be able to distinguish the kinds of trees. He had been eager to get out here by himself so he could start to figure out how these trees might be used, but Cathy had been with him constantly. So now he went back to his house and fetched his knife and set off briskly down one of the paths, glad to be more or less alone, heading for a little stand of thin and oddly white trees that he had mentally marked for later study. He was trying to altogether ignore the clumsy sounds of those cowering beings lumbering through the woods around him.

———◆———

There was a helipad on the opposite side of the front lawn, near the gate-house, and Liz later realized that she had heard Jack's helicopter when he left. That thumpity sound was vaguely familiar, but gone before she was fully awake. She could tell from the light that the sun would soon be rising, so she lazily got out of bed. Getting up early still felt normal to Liz, although she had dined with Jack on the two previous evenings and been exposed to electric light so now she was developing a sleep deficit. Today was the day all of that would change. Provided that another Clarice Prescott Richardson-like complication didn't arise.

Liz was ready to be an American again. She thought that now she even was ready to cope with being a rich man's wife. She actually loved the feel of Jack's house, the exquisite details, each room unique, the way the ocean and sky seemed to be actually part of the house itself. The atmosphere of Jack's house wasn't so much rich as it was extraordinarily peaceful and orderly, and in that respect it had a feel rather like an Atlantican village, Liz thought. There was the same complex sandalwood scent that she had loved in the salon on his yacht long ago, and the same quiet classical music barely audible in the public rooms. There were expensive paintings everywhere, but in fact the whole house felt like a work of art to her.

Liz was even getting used to the idea of being served by all those gentle people who seemed to be part of the house's décor. When she had mentioned under her breath the first night she dined with Jack that having people standing waiting to serve them felt creepy, he had told her that she was being elitist in not wanting these good people nearby. Everyone who worked here was a well-paid professional, many of them had worked for him for decades, and by the way, if she wouldn't accept a lady's maid then he was going to have to fire Clarice's maid, who was a single mother putting two sons through U-Mass Dartmouth. Liz didn't want that on her conscience, did she? Then he gave her the kind of half-smile that told her he had been just waiting to give her that speech.

Why ever had Liz been so phobic about Jack's wealth in the first place? He never had flaunted it. He had tried to protect her from it. All she could think was that her having attended a ritzy college as a girl so poor that she had to take multiple part-time jobs while other girls were spending their junior year in Paris had given her a persistent sense that life was a financial lottery she already had lost. And she had learned at Smith that there was a social music she was unable to hear that wealthy people learned to dance to as children. She wasn't pretty, either. Jack was prettier than she was. Even before she had had any sense of how extremely rich he was, Liz had found it impossible to believe that the actual Jack Richardson who had been named by *Time* magazine the richest American under the age of forty when he was only twenty-six could possibly choose her from all the women in the world. The richest girls at Smith had swooned over him, for heaven's sake! How could he possibly want someone like Liz?

But now she was past all those anxieties. For the first time in their twenty-five years together, she felt loved enough and safe enough to simply love him. Always before, she had been watching for his inevitable rejection so she could protect herself by rejecting him first. Why he had been willing to put up with such treatment, and why he had always come back and tried again, was something she never would comprehend. But apparently he still wanted her now. And she loved him beyond her ability even to give the extent of it adequate expression. This time, little Lizzie would not screw it up.

Rex hadn't been near electric light, so he was surely up by now. He wasn't in the village, so he would be in the woods, but Jack had told Liz not to worry when he was there. The woodland to the east of the house had been meant for bridle trails, but Jack hadn't had horses here in years, so now it was just an eighty-acre rectangle of thirty-year regrowth laced with long-unused paths. It was securely double-fenced and patrolled, so Rex was safe playing in the woods.

Rex also had a bodyguard now. There were twenty professional bodyguards on staff, and Jack had wanted two of them with Rex at all times, but every combination they had tried had upset him. Rex wanted their mind-energies nowhere near him. On his own, Rex had befriended a gardener whose mother was a longtime housemaid. And Jack had decided that since Rex would be well protected by perimeter security, for now he might have just one informal bodyguard.

Dennis Silvestri was a handsome kid a little older than Rex and less than six feet tall. He was Italian-dark, so to see them together reminded Liz of a pair of her mother's old plastic salt-and-pepper shakers. Rex really liked Dennis. He told Liz that Dennis was the only man from this other place he ever had encountered who had the gentle mind-feel of someone from home, without the stresses and aggressions and fears that made most men from this place so hard to be around. But Dennis wouldn't be here so early, so Rex would be alone in the woods, being watched by unarmed security staff required to stay at least fifty feet away from him.

One of the amusements of Liz's brief life in this fake Atlantican village was the moment when staff would appear with meals. The men in white jumpsuits were house-related, fixing and fetching things and serving, and they would magically walk into the village at what seemed to people living without clocks to be the precise moment when hunger set in. At breakfast there would be three of them, two with covered trays and one with pitchers of water and the orange juice that Rex had discovered that he loved. The funny part was that every service piece was solid silver. They had used wood initially, but the finishes used to seal it were upsetting to Rex. Then they learned that he was made uncomfortable by whatever he was feeling from plastic, and he had the Atlanticans' abhorrence of glass and crockery because they broke too easily. But Rex had found that silver was the perfect choice. It wouldn't crack like a wooden bowl, and it wouldn't rust like an iron pot! Rex thought it was distractingly shiny, but he had found that if you rubbed dirt on the outsides of silver vessels you could kill the shine.

As soon as the servers had laid their buffet, Liz took her boiled eggs and fruit and orange juice and more of that wonderful home-baked toast and went out to sit on the greathouse step. Having just come through an Atlantican winter, they were starting another winter here, but it was only comfortably chilly outdoors.

Liz had already lost her braids. Knowing that today she was going to be transformed into one of the beardless ones, yesterday Rex had cut her hair. And he had cut it short; Liz couldn't stop fingering it. Jack had been shocked when he saw her last night, and seeing that brand-new look on his face had made her realize that apparently nothing in their prior life together had shocked him. He was sure she must have done this to herself in a fit of temper that was all about him, so their otherwise pleasant dinner conversation kept roving back to what could be wrong, or whether after all she actually minded having a makeover and moving into the house, and whatever was bothering her she should please say it and he would not be upset. Thinking about his confusion last night was making her smile as she took another bite of toast.

Rex hadn't returned by the time the man in white arrived to fetch Liz for her makeover, but that was fine. He was as safe in his father's arms here as he had been when surrounded by a mercenary navy. Cathy was up and eating breakfast, and Liz was sitting in the greathouse with her when the man arrived. Liz stood then and kissed the top of Cathy's head and left Atlantica behind.

—•—

For someone whose only prior physical tending had been haircuts in the bargain places that cater mostly to men and children, Liz had an exhausting morning. She had expected a haircut. She knew there would be clothes to try on. But Jack had hired a stylist and ordered everything on the menu, so what began with a soak in her personal tub then progressed through massage and facial and shampoo and haircut and coloring and permanent and manicure and pedicure and makeup and clothing and shoes and handbags.

All of this was taking place in what was now Liz's personal suite, just across the twenty-foot hallway from Jack's suite. Liz knew that Clarice must also have used this salon off the gilt-and-crystal bathroom, but she found that she had no feelings about that. Clarice had been living here only because Liz had stupidly refused to live here, and now Clarice was fifty million dollars richer, so everyone had come out fine.

Liz realized as soon as she was led into the salon that she didn't want to watch this happen, so staff covered all the mirrors with sheets. And then, for what felt like forever, she submitted. The stylist looked to be in her twenties. Since Jack was paying for all of this, Liz didn't feel entitled to say, "Look, I'm six feet tall and fifty-five years old, so please don't make me look like an idiot." She couldn't say that. But she wanted to.

Liz was still avoiding mirrors when they began to show her clothing. She tried things on blindly and let the stylist tell her what looked good, since she had no idea what was fashionable now. What had been fashionable twenty-five years ago had been psychedelic prints and miniskirts.

It was midafternoon before Liz was dressed to everybody's satisfaction. "Please have a look, Madam," the stylist said then, and with a flourish she swept the sheet off a full-length mirror standing in the gilt-and-crystal bathroom.

Liz had been expecting to look like a frump with decoration artfully applied, but what she saw in that mirror was a serene and dignified and actually beautiful billionaire's wife. She was stunned. She scanned her image minutely, trying to figure out what they had done to make her look so completely the part that if she had passed herself on the street she would have thought herself to be a genuine post-post-post debutante. All she could think was that she had to show herself to Jack before she lost this illusion.

"Are you not pleased, Madam?"

"I love it! I'd hug you, but I'm afraid to get mussed. Thank you, everyone! I've, um, got an appointment now."

Liz was wearing shoes with little heels, which slowed her down since her feet were used to ponyskin moccasins. She knocked on the door to Jack's suite, and waited. She asked a housemaid in the hallway if she knew where Mr. Richardson was. "I'm sorry, Madam." So then down the staircase and through the foyer, dark wood and gold leaf, to pass another housemaid. "I'm sorry, Madam."

That library was the most spectacular place that Liz had ever seen, with books on three sides and three stories tall. The fourth wall was giant panels of glass that made the ocean view and the enormous sky an integral part of the library's décor. Especially since that wall faced south, you would have thought the heat gain would be overwhelming; but the glass seemed to have something going on that toned down the sun without affecting the view.

Liz stood and looked out at the terrace and ocean and the inconceivably enormous sky. This house was so completely of the man she loved that even though apparently he wasn't here now, there was a sense of him, expansive kindness and grace. It made her think of the light opulence of his yacht's beautiful pink-lit salon, and first meeting him, first coming to know him as they traveled south twenty-five years ago. They had sat together in that salon play-arguing with one another night after night while Liz had struggled not to sound like a fool and apparently Jack had been falling in love. And now, in what her younger self would have thought of as the entry to old age, Lizzie Brandt was unexpectedly beautiful and rich. The one trait seemed as unlikely as the other.

⇥ 11 ⇤

Until the sun was past its full height in the sky, Rex busied himself with using his knife to investigate the properties of the trees to try to find replacements for the basic uses that you would need to live happily in this village. Liz had told him that eventually he likely would want to move into the mountain of stone that you could see from beyond the houses, and where she herself was planning to live, but Rex was more comfortable with the idea of making a life in this miniscule village. He was enjoying the company of the woman whose home it was. Helpfriends would appear if something was needed, and they were happy to share their food. Rex had thought at first that there would be no way for just two or three to live together here, but it seemed to be happening.

Rex was finding that the awful, clanging pain in the plants that lay along the ocean path was also scattered here and there in these woods. You would be among trees that were happy enough, despite the fact that they seemed to be withdrawing their energies at what should have been the season of new grass rising; and then you would come upon a tree in as much distress as those along the ocean path. He was thinking now about how he might enlist Cathy in his quest to understand and resolve this pain of the trees.

Rex was coming to enjoy Cathy's company. She had been introducing him to concepts that she said he would need to understand, but the problem was that notions that were nonsensical seemed to be self-evidently true to her. So now he was asking her questions not so much to try to understand what was never going to make any sense, but primarily to try to open her mind so she could see the absurdity of what she was saying.

"But you've got to have laws!" she had said last evening in the great-house after supper. She found it so hard to go to bed when he normally would go to bed that he didn't mind staying up with her and talking for awhile by candlelight.

Rex said patiently, "Try see. All mind is one. You mind and my mind. Part of the sielrah. So is most disrupt the sielrah if mind go against mind. You see? Yes? So if I try make you do my will, I wreck unity of minds. You see?"

"But how can you get people to do anything if you don't have some kind of structure?" she asked in her soft voice that he was coming to enjoy.

"People do what they do."

"Then nobody would work, Rex. You can see that. I want to go lie around on the beach!"

"So you beach." He paused. He added, "Cold for lying. Better you walk."

Cathy slapped her forehead with the palm of her hand, which amused him. She had a tendency to express herself with unexpected meaningless gestures born of the frustration he was feeling in her. He had found this troubling when he first met her. Now that he knew her, he thought it was cute. He said, "Need bigger village. Enough people, one always do what all people need."

"The more people, the more chaos."

"Chaos come from mind apart. In unity of mind, no chaos."

This was actually the third tier of a discussion that had been going on since before their food arrived. Cathy had it in her head tonight to teach him something about the American system of government, of which she apparently was proud. So then he said, "Why need government?"

The question seemed to flabbergast her. "To enforce the laws! Don't you have a government where you came from?"

So then he said, "If I force my will, I harm the sielrah," and they were off to the races. All their discussions seemed to come back to that basic necessity to preserve the unity of minds, because without unity, nothing could be right. Cathy told him last night at the height of her frustration that if he couldn't get past this religion thing, there was no way he was going to learn anything.

Having skipped both breakfast and lunch, Rex was noticing that he was hungry. And here came Dennis, a man of about his age he had lately encountered in these woods who had spent all of yesterday with him. There was no other village nearby, so apparently Dennis had walked a great distance. It occurred to Rex as he watched his new friend approaching that he ought to ask him why he didn't simply move to this village.

"Hey, Rex!" Dennis called. "They said you didn't eat yet today? I thought you might like a Big Mac. Sorry I'm so late." He showed Rex a sack made of paper and removed from it a warm lump wrapped in stiffer paper. Rex opened that inner wrapping, and there was bread stuffed with something that smelled like low tide on a beach. Dennis was saying, "You never had one where you came from? See if you like it."

Rex took a bite of it. Before he could chew, there was a seawater explosion in his mouth and throat that had him reflexively retching. He was coughing, hacking, retching, bending to grab the tail of his tunic to try to clean out his mouth. Dennis was shouting, "Water! Who's got water?" The water helped to control the rank salty taste, but it couldn't get rid of it completely. Dennis was clapping Rex on the back. "Okay now, buddy? Want more water?"

The expression on Dennis's face, and more the confused feel of his mind, made Rex chuckle a little, still bent to wipe out his mouth. He said, "Nah eating the sea! Is all here eating that?"

"Sorry, bud. I keep forgetting. You okay?"

"We walk. Need friend now."

As they walked together down one of the trails that were all over these woods but led nowhere, Dennis was telling Rex companionably about a dentist appointment for which he had the morning off, followed by traffic that made him even later.

"You have wife, Dintz?"

"Just got engaged," Dennis said happily. He was munching on Rex's Big Mac. "I don't know if you know it, but your dad pays like nobody else. Now I've got this job, we finally got engaged."

"Is engaged meaning is wife?"

"Next year. We're still settling on a date." Then Dennis said through his food, "Do you have a girlfriend?"

"She wife other man."

Dennis gave a little snort and said, "Whoever he is, you trump him, buddy. That's what courts are for."

Rex glanced at Dennis. So much of what the man said was nonsense, but it was funny nonsense. Not like the deadly serious-seeming nonsense that Cathy was trying to drum into him day and night.

Dennis said, "Your dad is wonderful. My parents have a nice life thanks to him. Don't know if you know how good he is."

"Try making other happy. Hard for not happy."

Another snort from Dennis. "How can he not be happy?"

"Have chains, mother say. Many chains."

There was a trill of nervousness in Dennis's mind. He said, "Look, I'm not supposed to talk about anything personal. Sorry about that. You won't tell anyone?"

Rex stopped walking and turned to Dennis. The man was shorter than men usually were, but Rex was getting used to that. He put his hand on Dennis's shoulder and said, "You fear. No fear, friend."

Dennis was smiling nervously as they resumed their walking.

Rex said, "You loving you wife?"

"Of course! She's a hairdresser, but she's going for her degree. Your dad has a scholarship program. I'm not using it, so my mother got him to give it to Cecilia. Good man, buddy."

Dennis's chatter was distracting Rex a little from the black pain that had been consuming his mind ever since Myra had told him that Gaprelagh the beautiful had united with her new husband. It wasn't so much that she had entered his bed. Rex had expected that, and they were married. It seemed to be more the way her life was so easily resuming as if he never had been in the world. Of course, he had been hoping that would happen. He couldn't bear to think of her grieving for him. But he never had imagined such pain as this, nor could he conceive of its ever ending.

"You okay, Rex? You seem kinda glum today. Anything I can get you?"

"You go blissful village—you die, you wife sad?"

"I guess so. Life goes on, though."

Before them unexpectedly the woodland was ending, and they found themselves at a corner where woods and lawn met ocean beach. Rex stopped still, looking at that ocean. He could see no land at all, nothing but sea, but out just beyond what he could see would be home. Right there.

———— • ————

At one end of the library was a gigantic fireplace that still was dwarfed by the immensity of the room. At the other end were double doors into the drawing room, flanked on either side by human-sized fireplaces that each provided a focus for comfortable seating in conversational groups. One of these smaller fireplaces had a mirror above it. Liz was studying herself in the mirror, experimenting with hooking her hair behind her ears and thinking about a different part, when she noticed Jack standing halfway across the room behind her. She turned quickly, trying to smooth her hair back the way it had been so he could get the full effect. She said cheerily, "Hi sweetheart! Where have you been all day? Wow, you look gorgeous."

He was beautifully groomed, his beard and mustache neatly trimmed and his hair touched up to minimize the gray. He wore a suit like nothing Liz had seen before, probably silk, and tailored to fit him so perfectly that in it he looked younger and fitter. He was studying her from forty feet away. She bobbed a curtsey and started toward him.

"No. Stay there." As he reached her, he said, "You look beautiful, but you don't look like you. It was a mistake to use Clarice's stylist. I think she even had that pantsuit."

"Should I get rid of the makeup?"

"No, it's fine. You look great, honey. I'll get used to it."

"Where were you? I've been trying to stay perfect so you could see this, but it's been a struggle."

He took her face into his hands and kissed her, and then slipped his arm around her waist so they could study their shared reflection in the mirror. Liz was transported by that sight. How beautiful they looked together! She was astonished at herself that she didn't feel the need to balance this perfect moment with a wisecrack.

They sat down in companionable armchairs as he said, "I had a closing. I insisted we start at eight so I could be home early, but the lawyers had to run their meters." Then he added, sounding amused, "People know if there's enough money on the table, we can close deals in my penthouse and I'll show up. They never meet me otherwise. I swear, honey, they up the ante on some of these deals just so they get to do the penthouse party and I'll be there. Does that make me a whore?"

"Pretty much. And an expensive one!"

He was studying her, cocking his head, beginning to smile a little. He said, "You clean up nicely."

And so did he. Seeing now the way he liked to live, Liz was astonished to remember all those years when he had been willing to wear homespun wool in a hovel because she wanted to be there. My God, he must really love her! Then she had another thought.

"Do you still have the Picasso drawing hanging right next to the Rembrandt portrait in your penthouse?"

"It's investment art. We had to put it somewhere. You were the one who pointed out how ridiculous it was, and we've kept it that way ever since. Rembrandt, Picasso, Remington and Calder, all on top of one another. It's become legendary."

"Um, so what do rich people do all day? I've only been rich since sometime this morning, and already I think I'm getting bored."

Jack stood as he said, "Then let's spice it up. Come on, honey."

He positioned her in front of the mirror and drew a necklace from his pocket and fastened it around her neck, ducking to look in the mirror as he did that. He centered it and stepped back.

Liz recalled his taste in jewelry as over-the-top, but this necklace was a light and lovely combination of emeralds and diamonds, with the emeralds as graceful twining leaves and a rather large diamond at her throat. There was a recent time when Liz would have been outraged or pained or in some way discomfited by the fact that he must have done this dozens of times with dozens of women. Fairly recently, she might have told him off. But now that she was rich and beautiful, what she said was, "That's lovely! Thank you, darling."

"I thought emeralds would be nice. You have a little green in your eyes. But you can have any necklace you like, honey. The money stone is the diamond. It's just fifteen carats, but it's flawless."

Jack had a butler and a valet. Since they both came to work in black tie and they looked enough alike to be bookends, Liz had been wondering ever since she got here why for heaven's sake he had to have two of them. Yesterday, when she had asked the question, he had explained to her that the butler managed the house and the valet managed his person. She had told him then that whenever "hrastinit" finally made it into the dictionary, his picture would be its illustration.

Clay, Jack's valet, had slipped into the room as they were admiring Liz's new necklace. He cleared his throat. He said, "Excuse me, sir. I'm sorry. They're pulling your son from the ocean. "

Liz's eyes met Jack's in the mirror. She saw in the horror flooding his face that this was little Milly all over again. He was running, dashing out the door, tearing across the terrace. Liz hurried after him, but she couldn't run in those shoes so she kicked them off and ran in nylons. There was a little crowd down to the left on the sandy part of the beach, and now Liz was hearing wailing and screaming. But it wasn't Jack screaming this time. Security men in brown jumpsuits were trying to hand Rex out of a boat pulled up on the beach, and he was raging and fighting them. Jack reached him. He tried to hug him and maybe pin his arms, but Rex was fighting as only a healthy and fit man can fight. All the while he was wailing and screaming and trying to get back to the water.

The only other person Liz had ever seen break down this way was Jack, on the night little Milly died. She had had an Atlantican name as well, although Liz was having trouble remembering it now because he insisted on calling her Milly so everyone else also called her Milly. The baby had been a blond curly-top, her eyes so intensely blue that they were the first thing anyone noticed about her. Jack had arrived back before her birth, so he had the thrill of catching his daughter as she was born. He stayed on Atlantica after that, talking with Ted every few days by phone and leaving briefly only twice, Liz thought, in the whole of little Milly's life.

Milly had been barely two years old. Everyone was singing and dancing in the greathouse after supper. She was squirming in her father's lap, so Rain took her to play with other children her age in what had once been a clinic, but now was a big unfurnished room filled with toys made of wood and horn and bone so toddlers wouldn't get bored during those greathouse community evenings. Jack missed having Milly in his lap, so soon he went to fetch her. There was a back door to the playroom that nobody used, but inexplicably he found that door open. Then they heard him screaming. Above even the loud rhythm of tree-trunk drums and the beautiful chaos of Atlantican singing they heard those screams that Liz could not to this day get fully out of her head. They all ran outside. They found him crumpled on the riverbank with the baby's body in his arms, rocking her and screaming and screaming.

The sight of Liz's perfect baby lying in her father's arms with her eyes open and her face that looked so much like his forever frozen in surprise was so horrific that Liz blanked the sight. It came back to her only in glimpses, seasons later, perhaps as she was better able to process it. Her whole concern that night was for Jack, who at first couldn't be made to give up the body, and then without that little anchor he was in such anguish that he was stumbling around, screaming, throwing himself against things, so island-fit and so demented that Liz couldn't get near enough to begin to calm him until his arms and his legs and back were bruised and bleeding. He wasn't even able to convert his demented rage into something more like grief so he could begin to cry it out until the sun was close to rising.

Jack fell out of love with Atlantica that night. It surprised Liz at the time that he didn't insist that she and Rex go back with him immediately, but he seemed still to think that Rex was better off where he could live a free little-boy life. And as Jack was moving past the worst of his grief, Liz's own long grief was settling in. She had lost her first baby in an auto crash when he was just sixteen months old, and now the accidental deaths of Aaron and Milly seemed to be merging in her mind into a depressive hopelessness and a raw, keening pain. Jack spent all the fall seasons of that year seldom even communicating with Ted while he and Liz took long walks and he helped her deal with her loss.

In the depth of their pain at losing little Milly, they decided that having more children was not for them. Jack didn't care for intercourse anyway, and for Liz the risk of ever again loving a baby who could die seemed to be beyond what she could bear. She and Jack found that she was at her core more emotionally fragile than either of them had thought she was, while at his core he was actually stronger than the avoidant man they both had thought him to be. And their relationship considerably deepened that fall. He seemed to become protective of her, and careful about what he thought she could bear, in ways that never before had seemed necessary to either of them. With his patient counsel, Liz was able to do at length something that felt like re-absorbing her two lost babies back into herself, safe now and forevermore, cleaned out of her mind altogether because the thought of having lost them was so unbearable, but safely re-absorbed into their mother's heart.

So then Liz and Jack established a new normal in which Jack lived with them for a couple of Atlantican seasons each spring and fall, and when he was away he would send them notes through Desedala almost daily. Liz got used to it. She came to think it was working fine, until the day when Rex couldn't take it any longer.

Now Jack was trying to calm Rex down. Foolishly. Liz knew that when someone is in that condition, all you can do is try to keep him from hurting himself or someone else until he exhausts the worst of his pain. Liz thought as she watched Jack ruining his suit that she should have been expecting something like this. Rex had in recent days been talking about Gaprelagh the beautiful more and more.

Someone else also was wailing on the beach. It was Rex's bodyguard, the boy she thought of as Pepper to Rex's Salt, crying with every part of his body as he watched Rex fighting with the boss. Liz hurried to him and put her arms around him.

"Don't let him fire my mother!" the boy wailed as he stiffened in her arms. "Please, Mrs. Richardson! This is all she has! Please!" Liz was stroking his hair and whispering that everything would be fine, don't cry, while all he could do was beg that she somehow preserve his mother's job. Being held this way, he was quieting as she murmured to him. He said, sobbing and hiccupping, "I'm so sorry! I gave him a Big Mac! He needed water! I was getting him water!"

Jack had a full-time nurse on staff who took blood pressures and managed meds and coordinated visits from his doctors and administered EKGs for a man who had had two heart attacks and a triple-bypass by the age of fifty. Once security had Rex pinned on the sand, Jack's nurse gave him a shot of something. As Rex quieted, Jack stood up and roared, "Where is his bodyguard?"

Liz whispered to Pepper, "Honey, go home. I'll take care of it. Nobody is getting fired. Go now."

Pepper—now she recalled that his name was Dennis—darted off among the security men and was gone. Liz hurried to Rex, now lying quietly in the sand. She knelt, heedless of her clothes, and kissed his cheek and stroked back his hair and whispered that everything was going to be fine.

But Jack was still shouting. Liz stood and slipped her hand into Jack's, and he shuddered and quieted. He was looking around for Dennis. She said, "Sweetheart, he's fine. He's just upset. His wife got married. He's going to be fine." But someone was telling Jack that Dennis had left, which had him pulling his hand from Liz's and shouting again. Liz grabbed Jack's arm and shook it and shouted more loudly than she had intended, "Stop it!" He jerked his arm away, but he stopped shouting and looked at her. "Stop it, sweetheart. Think of Rex. You're upsetting him."

Security people were maneuvering Rex onto a stretcher. Jack let Liz lead him away, but not as far as the nearest wrought-iron bench. He was brushing sand off his sleeves. He said grimly, "Stay out of this."

Liz was checking to make sure her fifteen-carat flawless diamond hadn't been lost in the melee as she said, "Jude was your son, too, right? You adopted him? And he told me what his life here was like. He couldn't leave without permission. Always had to have two bodyguards with him. And what did he do? He threatened suicide, remember? Darling, you can't do this. If you treat Rex the way you treated Jude, he really will swim back to Atlantica."

"We pay a bodyguard to keep him safe—!"

"So, okay. He screwed up, but he learned a big lesson. I sent him home, by the way, so don't blame him for leaving. Dennis is Rex's first American friend. He really likes him. If you fire that boy, you'll be taking away the only friend—"

"His mother is a housemaid!"

Liz winced and glanced around. She said under her breath, "Shame on you. That's not who you are."

"Honey, I've got only one son—"

"I know. I understand how hard this is. But if you don't stop behaving like a jackass, you're going to push Rex away just as you did Jude."

He blinked. "Did you call me a jackass?"

"I'm sorry. For Rex's sake, you've got to forgive Dennis!"

Jack's jaw was set. He was looking away from her. He said, "I won't have this kind of relationship with you, Liz."

She paused, looking at him and thinking that now she understood what one of her roles in his American life was going to be. She said gently, "It's sad that nobody else has ever dared to tell you when you're wrong. I'm sorry." She stood on tiptoe and reached and drew his head down to hers a little so she could kiss him a peck on the lips. She said, "Fortunately, now you have someone who loves you enough to do that."

⇜ 12 ⇝

Liz had been carefully thinking through how she might introduce Rex to his father's home, but one option she never had considered was his immediate immersion in the infirmary, naked and strapped to a bed. Sea Haven's infirmary was on the east wing's first floor, opposite the kitchen complex. It was intended primarily for Jack's care, including an EKG machine and a dentist's chair, and even including a hospital-grade laboratory and a medical dispensary because all Jack's doctors came to him. The infirmary had driveway access in case an ambulance or a mobile MRI were needed.

Liz knew that Rex was going to be fine. Her primary concern was to use this episode as a teaching moment for his father, so she and Jack meandered up from the beach and into that end of the house while they discussed whether Rex had to have professional bodyguards now, or whether that was a stupid and ridiculous idea that would only further upset him. Liz was shocked to enter the infirmary, still chatting with Jack, and find Rex strapped to a hospital bed and naked above the sheet that covered him to his chest. Apparently they had managed to remove his wet clothing, but they hadn't convinced him to wear anything else.

Rex glared at his parents as they approached him. He looked dazed and frightened and angry, even despite the sedative. What Liz could feel of

115

Rex's mind seemed stridently chaotic but without recognizable emotions, although perhaps she just was getting past her ability to read emotions. She rushed to his bedside and slipped her hand into his where it lay strapped to the bed's side-rail. He tried to resist that, feebly. He said in Atlantican under his breath, "Take me home. I do not stay here."

"Be at peace, dear one—"

"You look beardless! You have no right to tie me!"

"I am your mother, no matter how I look. You are tied so you cannot hurt yourself. If you promise to be calm, I can untie you." She glanced up at Jack standing across the bed and added, "It would be a kindness to your father if we could speak English. May we speak English?"

Rex said to Jack angrily in English, "I going home!"

Jack murmured, sounding helpless, "I'm sorry, son."

The sedative was wearing off. Rex abruptly began shouting in two languages, "Take me home! I go home!" and flinging his head and yanking and kicking at his restraints and spitting toward Liz the horrendous epithet, "You are destructive of the unity of minds!" It sounded worse in Atlantican.

Liz tried to keep on holding his hand, and tried to stroke his hair despite the fact that he was biting toward her hand whenever it came near his teeth. She told him desperately over and over how much she loved him and everything would be fine, please darling, listen to me, stop it! I love you! Please!

Then, amazingly, Sigmund Freud hurried into the room past Jack and calmly put a stethoscope to Rex's chest, staying away from his teeth but otherwise ignoring him. Freud stepped back and studied Rex impersonally, prompting the boy to shout at him, "You eat seawater! Your smell offends the trees!" in outraged Atlantican.

Then Freud turned and touched Jack's arm and said, "Let's talk," and led him out of the room.

As they were leaving, Cathy was coming in. When she saw Rex and heard him shouting, she gasped a soft shriek and ran to him. Liz stepped back as Cathy took his hand and leaned and spoke to him. He stopped moving and shouting. Liz could hear her saying calmly, "I just thought of another reason we need a government, Rexie. I'm sure I'm wrong, but I need you to explain it to me." She hurriedly pulled up a chair and sat down and said, "Um, ah—It slipped my mind again." She slapped her forehead with her hand as she said busily, "It'll come back. I was looking all over for you. Where were you all morning?"

Rex gave her a little smile and said, "I swim. Like cold swim."

Then Freud came hustling in again, took a syringe from his pocket and shot a droplet from it upward to clear the needle of air, and gave Rex a shot in his upper arm. He said to the women generally, "Let him sleep," and rushed back out.

Liz hurried to Cathy's side. Whatever shot Freud had given to him was making Rex wilt and fogging his eyes as he looked from one to the other of them desperately. As soon as he seemed to be more or less unconscious, Cathy's apparently cheerful face resolved into wailing. Liz caught her in a hug and drew her away from the bed as she whispered, "He'll be all right, sweetie! I promise," while Cathy cried all over Liz's expensive pantsuit. Thinking of that had her reflexively checking to make sure her fifteen-carat flawless diamond was still there. Then Liz noticed Jack's butler over Cathy's shoulder, gesturing professionally with his eyes. She moved Cathy to sit on the chair by Rex's bed, asked the nurse to stay with her, and followed Carlson out of the room.

Liz knew that the fellow who looked like Freud had to be Shrinky Chuck himself, and she realized before Carlson opened the door to the formal sitting room that already she despised the man. She was struggling to get past that. When Liz was ushered in, Jack turned from pacing and looked at her with his face stark and his eyes hopeless and said, "Rex is having a psychotic break. They're going to hospitalize him." Jack opened his arms to Liz as she approached him. But then she grasped what he was saying, and she turned and began to do some pacing of her own.

"Sweetheart, think of every woman you've ever loved. Now, imagine you're his age, and you're married to that perfect woman who's every woman you've ever loved, and you even have a little boy. Now, imagine that just because of a stupid accident of birth and the way this disgusting world is, you can't stay with her because in order to protect her you have to go halfway around a world you didn't know existed—"

Chuck said, "We have no time for this—"

"Shut up. If you touch my son again, I'll have your license." Liz went on, speaking to Jack, "Now, imagine that because you don't want her to be alone, you've made her think you're dead so she can remarry—"

Chuck said irately, "Where did you go to medical school?"

"I went to mommy school!" Liz faced Jack and said, "His wife has been the center of his world since they were toddlers. She's just remarried. That might give anyone a bad day, don't you think?"

Chuck said impatiently, "The ambulance is on its way, Jack. We've got no time for this nonsense!"

Liz thought briefly, then approached Jack and adopted a different, pleasant tone.

"Mr. Richardson? I am so grateful your people were able to save my son! And thank you for allowing him to be in your infirmary here. Nice house, by the way. Now, um, I hope you'll let him stay for a few days. You see, he has no father and I am his only relative, and some lunatic is trying to have him committed for being sad." She opened her stance to include Chuck as she added, "If anyone removes him from this house without my permission, as my son's only relative I will spend every cent I have and can raise to sue every person in this room but me for everything you've got."

She fingered her fifteen-carat flawless diamond and craned to look toward it, although it was too close to her chin for her to see it. She glanced at Jack and said, "How many lawyers could I hire with this, sweetheart?"

Then she lifted her head and looked at him. His face was a picture, perfectly poised at the point where pain and confusion and humor meet. They looked at one another and broke into laughter simultaneously, which each realized was such an inappropriate thing to do that they tried to stifle it, which each noticed in the other, so then they were laughing so hard that she fell into his arms. Then they couldn't stand up, so he managed to get them to a nearby sofa. He sputtered, "Don't look at me!" when she looked at him, because the sight of her face would set him off again.

Liz composed herself enough to say, "Is there room in that ambulance for three, Chuck?" which had Jack guffawing.

Eventually Jack was sitting up, wiping his eyes, composing himself. He said to Liz, trying to sound sober, "We've got to do something for him, honey."

"I hate to mention this, but there was a night when you were going through the same thing he's going through now. You remember how bad it was, and how you got over it—"

"I'll never get over it," he said, sounding immediately grim.

"Would it help you to know she's fine? We've seen her?"

Chuck started to say, "What's it going to be, Jack—?" but Jack waved him off, looking at Liz.

"You've seen her?"

"Rex took it really hard when you didn't come back. Sorry, darling. One night I was sitting with him and he was crying, and a glow appeared. It was a shimmer. I could see just the shimmer, but not who it was, but he told me it was little Milly as a beautiful woman who looked just like you. He was enraptured. Then I could hear her in my mind." Saying that made tears start in Liz's eyes at the remembered wonder of that night. "Little

Milly said you loved him but you couldn't be with him. But she said the Teacher was here for him in your place." Liz tipped up her chin.

Jack said, "You're kidding."

Chucky Freud said with a wary glance at Liz, "What's it going to be, Jack?"

Jack said, wiping his eyes with a handkerchief that Clay had just brought him, "It looks as if she's your new boss. How do you want to handle this, honey?"

⊰ 13 ⊱

Liz opened the infirmary door and began to lead the men in so they could strategize about Rex's care. They stopped dead in the doorway, staring. Rex and Cathy were lying spooned together in his bed with his face buried in her hair. From what they could see, she also was naked. They looked as if they were asleep, but then Cathy's hand came up to stroke Rex's cheek and beard behind her head. Beside the door, the nurse leaned and whispered, "I'm sorry, sir. She insisted." But Liz put a finger to her lips and smiled reassurance at the nurse as she pushed the men out and closed the door.

Back in the hallway, Liz said to Chuck, "See? That's what he needs."

"Sex?"

Liz muttered to Jack, "I think I'm starting to hate Americans."

Jack said, "I didn't know they'd gotten that far," in a look-what-a-stud-my-son-is kind of voice.

Liz said to Chuck, "Do you actually try to look like Sigmund Freud?"

He said in a voice of clinical interest, "Do I look like Sigmund Freud to you?"

Liz waited until Rex was awake, lightly sedated, and calmly talking with Jack and Chuck before she crooked her finger at Cathy, now sitting primly in a robe nearby. Cathy joined Liz in the hallway, and they went

121

to the informal sitting room and sat down together on a loveseat by tall windows that showed a navy-black sky and a thin remnant of orange sunset along the western ocean edge. Liz said to the girl, "Thank you."

"He talked about how he liked to sleep that way. He misses his former wife terribly! I thought he could think that was who I was."

Now Liz had no idea how to begin this. In America, marrying after such a short acquaintance was unheard-of, but where Rex had grown up it was a commonplace. People on Atlantica decided somewhere in their latter teens that it was time to go courting, and as soon as they found someone they liked who also liked them, they got married. And they married permanently. Marriage there was so different, though. Every adult had a separate house, children older than toddlers lived in the childhouse, and each adult had several deepfriends with whom to carry on what amounted to intense nonsexual affairs. Marriage was for perfecting a union that was the basis of the unity of all human minds, and it was for sharing the rearing of children. It was a partnership that reinforced the fact that all humanity is a universal partnership. But they knew that marriage couldn't also carry the whole burden of intimate emotional support, nor could it last for long if married people had to live as if they shared one skin.

Liz thought for a moment about trying to say all of this, but of course a truly Atlantican marriage wouldn't work here, anyway. And for Rex and Cathy to get married so soon in a place where marriage was not taken seriously carried the risk of being disastrous. But Rex was Atlantican enough to really need to be married now. He couldn't be emotionally healthy without it. Liz guessed they would just have to figure this out as they went along. She said, "Do you like Rex better now?"

"Oh yes!" Cathy tried to suppress a grin. Liz loved seeing that. "You were so right. He's such a sweet guy. I think he really likes me, too."

Liz smiled. She reached and took one of Cathy's hands in hers and said, "Sweetie, I have a favor to ask. It's a rather big favor. Where Rex grew up, everyone his age is married. It's not a rule or a custom. It's more they feel discordant without a spouse, as if that connection in marriage helps them unify all their minds into one." Liz paused. Well, okay—go for it. "I think it's been almost a month now he's been without his wife. Here he is, so far from everything he knows, and on top of that he doesn't have a wife—"

Cathy said, "I would marry him. Would that help?"

Well, of course she would marry Jack's heir. Here was that damn stupid useless money thing again. Liz said, "I can't make that happen. Not so quickly. But I think I can persuade him you and he are married under American law. That would be a good start, don't you think?"

"You want me just to sleep with him?"

Cathy had such a childlike air that for her to say it so frankly made Liz wince internally. She rushed to say, "We'll do a little ceremony so he'll think he's married. Then I hope he'll start getting better. As he gets better, perhaps we can make it happen for real."

———◆———

Liz found Jack and Chuck play-arguing at Rex's bedside about whether or not the United States should invade some country called Iraq, which seemed to Liz to be such a ridiculous, off-the-wall thing for them to be fussing about now that Liz met Jack's eyes and then rolled hers. Liz had insisted that Chuck medicate Rex so lightly that he would be calm but his mind would still be clear, and she had to admit that the man knew his trade. Rex looked at his mother when she walked in. He seemed a bit drowsy but reasonably alert, and what she could feel of his emotions seemed peaceful.

"How do you feel, sweetie?"

"Where is Kethy?"

"She's taking a shower. She'll be back. But meanwhile, I want to talk with you about something." Liz pulled a chair close and sat down in the glow of the overhead light that glittered in Rex's hair. She glanced at Jack in the gloom across the bed and said, "Maybe you could go fight your war someplace else?"

"We're monitoring his meds, honey."

Liz and Rex were two of very few people whose minds interested Jack enough for him to want to spend time play-arguing this way. The fact that Chuck was apparently someone else whose mind Jack enjoyed gave Liz a new respect for the man.

"Okay, stay there. But butt out, please."

A man in white came in then with Rex's evening tray of boiled eggs and fresh spinach and carrots and strawberries. Not having eaten all day, Rex was certainly hungry, but Liz took the tray and set it aside for a moment. To Rex, she said, "Sweetie, it pains me terribly to see you in pain. I am so sorry! But I have an idea that might help. I know you're married to Gaprelagh the beautiful forever, but since we're in this other place it's possible for you also to have a temporary marriage." The Atlantican compound noun for a foreign marriage literally meant "temporary happiness." Liz went on, "A temporary marriage wouldn't interfere with your real marriage at all. And because your connection to the sielrah is so strong, through your temporary marriage you can help to build a sielrah for this other place."

Rex was looking at her calmly. What she could feel of his mind seemed calm. He said, "No woman do to me temporary happiness." He used the Atlantican noun.

"Well, true. It would be a great sacrifice. She'd have to love you very much."

Jack was struggling to keep a poker face. Liz turned firmly away from the possibility of seeing him as she said to Rex, "Here the custom is that a woman who loves a man enough to enter a temporary marriage will speak to the mother of that man. And darling, Cathy has just asked me if you would do a temporary marriage with her. Isn't that wonderful?"

He folded his arms. He set his jaw.

"Kethy needing husband. We deepfriends." Another Atlantican noun was necessary.

"Well, um, sure. A temporary marriage here is a lot like being deep-friends at home, but it's living as if you're married." She thought, *if you know what I mean.* She said, "But you can also have children. It's like deep-friends, but you can have children."

The fake wedding that Liz had envisioned was delayed until three days before Christmas, and then it was a genuine wedding because for the first time in all their decades together, Ted was able to say no to Jack. Having heard nothing about it, but being told by his daughter when she came home for the weekend that after having known one another for less than two weeks, she and Rex were going to be married on Monday without a prenuptial agreement and without her parents there as guests, Ted smelled a rat the size of Manhattan. He showed up at Sea Haven that Monday morning with a draft of a prenuptial agreement, and he told Jack that if this was going to happen, it was going to happen right.

———————•—•———————

For an at-home wedding whose participants would be celebrating at the family's twenty-seat dining table with half the table left over, Rex's wedding soon became gigantic. Ted's insistence on a prenup followed by an actual wedding had come as a surprise to Jack that Monday morning, but he spoke with Rex and Cathy separately, he decided this was what they wanted, and he spent half a day behind closed doors with Ted and two sets of lawyers to get the legal stuff out of the way. Jack was apparently phobic about ever again getting married himself, but he seemed to enjoy the idea of a wedding. Once he was on it, he kept thinking up details.

Liz was in her sitting room with her stylist one morning, selecting a mother-of-the-groom gown from five dresses in various shades of red. All these bedroom suites were inverted, with internal hallways leading to bright sitting rooms against the outer wall, and with windowless bedrooms toward the inside, each with a large bathroom and a dressing room beyond. Her sitting room was full of morning light that made the gowns laid across the back of her sofa look brilliantly garish.

Jack strode down the little hallway, calling, "Cover up, honey!" You could tell this was a weekend day because he was wearing slacks and a polo shirt. He stood and briefly studied the dress alternatives, touched a bright-red brocade and said, "That one," then said, "Thank you and please excuse us," to the stylist. The woman gathered her dresses and bowed and smiled out of the room.

Liz said, "That was easy," and put her arms around Jack's neck and kissed him. He broke the kiss, went to sit down on her sofa, and patted the cushion beside him. Liz sat down, searching his face.

"Is something wrong?"

He handed her a flat square velvet box that had to be another necklace.

"But darling, I love the one I've got! How many necks do I have?"

"Open it."

She lifted the cover, wondering, to find a birth certificate folded inside. It turned out that Rex Richardson had been born to Jonathan J. Richardson, Jr. and Elizabeth B. Richardson in Pilgrim Cove, Massachusetts, on August 28, 1978, at 8:59 in the morning. Liz lifted her eyes to his, slowly grinning.

He said, "A mother-of-the-groom present."

Liz gushed, "Thank you!" and tried to throw her arms around his neck, but he was struggling to take another box from his pocket. He handed her that one as well, and she opened it. Inside was a gold ring set all around with rather large diamonds.

"Try it on. You can have platinum if you prefer. I like the gold."

Studying the ring without removing it from the box, Liz said, "It's beautiful!"

"Try it on, honey."

"This is either an efficient way to do a dozen engagements at once or a spectacular wedding ring."

"When we married on Atlantica, I never gave you a wedding ring. Shall I place it on your finger?"

He was beginning to do that as he spoke. Liz studied the ring on her hand. It was a bit tight, but once it was on her finger she thought she would never take it off again, anyway. She smiled at him happily, said, "Thank you," a second time, and again tried to give him a celebratory hug and kiss. He slid out from under her arms and stood. She sat looking up at him, loving the sparkles of white in his sun-struck hair and feeling freshly stunned to think that little Lizzie Brandt had the joy of sharing her life with this man.

Jack paced a few steps, then faced her and said, "Switch your mind to business, honey. No, cancel the 'honey'. Ted gave me his notice yesterday."

"Oh. Why? But Cathy and—"

"He wants to retire. It's fine. I was expecting it. But now I've got to choose his replacement." Jack paced a step to the fireplace mantel between the windows and turned and said, "There are four men at Larkin who've been grooming themselves for twenty years so one of them could take Ted's place. But now I have someone else in mind." Jack had a general air of calm confidence that was not easily ruffled. Liz couldn't recall that she ever had seen him keyed-up this way over basically nothing.

He went on, "Having to get you that birth certificate made me think back to all the times you've outmaneuvered me. Before I stopped doing interviews, there was a profile in the *Times* about the boy-wonder negotiator. I think I was in my early thirties. Someone interviewed for the profile said I was the best negotiator he'd ever seen because I think in four dimensions while everyone else thinks in three. But now I look back and I see that you've beaten me repeatedly. And you're so slick about it I hardly feel checkmated. You just get me to do what you want as if it were my idea. Living on Atlantica. Letting my only son grow up out there. Getting you that American birth certificate with my name on it, which I swear was the last thing I wanted! You have no idea how Rex's being my son limits our planning options. And then you got me to go easy and not fire that incompetent bodyguard fool who now is going to be my son's best man? Come on! Having to sit across a table from my own employee and agree to his demands, and even a press release announcing the marriage? I haven't done a personal press release in thirty years! I swear, even though you weren't in the room, you were pulling his strings. That's not Ted. To stand up to me that way? But you're always so slick, I never notice the check when it happens. I just look back and realize you got me again. If I think in four dimensions, you must be thinking in five!"

This was unexpectedly sounding bad. Liz swallowed. When he paused, she said, "I'm sorry. I don't mean to—"

"Don't apologize. I'm not upset. I'm offering you a job." He sat down on the edge of one of her side chairs as he went on, "The brilliant thing is you're my wife! Who can speak for a man better than his wife? You'll get more respect than Ted ever got because you're my wife. You used to be flighty and insecure, let's be frank. I never would have thought twenty years ago I'd be choosing you to replace Ted, of all people. But the way you look now, and the way you think—I loved the way you told off Shrinky Chuck, by the way, and even made it funny! The woman you are now is so perfect for Ted's job that I'd be looking to hire you no matter what your name was."

Liz was going to have to remind him that she wasn't a lawyer. But as Jack had been talking, she had been studying that wondrous birth certificate. She said, "Sweetheart? He was born in I think June of '77. You've got him too young here."

"So he'll celebrate an extra birthday. You have no idea what we had to pay to get both a hospital and a town to risk whatever regulatory issues they had and backdate fake records! The friend of one of my lawyers who got it done had a daughter on whatever date is on that certificate. Liz, did you hear anything I said?"

"But I'm not a lawyer, darling."

"Ted hasn't practiced law in thirty years. What he does is speak for me. He stands in for me with his cellphone on the table. He'll say, 'I don't know if Jack will go for that', or 'He'll have my head if I call him to suggest that'. He gives me a layer between. The key is he has to do exactly what I tell him to do, but lately he's been thinking for himself. That would be fine if he could think strategically, but he can't. I think maybe you can."

"But I don't know anything about business. I'm afraid I'd embarrass you."

"This is a serious job, Liz. You'd be president of Larkin, with five division presidents reporting to you. That's fine because they'd actually still report to me, but on paper you'd be one of the half-dozen most powerful businesswomen in the world."

"It's full-time? I'd have to work full-time? And I was just getting used to being rich and lazy." Liz gave him a puckish smile.

"Before you tell me if you're interested, there's something you should know. Liz, I'm a bastard in the office. Nobody speaks to me unless I ask for it. Nobody uses a phone or speaks above a whisper in the hallway. I've fired good people because they entered my office wearing sneakers or chewing gum. So no affection, no personal discussion, no familiarity at all. I can't bend the rules for you without wrecking discipline."

Liz was smiling at him, cocking her head. This suddenly felt like seeing a beloved little boy trying to act grown up.

"Don't look at me like that! I swear, if you make me laugh even once I'll fire you. I mean that."

"Are you serious? You really would choose me over someone else? That's so hard to believe! Is it so you don't have to pay someone? A wife works for free?"

He gave her an exasperated look. "Anybody else would be quaking in his shoes and desperate to get this job. If you can't take it seriously, maybe you're not the right choice after all."

"It's full-time?"

"No. It's piecework. Of course it's full-time! You don't leave the office when I'm there. You don't speak to me unless I speak first. I mean it, honey. I run the tightest ship there is. A lot of good people can't do it. Those who can, make a lot of money."

"Can I try it first?"

"We can try it for three months. If either of us thinks it isn't working, I'll have someone else to tee up. Ted's given me until the end of June." Jack added, "Always remember, nothing about business is funny."

"I get paid?"

"Ted makes a million dollars a year plus bonuses. Would that do for you?"

"Well, that would be plenty if we had an American marriage. Sure. But we've got an Atlantican marriage not recognized in the United States. So I've got to be playacting, too? Pretending? So, maybe five million?

He snapped a look at her.

She gave him a little smile and said, "Check?"

He said crisply, "Five million it is!"

⊰ 14 ⊱

The greathouse of Rex's father's village was full of the stressed and worried energies of flowers cut off from their roots. They looked and smelled beautiful, though. Rex and Dennis were wandering the room together, dressed in black clothing, waiting for Cathy and her parents to arrive.

Rex was actually more comfortable living inside this stone mountain than he had been in the little village outside. He liked the softer human energies, the quiet music, the delicate scents. Even many of the people who lived around here were sensibly dressed alike, and the notion of stacking people's houses inside the mountain seemed handy to him. He especially loved this enormous greathouse that had the whole sky actually inside the room.

Dennis was turning out to be more of a help to Rex in comprehending this other place than Cathy could be. While Cathy kept trying to get him to accept things that would never make sense, Dennis simply answered his questions. He was never impatient with Rex for having asked them. Rex's friendship with Dennis was beginning to have the same feel for him as had his closest friendships back home, the same wordless understandings, the same deep acceptance. And Rex's ability to read emotions made him know that Dennis was getting the same kind of validation from being with him.

Rex found so many things about this place astonishing, and he could freely say that to Dennis. Kindly Dennis would say something like, "I feel the way you do. Who lives like this?" When Rex asked him whether there was a lot more beyond the fence, Dennis said, "There's millions of people out there. But don't worry, when you get there you'll be ready to deal with them." Rex asked him why there even was a fence. Was it there to keep us in or to keep them out? Dennis hesitated for a breath. Then he said, "I think it's just to keep us apart."

Dennis was marveling now, "Do you ever get used to all this, dude? I didn't think so many books existed! I'd ask if you thought your dad would rent this out for our wedding, but I don't think I've got the coins."

"Is okay you girl not here?" Rex asked as they paused by the window-wall to admire the sky.

"Sure. Sorry about that. Her dad did time, but he's okay now. I guess your dad's pretty strict. Your mom told me she's going to be the maid of honor instead. Pretty fancy wedding for just eight people."

"Is very small village. You live here, Dintz?"

Dennis smiled and said, "I couldn't afford the rent."

Rex enjoyed listening to Dennis. Everything his friend said to him felt like another gentle affirmation, and Rex was grateful for the practice Dennis gave him in conversing in English.

A woman and man were appearing here every day now to sit with Rex and teach him to speak better English, and he thought it was kindly of them to be helping him. They were especially beardless, though. The chaotic intensity of their minds and their base fear tended to batter his own mind, so he needed to pause often and go outside and walk around for a bit. He couldn't go far, because whenever Rex went outside now there would be men standing between him and the ocean and moving whenever he moved. Rex knew they were worried that he might again seek to rejoin Gaprelagh in the world, and he had tried a few times to tell them that if he decided to go home he would arrange it with his parents and he would never again do something so foolish as wading in and starting to swim, but that hadn't seemed to make a difference to them.

Rex said to Dennis as they wandered the room, "You know time, Dintz?"

Dennis glanced at his wrist and said, "Eleven-thirty. Another half-hour."

"No. Is how can a past? Always is now! How can a future? Now is now."

"I guess they don't have time where you came from? Boy, that would be nice."

"Is nice. Time idea is hrastinit. Why they have it?"

"I thought about this. The last time you brought this time thing up, I thought my head would explode. Rex, imagine you're a twig floating down a river. You're by this big rock, then you're by this other rock, then you're down by this tree. Can you picture that?"

Rex thought about the river and the twig. "I am the twig?"

"And time is the river."

Rex thought for a moment. "Okay. So why caring?"

"I guess because the river is real. If you're in it, you've got to deal with the fact it's flowing."

"But if is a pool?"

"If there's a pool and the water's not flowing, then you're right. There is no time."

Rex considered that. "Okay. In people's world, the twig in the pool?"

Dennis clapped him on the back and said, "If your people already made it to the pool, my friend, then I can see why you'd rather be there."

Rex's parents were approaching them. His father was dressed as he and Dennis were dressed, and his mother wore a long garment the color of the red flowers around them that made her appear to have no feet. Rex was used now to this difference of clothing every day, and he was becoming used to the fact that he hardly recognized his mother anymore by eyes or nose, so different did she look and smell. But she still sounded the same, and her mind felt the same, if even looser and more fluttery. As they came within earshot, both of them smiling, Rex said to them, "Time is river. Home is pool, so no time."

Liz gave him a hug and said, "How did you figure it out so soon?"

"Dintz figure out." He shrugged. "I dealing with river."

Jack said to Dennis, "He's using professional bodyguards. I'm sure you understand why." Rex felt a startle in Dennis's mind, followed by a rush of fear. Then Jack said, "Your new job is to be his tutor for things like time. How much am I paying you?"

Dennis cleared his throat and said, "Ah, fifty, sir?"

"Now it's sixty. Thanks for your help with that. Be sure to tell someone your new number, because I won't remember."

Jack turned to greet the very beardless Ted, who was grinning, an expression that apparently had been so rare for him before today that the set planes and lines of his face were having trouble accommodating it. Rex had found this man Ted to have the most chaotic, stressed and fearful mind of anyone he ever had encountered, so the sudden relative placidity of it surprised him. As the men began talking, Liz said to the woman wearing green who had entered with Ted, "Linda, I don't believe you've met our son. This is Rex, and Rex's friend, Dennis. Rex and Dennis, Linda Armstrong is Ted's wife and Cathy's mother."

Rex wasn't good at the beardless hand gesture, as he could tell by an occasional blip in the other person's mind. Linda looked like an older version of Cathy, which meant that she was beautiful. And despite that little blip when he tried to shake her hand, her mind had a wonderfully soft and confident feel to it. Rex said to her gravely, "Thank you for Kethy. I know is big sacrifice, she doing temporary marriage with me. I promise I never forget." The sharp startle in Linda's mind, and the plain astonishment on her face as she glanced at Liz made Rex realize that he must have violated some unanticipated custom in speaking so plainly. He said quickly, "I am sorry. No live this village long. Forgive I speak so." He glanced at Liz, she nodded her agreement that he didn't have to stay with them, and he said, "Excuse please," and moved away with Dennis.

Rex was trying to get used to all these details of words and gestures that were required in this other world so people could show one another that they meant to be friendly. But why not simply show that by feeling it? The most hrastinit things about being here were turning out to be all these confounding complexities required for interacting with other people.

Jack called, "Rex! Let's get started. No need to wait for noon." He was positioning Cathy's parents at one side of the big fireplace, moving them with his hands on their arms to get them to stand just where he wanted them. There were two men standing in the middle now with their backs to the fireplace, one all in black and one in white with a bright sash about his shoulders that hung almost to the floor.

Liz said to Jack, "I've got to stand over there, sweetheart. I'm the matron of honor."

"You're with me. Dennis can be the matron of honor. You don't mind, do you?" he said to Dennis. "We want the pictures to balance."

Then there were people fussing and flashing things as Rex stood with his parents and Dennis stood beside Linda with Ted beyond her. Ted soon hurried from the room, and the seven people in black who had been making chaotic little noises for awhile in the opposite fireplace corner began together to play sweet music that made Rex think of birds beside a rippling stream.

Cathy entered from the drawing room with Ted. She was enveloped in so much shiny white fabric that her father couldn't walk close beside her. Even her face was covered in cloth. Rex watched her approach with a rising unease born of the fact that none of this was making sense and he couldn't even see her face. Suddenly, though, he was feeling her mind, that soft childlike sweetness that made him think so much of his Gaprelagh. As she came closer, her father helped her lift the cloth, and Rex was seeing her face with a shock of feeling that swelled his chest and had him grinning at her. She smiled back at him with the sort of look that she would give him when she could tell he was being more obstinate than he needed to be because he was enjoying flustering her. How he loved that look! Rex's impulse was to stop this foreign wedding, defend her even against himself, and make it his mission to find for her the genuine husband that she deserved. But then he couldn't bear to do that.

Jack and Liz spent the month before she started her job fretting about how they could pull this off. Never to catch one another's eye and realize they were sharing the same irreverent thought and trying to avoid a small chuckle, which each would then notice in the other so they ended up laughing? That had been a game of theirs at least since their Atlantican wedding, Liz thought. How do you break a habit like that?

She really did want this job. She had graduated from college as a first-grade teacher because she needed a way to make a living, but she hadn't liked teaching. A few years of it had made her confident that her mind was shriveling from boredom and from what felt like forcing it to rev in such a low gear that she was losing her ability to think in words of more than one syllable. Soon after meeting her, Jack had wonderfully offered her a job as his assistant; but then she had gone native on Atlantica, which had scotched that. She had been sorry about it later. Loving Jack as she had come to love him, she had later thought it would have been nice to have been involved in the business part of his life so she could have come to know him from that perspective. So now, quite unexpectedly, that lost opportunity from decades past seemed to be coming around again, and with designer clothes to boot.

But the no-laughing rule was a problem. Jack kept fretfully insisting that even one mistake would have to get her fired, because Larkin and its affiliates employed more than five thousand people worldwide, and that entire rigidly-controlled community would be watching for her to make a mistake. If Jack bent the rules for Liz, there would be an international sigh of relief and everything would dissolve into chaos.

So they practiced. They shared every meal with the understanding that this was a business meeting. They practiced not looking at one another directly, while not thinking about not looking at one another, and they practiced his saying outrageous or intentionally funny things so she could practice not reacting. They practiced having him sit at the desk in his sitting room and having her walk in and sit down facing him without giggling. But all that practicing seemed to Liz to have been a waste of effort when at last she entered Mr. Richardson's office on the morning of her orientation. He looked and acted so different from the man she loved that interacting with him familiarly seemed inconceivable.

His personal office was on the second floor of a surprisingly large brick office building that was just west of the main house's west wing. It was pretty much what Liz would have expected, all raised paneling in a light fruitwood and too many dark and expensive-looking paintings. As she was ushered in and she sat down in one of his guest chairs, Jack said without lifting his eyes from perusing her signed induction documents, "Good morning, Mrs. Richardson. Do you have any questions?"

"No sir." No impulse to giggle so far.

"Did you very carefully read the privacy agreement?"

"Yes sir."

He lifted his eyes, looked directly at her, and said, "Do you understand that for you ever to reveal anything about me or my businesses to anyone will get you fired? If you ever in your life reveal anything material, you've agreed to repay everything that any of my businesses ever has paid to you?"

"Yes sir."

Like I would do that, Jack! But then she caught herself. Mustn't think his first name.

Jack went back to looking through the documents that had been delivered to Liz at the house the previous afternoon for her to read and then carry up the little walk between the house and the office building this morning so she could sign them before a notary. He flipped the last page toward her and said, "To spare us both grief, please read this list of rules several times a day until you've internalized it. I'm paying you more than you could earn elsewhere in part to make it worth your while not to distract me."

Liz half-stood, leaned, and took the list from his desk.

He said, "Stand and walk. Move with energy. Watch your posture."

She thought, *Good grief.*

Jack sat back in his chair and looked at her as if he never had seen her before. He said, "I'm going to ask you to forget everything you think you know. I don't do things the way other people do, and I'm not hiring you for what you know. I'm hiring you for the quality of your mind. I expect you to pay careful attention to everything I tell you. I want you to learn to think as I think. Can you do that?"

"I'll try, sir." Liz had practiced seeming to look at him, but with her eyes off-focus. Now she briefly risked focusing on his face. It seemed to her that he was relaxing a bit, and so was she. Maybe this really could work.

"I'm going to tell you a little about me and my businesses so you'll have a framework on which to hang our discussions. I want you to know how the world looks to me, so it can begin to look the same way to you. I'll welcome questions on specific matters in the course of our work together, but this background information won't need elaboration.

"My father was one of the reasons we won the Second World War. He ran a couple of companies that supplied the auto industry. He helped American manufacturers turn on a dime and retool to make tanks and jeeps and planes. He was barely thirty. By the time he died at the age of fifty-five, he and my mother had left me a combined estate worth more than half a billion dollars." Jack seemed to be relaxing even more. He had told Liz that everyone he hired for a senior position got more or less the same spiel, so she settled in more comfortably to listen.

"My father ran businesses. I run money. I will be sixty-two next week. In the thirty-five years since my father died, I have built my inheritance to be worth something like twenty-three billion dollars."

Liz blinked when he mentioned his birthday. She had asked him long ago when his birthday was, and he had told her that birthdays were depressing and nothing to celebrate. But hearing that it was at the end of January made her forcefully recall that his mother had died when her plane crashed in a snowstorm on the weekend before his twentieth birthday. Liz felt a little rush of pity for him, to realize that Milly had taken from him even the little pleasure of celebrating birthdays.

Jack went on, "You're the nominal president of Larkin International. That makes you my senior employee. The Larkin parent company controls five divisions, only one of which is based in the United States. I should add that although we call them divisions, they are in fact six independent companies contractually tied together. The only one in which I'm still active is a hobby. I play with doing rollups of small businesses, and for that I need an end-stage negotiator. That was your predecessor's primary job in recent years. For the next few years it will probably be yours, although doing rollups is less profitable than it was ten years ago, so I expect to be winding it down before long.

"I began my career as a turnaround specialist. It was a lot of work, but I made a lot of money. Now most of what I've made is invested so profitably in trading stock options and currency spreads that when I borrow from my offshore funds to buy something in the United States, I cut my returns. That's why I call this a hobby. I like playing with businesses.

"But here are some things I do differently. I never use outside leverage. I don't use outside professionals. I have no interest in any business worth more than a quarter of a billion dollars, and in fact I like the little ten- to fifty-million-dollar business that somebody spent his life building. Now he wants to retire. I give him a payday. Then I send in my team and clean it up and put together a number of similar regional companies and roll them up. We either sell the resulting business or take it public. I don't do tech. I don't understand it, and I have no interest in learning about it. At the moment I'm playing with auto service businesses in the northeast quadrant."

Liz had no idea about a lot of what he was saying, but he wasn't hiring her for what she knew. She hoped the quality of her mind would help her figure it out.

"My father was the smartest man I've ever known. He told me he was there in the thirties when American freedom started to die. He could see how it was going to end, but he didn't know how long it would take. He began moving our assets offshore while he was alive. Larkin is a Swiss company. One of its divisions has no U.S. nexus, and three more will eventually be clean. We can abandon the one here if that becomes necessary because its assets are pledged to offshore affiliates." Jack paused, then seemed to do an internal shrug as he added, "I'd been thinking about giving my son direct ownership of our trading company with no U.S. connections, but apparently the fact that he's my son and U.S.-born makes that risky. We both may eventually renounce our U.S. citizenship."

Liz blinked. Okay, that had been a trap, and she realized there were likely to be others. She kept her face blank, but that was when she began to grit what felt like deeply internal teeth.

"Thirty years ago people thought I was paranoid for being wary of the federal government. Lately they're starting to see me as prescient. Reagan could have arrested the slide—" Here Jack was the one who blinked, and Liz realized later that he had been thinking through the fact that his informing her that one of the greatest presidents of the twentieth century had been someone she would recall as a B-grade movie actor might have broken the no-laughing rule right then and gotten her fired in less than a day.

Jack went on, "He saw the risk, but he was too old and becoming senile. The first Bush never listened to me because I'm a Democrat. I gave Clinton enough money that he gave me an audience, but he was too optimistic by nature to take what I was saying seriously. Now another Bush is in office. He's open to dealing with a Democrat, but this terrorism scare has thrown him off stride. It's going to take someone on a mission to arrest the slide at this point, and I don't see that in him."

Liz had no idea who these people were. She realized that in order to do this job, she was going to have to catch up on the recent world history she had so blissfully ignored.

"Three of our offshore divisions partner with local companies to establish and build businesses all over the world. We supply the capital. The locals supply the expertise. I hadn't meant to go in that direction since running the money is cleaner, but there are opportunities in developing countries too good to ignore. And the men running those divisions are doing wonderful work."

After Jack's induction spiel, he and Liz met individually with four of his division presidents. Three of them had flown in for this meeting from their homes in other countries, having been informed only days ago that Ted's successor had been selected so the race for the top job was already over. They all looked rather pale and shell-shocked to Liz, even the Asian man from Singapore and the man from India and the South African fellow with the musical accent. Not only had the boss hired a female from outside without giving them a chance at the job, but she was apparently his longtime wife and the mother of the grown son no one had known existed before this morning. So, who was Clarice Richardson then, the woman they had long known as his wife?

Jack gave them all this new information matter-of-factly. Liz came to wonder during those meetings whether his treating four powerful, useful men as just the employees that they were was a deliberate way to keep them to heel.

And she wondered why they even wanted this job, which was seeming to her more and more to be just an overblown assistant's job. Something Jack thought she could do? Come on! How was that a promotion for them, and requiring an international move besides? All she could think was that this was a game for them just as much as it was for Jack, so his treating this job as a prize had made them automatically want to win it.

Where Jack was concerned, meeting these rivals for her job made Liz realize that his primary reason for choosing her likely had been that he trusted her. He trusted almost no one, but he had trusted Ted. And now, after all their years together, and despite all the ways that she had complicated his life, apparently he trusted Liz as well.

⚔ 15 ⚔

Having lived here for two months now, Liz knew that Jack needed to decompress between coming down the walk from the office building at six and coming downstairs to dinner at seven. As they entered the house and the front door closed behind them after their first day of working together, rather than turn to her so they could fall into each other's arms in laughing celebration, Jack said curtly to Liz, "See you at dinner," as he headed upstairs.

A housemaid approached Liz while she was giving him a courtesy space before she went upstairs herself. The maid said, "Excuse me, madam. The younger Mrs. Richardson asks if she might have a word with you. She is in the formal sitting room."

Liz saw as soon as she opened the door that Cathy was hiding out in here to cry privately. She hurried to sit beside Cathy and put her arms around her as the girl was finding a dry place on what Liz noticed was one of Jack's monogrammed handkerchiefs, likely brought to her by his kindly valet. Cathy said without looking at Liz, "I'm so sorry. I really tried, but I love him so much! I can't stand anymore that he doesn't love me. I mean, how would you feel?" Just the thought of that brought another spate of crying.

"Of course he loves you!"

"I have to leave. I'm so sorry. I called my father and told him I just want to forget the whole thing. Rex doesn't owe me any money. But—but—but he said I have to enforce that thing we signed. The prenup? But then if I leave, Rex has to pay me fifty million dollars? After less than a month? I can't do that! His father will be mad. I can't do that to him."

"Oh sweetie, of course he loves you. Uh—did you say you can't leave because you don't want fifty million dollars?"

"I don't want to hurt him!" Cathy blubbered. She looked for another dry spot and delicately blew her nose.

"Sweetie, if everyone else can see he's head over heels, why can't you see it?"

"He thinks I'm ugly! He won't have sex with me." She glanced at Liz and added, "This is so embarrassing."

Liz said, "Oh," thoughtfully. She broke their hug and sat up so she could think more clearly. She said, "I'm sorry. He loves you. He's just confused. I'll ask his father to have a talk with him. Where is he now?"

"He went to the staff parking lot to see Dennis's new car. Apparently Rex has never seen a car?" Cathy glanced at Liz uncertainly. "The body-guards didn't want him to go. He said they were hrastinit and went anyway. They thought it was a swear."

"I'll talk to his father. You go have a nice bubble bath before dinner. And don't worry," Liz said as she stood. Although now she herself was worrying mightily.

———— · ————

Jack was busy at the desk in his sitting room. He hadn't turned on the room lights, so the only light came from the fat brass lamp on his desk that made Liz think of the lamp in his study on his yacht, and the night of their first-ever confrontation. Jack said without looking up, "If only one wing of the house is on fire, please call the fire department. You know I need more time."

"I'm sorry. This is even more important than a fire."

He looked at her. She had become used to seeing the business Jack Richardson disappear into his suite and then reappear transformed to the normal love of her life an hour later, but this in-between Jack was new.

He said, "All right," and sat back and looked at her.

Liz brought up the room lights halfway and went to sit down in one of his guest chairs. As she did that, he said, "Good job today."

"Thank you." She gave him a little smile. He had told her that since he was so focused in the office and he didn't want to mix office with home, she was unlikely to get much feedback, so this felt like a gift. She said, "Darling, will you please talk with Rex? Cathy just told me they haven't consummated their marriage. She thinks he hates her."

Jack gave Liz a patient look.

"Their love life is more important than having the house burn down?"

"She was crying! She said she's so sad that she wants to leave, but Ted won't let her leave without taking the money. She doesn't want you to get mad at Rex."

"What ever did you do to Ted? For forty years he was the perfect foil, and now look at him!"

"Please speak with Rex. I thought before the wedding he was seeing a foreign marriage as more like deepfriendship. I told him it was the same as deepfriendship, but you get to have children. I guess now he thinks that happens by magic."

"You broke it, honey. You fix it."

"All he needs is for you to tell him sex is okay—"

"You tell him it's okay! I am the worst father in history. Now I'm just beginning to build a relationship with my only child, and the last thing I'm prepared to do is get involved in his sex life. Which is none of my business."

"I can't talk with him. Wrong gender."

Jack finished typing something on his computer as Liz watched her hose-covered toe find crevices in his desk carved from three-foot-wide boards of Venezuelan mahogany. So this was where that fancy desk from his penthouse had ended up.

As Jack stopped typing, he said thoughtfully, "I've never said this because it would have set you off, but you were the best lover I ever had. And as we know, that's saying something." He paused so she could react. She didn't look up. He went on, "You understand that sex happens in the mind. Most times, when I told a woman I didn't do intercourse, she would just go down on me, but you came up with creative ways to play with my mind. Wondering what you were going to do became part of the game—"

"I can still do that," she said, watching her toe. When he said nothing, she looked at him and said, "Are you seriously giving up sex for the rest of your life? This is checkmate, right? You're getting even for our whole life together?"

"No. I can see the check, but there are ways out of it. Shrinky Chuck believes I'm not attracted to you because you've become my pure second chance with Milly. Once again, he is full of it. Sex feels like Atlantica to me now. Atlantica drew me in, then it killed Steve and it killed my baby girl. Sex drew me in, then it killed both my parents. People I loved more than life itself."

Jack's mother had died in a plane crash while she was trying to interfere with his seeing someone else, and then his father had suffered a heart attack during lovemaking. So Liz had no answer for that. She said sadly, "It's just ironic. This is absolutely the dead-last problem I thought you and I could ever have."

"Just give her some coaching, honey. If she brings him up and down a few times, he'll stick it anywhere." He glanced at her and added, "As we know." Then he winced and smiled a little and said, "Tell her to do to him what you did to me to get little Milly."

"I can't tell her that!"

"Sure you can. Just don't tell her we ever did it. And for heaven's sake, don't tell me you've told her. I need to be able to face them at breakfast."

———◆———

There was a gym near the end of the first floor of the west wing, not far from the ballroom entrance that could serve as a short cut to the office building. With Jack's permission, Liz soon developed the habit of going down at lunchtime and working out rather than accepting a lunch tray. Her nice suits were getting tight, which was no surprise in a household in which six-course meals were the norm. Liz kept shorts and a tank top and sneakers in a gym locker. She would hurry down and change quickly and work out a little, trying not to break much of a sweat. Fresh snow glinted blindingly beyond the window wall. As Liz was spinning, she was craning to enjoy the broad blue sparkle of the ocean beyond the broad white glitter of snow that had turned the formal gardens down the hill into a regular grid of bumps.

Jack called, "Honey?" from behind her. She startled and got off the machine.

"Sir? Permission to ask whether I can ask a question? If it's during the work day, is this room technically house or office?"

He was wearing a business suit. Don't giggle.

He cocked his head at her, beginning to smile. He said, "I hate it when I can't tell if you're being funny deliberately or by accident."

"House, I gather. So kissage is appropriate." She stepped and put her arms around his neck and gave him a nice generic sort of kiss, having to rise on tiptoe to do it because she was wearing sneakers.

As they pulled two tall stools to where they could sit side by side and look out at the sparkling view, Jack said, "Ted tells me you're doing well. That doesn't surprise me, but on the other hand, it amazes me. Perhaps you complete me in this part of my life as well."

"For five million a year, I should tell you I'm suffering, but I love it.

147

Feels like a smorgasbord of interesting things to learn. He really said I'm doing well?"

"You're going to hold me to that five million, aren't you?"

"Damn straight I am. We unmarried-in-the-United-States ladies have to provide for ourselves."

He glanced at her, not quite smiling. He said, "Clarice is breaking the privacy agreement. Not much, but enough that we may have to take back some of the money. We've sent her two warning letters, but apparently she doesn't believe I would actually do it. So I'm being advised to set a counter-fire."

"Is that legal jargon or business jargon?"

"Neither. I came to a place in the sentence that needed a word, so I thought up a word."

Liz glanced at him, smiling inwardly. The sun-struck snow was throwing glints that sparkled in his hair and eyes. The hair at the side of his head that she was studying had considerable white in the mahogany now, but his beard had little white. She thought she liked him better without the beard, but seeing him in it sweetly reminded her of their long Atlantican romance. And if this sort of visit were going to become a regular thing at lunchtime, she was going to find it hard to lose weight.

He was saying, "They want to run interviews in *The Wall Street Journal*, *Forbes*, the *Times*, and maybe the *Globe* about the new president of Larkin and also her son no one knew about. They'll explain that we were married whenever, we lived apart for eleven years because you took him to be schooled in some exotic place or whatever, and now our family is back together and you're the new president of Larkin. It was helpful to my image when Clarice went to parties. Seeing you and him will be even better. And it may make Clarice go away before we have to nuke her."

"This is a trap, right?" Liz said, looking at him.

"How is it a trap?"

"'Hello Mrs. Richardson, just like to ask you a few questions about your husband. What does he like for breakfast?' 'Toast with marmalade.' Zap! Contract broken, no five million dollars and take a hike."

Jack smiled a little, looking back at the snow. He said, "Good point. But they'll figure it out." He slipped a folded sheet of paper from an inside breast pocket and said as he handed it to Liz, "Public Relations has been after me for the past two years to do a twentieth-anniversary edition of *Strange Dogs*. I always told them you refused. So now that they know you're here, this is what they emailed this morning."

Sir, We have been informed that your Strange Dogs and Their Masters *will be No. 6 on the* Forbes *list of "Ten Books That Made the Eighties the Eighties" in a 2003 Issue. They think Aug or Sept. They are asking to profile the authors. Our Sandra McMullen did original publicity for the book, and she found two interviews where you said Elizabeth Lyons was your secret wife raising your secret family on a secret island! We thought you were kidding. Advise you and your Mrs. do a joint interview. Advise you do a new edition of* Strange Dogs and Their Masters *to capitalize.*

"Didn't we have fun?" Liz said softly. "I remember that time as one continuous giggle."

"I remember dictating it to you with a baby girl on my knee. Bringing all that back now is the last thing I want."

"Oh, but—"

Then they heard Rex say from behind them, "Good! Both together."

They turned to him so quickly that Liz stumbled getting off her stool. Rex and Dennis were standing in the doorway to the gym, dressed like teenagers in jeans and T-shirts and sneakers. Both of them had shaved off their beards. As they entered, Liz said, "Where's your beard, honey?"

"I thought shaving might be good for Cathy. But not enough."

They had been noticing at meals that he was speaking much better English now, but Liz found it astounding to hear him use past tense and good pronunciation so easily. She said, "That's wonderful!"

"She say she leave me. Left me. You find this is wonderful?"

"Cathy left?" Jack said with a questioning glance at Liz. She winced a little apologetic glance at him, and he gave her a glare.

"She'll come back, darling!" Liz said hurriedly. "I'm sorry. It's just a misunderstanding."

"She has fears of Myra. I tell her shimmers will not harm her, but—"

"Myra?"

"Your mother wake us this morning. Cathy find this is troubling. Myra come to say that—To say—" He stopped talking and cast his eyes upward, pouting. He went on, "She tell me my wife love new husband. My child consider he is his father." Rex looked levelly at them both.

Liz was astonished to see that her son was so strong. She didn't rush to hug him. She let that calm face stand on its own. Then she said, "My mother came to you this morning?"

"Oh yes. She is frequent guest. She visit you, but you ignore her."

Rex had been working hard on grammar and pronunciation. He still had a musical Atlantican accent, full of tones and notes, but that was pleasant to hear and it was going to fade.

Liz said, "I can't see her!"

"You can see her. Let eyes go off focus. See with your mind. Shimmers easy to see."

"Come and pull up stools and enjoy the snow with us, darling."

"No! I want to learn money. Denetz and Cathy try, but is so hrastinit beyond hrastinit I cannot make sense. They say you are able to teach it, Jack."

This startled his parents. They glanced at one another.

"Enough! I am here—were here—three of your months, and I learn nothing! I see on TV in staff room there is much to this place beyond the fence, but—"

Rex stopped talking. He looked quickly at Dennis, then at Jack. He said fiercely, "Why when you look at him he has fear? Why do they all fear you?" Rex's voice was rising. He said angrily to Jack, "What do you do to all these people, that if you look at them they have fear?"

Jack said nothing. Liz slipped her hand into his.

Rex stepped, turned, and pointed at Dennis. He said angrily to Jack, "Tell him now he has nothing to fear. Tell him in front of me!"

Dennis was looking at the floor, saying under his breath, "It's okay, bud. Don't push it."

Jack lifted his chin and said quietly to Dennis, "Don't worry, son. I won't hurt you."

Still looking at the floor, Dennis said, "Please don't hurt my mother, okay?"

"Why would I hurt your mother?"

"Sir, I'm sorry. She doesn't want me to be Rex's friend. She's afraid I'll make a mistake, and you'll, um—I'm sorry."

"Why do you do this, Jack?" Rex said angrily.

Jack said to Dennis, "Tell your mother she has a job for life, and a pension whenever she wants it. And your job is safe, too," he added, glancing at Rex, who was glaring at him.

Rex ranted, "When do you teach me? Cathy and Dinitz teach me much, but you teach me nothing! I am a child to you. But I am not a child you can lock in this house. I am the light of the world! I will know the truth, and the truth will make me free! But I see you only to eat, and you go away all the day and you teach me nothing. How can I be the light?" His eyes narrowed as he looked at Jack. He said, "What is it you do all the day that is more important than teaching me?"

Rex had always had a sharp, sudden temper rather like a relief valve, expressed and quickly over. Liz had never seen him sustain a rage except on Jack's last awful day with them on Atlantica, when Rex had at last reached the end of his long patience with his father. She had the uneasy sense that might be happening again. But despite her fears, she was enjoying hearing her child unexpectedly so easy with English. In this light, his hair was the color of gold metal and his face looked as if it were lit from within. Without the beard, he resembled his father even more.

Rex was telling Jack, "You cannot keep me here. You teach me, or I find a way to die. Never think that I am not able to die." Then he shouted at Jack, "Shave you beard! I am not comforted to see man in a beard who looks at people and they fear! Are you not ashamed?"

Liz squeezed Jack's hand. Had he not been here, she would have told Rex that the way his father affected people and the house around him were pretty much all he needed to know about money.

"And I want a car! Dinitz have a car."

"We have one on order for you," Jack said quickly. "They take awhile to build. But you can use my old car. It's a '95 I think, but hardly used. It's black. The new one will be midnight blue."

"I have it now? I go drive now?"

"We've got three drivers on staff. I'd prefer you use Peters unless I need him."

"I have Dinitz—"

"Ah, no."

Rex said to Liz, "My Cathy tell me she love—loved?—me too much to live with me because I have real wife so never can unite with her. So, why do this? Flowers and clothes? Is over because we love too much?"

"It's not over, darling," Liz murmured.

"I am beardless now, but still one with the sielrah. I do not lose it as you have, Litz. Liz. My wife teach—teached—me to preserve the sielrah of my mind from energy of people who have no connection to life. Now I must understand how to help them. Yes, I understand there are many more people. I am not a child! I see from TV—" He said angrily to Jack, "Why you never show me TV so I can learn? I see many people who are the ocean. But if we bring in them a connection to the sielrah that they feel themself not alone, they do not swamp us."

Liz said quietly to Jack, "We'll finish the carwashes and lube shops. Try to get Ted to stay another year so he can hold a cellphone. He and I can finish it, darling. Take off your suit now and teach your son."

⤜ 16 ⤛

Cathy returned to the house the following evening. Rex, Liz and Jack were still at the table, cleared now of the remnants of dinner, and Jack had just said, "Think of it this way. If more people in Morakan liked making shoes, and in Samitkan they liked making cheeses, they would trade off, wouldn't they? So then if the Morakan cooks wanted more cheese one day, they might want to give Samitkan something to keep track so later they could give them back more shoes in return?"

Rex had then said, "Morakan gets cheeses now. Samitkan gets shoes later. Why is that not make more sense?"

And then Liz had said, "You know, now money doesn't make sense to me, either."

Rex was looking at Jack in triumph when he saw his father's eyes move. Then he could feel Cathy's mind nearby, so he was already standing as he turned and saw her in the archway, looking sweet and lovely but feeling a bit fluttery. Rex ran the length of the table and caught her in a hug and bent and touched his mouth to hers in the greeting she liked. He lifted her in his arms and buried his face in the curve of her neck and smelled her soap and the sweet familiar scent of her skin and set her down again. With his arms still around her, he bent and whispered to her, "I love you only as I should. Please stay, beautiful one."

154

Cathy looked up at him so sweetly, and she gave him her little smile that ended in a tentative bite of her lip. The way she did that enchanted him. The sweet, soft feel of her mind filled him with such unexpected joy that he was struggling to suppress a grin. She said, "I want to stay. I love you the right amount too, Rexie. I just, well, there's this ceremony thing we have to do before it's three months or we can't be married anymore. We don't have much time left. Do you have time now?"

None of that first ceremony had made sense to Rex, so to hear there was another one gave him the urge to blurt, "How many more, so I can prepare my mind for all this further hrastinit?" Instead, holding her against him, thinking that never to be able to feel her in his arms again would be a black river of a future impossible to contemplate, he said, "Please, we do it now. Then come home."

They said goodnight to Jack and Liz, still sitting at the far end of the table, holding hands and smiling at them. They had developed a game of running up the stairs in the Atlantican way, where they had to arrive at the top precisely together or the game was lost. They started down the broad hallway past his parents' rooms, and down past two further doors to their own rooms. Jack had opened the second floor of the west wing for them when they were married, but that part of the house was dismal after thirty years bereft of people, so after one night there they had moved back to these rooms where Rex had been living since he moved into this house, still far enough from Rex's parents' rooms to give everyone privacy. And since Rex slept so much better with Cathy in his arms, they were living in one suite. Halfway down the broad hallway, Rex couldn't stand anymore not having Cathy in his arms so he swept her up and carried her as if she were a child. He buried his face in her neck so he was breathing her in, and she squirmed and giggled. He set her down in their sitting room and made the light appear, automatically shielding his personal energy against that little shock of electricity surging.

THE LETTERS FROM LOVE SERIES

Cathy said, "I'll be right back, honey. You go take your shower."

Rex was used now to this miracle of a warm-water shower. Standing in it for awhile and letting his mind go blank was a wonderful way to prepare himself for sleep, and it gave him time to do what was necessary to let him sleep comfortably with Cathy in his arms. Even with this preparation, one night while he slept she had found him to be ready for union, and she had moved herself against him so as he awakened it was being completed. He came to awareness confused about where he was and who she was, and then he was so embarrassed as his mind cleared further that he shouted at her never to do that again. He was sorry now that he had shouted at her. By the time Rex found Cathy in the bedroom, she had lit candles around the room and spread a sheet on the bed over the coverlet. She was wearing a white something, but her skin could be seen through it. As she passed a candle, he saw the silhouette of her body. He said to her, "What is this ceremony?"

"Oh, it's nothing, honey. Just a little nuisance thing. I think you'll enjoy it. But we have to do it or we can't be married and I can't live here anymore. Lie down in the middle, as close to the middle as you can. Are you comfy? Spread your arms out now. That's right."

He lay with his arms spread and lifted his head to watch as she came back with what appeared to be ribbons. Pink ribbons. She was tying a ribbon around his wrist, saying busily, "I'm supposed to really tie you, but you'd hate that so we can do it this way. But you have to promise you won't move. Pretend you're really tied. If you move even a little bit, we have to start over."

Rex ended up with ribbons on his wrists and ankles, and now he was supposed to lie still. He enjoyed watching her doing whatever she was doing, with her body under the cloth intermittently visible. Where Rex had grown up, people went naked all summer long. Nothing about casually seeing a naked body had ever seemed remotely erotic to him, except maybe a little bit right now. She crept up onto the bed and knelt and began slowly to rub his right arm and shoulder with oil slightly warmer than his skin.

"Is it too hot? It's supposed to be hot, but not too hot."

"It's fine." His nose was developing an itchy spot. He was trying to block that.

She had oiled his arm and shoulder and chest, and she was moving slowly down his belly. He was surprised to feel how this ceremony was affecting him so soon after he had released tension. He wanted to scratch his nose and cover himself below because this was becoming embarrassing, but then she would have to start over again. Instead he said, "I cannot believe this is a ceremony! My parents did this?"

She was concentrating on doing her slippery stroking as she got closer, and it was affecting him more, and he was wondering whether she would be oiling that, too. She said, sounding intent on what she was doing, "Didn't they get married out where you came from? Do they do this ceremony there?"

"No." He had a desperate need to move his legs. The more he thought about trying to stop what was happening, the more it was happening. There was enough now to begin the union. He said, "I'm sorry."

She was concentrating so intently on what she was doing that she seemed not to notice until she reached his lower belly. Then she straightened to sit on her heels and said, "Oh dear. That's not supposed to happen." She slipped off the bed and headed for the door as she said over her shoulder, "I'll give you a minute. Don't move now! We don't want to have to start over."

He called after her, "Your people are crazy, do you know that?"

He didn't dare even to scratch his nose because she had left the door open and the thought of maybe having to start this over was making his head throb. He kept his mind fixed on those freezing showers in the bathhouse in the little village outside, and gradually he became soft again.

"Are you there, Cathy? Come back now."

She had re-warmed her oil in the box for warming food. She knelt on the bed on his left side and began slowly to oil his left arm, saying, "I've got to be careful to get all your skin," as it began to happen again. And just his knowing it was going to happen, and trying to avoid letting it happen, had him fully ready when she was still oiling that side of his chest. His legs were trembling with his need to move them. His jaw was clenched so he wouldn't say anything, because to have to start this over again would have made him lose his mind. Finally he had to say, "Leave again," or he might have released, and that would for certain have meant this whole stupid hrastinit clueless ceremony of these benighted fools would have to start over again.

Losing it took longer this time, perhaps because it had just occurred to him that she might have to oil his legs as well. Finally he was able to call, "Come back, Cathy!" As she entered the room he said, "Please finish quickly. I am not able to start over."

"Not much more, sweetie." She started oiling midway down his belly. Very soon she was saying, "Oh dear," again.

He looked at her, feeling beaten. He said wearily, "Please go away again," because just her being so close to him was giving him an increasing need to do what he must not do while his wife was alive, for fear of damaging the unity of minds.

Rex was becoming ever more desperate to understand how to better tend his connection to the energies around him and preserve what was left of his mind-sensitivity. The only thing worse than losing Cathy from his life would be joining his mother in losing the last of his flame within. And where Rex had grown up, for a married person to make the union outside of marriage would have been unthinkable, an assault on the sielrah, a fatal stupidity like stepping off a cliff to enjoy the momentary pleasure of walking. But then, Rex's having made Gaprelagh believe that he was dead had induced her to do that, hadn't it? So, what could now be right?

Cathy touched her lower lip adorably with one finger. She said, "You know, there's a different way to finish this. Your legs are so long, this could take forever." Just hearing her confirm that his legs were next made Rex close his eyes and moan a little. She added, "I don't know if you can manage this."

"Yes! I can!" Just having her there so close to his hip, right there, was making the pleasure of it tip toward aching. He said, "Please move away." Then he said, "Please do whatever you can to end this."

Horrifyingly, she was slipping the cloth she was wearing aside and straddling him, saying, "Remember, you can't move at all or we have to start this over." He was inside of her, but just a little. She said sympathetically, "I'll try to move as little as I can."

But that was worse. Being in her so little and having her moving so little abruptly ended the ceremony, so he had her under him, and he was thrusting but she was too small and he was unable to thrust far enough or hard enough and babbling, but realizing she couldn't understand but there were no words in English and when the release came it was so bright. He stopped moving, not even supporting his weight, but knowing that was all right because she was whispering to him, stroking his shoulders, wrapping her legs around him. Until he went soft, they were still connected, and he found with a joy that had him grinning into the curve of her neck that the union was the same here as there and the sielrah was in it and now he was whole again.

Mrs. Richardson Steps Forward

New York—*Elizabeth Richardson is an imposing presence, more than six feet tall in heels. Here in her triplex penthouse overlooking Central Park she welcomes a guest with easy grace. Mrs. Richardson is the newly-named president of Larkin International, the holding company of reclusive billionaire Jack Richardson. More surprisingly, she is his wife of twenty-five years and the mother of his only child. Hers is an amazing story.*

"*My husband grew up with wealth,*" *she begins as a maid pours tea.* "*When Rex was born, we wanted something better for him. So our son and I have lived for the past two decades on our private island, without bodyguards and without restrictions. He got to be a little boy. He grew up wild and free!*"

Where is the family's island? Mrs. Richardson won't say. She is mum about the location of the family's other residences, too, and she says that this beautiful penthouse full of museum-quality art is just a place for conducting business.

"*My husband and I prefer to live simply and privately, surrounded by family and friends. I grew up without money. This kind of place is not me at all.*"

How did this unlikely pair meet?

"*I was hired as his assistant in 1976, and I got lucky.*" *She smiles at her guest over her teacup and adds,* "*I'm not talking about money. My husband is the kindest, smartest, most extraordinary man I have ever known. And the funniest! We have no television at our island estate, so when we are there we have just ourselves for entertainment. After twenty-five years, I still can't get enough of him.*"

When asked about their son's education, Mrs. Richardson explains that he was homeschooled on the family's island. "*And now that I have taken on his business burdens, my husband has the pleasure of completing Rex's education so he will be prepared to assume control and allow his parents to retire.*"

But how was Rex's mother made ready to take on the burden of managing what Forbes *estimates is a nineteen-billion-dollar fortune? She says,* "*My husband and I have worked together since the seventies. And he remains a very active Chairman of the Board. This new phase of our lives is turning out to be fun for all of us!*"

Mrs. Richardson is the co-author of her husband's 1981 best-seller, Strange Dogs and Their Masters. *Their book is a summary of business wisdom gleaned from Jack's years as a turnaround artist. In the past twenty years, it has sold more than five million copies in fourteen languages, and it is still on the reading lists of many M.B.A. programs.* Forbes *recently estimated that using the techniques articulated in* Strange Dogs and Their Masters, *Jack Richardson has created more than a million jobs in the course of his career. His co-author says, "My husband has had to add a disclaimer to the book. Federal regulations have become so intrusive that a lot of what worked best in the seventies can't even be done today."*

When asked about socialite Clarice Richardson, who long was thought to be Jack Richardson's wife, his true wife chuckles and reaches for a cookie. She says, "There were rumors that he was secretly married. After a much-too-public early life, my husband wanted privacy. He was advised that the best way to end the rumors was to produce a wife. We didn't want to go public with Rex until he was an adult, so Clarice was hired to give us a social presence. She did a wonderful job! It was a private joke, since we all knew that eventually my husband's real wife and son would make our appearance."

Mrs. Richardson has a strong, serene face. She doesn't look all of her fifty-five years, but she does look as if she has had nothing done. She tells her guest, "I have lived for twenty years mostly outdoors. There are natives on our island, and we have made improving their lives a central goal of our own. Wrinkles come with the territory! But my husband has rejected the idea of plastic surgery for me. He says he prefers me as I am."

Her guest is surprised to hear her mention natives. "Oh yes!" she says. "Wonderful people. Two American families have made caring for their needs our charity for generations. I have close friends among the people there, as does Rex. He has a bit of an accent even now, since English was not his first language."

How reclusive is Jack Richardson?

"He can't go anywhere in public. We try, but he is 6'8" tall and instantly recognizable. So we enjoy our lives mostly at home. He is a wonderful horseman with a lot of interests. He even has a forge, so when he needs to work off steam he can go and pound metal."

Will this Mrs. Richardson take Clarice's place as a prominent figure on New York's social scene? She says, "I don't think so. After all, I have a day job!"

The profiles in all four publications carried a picture of Liz in the ladies' sitting room in the penthouse wearing a simple Chanel suit and smiling confidently. Two of the articles ran on the last Sunday in March. Since *The New York Times* and *The Boston Globe* both were delivered to Sea Haven, Jack and Liz each had a version to read as they shared a late breakfast, having waited half an hour for Rex and Cathy to come down before concluding that the kids were sleeping in. The interviews had been conducted separately, but all four articles were much the same, although *Forbes* included an overview of Jack's business history and the *Times* reporter had tried to get Liz to talk about what the reporter called Jack's playboy past. In answer to her questions, Liz had said, "I have no idea. He's been nothing but a family man since we met."

Liz had refused to be interviewed until Jack signed a waiver of his privacy contract. "I won't betray you, darling, but I'm unmarried in the States. I can't afford to lose my job." So Jack had been mildly concerned about what Liz might say. She thought he even wanted to forget this whole thing. But a week before the interviews were to take place, rumors surfaced that Liz had assumed control of Larkin because Jack had become mentally unstable and was in a private psychiatric hospital. Jack was sure the rumors were coming from Clarice, and detectives were trying to trace a connection. But with this betrayal out there, Liz's interviews had to be conducted after all.

"They're pretty good, don't you think?" she said to him as she read the *Globe* version.

"You make me so normal! I've spent half my life trying to be Howard Hughes, and you make me sound like Ward Cleaver."

"I thought that was the goal?" She could see from his face that he was kidding her, but still he wasn't as pleased as she had thought he would be. Apparently even good publicity made him uncomfortable.

He said as he read the *Times* version again, "What gets me is the way you make our lunatic past make sense. 'I majored in education at Smith, so I homeschooled him where he could have a free childhood.' What a wonderful mother! 'And meanwhile, my charity was caring for the people on our private island.' What a saint! And, 'We have our island so we can vacation in a place where my husband can relax without security.' How sensible that is."

"But isn't that what I was supposed to do?"

"Of course. Public Relations must love this." He was scanning the article quickly. Then he said with a little ironic smile, "You got me again."

Liz looked at him.

"Count the number of times you say 'husband'. And you don't use my name even once."

"I—what?"

"Honey, you know I never wanted to be married. Especially after Louise! That we managed to do it on Atlantica is a wonder to me. Please let that be enough."

Liz was protesting, "That was the reporter. I used your name in the interviews," as she began to feel deflated. She had known he didn't want to get married again in the States, but she hadn't realized that their back-and-forth about it was more than a lighthearted game to him.

He added, going on to skim headlines elsewhere, "I need you to talk with Rex. He's obsessed with this sielrah thing. Jude lost it, and only then could he really settle in here. Tell Rex when he loses it, he'll be a better man for it."

Liz looked at Jack. One of her mental games had become a morning internal check to see whether she loved him just a bit more or just a bit less than she had loved him yesterday. Her base wonder was the simple fact that after all this time, and even with all that she had done over the years to complicate his life, he continued to want her there beside him. She had grown past her old worry that he might cast her out at any moment, but still, their relationship was so deep and so good! Without marriage. Even without sex. She thought, *More.*

"Darling, when you were the boy-wonder negotiator, how useful would it have been if you could have read the emotions of those poker-faces across the table?"

His eyes slid beneath his lashes. He looked at her.

"Don't suggest he lose it until you're sure it won't be useful to him later."

⇥ 17 ⇤

As Jack's silver Bentley limousine approached the Larkin building, Liz could see that there were photographers waiting. With most of its employees now based in other countries, Larkin was down to fewer than seven hundred people in the United States, including forty-four in legal, thirty-five in accounting, another twenty-three doing advertising and public relations, and just over five hundred people in its Levigard Holdings affiliate, who worked in teams doing business rollups and acquiring and managing real estate all over the United States. Levigard was based in an office building in Hartford, Connecticut. When Jack had first heard Liz's mother's maiden name, he had been delighted to have an interesting new family name to attach to what had been only Larkin East before.

Larkin's public relations people had let them know on the Monday afternoon following Liz's debut in print that she was unexpectedly a star. They had been deluged with requests for more interviews with her, guest TV appearances, even a seven-figures offer to publish her autobiography. So now Liz had her own publicist to strategize all her moves. A personal trainer was helping her learn to make the most of her time in the gym. Coaches were teaching her how to sit and stand and walk in high heels, how to shake hands, and how to go through doors. A more expensive stylist was refining her look, using more expensive clothes. One of the ironies of life was that if you could afford to buy expensive clothes, you could some-times get them for free if you were going to be photographed in them and your bagman carried cards identifying the designer.

Jack's car seemed to Liz to be precisely in his taste, with a skin of bright stainless steel, with a powder-gray leather interior and burled wood inlays and smoked windows etched in graceful patterns. There even were bud vases that held fresh roses. The only person riding with Liz was a handsome young man named Jason, a bit shorter than she was in heels, who had been chosen to complement her look. He was a trained bodyguard, but his primary function was to fetch and carry and open doors and hand out those designer cards. Today it was Ralph Lauren.

Liz had met her bagman just yesterday. Today, two weeks after she became famous, she was going to make her first post-articles appearance. The old Liz would have been shaking at the thought of leaving a car worth a million dollars and having her every clumsy move immortalized. But now she had coaches who had taught her how to leave a car, how to walk briskly but not hurriedly, and how to set her face in a way that looked dignified but not cold. Besides, it was going to take her maybe half a minute to cross the parking lot from where Jack's chauffeur was parking now. Ahead of them, four bodyguards in dark suits and sunglasses were leaving a black limousine, looking around and positioning themselves as Peters opened her door.

The trick to gracefully exiting a limousine was to be on the edge of the seat and against the door when it was opened. Then take Peters's hand and swing her feet through the doorway and position them while Peters blocked most of the view. With his support, slide off the seat and lean out to be free of the doorframe and stand, all in one smooth motion. Then Jason slid the handle of her briefcase into her free hand, Peters stepped back, and Liz began her first walk for photographers. She lifted her chin and set her eyes on the middle distance, envisioning Rex smiling at her.

Actually, it was Jack that they had first suggested that she see, but she had learned that if she thought of Jack while trying to be dignified, her mental Jack might cock his head and give her a look that made her snicker. Jason opened the Levigard Holdings door for her, she walked inside, and that was that.

Liz had intended just to introduce herself and answer a few general questions. But Art Carey, the Levigard president, had met Liz on her orientation day and had extended this invitation, and now he was determined to show her how they would be working with her. So for an hour and a half Liz had the seat of honor as the heads of eight work teams did PowerPoint presentations that described the whole process of doing business rollups as Jack did them. It turned out to be a wonderful education. Carey sat beside her, whispering occasionally. He was a ruddy-faced man in his early fifties who had the look of someone who ate too well and exercised too little, so although he wasn't fat, he had a lumpish, oily look about him. He treated Liz perhaps too familiarly; when she didn't catch his comments, she didn't ask that he repeat them.

After the show was over and the lights came up, Liz had an overwhelming need to stand. She was the only woman in a room that felt too small for the level of testosterone emanating from a dozen ambitious men. She walked around the table to stand before the pulldown screen while she tried to remember the things Jack had suggested that she say.

"Thank you, gentlemen. That was a wonderful education. My husband's mind is so far ahead of mine that he seems to have skipped a few steps when he described to me what it is that we do." There were nervous chuckles in the room. Besides Carey and his senior people, these were team leaders in their forties and fifties, intensely career-focused. Since they worked for Jack, they were very well-paid. Liz tamped down a thrill of wonderment that little Lizzie Brandt was their boss. Well, on paper, anyway. The presidency of Larkin was a figurehead position to give Jack what he called his "layer between," but the subtlety of the fact that Jack still called the shots seemed to have escaped these men. They were raptly listening.

"I'm sorry that we seem to have surprised you. We weren't sure when it would happen, but we knew that at some point my husband was going to want to step back so he could prepare our son for the role he will be playing. And—I know it's trite to say this—he's worked hard all his life. Now he has some roses to smell." Another few suppressed chuckles could be heard as Liz went on, "I'm going to ask you to begin our work together with the same discipline and dedication that you always have shown him. It isn't just me he's expressing confidence in. He's also expressing great confidence in you. With all that said, I'd like to begin our relationship by entertaining your questions."

Liz had told Jack she was going to do this. He had all but forbidden her to do it. He thought that letting them question their first female boss would be a sign of weakness. As Liz fielded mostly softball questions about how she liked her job so far and what her son was really like, the men in the room gradually relaxed, made little comments to one another, laughed with her when she said that she first was attracted to Jack because finally here was a man she could look up to. By the time she was shaking hands by the door and mentally preparing to again face cameras, Liz was seeing her having dared to make herself more human to them not as a weakness at all, but as a strength.

Beyond the ballroom on the first floor of the west wing was a large conference room. After Rex insisted that his father get serious about teaching him, Jack set about doing that. He had a whiteboard hung, and the conference table was now against the opposite wall to create a space where he and Rex could wander and mind-wrestle because both of them thought better on their feet. But money was still a problem. No matter how Jack tried to present it, after weeks of afternoons in this conference room there still had been no breakthrough comparable to Rex's eureka moment on time, to the point where Rex was beginning to think that there actually was no sense to be made of money.

As Jack presented money to Rex, it was numbers with too many zeros for the numbers to look meaningful. It was little pieces of paper and metal that looked to Rex to be entirely useless. It was another of those things—like laws, like religion—that people here had thought up to complicate their lives in order to distract themselves from what was important. Yet Rex's kindly efforts to help his father grasp the fact that money was useless, so his trying to attach importance to it was a foolish waste of a nice afternoon, seemed just to really irritate Jack.

Still, Rex was enjoying spending time with his father. Before his need not to lose him again had prompted him to say things that had separated them for more than a decade, Rex had loved to hone his mind against Jack's. Night after night, before the fire in the little house his parents shared, the two of them had brainstormed answers to questions that had interested Rex as a child. Why does fire glow? Are stars tiny and close, or larger and far away? Why does plant energy feel so different from pony energy, and why is human mind-energy so different from them both? Rex had realized even then that Jack was pulling his punches a little. But still, Jack had been willing to pin his eight-year-old son when he caught him in a logical error, which chest-swelling fact had kept Rex coming at his father eagerly night after night. Jack was saying to him now, "Okay, fine, then let's try this. You know there are many different countries with different economies and different kinds of money, right? So then if . . . ."

Rex nodded, but he wasn't listening to Jack because beautiful Cathy had entered the room. She was settling into one of the armchairs that had appeared by the door when Rex had insisted that she and Dennis must have the right to go wherever they pleased as part of the process of developing their minds.

Rex couldn't be sure how much mind-sensitivity he had lost because the loss wasn't constant: one minute he would be fine, and the next minute he would be feeling almost numb. Days ago, in desperation, he had approached his mother after dinner as she read a business report in her sitting room, and he had asked her what Jude had said about his own loss of connection to the sielrah when as a young man he had lived in this house.

Now Rex wished that he had talked with Liz sooner. Jude's insight had been that he thought our minds didn't generate the unity of all human minds, but instead our minds received it. As it had been weakening in Rex, now fully there and now mostly gone and now mostly back again, it had indeed felt to him as if he were losing his connection to something. Where he grew up, the sielrah was a web of mind-energy of which your mind was an integral part, and whether your mind generated or received it, the important thing was the fact that it was a dense and palpable web of mental connections with other people. Perhaps the great net of mind-energy was strengthened when more minds were connected with it? If that were so, then the reason he was losing contact with it now could be the fact that in this place he seemed to be the only one who was aware of it.

So then Rex asked his mother how she had managed to develop the ability to connect to the sielrah when she had moved to the people's world as an adult. She told him that the key to developing that ability seemed to be personal autonomy. Freedom of mind. Following your own wishes at each moment. She had found that getting in touch with herself so deeply was harder than it sounded, but awhile after she had begun to live that way, unexpectedly and wonderfully she had gotten her earliest whispers from the plants around her.

Rex concluded that in order to keep any mind-sensitivity at all he was going to need other sensitive people here. Cathy and Dennis were curious to try to develop their minds as Liz had developed hers, so now they both had such complete freedom to move in their environment that even private rooms couldn't be off-limits. That was where Jack drew the line. Rex fretted, but he had to agree that if a door were locked it might be treated by your mind as just a physical barrier and not an impediment to your freedom of mind, which meant that Jack's suite and the back of the office building facing the western end of the house were now locked at all times. The front of the office was fenced off because it had street access for employees. Of course, that ten-foot-high wrought-iron fence around three sides of Sea Haven and the razor-wire-topped chain-link fence twenty feet beyond it continued to bother Rex, but there was nothing he could do about the fences, so he decided to assume that fences might be treated by people's minds as more natural barriers.

Cathy had been trying for the past few days to learn to live in personal freedom. So for her to wander in here now with her knitting-bag so she could sit by Rex, and to choose to do that above all else, was a gift that had him smiling at her. Jack was saying to Rex, "You haven't heard a word I've said, have you?" as Liz came into the room.

It was unusual now to see Liz before dinner because she had taken over doing whatever it was that Jack used to do all day. But now, here she was at midafternoon, looking fussily dressed and weary. Her mind, though, felt as if it were toughening, perhaps becoming a bit more like Jack's mind, with less of the tentativeness that used to be her own mind's signature feel. Liz said to Jack as she dumped herself into the armchair next to Cathy's, "I think I deserve a raise."

Jack said to her with the indulgent, entertained look that his face generally assumed when he was interacting with Liz, "How did it go?"

"Great. They finally taught me what we do. That's a help. It boggled them that I was willing to come to them, and not the other way around. I told them nothing was going to change except I intend to keep going there from time to time. Oh, and the naked Fridays once a month for the boss's entertainment. All they could wear was their ties. That seemed to rattle the older ones, but the younger –"

Jack was across the room and pulling her from her chair and rocking her a little in his arms and kissing her for such a long time and apparently so enjoyably for them both that Rex thought as he watched that perhaps after all there might be something to this kissing idea. Where he had grown up, people kissed babies and children. For adults, touching mouths that way would have felt like a bodily invasion, he thought. Personally disrespectful. Harmful to the sielrah. But as he watched his parents, he was reconsidering.

Liz was a little out of breath. She said, "That was nice! I thought you had forgotten how," and crossed the room to kiss Rex's cheek before she settled again in the armchair beside Cathy's and whispered to her as she admired her knitting.

Rex said to Liz, "You took Peters? He can't drive me anymore?"

"Your mother's going to work now, son. But we've found you another good driver. He starts on Monday."

"Why can't Denetz drive me? Peters won't let me stop. All I can do is look out the window? I want to talk to people. I want to feel minds!"

Rex's parents exchanged glances, and seeing that annoyed him. When did boys become men in this place? Back home it happened at marriage, but Rex had been married twice now, and apparently he was still a child here. He said evenly, "My driver will do what I want him to do. Or Denetz— Dinitz—will drive me. Or I will drive myself!"

"How's the money thing going?" Liz said quickly.

"It's going wonderfully. Rex taught me today how to tell if a number is prime, but he still thinks a ham sandwich should be free."

Rex felt mildly irritated at his father for having put it that way, but he didn't say so. He and Jack were both hugely frustrated at this point, and annoyed with one another, too, since each thought the other was being obtuse. Rex already understood every smallest ridiculous thing that Jack was telling him about all these numbers and converting them into other numbers and tying various numbers to various places. He got all that, but he still couldn't see what it had to do with anything. How could it be his fault that none of it mattered? Or if it did matter, wouldn't Rex be able to see that by now?

Liz stood again and started to walk. She kicked off the shoes with pointed heels that she generally wore now, clumsy-looking but meant to make her taller. She said generally, "See if this helps." To Rex she said, "I realized this morning that what's confusing you isn't money. It's ownership. Jude used to say the whole idea of people being tied to objects was insane. Is that how you feel, too?"

"They aren't tied. What's insane is pretending they are."

"That's what I thought. Okay, sweetie, whose house is this?"

"It's Jack's house."

"Why is it Jack's house?"

"He's using it."

Liz gave Jack a quick confirmatory glance as she said, "Now, baby, suppose everything your dad uses is taken out of this house. All of us leave. It's entirely empty. Now whose house is it?"

That was a stupid question. "It's nobody's house. Until someone chooses it."

Liz looked at Jack and pointed at Rex and said with mild triumph, "That's your problem."

"So he's a communist? Socialist? What?"

"No. Just the opposite. Atlanticans don't own things in common. They don't recognize even the concept of ownership. Let's see if I can fix this." Liz paused to look out the window-wall at the sunlight breaking through and sparkling on the rain that was still falling. She said to Jack, "As you know, personal freedom is the core of their system. They've figured out that for someone to impose his will on someone else is a big thing that gets in the way of human unity. Only when each individual is autonomous and free can their minds unite. Isn't that right, sweetie?" she said to Rex.

He nodded once. He glanced at Cathy. He wasn't sure where this was headed, and if it might trouble her mind he wanted her not to be here. His mother was telling his father, "Communism and socialism are coercion. This is the opposite of that. This is people so perfectly free and able to unite their minds that they can trust one another completely. It's a tripod. Freedom and unity and trust. I think you can't have any one of them unless you develop all three together. That was the mistake Steve made with his Farm. He thought just giving people freedom led to everything else."

"So now you're telling me Rex will never understand money if money exists?"

Liz smiled at Jack indulgently. She said, "Cute, but not quite. Jude and I talked a lot about this. We're the only two people who've ever lived both there and here, and it boggled us to know that something does develop in people who live the way Atlanticans do. It has to be normal, right? They all develop it? And when I was there long enough, so did I. And so did you! Remember when you could feel how the trees felt?"

Jack looked away as he said, "Something like that." Rex could feel his father's rising irritation, and the hold that he was trying to keep on it.

"We concluded that the problem was civilization. People on Atlantica apparently are living the way people are supposed to live. They're wild. In a state of nature. I don't know if that's true, and someone should study it—"

"Where is this going, honey?"

Liz said to Rex, "Think of money as necessary when people have no connection with one another, and they're always interfering in other people's lives so nobody trusts anybody else. They have so little left of themselves that they try to cram their lack with an abundance of objects."

She was walking around, briskly picking up things from here and there, a pad of paper from the conference table, all the markers and the whiteboard eraser, even Cathy's knitting from out of her hands. She said then, "Oh no! Now I've got all this, and I still feel empty. I've got way more stuff than I ever should need now, but I don't feel any freer or any more connected to and trusting of others. Obviously, I must need even more." She turned to Cathy and said, "Sweetie, I've got this nice half-knitted scarf you might like. Do you want it?"

Cathy was smiling. "Sure!"

"Okay. I don't need it, but now it's mine, so since I'm not connected with you by mind enough to want to support you the way I would if we were connected—I don't mean that, of course," she said to Cathy hurriedly. "But this is mine now, and I still feel empty, so I need to be able to get more stuff. So I won't freely share this knitting with you. Instead, I'll sell it to you for a dollar that I can spend to buy more stuff for me."

Cathy handed Liz an imaginary dollar. Liz handed her back her knitting. Then she turned to the men and held up her imaginary dollar and said to Rex, "That's money."

Oh. So money is a replacement for love and trust freely given? That's all it is? Rex still couldn't see why money would be necessary, but he thought that at least he could grasp it as a concept. He said, "But why would they settle for objects and money if they can have freedom and unity?"

"They can't have freedom and unity. That's the point. And since they can't own even themselves, and they can't own a connection with other people, the only thing left for them to own is stuff. They try to fill their emptiness with objects. Or money, which is another kind of object."

Rex was finding it impossible to conceive of the horror of having to live that way. He glanced at Cathy. He could see and feel that she was unbothered. Jack said to him, "Did that do it for you? Do you understand money now?"

Rex said, as outrage was rising in him, "Then why do you need so much of it, Jack? Money and objects? Why do you not rather have people?"

Jack started to say, "I don't need it, really. It's just—"

But Liz broke in. "Rex, sweetie, please understand that your father's money is a great gift! Learn all you can, and build up as much more money as you can, because it looks as if we have a bigger job ahead of us than saving just our people's world." She sighed. "Someday we're going to need every bit of all the money you can make to fight for the freedom of all humanity." She bent and scooped her shoes from the floor and said to them all, "I need a bubble bath," as she left the room.

≼ 18 ≽

Rex and Dennis conceived a habit that spring of going for Friday afternoon drives. Their first driver was Peters, Jack's personal chauffeur, who had been caring for cars and running staff errands in a black Mercedes station wagon because Jack almost never left Sea Haven except by helicopter. Peters had inherited this job from his father, who had taught him so rigorously the trade into which he had been born that this Peters, only in his mid-twenties, had Dennis snickering to Rex that the kid was a pastel Christmas nutcracker. Whatever that meant. He wore a uniform in the same pale gray as Jack's car, with a bib front trimmed in stainless-steel buttons and a matching peaked cap and matching leather gloves and a rigid face and demeanor that seemed to make Dennis need to give him occasional verbal pokes.

This Peters ran the car precisely as his father had taught him to run it. Staff rode on jump seats, and they wore seat belts. As family, Rex rode on the comfortable back seat, and he could do as he liked. This was a problem, since Rex treated their early drives as thrilling sightseeing excursions that had him flipping from one side of the car to the other, drinking in whatever he saw and asking Dennis so many questions that Dennis was repeatedly taking off his seatbelt and shifting to the opposite jump seat in order to better see whatever Rex was seeing. Peters had dashboard indicators, so he would sharply slow the car until Dennis was back in a seatbelt.

Cathy was eager to join their first excursion. But Rex spent it bouncing back and forth from window to window, astonished by traffic lights and trucks and buildings and cars and bicycles and people and skateboards and power lines and a train, flabbergasted by so much road and distance, asking questions that forcefully reminded Cathy that her husband knew nothing about anything. She declined to join them on their later drives, and Rex was relieved not to have her along because watching him learn was stressful for her. He was trying to learn as quickly as possible, so having to cater to whatever she was feeling only would have gotten in his way. By the time Rex's new chauffeur, Clark, replaced Peters in Rex's car a month later, Dennis had bought a map, and they were planning their drives around answering Rex's questions. But still, they never stopped for long, and Jack had forbidden them to open car doors.

One Friday afternoon late in the season of new grass rising, they decided to drive north as far as Springfield, Massachusetts. Rex was trying to better understand how Americans lived, so he had Clark drive slowly through neighborhoods, frequently slowing down still more so Rex could get a better look. He had lately begun to notice the vast differences in people's homes, and the fact that his father's home was so much bigger than any other house they could find was confusing to him. The way people's houses varied so much in size and appearance, but within neighborhoods they were fairly uniform, perplexed him. In one area where the people generally had the brown skin and eyes of those in his home-place, Rex noticed a man of about his own age who was doing something blue to a small white house close beside the road. Rex was so interested in what the man was doing that he asked Clark to drive past that spot again, more slowly. The man glanced over his shoulder, then stood and stared as a black Bentley limousine rolled by. By their third pass he was back to work, but he paused and watched the car as it again approached him. Rex called to Clark, "Stop for a minute." Clark was so much friendlier than Peters that when he was driving they rode with the partition down.

Rex wanted to get rid of the glass in the door so he could talk with this guy, who looked quite a bit like one particular friend of his back home. He knew there was a way to make the glass slide down, so he was punching buttons on the door's armrest when he heard the door unlock. *Oh. Even better!* He opened the door and stood out cheerfully as he heard Dennis call from behind him, "Rex! Wait!"

The man was eyeing Rex warily. Rex was surprised by the feel of his mind, which was stolid and calm and without perceptible aggression, although it was filling with a creeping fear that felt like water seeping through crevices. Rex said, "Hello. I want to know what you're doing." And that made the seeping fear become a flood. The man stepped backward, staring. He had a brush in one hand and a bucket in the other. Rex said, "Please, friend. I want to know how to do what you're doing. Will you teach me?"

The fellow said warily, "This a joke, man?"

"My name is Rex. Do you have an American name?"

"Clarence."

"Well, Clarence, I like your blue house. What are you doing to make it blue?"

"Uh, paintin' it?"

"Will you teach me that?"

Clarence was eyeing the car and then looking at Rex, then looking at the car again. He was smirking a bit now. His fear was abating; his mind felt just lightly confused. Amused. But stolid: Rex liked the calm, centered feel of his mind-energy. Clarence knelt and dipped his brush into his bucket and began to paint, and Rex hunkered on his heels beside him, eager to watch. Then he said, "Will you let me try?"

"Uh, you want to paint my Ma's house?"

"Would you mind?"

Rex knelt then and tried it, the dipping of the brush, the getting rid of drips against the lip of the pail and the careful stroking, dipping again, stroking, having Clarence correct the way he was holding the brush, and all the while he was chatting with Clarence about the fact that he only just moved here so forgive him for not knowing basic things, and he just got married, and asking if Clarence were married and was this his house and had he lived here long. Clarence was relaxing into their conversation, beginning to answer Rex's questions, saying that he had a girlfriend and a baby, but he couldn't find a job but his mother was letting the three of them live with her if he fixed up her house, and he was finding that he liked carpentry and painting so much that he was thinking about trying to get a journeyman position. The feel of Clarence's mind-energy was becoming ever more calm and mild. But then Rex heard Dennis speak from behind them.

"Clarence, this has nothing to do with you, so don't be alarmed," Dennis said pleasantly. "We've blocked your street until security arrives. You'll be seeing police until Rex's bodyguards get here, but just ignore them. Everything's under control."

There was a sharp ping of stress in Clarence's mind. He looked at Rex, startled. Then came the fear. Rex looked around quickly, and sure enough, there was a car with lights flashing blocking the street three houses down, and another one in the opposite direction. Still amiably painting, Rex started to say, "I'm sorry. My father's—"

"I didn't do nothing!" Clarence said hurriedly, standing and backing away, staring.

Dennis was approaching him with a piece of money in his hand, saying, "You taught Rex to paint. He'd like to pay you. Will a hundred bucks do it?" Clarence wandered back uncertainly, looking at Rex, then at Dennis. Slowly he took the money. Dennis said to Rex under his breath, "Let's go.

Now we're not allowed to brush our teeth without bodyguards. Good to meet you, Clarence!"

The door to Jack's suite was locked. Liz was briefly irritated. She knew that of course it had to be locked because otherwise Dennis or Cathy or Rex might wander in as they accessed their innermost feelings, but Jack had locked her out and this was ridiculous. When she knocked, he came up the hallway in his stocking feet and opened the door. Seeing her made him cock his head and smile and say, "How was your day, honey?"

She led him back down the suite hallway to his sitting room full of late-afternoon light, where she sank into his big, soft sofa. He followed her.

"Why are you up here so early?" she said as he sat back down at his desk. "Where's Rex?"

"He and Cathy are doing what they feel like doing. I'm catching up on emails. How did today go? You're home early."

"They wouldn't budge. I walked out on them."

He gave her a sharp look and said, "Ted approved of that?"

"I did the phone thing and told him where we were and asked if he concurred that without absolute noncompetes for five years it was worth half. He knew the answer I was looking for." She had her left shoe off. She rested her left calf on her right knee because there was a spot on her foot that she had been meaning to scratch all day.

Jack said, "That's attractive." Then he said, "You're not ready to make these decisions, honey."

"But I've been at this for, what? Six months?" Now her other foot needed scratching, too. "I can do these penny-ante deals in my sleep now. I've done eleven. This is the first one I've dumped. All we're doing is finishing what they already had teed up when I started, and it looks like the carwash company isn't going to be worth what it should be worth. I never imagined I could think this way so soon, darling, but it's starting to get boring."

Jack was studying her, smiling indulgently. He said, "'Penny-ante deals'? 'Teed up'? Listen to little Lizzie now!"

"They'll be back. They need to sell. I smelled a rat last week, so I had them do a more detailed check. He's got a brother-in-law with a big gas station. So he builds this nice eight-shop lube chain and sells it to us and uses our money to build a competing chain on top of us?" She had one more spot on her left foot that needed scratching. "I told him I could meet with him any day next week, but we've got to have those noncompetes. After next Friday, we move on."

With both feet now happy, Liz tried to draw them up beside her, but the mauve Chanel suit that she liked so much that she had already worn it three times was too constricting. She thought of slipping off the skirt so she could be more comfortable, but she was appalled to realize that doing that in front of Jack didn't feel right anymore.

When they had first met, Liz had mightily resisted having sex with her rich and famous boss, never mind that they were falling ever more desperately in love and she was so profoundly attracted to him that meeting his eyes could cause genital tugs and the unexpected sound of his voice gave her butterflies. Months later she gave in, and they spent a whole eight days and nights doing nothing but making love and sleeping. Laughing. Talking. Very little eating. And for all those eight days Jack never even spoke with Ted or went near his office. There was one twenty-four-hour period when he climaxed seven times, while basically she was climaxing continuously. He was so eager to please her that he even put aside his squeamishness about intercourse, and Rex was the wonderful result. So the fact that slipping off her skirt in front of him felt awkward now was distressing to Liz, especially in view of the fact that she had an additional itch that only he could effectively scratch. She said to him, "Now I get why you found all this money and doing deals so sexually stimulating."

He looked at her.

"I'll bet when you did some billion-dollar sale of some company worth less but they overpaid so they could close in the penthouse and meet you in person, I'll bet when you finally got that done you needed a few girls to get it out of your system."

His face winced as he looked at her. He said, "Tell me."

"Oh, his young-turk lawyer kept flirting with me. It's a way to take me down a peg, if they can make me squirm but nobody else knows why."

His eyes slid away from hers. He said, "You're right. I think that's most of why I started hiring women. To have them there when I needed them. You can't act on it, honey. You know that."

"Shall I get the oil and ribbons?"

"That works just once. Until suddenly the game was over, I had trouble keeping a straight face so you wouldn't insist we had to go back and start the whole damn thing over again." He glanced at her and added, "It worked for them, too, didn't it?"

"But you haven't tried my latest variation, with the circus ponies and the velvet whips."

"Thanks for that mental picture!"

"Darling, this isn't only your decision. I've come home horny because some bastard kept licking his lips and going down on his pen and smirking at me sideways as he did it. Now here's my more-or-less husband, and we've got two hours before dinner and our children are rolling in the hay right now, and you're not interested? What is wrong with this picture?"

He looked at her. He compressed his lips, then bit his lower lip thoughtfully.

"Come on, Jack. You're being ridiculous."

"It's really that bad? I think women keep their sex drives longer than men do."

"It gets worse, actually. Until menopause you're too focused on the pregnancy risk. Please, darling. I can't stand to think that at only fifty-six I've become a nun."

He was looking away from her again, his face troubled, apparently thinking. Without looking at her, he said, "You can't risk an affair. You do realize it's the money they're after? I always knew that. And whenever I'd give in to a whim, there always was a messy aftermath." Then he looked at Liz and said frankly, "Choose someone. Put him under contract. Don't choose anyone I'll ever meet, and I don't want to know about it. Don't make me wonder where you are. Just do what you need to do."

Her jaw went slack. She stood as she blurted irately, "What? Are you kidding?"

Her reaction surprised him.

"I gave you permission. What, that makes it less exciting now?"

Liz went to him, thinking about drawing him to his feet, but he resisted when she tried to pull back his chair. So she took his face into her hands and began to kiss him, softly at first, then with little nibbles and more and more ardently, which had him pushing his chair back from his desk and rocking it backward and accepting her into his lap and his arms. Liz had the thought that together they weighed a lot, and if this chair went over backward it would be embarrassing if not painful. But the chair seemed to be holding, and he was losing himself in his kissing now, breath purring and mouth working wonderfully. She was squirming a little in his lap, helping him decide that maybe this was a good idea after all. But he just kissed her on and on, right on the edge, where the delicious feelings aroused could be an end in themselves. Liz broke the kiss finally and whispered to him, "Let's do it, darling."

He cuddled her in his arms.

"I love you so much. You do understand that, honey? I just need more time."

"But this is getting ridiculous. I've been here for nearly a year! And telling me to hire someone? That's not how women think!"

He smiled at that and tried to kiss her again, but she struggled out of his lap. As she turned up the hallway toward the door out of his suite, she called back to him, "See you at dinner!" She paused, then called more loudly, "Got to start screening applicants!"

ᚷ 19 ᚷ

This place also had a season of leaves falling, and here the season of leaves falling was beautiful. In the people's world, any trees not evergreen would drop shriveled leaves that had little color; but here big leaves turned bright red and yellow and fluttered down to carpet the earth with such brilliance that the leaf-covered ground seemed to radiate light. And these leaves had such a wonderful smell, like the season of dry grass but with rich floral accents.

Rex had told Jack that today he needed to be outdoors. For months they had spent most of their afternoons talking about things like rates of return and stock options and commodities and currency trading and commercial real estate analysis. Rex had tried, but he couldn't make himself begin to care about any of it. From what he understood, there were people who used these concepts to increase Jack's money, and in some ten-season cycles some of these people were able to increase what they were managing by double. This fact delighted Jack, that a billion dollars became two billion dollars a year later without his having to do anything, but it did nothing for Rex. Jack introduced new concepts almost every day that built on concepts from the previous days that Rex had half-heard and less than half-understood, so the more time Rex spent at these billionaire lessons, the less of any of it he retained. Cathy and Dennis had their personal freedom, but Rex had been fretting and re-testing all summer to be sure he wasn't losing his flame within because he spent most afternoons bored out of his mind. So, seeing those leaves bright beyond the windows finally made him tell Jack that he was taking the day off.

Dennis had lately moved into Sea Haven, directly across the hallway from Rex's and Cathy's suite. He was enjoying being part of Rex's project so much that he and Sissy had decided to put off their wedding for another year to let her concentrate on her college studies, and let him concentrate on learning how to access the sielrah. Although Rex wasn't calling it the sielrah anymore. The word had no easy English translation, but it meant something like "the further perfection of the unity of minds." Without unity of minds here, the word was meaningless. So as Rex tried to help Dennis and Cathy understand what it was that they were trying to develop, he took to referring to it simply as "mind." The ability to access the living energies around us.

Cathy wasn't going to be with them this morning. She had the sickness of coming motherhood, so she was reading on the sofa in her sitting room. Rex thought that anyway she never had cared for the effort that was needed to be part of this project, but rather she had been working with them a little just to please her husband.

Rex was still troubled by the fact that there were places here and there in the woods where the trees were suffering. Liz had told him that when she had been just beginning to join the sielrah on Atlantica, she had first been able to access plants, and only later had been in contact with people. Dennis thought he was feeling the grass a bit now, and it had occurred to Rex last night that perhaps if that were true then it might be those trees in human-like pain that Dennis would feel before he felt human mind-energies. So, right after breakfast, Rex and Dennis slipped out the door at the end of the east wing beside the infirmary and started down a path that would lead to those three trees in pain at the edge of the woods. Rex had come to understand that apparently the grass was suffering just in sympathy with the trees, since the only distressed grass was a strip about as wide as a man is tall at the edge of the woods by those trees in pain. So the problem was the trees. There had to be a reason.

"Can you tell which tree it is?" Rex asked Dennis as they approached the first of them. "There are two on the edge of the woods here that are a little troubled, and one that's really suffering. I've never felt a tree do that." Rex could feel the tension building in Dennis's mind. He said, "Relax, little bud. Don't try. Just open your mind without expecting anything."

Then Rex was stepping backward. When he was far enough away that he couldn't feel Dennis's mind so he thought Dennis wouldn't be affected by his, he dropped to sit cross-legged on the grass and withdrew his mind into the void as an additional precaution. He was so deeply in the bliss of it that he was startled to find Dennis there beside him and tugging at his arm, saying, "That one! Is it that one?"

Rex opened his eyes and looked up, then looked where Dennis was pointing. He smiled as his conscious mind came back.

"How did you know?"

"I don't know. But it's that one, isn't it?"

Could Dennis do it again? Rex got to his feet, saying, "Let's go find another one!"

But Dennis was studying the tree, stepping up to it and back and walking around it. He said, "I think it's got something stuck in its roots. Maybe it's a body!" There were two gardeners in green jumpsuits up by the edge of the terrace, tending a border of yellow chrysanthemums. Dennis called to them by name and said, "Do you have a shovel?" He added with a twinkle in his voice, "I think we found Jimmy Hoffa here!"

The more Dennis dug, the more he uncovered random personal items, a shoe, a toaster. Finally he said, swiping at his brow with his forearm and then standing the shovel and wiping his face with the tail of his shirt, "I think the tree squashed a house with everything in it. Would that upset the tree? Maybe its roots can't spread?"

Rex called to the gardeners, "Excuse me! Will you ask Carlson to send my father down here?"

It was occurring to Rex that what he was feeling in those trees might in fact be human emotional pain, picked up from buried possessions and filtered through the trees and wrecking the sweet green feel of them.

They had to wait awhile, but there came Rex's parents on the path around the end of the east wing, holding hands and talking. His mother was smiling. Having lived with Liz's long sadness back when she had been without her husband, Rex was freshly warmed now whenever he saw them together. He watched Jack say something to Liz, then as she spoke he listened and glanced at her, looking entertained. If Rex managed to do nothing else in this journey he had undertaken to save his people's world, this one act of bringing his parents back together was beginning to feel to him all by itself to be worth all the pain his journey had caused him.

Liz called, "What's wrong, sweetie?"

Jack said as they came closer, "Is that the bad tree?"

"Did you hurt people here? I'm not angry," Rex added as he caught the What-now? look on his father's face and felt his mental ping of stress. "I think this tree is in pain because somebody buried possessions that carry emotional pain. Plants are affected by human emotions. I'm not angry. Just tell me why these things are here."

Liz said, "Is that a bulldozed house?" She looked at Jack. She said to Dennis, "Is there enough there to be a house?"

Dennis was shy around Rex's parents. He just said mildly, "Could be, Mrs. R."

Rex was looking at his father expectantly. Jack said to Liz, "I was in a hurry in the beginning. Buying houses with their contents was easier. It seemed fairer, too. It gave them a premium." He sighed and added, "A lot of the houses were bulldozed at once. We were establishing the building site." He said to Rex, "I'm sorry, son. The last thing anybody thinks is it will bother a tree if you bulldoze a house."

Liz said, "They just left it here?"

"I didn't tell them to take it out. It was the sixties, honey. I was twenty-five years old and full of it."

Rex could feel Jack's mind cringing with discomfiture. His father was expecting another self-righteous lecture from him. Rex's old child-hood habit of freely expressing rage at his father had carried even through this past summer, when over and over he had let Jack know that these numbers were meaningless, and wasn't Jack ashamed that he cared about numbers instead of people? Yet Jack never retaliated, no matter what Rex said to him. Back in the people's world and now here, Jack seemed almost to feel that he deserved to be the target of his son's anger. Rex knew that his childhood rages at Jack had always had at their root the fact that his father kept leaving him, so over and over Rex had felt abandoned. But now Jack seemed to have developed an obsessive, indulgent love for Rex that put him again where no child should be, no longer loved too little but perhaps loved too much. One was as disruptive to the unity of minds as the other. And Rex was realizing only now that the self-indulgent anger he still carried toward his father for living the life he had chosen to live might in itself be the reason why Rex was losing his flame within. Give it up. Let it go.

Rex said, perhaps the first time in his life that he had used the word, "Dad, everything is emotional energy. You see things as solid, but they're not solid. It's all energy. That's all there is. These people didn't want to give up their house, and the pain of that is still in the objects. Things that have been loved by people are just emotional energy anyway, so they often pick up people's emotions. Emotions are energy!" he said, responding to the look on Jack's face. "Everything is emotional energy. Where I grew up, even children know that." Rex sighed and added, "We'll figure out a way to fix it."

———•———

Even though Liz hadn't told Public Relations that she was going to Levigard Holdings today, a photographer was waiting as Jack's limousine arrived on a random morning in early December. He was photographing the car. Liz was long past her embarrassment about arriving this way, the Cadillac limousine carrying four bodyguards in front of Jack's stainless-steel Bentley limousine. Like Jack's house, his over-the-top car looked improbably lightweight and pretty for something that weighed eight tons and was built to withstand a mortar hit.

Ted's black Mercedes was already at Levigard, parked unobtrusively beside the building. He and his two aides were alighting from it and skulking toward the side door, where Ted had arranged for someone to let them in. Liz slipped to the left against the car door, took Peters's hand, then swung her legs out and positioned her feet as Jason handed her the prop briefcase, and she stood out in one motion and began to walk toward her imaginary Rex. There were eight people sitting waiting for her in the conference room that morning. Liz bent for the appropriate cheek-kiss from Ted, and bent to receive a kiss from Art Carey as well, then took her seat at the head of the table. She said to Ted, but for the room in general, "Aren't these offices nice?"

This was Ted's first time here. He said automatically, "Very nice."

Liz cleared her throat and said to them all, "It's time to talk about what comes next. You know that for the past year we haven't acted on anything your teams presented. We've just been finishing what my husband started, and there are only two of those transactions left. We'll have more than a hundred lube shops and another sixty-odd car washes that your people are nicely upgrading and re-branding—thanks!—and they'll soon be ready to sell or take public. But you're telling us now there isn't much call for such a big chain from a single buyer, and the lawyers are telling us they can't find a way to shield my husband from personal liability under the new Sarbanes-Oxley Act. They're still working on that, but for now, going public isn't an option, either.

"So we're going to close this last rollup by creating a franchise company, which was Mr. Smith's idea—Thank you, Charlie! Once the franchisees are in place, we believe there will be a market for the parent. But my husband has no interest in doing more business acquisitions. He will soon be sixty-three years old, and a grandfather." Liz glanced at Ted, who barely cracked a rare smile at her. Liz added, "Consider this private information about Mr. Richardson. We expect a grandchild in March." She cut through their murmured congratulations by adding, "But while one era ends, another begins."

For Liz, this wasn't about saving their jobs. It was about keeping Rex from losing his mind. At this point, he was coming to her suite two or three times a week as she was returning from work so he could pace and complain and get it out of his system enough so he could be pleasant at dinner. He hated the financial shenanigans that Jack enjoyed, he couldn't make sense of why it wasn't just numbers with too many zeros to let you play games with them, and he was so bored that one afternoon he told her he had done nothing but watch a ladybug meander up a chair-back and over the top and down most of the other side before it opened its wing-covers and flew away. That process had taken the ladybug much of the afternoon, and during all that time Rex had sat slumped at the conference table with his head propped on his fists while Jack talked and made occasional marks on the whiteboard. Rex was beginning to conclude that if this was what he had to do to save his people's world, then maybe he should just go home now and enjoy whatever time their world had left. Of course, whenever Liz asked Jack how Rex's business lessons were going, his answer was, "Fine."

Liz said now to those at the table, "As you know, our son is being groomed to transition into heading Larkin, but he has no business experience. So our plan now is to turn the business team at Levigard Holdings over to Rex so you can teach your future boss what he still needs to learn." Unaccountably someone clapped, so then they all were clapping. That trailed off when Liz didn't smile. She went on, "We need to help him build something. His request is that it involve people and cars and fewer zeros—" She smiled then and added, "He's been getting his fill of international finance from his father," at which they all chuckled a bit, since she had meant that to be funny.

"You'll find that Rex is a more hands-on guy, and he's a regular guy. He's fun to be around—" Someone laughed a snort because of course she would say that, being his mother, so she added, "If I do say so myself. Ted Armstrong will be his coach. I'll remain as interim president of Larkin until he feels ready to take that on. Remember, Rex wants people and cars and less financial manipulation. Give him some ideas for a project he'll enjoy."

⫷ 20 ⫸

Liz had come to conclude that ambitious young men were naturally wired to compete with older men and to dominate women, so when they had to sit in negotiation with a powerful older woman who was winning points, it seemed to cross enough of their wires to make a few of them go mad. It was always the handsome ones, and perhaps the most ambitious but frustrated ones. Junior lawyers, usually. They would try to catch her eye, smile or wink at her, perhaps touch her unnecessarily when they handed her documents. It was a game. If she reacted at all, they felt back in control, and then they could ignore her thereafter. Polite handshakes to end the meeting. Sometimes, though, it was personal.

The last of Jack's deals that Liz took to final documents was the purchase of a chain of four large lube-and-muffler shops in eastern Massachusetts. The meeting location was just close enough, and flying would have been inconvenient enough, that she chose to go in Jack's car. This was the last of her seventeen deals to purchase little chains of lube shops and car washes to add to the hundred and eighty or so locations that were in the process of being upgraded and branded. They would have to be franchised out because the initial public offering that Jack had expected to do had been rendered impossible by the federal government.

There were three issues still on the table, none of which individually was big enough to blow up the deal. Liz thought it was ridiculous not to be settling these last details through lawyers, but Jack had told her that people selling the product of their whole lives' work were happier when they could interact with the buyer a little on a personal level. He could stroke them. They could come to like him. Then if Jack later needed them to bend on something, it would be harder for them to refuse. Jack had long ago discovered that sympathetic Ted could do as well at making these connections if Jack were reduced to a cellphone on the table, which had given him a formula that had worked well for decades.

The seller in this case was a thickset, ruddy-faced and amazingly vigorous eighty-year-old who enjoyed negotiating so much, and who seemed to be enjoying Liz so much, that what should have been well over by noontime ended up taking them most of the day. Liz didn't mind. After all, this was the last one. Research had revealed that Mr. Baldini had tried for years to pass his business to his wayward son. Now Baldini's wife had health issues, so the dad was giving up and selling out. Liz found him to be so old-fashioned charming that she was patient with his long stories and his reluctance to finally settle anything, and with his attorney's permission she even took him to lunch in Jack's car. It was late February. Snow was on the way, but Mr. Baldini promised to get serious after lunch. Liz hoped to be on the road by three, and home in time for dinner at seven.

At just past two, the son showed up. He held five percent of the stock. And he was so bitter about Liz's taking the business that he thought should have been his by right that as she was working out with Mr. Baldini and his lawyer how to handle obsolete equipment and excess inventory, the son sat beside his father, leering at Liz and performing cunnilingus on his pen. By a quarter to three, Liz and her legal team had guided their seller and his lawyer through offsetting the valuations with a token reduction in the stated price. She hadn't needed to involve Ted. But as they were standing and moving around the table for handshakes, the son drawled that he wasn't willing to agree to any reduction at all.

Liz understood that the twerp was trying to drive off his father's buyer, which would mean that Mr. Baldini never could retire. They already had the son's signature on preliminary documents, and there was a come-along, take-along provision in a shareholders' agreement that was probably enforceable. Again without involving Ted, Liz bent and hugged her new friend and whispered, "Enjoy your retirement," and she got herself and Jason out of there.

Jack's current chauffeur was the third of his chauffeurs named Peters, the first of whom had also served his father. This grandson was not much older than Rex, and he was so nervous driving that expensive car in even just a few inches of snow that it took him more than five hours to get them home. It should have taken not much more than three.

Sitting there with Jason in the car for hours gave Liz too much time to think. As always happened when one of those jerks got sexual, she was both angry and a bit turned on. It was getting dark, the partition was up, Jason was under contract, and this felt so easy. After ten months of his waiting on Liz with such deference that he rode meekly on the left-side jump seat or in the first-class airplane seat next to hers and they never had a conversation, for her to command a little sexual play to distract her on the boring ride home might be just an extension of his job. More or less? After all, Jack used to sleep with his secretaries.

But of course she didn't do it. She never came close. Instead, what she did for all those hours was to build up a roaring head of rage against the man who had put her in this position. What did he even do all day long, beyond occasionally checking on the various markets that were making him vastly richer by the day? When was the last time he had left Sea Haven, other than an occasional helicopter ride to the penthouse? While Liz had spent the past year working and putting up with creeps out to settle scores, what had Jack been doing? Who was he, anyway? What had happened to the man she loved? It seemed to Liz, as she thought about it, that Jack's apparent decision to give up sex had also been a decision to give up living.

Liz didn't get home until nearly eight-thirty. She went directly upstairs and knocked on Jack's door. He came up his little hallway and opened the door, saying, "There you are. Did you eat, honey? Would you like a tray?"

Liz turned on him once they were in his sitting room. She said bitterly, "'Thank you, Liz. Five miserable hours of riding in the snow with a kid who would have been glad to do you a favor, but you came home to me instead, because . . . ' Because why, Jack?"

He looked at her. She realized as she saw the confusion in his face that he was so used to her constant affection that he had no idea why she was upset. Then he tried for a joke. He said, "Not him," blandly.

Jack's off-the-top-of-his-head notion of several months back that if Liz needed a lover she should hire one had developed into a game for him, made more enjoyable by the fact that Liz found it so emphatically un-funny. So now on occasion he would see a face in a newspaper ad or on a magazine cover and say, "What do you think, honey?" or "I don't know. Not really your taste." And that was funny to him.

Liz said, "I want you to kiss me as if you mean it. I want you to take me to bed. Right now."

He cocked his head and smiled a little and said, "I gather the deal went well?"

"When was the last time you left this house?"

He was catching on belatedly. He went and sat down at his desk and tried to go back to whatever he had been doing. She followed him.

"You're Howard Hughes with a better manicure! Are you proud of that?"

He said grimly, "I won't do this with you."

Liz had been gaming this confrontation on the ride, thinking it through in detail out of boredom. She hadn't expected that she actually would do it, but now, to her own surprise, she began it.

"Mr. Richardson, I'm about to give you what may be the biggest check of your life. I love my man beyond all reason, and I won't let you kill him without a fight. You set yourself up, sir. You let someone who loves you as much as I do know too much about you."

He was sitting in the warm light from his desk lamp, probably not seeing her well in the gloom of the rest of the room. She was glad about that. What she was about to do to him was making her feel at once courageous and despicable.

"I want you to make love to me right now. Right now, Jack. No? Then tomorrow morning I'll be calling a few of those reporters who keep leaving me messages. Tell them little things. Tomorrow night I'll be back in a negligee and smelling good. Still no? I'll have to make a few more phone calls." She paused for drama before she said, "It should take me a few days to get to Milly, but I will get there if you—"

"You signed a contract!"

"I did. But here's why it's check, Mr. Richardson. I don't give a damn about your money. Take it all back! What do I care? All I want is my Jack! You're turning him into an old fart, and I hate you for it!" He was standing up from his desk again. "Do you see a way out of it? I do. You can have me killed, darling. That's your only way out." She drew a breath and added, "If my Jack is still somewhere in there, at least he knows how hard I'm fighting for him!"

But then Liz was struck by a horrendous realization. She said, tears starting, "The check is really on me, isn't it? I've threatened you. Now I'm out of your life. But I already quit," she managed to say, with her mouth distorted by crying.

Jack lifted her in his arms. Some calm part of her mind was amazed that he could do that. He carried her into his bedroom and laid her on his bed and settled in and began to kiss her while he was undressing her by feel, not looking, kissing. But she couldn't stop crying. All she could think was that she had just stupidly broken his trust, and he never was going to feel safe with her again. He was whispering to her. She was wailing and embarrassed, but unable to stop crying.

He had a way somehow that once she had climaxed he could keep her there so it kept on happening, each bigger than the one before it, three or four times, almost on the edge of painful, until all she could do was to squeeze tight and ride it, sometimes right into sleep. She woke up once in the night. Of course he wasn't there. She was wrapped in probably expensive fur, and she pushed it away from her face so as not to get it wet because once she was awake she was crying again.

<hr />

Liz was awakened by a soft, polite knock. It was morning, she was alone, and all of a sudden she felt as if she were back on his yacht. How could it have been so long ago? She and Jack had spent their first-ever evening together talking in the salon from right after dinner until after two o'clock in the morning, while Monica—was it Monica?—had fallen asleep on his shoulder. Liz had never before made such an intense and immediate connection with anyone. But then the next night he made a pass at her, she told him off, and she cried herself to sleep over the fact that they were already so close that they were completing each other's sentences, but the whole thing was completely impossible. Now she was feeling that her assessment back then had been right. Their ending just had taken awhile.

There was another polite knock on Jack's bedroom door. What had she said when Ted knocked on her door that next morning, when he came to apologize for Jack? She mumbled aloud, "Go away." Now what came next?

She had rehashed this conversation so many times in her head. He would say, "Are you decent?" She would say, "I'm obscene," and he would say, "Get decent. I'm coming in." But he wasn't saying anything.

Then came, "Are you there, madam?"

That was Liz's personal maid, the single mother putting her sons through college. And losing the help of this kindly woman who faithfully woke Liz up each morning, who did her hair and makeup, took care of her clothing, shopped and tidied and fetched and handled her details was going to be yet another result of Liz's having stupidly lost Jack's trust.

Liz got up, found her clothes where Jack had flung them, put them back on, and opened the door. She wandered out of his suite and across the hallway into her own suite as Dolly said from behind her, "Shall I begin your shower, madam?"

But Liz was crying again. She flopped onto the sofa in her sitting room, unable to see anything but the fact that Jack fired people for chewing gum, for heaven's sake. How much faster would he fire her for threatening him? But it wasn't even really the prospect of being fired that Liz found upsetting, so much as it was the fact that over twenty-five years she had fought so hard to teach him that he could trust her. He probably at this point trusted no one else. What she had done last night in a careless moment had destroyed that for both of them. And there was no fixing it.

Dolly had awakened Liz at seven, as she always did on weekdays, but there was no way Liz was going to work. Dolly brought a box of tissues and ordered breakfast sent up while Liz moped and blubbered on her sofa. How like Jack it was that he had made love to her that one more time to put a bow on it, but of course he hadn't climaxed with her. He had gone off to sleep somewhere else. But with whom? It didn't matter now. It was just so like him to have stayed long enough to end it with her neatly.

Eventually lunchtime came as well, and seeing her lunch tray arrive confounded Liz. She was still here at lunchtime? But why hadn't Jack sent people to deal with her by now? She couldn't recall ever seeing him leave anything to chance this way, but perhaps he was giving her a courtesy space. He was letting her leave on her own terms, with dignity. To leave, though, she would need a car, and she didn't have a driver's license so she also needed a chauffeur, but everyone here answered only to Jack. Perhaps he hadn't considered that. And what about Rex? Was he going to have to take sides? That was the last thing Liz ever wanted. Rex belonged here. She didn't want him involved. What she wanted to do was get out of here cleanly. She could waitress. Maybe she could after all go and find some nice lobster restaurant in Maine.

———————◆———————

Liz was semi-napping on the sofa when Jack came in. She could tell from the light that it was past midafternoon. Her eyes were blurry from too much crying, but she could see that it was Jack and he was wearing a suit. She groped and fumbled to sit up, feeling foggy and rubbing her eyes. Jack squatted on his heels to be on her level and said, "Are you all right?"

"I'm so sorry. You know I'd never do any of that."

"I know." He stood again as he said, "Have you been crying? I thought you'd be gloating. I imagined you taking an all-day bubble bath. And it took all day to get the stone. They had to fly it in from L.A."

"What?"

"You got me again." He was smiling a little. Then he said, "You look horrendous. What happened?" He drew her to her feet and put his arms around her and rested his cheek against her hair.

Liz said softly, with her cheek against his lapel and vaguely worried that she was getting makeup on it and wondering why she cared at this point, "I'm fired, right?"

"That's one way to put it. I'm surprised you're upset. I thought you knew you had me again. You were thinking in six dimensions." He set her down sitting on the sofa. He sighed and tugged at his pant-legs, protecting creases, and he went down on one knee before her as he was fishing a little square box from his pocket. Liz watched all this in wonderment. The look on his face made her know that he felt ridiculous, but he was trying not to feel ridiculous. He took her hand and said, "If I'm skipping some steps, please let it go. Liz, will you marry me? Please."

She giggled a little and covered her mouth with her free hand, looking at his face as he looked at her in all her hideousness. She almost said, "This is a joke, right?" But she reached and cupped his cheek with her hand and leaned and kissed him on the lips and said, "Of course."

"I think I'm supposed to have given you this already." He opened the ring box he had taken from his pocket, and there against white satin was an enormous diamond. He said, standing again, "I wanted the biggest diamond that wouldn't embarrass you. They said ten carats." He and she both said "Flawless" at the same time, and they looked at one another. He slipped the diamond ring on her finger above her eternity ring, and he sat down to her left with his right arm around her shoulders and took her left hand in his and held it up so he could study the diamond.

Liz glanced at his face. It was calm and peaceful. Nothing about this moment felt real. She said, "Because I'm thinking in seventeen dimensions, I sometimes forget what I did at dimension six. What ever prompted you to do this?"

"After you went to sleep, I went out and walked on the terrace for awhile. In February. I think it's too big. I'll get you a smaller one, too. Three carats?" He went on, "The worst thing about my childhood was not what you think. More and more, I think it was the way she taught me to be afraid. She never let me forget the way she lost my brother. He was two weeks old. Someone dropped him. Just a stupid accident. But she was so sure something was bound to happen to me, too, that she never let me out of her sight. I never had a friend before Andover. I couldn't play outside without bodyguards. Steve said when he met me I was already an old man. At fourteen."

Jack glanced at Liz as he said, "The core thing that makes me need you is not that we mind-connect and we get each other's jokes. The core thing is that you're never afraid. I think I originally fell in love with you because except for Steve, you're the only person I've ever met who wasn't afraid to stand up to me."

Liz wanted to tell him that when you have nothing to lose, you also have nothing to fear. She hoped she would remember to say that later.

"Last night you told me you were beating me up because you were fighting for me. I realized out on the terrace in the cold that every fight we've ever had was basically you fighting my mother. Until now, she always had to win." Liz turned the hand that wore the diamond so she could grasp his. "She taught me to be afraid to trust anyone enough to get married. Then, of course, Louise reinforced that lesson." Liz glanced at his face. He looked soft and thoughtful. He lifted her hand so all those diamonds caught the late-afternoon sunlight through the window behind the sofa as he said, "This is for you, Milly."

⤙ 21 ⤚

Rex was glad this wouldn't be his first time delivering a baby. That first time had been frightening, even though he had witnessed so many births in childhood that he had begun the process when his own time came with a certainty that becoming a father would be easy. But feeling close-up the pain of someone he loved, and being unable to protect her, and even feeling a little bit that he had been the cause of her pain, had distressed him so much the first time around that Gaprelagh had ended up comforting him more than he had comforted her as they did their walking. And Cathy was so much smaller and frailer that Rex was beginning to feel frightened for her as they walked the lower east-wing hallway with arms about each other and he chanted in his mind what he could remember of a childbirth counting-song. Could a woman from this place give birth as easily as women gave birth in the world he had left?

Rex had promised Cathy after their visit from little Milly last night that the birth of their daughter would be the moment when she would become his true wife and this place would become his true home. And Cathy had agreed with him in return to let him name their child. He had moved past his worry that in taking a wife here he had violated the unity of minds. Indeed, Cathy and Gaprelagh seemed somehow to have melded for Rex without his realizing it was happening, so now when he thought of either of them it was Cathy the beautiful he would see. Myra was still reporting to him whenever it pleased her to show up, so he knew that whatever place in Gaprelagh's heart had once been his now belonged to a man who loved her and was a good father to their son. While once hearing this would have wracked him with fresh pain at his ongoing ordeal of separation, now he found himself feeling glad that her pain of having lost him had passed.

Rex could feel another deep cramp developing in Cathy's body. She hesitated. He murmured to her, "The pain will be less if you walk with it, beautiful."

Apparently this was not the way that women from this place gave birth, as Cathy's father had been reminding Rex daily. But Rex and Cathy had discussed the fact that they couldn't know which aspects of the child-birth customs of the place he had left were essential to the development of the baby's mind, so she had agreed that they could take no chances. She was trying to give birth without drugs; she was walking rather than lying down for labor; and there was a birthing-stool made of new wood from an especially peaceful tree standing ready by the fireplace that just had been installed in an outside wall of the infirmary. And of course all of them were wearing woolen clothing from Rex's childhood home that had a strange smell, like spent flowers but more complex and much stronger, because another of the trees that didn't grow here was the one whose bark could be ground and added to wash water to minimize worm-damage to wool.

Rex's baby sister had drowned as a toddler on Atlantica long ago. She had visited him occasionally, but he hadn't seen her in years until she came to him the previous evening. Rex felt the mind-energy of an approaching shimmer, not able yet to tell who it was, knowing only that it didn't feel like Myra. He knew that the fact that he conversed with people Cathy once would have thought were entirely dead somewhat troubled her, and he was trying to help her get past that so he called to her and she came padding into their sitting room and climbed into his lap, somewhat clumsily.

THE LETTERS FROM LOVE SERIES

The mind-energy of this shimmer felt like little Milly now, but as she began to appear he could see that she no longer looked like little Milly. Now she had the black hair and brown eyes and skin of people from his home-place. Rex whispered to Cathy, "Let your eyes go off-focus, beautiful. See with the mind behind your eyes." He smiled at his sister, who was smiling benevolently upon them both. He could have spoken to her by mind, but for Cathy's sake he said aloud, "Thank you for coming, baby girl! And thank you for looking like someone from home." Shimmers could choose to look however they liked, so her looking this way felt like a gift to him.

You are grown now. You no longer need the comfort of having me look like one of your family of this lifetime, so I have resumed my eternal appearance.

Rex was whispering eagerly to Cathy, "Can you see her? Can you hear her?"

Cathy nodded a little, eyes wide.

As you know, your baby is female. She will be well born, and she has planned a long life. Be at peace about her. I will put into your mind at her birth the name that she has chosen.

Rex was hugging Cathy tight.

Know that I lived a brief lifetime as the child Milly so I could establish a stronger bond with you, dear brother. You and I planned before we were born that I would now become your spirit guide.

Rex murmured, "Thank you," but there was no need to thank her. To guide an embodied being was a privilege from her perspective, an opportunity for her own spiritual growth.

As your guide for this stage of your life, I go within. You will no longer see me. But listen for me. I will never leave you.

"Oh my God!" Cathy murmured.

"She's going," Rex whispered.

"She's going to be inside you?"

Rex helped Cathy off his lap. He stood and lifted her and carried her back to bed, being careful of her enormous belly. On someone so little, her end-stage pregnancy looked as if it had to be painful. As he tucked her into bed, she said, sounding worried, "You're letting her be inside you?"

He sat on the edge of the bed and took Cathy's hand and said, "Each of us has spirit guides who once were in bodies. How else could they know how to help us? They work within our minds. No harm comes from them." But she still looked worried. He went on, "Please try to understand this, beautiful. We are not separate. We are all one. When the Teacher says we must love each other as ourselves, he means it literally. So for her to join my mind in order to guide my spiritual growth is no invasion. Can you see that? Please don't worry about it."

"Do I have someone like that, too?"

"Nobody can be in a body without a guide. Many people have more than one."

Cathy shuddered delicately and said, "Come to bed, Rexie. I need you to hold me."

Now here came Ted and Linda down the hallway from the front door, with Ted briskly rushing ahead when he caught sight of Rex and Cathy. He was eyeing their woolen Atlantican clothing with a look on his face that omitted the actual eye-roll. As he reached them, he said hotly, "What are you doing, Rex? We've talked about this!"

The fact that he and Ted had worked together for the past month and had become friendly seemed to Rex to be a disruptive complication now, because from the moment Ted learned that they were planning a home-birth, he had been set emphatically against it. Rex told Ted as they continued to walk, "We have a doctor and a nurse. There's an ambulance at the door. Giving birth is no more a health problem than eating is a health problem, but we've done everything you asked us to do." As Ted started to protest, Rex said beneath his breath to him, "You should be here, but if you're disruptive you won't be here. That will be your choice."

"Where's Jack?" Ted asked grimly.

"They're playing in the infirmary."

Well, they really were playing. Rex had long seen the things his parents did as not actual work, because they never produced anything. It was play-work, to give them the illusion of doing something useful. But since they had decided a month ago that their marriage needed an additional ceremony, even they seemed to be seeing everything they did as playing. Rex had begun to feel more like their responsible parent than their child.

Ted hurried off to find Jack. Linda was walking on Cathy's other side, and they were murmuring together.

Rex had come to love his mother-in-law, the soft and confident feel of her mind, the graceful way she dealt with people, the fact that she had from the first treated Rex with kindness and respect. She had seemed to ignore his early, clumsy efforts at learning how to live in this place, while he knew that she had noticed them all, because often she would give him cues. He had learned early in his marriage that if he felt awkward when Linda was around, he could glance at her and she would pointedly pull a tissue and dab at her nose or stand up and then sit down again carefully or set down and again pick up the correct fork, all while not seeming to look at him. Rex had come to hope that as Cathy grew older she was going to become more like her mother, keeping her same soft and gentle feel and her same fundamental sweetness, but growing more peaceful and confident. Stronger.

Rex, Cathy and Linda were approaching the infirmary door as Ted came rushing out. Rex could feel that Ted's having found Jack wearing homespun Atlantican wool had not been a happy surprise for him, no doubt made worse by Jack's saying as he followed him through the doorway, ". . . I'm sure we've got more." And calling back to Liz, "Do we have clothes for Ted and Linda, honey?"

The five of them met in the hallway. Cathy needed to walk. Rex said quietly to Ted, "Whatever you have to say to me will be said after you have held your grandchild," and he helped Cathy turn so she could keep walking.

———————•—•———————

Cathy's labor took them most of the day. By the time the doctor confirmed that she was ready to deliver, she was weary and grim and never out of her husband's arms. Rex was less surprised than the others that she had managed to get this far without drugs, but he was weary, too.

Rex really liked this doctor. He had interviewed four, and had found a young man with the same sort of cheerful, good-hearted mind-feel that had made him choose Dennis to be his friend. Having Dennis here for the birth was additionally upsetting to Ted, but that was one place where Rex wouldn't budge. Dennis had worked so hard at not working hard to develop the powers of his mind that he and Rex had the beginnings of an actual sielrah, a wisp of that feeling of mind-energy connection. Feeling it begin to be always there, Rex now dared to believe that if all the minds here were similarly free, they might even in this discordant place be able to build another great net of minds, a basis for universal human unity.

Dennis was reading people's emotions perhaps as well as Rex could read them now, given the fact that Rex's sensitivity had weakened so much. While Rex had learned to largely block the ugly stridence that often came from Ted in order to be able to work with him comfortably, Dennis had felt Ted's distress today and spoken with him, and he had turned his chair so now he wouldn't be able to witness the birth. He was facing Linda where she sat on a couch, and she and he were conversing. Rex heard Linda laugh gently.

Rex helped Cathy off the doctor's examining table and held her briefly and kissed her and told her he loved her. Then he helped her onto the birthing stool and showed her where to place her feet and hands and how to hold her body. Linda came hurrying to support Cathy as mothers always supported their daughters, seeming to know without being told that Cathy needed to move freely, but she could be helped by having her mother's arms around her upper body. Rex smiled up at Linda from where he was kneeling, watching, ready to catch his child. He said to Cathy as he watched for the baby, feeling her body's sensations almost as if they were his own, "You want to push, beautiful. Go ahead and push. Nearly done."

Behind him the doctor was saying to the nurse, "Why doesn't everybody do it this way?" as the crown of the baby's head appeared. Rex had a hand beneath her head, and he was drawing it toward him, ready for her body to drop into his other hand. With her legs not yet born, the baby was flinging her arms wide in spastic amazement and screwing her eyes tight and screaming. Then all of her was born into Rex's hands, and he lifted her into her mother's arms. Where Rex had been born, the mothers would be naked and able to give their babies skin-contact, and that would generally quiet them quickly. This baby quieted anyway as Cathy gathered her limbs against her body and held her, and then Cathy looked at Rex. He was feeling such a sudden welling of emotion that he grinned at her foolishly. Still kneeling, he put his arms around all of them, Linda too, and he laid his head gently on his new daughter's chest, feeling the wonder of her first trembling breaths.

Cathy would hold the child still connected to her body until after the cord had stopped pulsing, so Rex stood then and waited and thought about what little Milly had instructed him to do once he took the baby back. There was a usual process to be followed now in which the grandparents would hold the child in order, the mother's mother and father first, and then the mother and father of the father. Reversing that order when he was trying to do this perfectly was troubling to him, but his sister's spirit had insisted. So once the cord was cut, Rex took his child back and carried her, still streaked and grubby from her birth, to where his parents were sitting on one of the small couches with which they had furnished the infirmary for this event.

Rex said to Jack, "It's your turn to hold her." Jack slid his foot down off his knee and struggled to sit more upright, glancing at Liz. He accepted the naked baby, who was sleeping. Liz showed him how to support the little head. They were grinning. Rex said to Jack, "Her name is Millicent Larkin Richardson. This is the Milly you will get to keep."

⇥ 22 ⇤

After having worked hard all his life, late in the winter when he turned sixty-three, Jack found that he had evolved himself out of a need to do much of anything. He told Liz his obsolescence happened so gradually that he didn't much notice a change until Liz finished that final lube shop deal, so now she also was out of projects. Ted had finally retired altogether, and Jack was managing his division presidents, so he told Liz that she could just take a break. Their routine soon became breakfast with the family, light working in his suite until lunch, and after lunch probably taking a walk. When they had been together on Atlantica, they had walked most afternoons for two or three hours, just talking and enjoying one another's company. They couldn't walk so far here. Even with nearly two hundred acres to explore, their walks kept running into fences.

Liz came to treasure those lazy mornings. Jack would begin with early calls to some of his international division presidents, and since Liz was still nominally the president of Larkin, she would have some of the happy-guilty sense of a child playing hooky as she sat perched cozily on his sofa, writing her memoirs on her laptop and listening to his half of their conversations. She learned a lot, but in pieces, and things kept surprising her. Apparently the Larkin division in Singapore was working now on opening Kentucky Fried Chicken franchises in seventeen Asian cities; the division in India was getting into managing teak forests; and the one in South Africa was buying commercial land near certain African cities and banking it by partnering with local companies to build storage facilities.

One morning early in May was so lovely that Liz opened the window behind the sofa. Through it came a breeze bearing a faint sea-scent and the musky-sweet smell of the lilac bushes in giant pots below the window. There was a big greenhouse to the west of the house where seasonal trees and shrubs could relax until it was their turn on the terrace. As Liz sat down and picked up her computer again, she said, "Let's sit outside. You've got a laptop, right?"

"It's not powerful enough." He paused. He said, "Damn, we're still moving the market."

"You'd think that would be a good thing," Liz said, mostly to herself. She was trying to remember what her father had looked like. "Shifty and beady-eyed" seemed wrong. "You know, 'Yay! We're finally moving the market.'"

"Not in this case, honey." He was studying his computer screen. "That's what the new beta was supposed to fix. I think it made it worse. Don't you think it's ridiculous so little money is the limit? Who knew the world was so small?"

No matter how many diamonds of no matter what sizes Liz now possessed for no matter which fingers, she still felt stricken with insecurity whenever she thought of Jack as wealthy. Even now, what he owned seemed to own him instead, so the best she ever could be was second-place. It had been only on Atlantica that she had felt herself to be primary in his life, although she realized now that even on Atlantica she alone would not have been enough. It had been that combination of herself and Rex and being able to forget about being different for awhile that had made him happy wearing homespun wool and logging with rough men in the woods. Nobody there had ever heard of money. And Jack had felt loved enough and safe enough with a mercenary navy standing by not to need to live surrounded by security. Liz no longer really missed a place that was seeming to her in retrospect to have been too much roughing it. But seeing Jack reduced to fretting about not being able to achieve better returns when he already owned ridiculously more than he ever could use a million times over made her wonder whether he might sometimes miss their carefree Atlantican life.

To change the subject, she said, "I talked to Linda. She says tea-length. And wouldn't you know, with a closet full of designer clothes I am fresh out of tea-length."

"Buy something. If we can't put it to work, we may as well spend it."

Baby Milly was going to be christened in Cathy's childhood church at the end of May. They would be leaving Sea Haven by car and driving to Ted's home in Oyster Bay, where approved publications would be taking photographs and a light Saturday supper would be served to Ted's and Linda's friends. So far, Liz's jokes to Jack about hiring an Army division to handle security and how surprised he was going to be to discover that roads were now paved with asphalt were falling flat.

Jack said, sounding preoccupied, "Are we actually getting married? Or are you just collecting diamonds?"

He had recently given Liz what he called an everyday ring, a four-carat emerald-cut in a plain gold setting. Still too large, she thought, but beautiful, and looking more like a real engagement ring.

She said, "Since we're geriatric, don't you think a big wedding would be stupid?"

He was typing something, working rapidly, with his reading glasses halfway down his nose. He said, "What about getting married at the christening?"

"Do they do that?" Liz hadn't thought about it. To be frank, she was enjoying being engaged. She had never before been engaged, while it seemed to her that she had always been more or less married.

Jack said distractedly, probably reading emails, "I told Ted the christening has to be private if he wants us there. He gave me lip about it, so I told him we were thinking about getting married at the same time. That has to be private."

Liz looked at Jack sitting at his ornate desk, studying his computer screen down the length of his nose to see it through his glasses. He had rediscovered on the day baby Milly was born how comfortable those ponyskin moccasins were, so now he was wearing them as slippers. Something about the vulnerable way he looked made her say, "We don't have to really do it, darling. The thought was enough."

"Don't you like the idea of a Catholic marriage? Let's do it. She would have hated it."

———•———

With Jack and Liz now out of projects, the first floor of the home office building had been adapted to the needs of Rex's Levigard Holdings team. That space had been meant for support staff, so Liz and Jack had only ever seen it as a big room full of cubicles. They were amused to get an email from Rex at the end of the morning, addressing them as the president and chairman of Larkin International respectively and requesting their presence at a concept presentation on the first floor of the office building at two o'clock this afternoon.

"What, we've got to wear suits?" was the first thing Liz said.

"They wear jeans. Ted says it looks like a frat house."

"How come he never told me that?"

"You haven't spent your life convinced that the hallmark of discipline is suits. He wanted to warn me. Let's dress. That'll show Rex we take him seriously."

So at two, they took the meandering walk from the front door of the house to the back door of the office building. Jack was tugging to widen the neck of his tie. Liz was feeling a bit wobbly in heels. The back door led to a vestibule with an elevator to the right and a staircase to the left and a single internal door that opened into a first floor that had been entirely emptied of cubicles. It felt enormous and full of light. There were random long tables, folding chairs, couches in conversational groups, a ping-pong table, banks of computers, and a big fish tank. Cathy sat beside Ted on one of the couches with baby Milly on her chest as they watched eight young men fighting an aggressive play-war with brightly-colored inflatable swords.

As people noticed Jack standing there, the war fizzled. Rex, flushed and grinning, tossed his sword and crossed the room and hugged each of his parents. He called out generally, "Time to get serious," as he led Liz and Jack to two chairs side-by-side next to where Ted and Cathy were sitting. Even Ted was wearing jeans.

Twenty feet or so in front of them was a long table. Six casually-dressed people in their twenties and thirties were moving to sit in a row on the tabletop, facing Jack and Liz. In front of them Rex was pacing a bit, unable to stop smiling, looking keyed-up and pleased. He began by saying with wry self-deprecation, glancing at his team behind him, "I know you all think I'm lucky, but my luckiest thing is having the help of all of you. Thank you, Mom and Dad. Thank you, friends."

Liz was astonished to hear him refer to his parents as Mom and Dad, when even as a child he hadn't done that. It seemed to be a subtle, perhaps subconscious way for him to align himself with the power side of the room. Rex said to his parents, "These people have been taking my ideas and helping me make them into a business. I want to do a business about people and cars. People, because people are all that matters. Cars, because I like cars." He glanced privately at Dennis, who was sitting astraddle an inverted chair on the far side of Ted.

Liz had developed a habit of automatically checking the status of Rex's accent. After eighteen months here, he spoke English fluently, perhaps not surprising when he had been bilingual for the first decade of his life. Now, though, even his lilting Atlantican accent was fading.

Rex said to Jack, "You know I knew nothing when I started. The ideas you'll hear today were shaped by my friends here. But I led them. These are really my ideas."

Liz thought, *Smart. If his ideas bomb, his father won't blame the others.*

"What I want to do is one-stop car centers." Rex glanced at someone sitting on the table. "People can find everything they need about cars in one place. And because some people have less money than other people have, we would charge them less." Again, a quick check behind him. "You have some car businesses that would be good for doing this. It would take a lot of land with each center. We think twenty acres for each." Another glance at someone. "We're thinking of calling it 'Free the People'."

Behind him, a tall young man with dark-red hair and the remnants of freckles slid from the table-top. He said, "May I, Rex?" and Rex stepped back. He looked relieved.

The lad appeared to be less than thirty years old. He stood calmly looking at Jack and said, "Sir, my name is Bobby Ingersoll. It's good to meet you. And Mrs. Richardson." He nodded at Liz. His voice was so young-sounding that it cracked a little now and then, but the man behind the voice seemed more and more tough and confident as Liz listened to him. He said, "What Rex wants to do is lease some of the larger lube shops you own where we can control enough land, and build each of them out with general service, auto parts, gas and car wash of course, used car sales, and a car-themed novelty shop and restaurant. If there's space, we'd add a go-kart track. Maybe a theater. Make it a destination. And we'd use the warehouse club membership model, but go it one better. Rex wants to charge as little as we can, and give any profits back to the members."

Liz glanced at Jack, who was studying Bobby closely. When he paused, Jack said, "Are we related?"

"Apparently. You're thinking you don't want to run a charity, but this won't be a charity. You'll get to bank the land, you'll get market rents, and you'll get an override on sales. The operating entity will be Rex's. He doesn't want to make a profit—"

"How are we related?"

"Your mother was my father's aunt. We're cousins."

Jack's face blanked. "Is that why they hired you at Levigard?"

"I didn't trade on it, if that's what you're asking. I know I look twelve, but I'm twenty-nine. I've got a Wharton M.B.A. I want to work for you. I've admired you all my life."

Liz slipped her hand into Jack's. She was wishing this were happening more privately.

Rex stepped forward then, saying, "I didn't know!" He clapped Bobby on the back and added, "Welcome to the family!"

Jack lifted his chin, looking at Bobby. He said, "Do you believe what you're telling me?"

"Yes. We've done some market research, but we'll do more once you approve the concept. We'd pitch it at the Wal-Mart and Target economic level. They've got some discretionary money, but no time. And they love their cars! This could be just the start," Bobby added with a glance at Rex. "We think this 'Free the People' concept with clean facilities, competitive prices, profit-sharing, and easy one-stop shopping could be replicated for home improvement and decor, for example. There isn't enough profit in food, but we could do it for clothing and personal items. We'd love to do it for banking, with lower-rate mortgages and car loans and small-business finance. We'd have a Free the People bank office at each location, but we think federal regs will get in the way."

"Where did you grow up?"

"Charlottesville. They carved up the old homestead." Bobby grinned unexpectedly and said, "It really is good to meet you, sir," and he stepped

218

and shook Jack's hand. Jack disengaged his hand from Liz's quickly and stood so they could shake hands properly.

Jack said, sitting down again, "Have you thought about the startup?"

"We've chosen seven candidate parcels, all within a reasonable drive of here. We'll get it down to one and do a pilot. If you're willing, we'd like to plan for a second- and third-tier expansion."

Jack said to Ted, "Did you know we were cousins?"

"How would I have known?"

To Bobby he said, "How much am I paying you, son?"

"Eighty thousand dollars a year, sir."

"We'll double it. I want you to teach Rex what you know."

⫷ 23 ⫸

The only thing Jack balked at was allowing Rex and the baby to ride together, so Rex and his posse of two rode ahead of them in his black armored Bentley. Cathy rode with Liz and Jack in the silver car, with Cathy to Liz's left and Jack to her right, so when they arrived at the church Cathy would emerge first and Jack would be last. In front of and behind the passenger cars were black Cadillac limousines, each carrying bodyguards. Liz assumed that on this joyous day her family must look like a funeral.

She was minimizing the teasing, even though Jack seemed less emotionally fragile than she had expected him to be. In fact, he looked quietly pleased as they drove up Shore Road and down 95. In Liz's mind, this had come to loom as a monumental day in his life, since after having for a couple of decades done very little publicly, he would now all on the same day be traveling some distance by car, allowing photographers, attending a social function, and by the way getting married. Jack was turned a little for better conversation, glancing now and then at Cathy, who had begun to nurse baby Milly beneath a gaily-printed covering. Cathy was falling asleep.

Jack said quietly to Liz, "I remember watching you nurse Rex. Now there's Rex's baby. Where has the time gone?"

"Rex would tell you there is no time, even if you point out how much time has passed. What's funny is when I lived there, I didn't feel time passing, either. When Ted showed up, if you'd asked me how long I'd been there I would have guessed maybe eight or nine years. But it was, what? More than twenty?"

Jack took Liz's hand and lifted it and kissed a few fingers, looking at her thoughtfully. He said, surprising her, "I felt it for both of us."

She had no idea what to say to that.

Then Jack remarked, "Ted's going to have a wedding cake. I agreed we'd do a wedding dance." He paused as if thinking, then added, "Our wedding song is my mother's favorite song. 'Be My Love.' Ted says the singer chose the song, but I like to think my mother had something to do with it. Perhaps she's giving us her blessing."

Liz was so used to knowing how integral Milly was to Jack's emotional life that she just glanced at him and smiled a little. Perhaps another woman wouldn't have liked the idea of his thinking of his long-dead mother on his wedding day, but after all of Shrinky Chuck's efforts to get him to hate his mother, Liz just was glad that he still thought of her kindly.

And Liz was beating down the urge to remark that after having been Atlantican-married for a quarter of a century, today was their first time in a car together, their first time going to a party together, and now apparently their first dance together. She had the strong sense that Jack was trying to feel normal, so she also stifled a crack about how they should have invited Shrinky Chuck to their wedding for the fun of watching his head explode.

Chuck had been shocked to learn that Jack had gotten engaged without first discussing it with him. When he warned that for Jack to bring Milly and anti-Milly together this way could cause what Liz later snidely referred to as an emotional singularity, Jack told him it was time they took a break.

Jack lowered the partition when he became annoyed that interesting things kept appearing in the side windows, then immediately disappearing. Liz checked to make sure that Cathy was well-covered, in case she was now in Peters's line of sight. Then she noticed through their windshield and through the little back window of the car ahead that Rex and his friends seemed to be roughhousing. Heads were bouncing and appearing and disappearing. Dennis had a calming effect on Rex, but adding Bobby seemed to have made them go manic.

Rex had just been telling Liz yesterday that Dennis was developing so much awareness that they had the beginnings of a sielrah going, which fact delighted him but made her uneasy for reasons she couldn't precisely articulate. Perhaps it was just another reminder that something had to be abnormal about people who didn't develop Atlantican awareness. But that possibility was too immense to contemplate.

Jack noticed the bouncing heads and said, "What the heck are they doing?"

"Bobby seems to be a bad influence."

"But he's brilliant! What an amazing kid. I went up and talked with him yesterday while you were at the dentist. Apparently I have six cousins in my generation, and another twenty-three in the next two combined." Jack took back his hand to scratch his head, then slipped it into hers again. "And he gave me a new perspective on why I had no family growing up. Milly always said they'd disowned her. But according to Bobby, she was the one who ditched her family. Why does hearing that not surprise me?"

"That's wonderful, darling. You've got a family after all."

"He tells me I'm the family hero. Who knew? They do a reunion every other year. Is it still a reunion if you're meeting people for the first time?"

"You're lucky. You've got a family. I don't have any family but us." Liz added, gazing out the window, "The Nazis took care of that."

The closer they came to that church, the more oddly glum Liz was feeling. She was coming to see, with the die already cast, that the thought of becoming American-married was making her feel owned and swallowed and stripped of who she really was. For them to be just Atlantican-married, with the lovely addition of now being engaged, had made Liz feel enough committed to Jack, but still enough independent of him, to establish a comfortable equilibrium. They had united their lives, but she remained her own person. Jack had always had a basic aversion to marriage that, yes, had a couple of times given way to impulse. But his reluctance to marry had seemed to Liz to be hardening over time. She realized as their car left the interstate, coming ever closer to that church, that she had been counting on his marriage phobia to keep today from ever happening.

Peters idled briefly in the parking lot while security checked the church and unloaded the first limousine. When accompanying Liz on her business jaunts, these bodyguards had seemed to be just power-props; but apparently when they were guarding Jack they became a lot more serious. Rex and his friends were out of their car now, straightening their own and one another's jackets and ties as they chatted with Father Jamar in the church doorway. Father Jamar was tall and brown and with a prominent nose, so with the right hair and beard he could have been Atlantican. He had co-officiated at Rex's wedding. Rex had enjoyed teasing him afterward.

"Teacher say call no man father but Father in heaven! You picking that name for you? Why you no caring what Teacher say?"

"Oh, well, it's a tradition," Father Jamar had said. He had a mechanical-sounding African accent, but his voice was soft and friendly. Liz liked him, too.

"But what Teacher say if we put traditions above what he teaching us? Bad, right? Gotcha there?"

Liz could see from a distance that the good-hearted teasing had resumed while they waited.

With everything secure, Peters approached the church and parked ten feet or so from the door. There were photographers around, but with so little room between car and church, whatever pictures they got would be awful. Rex opened the door and reached in and took the baby, then handed

Cathy out of the car himself. They moved into the vestibule as Liz slid to the edge of the seat. With an assist from Peters, she stood out correctly, and Jack followed her. There was a big church vestibule that included a baptismal font to one side, all of it complexly lit by stained-glass windows. Liz found Rex competently holding Milly while Cathy removed the baby's bonnet and straightened her rumpled christening dress. Then Cathy decided that Milly also needed a diaper-change.

While they waited for the christening ceremony to begin, Rex and his friends explored the church. Then Liz heard a commotion from the sanctuary. Rex's voice. He was shouting, "What is this? Jamar!"

Liz and Jack glanced at one another and rushed to the archway.

The sanctuary was confusingly full of colorful blocks of stained-glass light. The three had wandered down the center aisle, and from where Liz stood she could see what they had found. Above the distant altar was a full-color statue of a bleeding Jesus nailed to a cross. Several bodyguards had already reached Rex. Jack and Liz hurried down the aisle. Rex was shouting, "What is that thing? What kind of place is this?"

Then Liz heard Dennis say to him, "Uh, dude? That's supposed to be the Teacher up there. You know that, right?"

Nimble Bobby was already standing on the altar in his stocking feet. Two of the bodyguards had climbed up on chairs behind the cross in too little light, reaching above their heads, trying to figure out how to take it down. Father Jamar came hurrying down the aisle, shouting, "What are you doing? Get down from there! That's an altar!"

Rex turned on him and shouted into his face, "You've defaced your own altar! And you mean that thing to be the Teacher? You don't know the Teacher if you think that pleases him! You have children coming here? You want children to see that?"

Jamar looked at Liz, weakly.

Jack said to Jamar, "It's coming down. That's not negotiable. What's negotiable is your price for never putting anything like that up again."

Dennis had his arm around Rex's waist now. He was edging him away, talking quietly. Then Cathy appeared. Looking at her face, Liz could see that she was immensely relieved that her parents had decided this morning that they were too busy with the party to attend the christening. Liz took the baby from her, saying, "We'll get this straightened out. Go hug your husband."

Jack was holding a cream-colored check against the top of a pew and bending to sign it. He held his hand poised, looking at the priest. Then he handed him the incomplete check. He said, "You'll be getting a contract from me next week in which you'll promise never to hang anything like that again. Fill in whatever number will make signing it worth your while." To Liz beside him, holding Milly, he said, "There was one in my church growing up. I had nightmares."

Rex was approaching them, looking calmer. He had an arm around Cathy and an arm around Dennis. Beyond them, two bodyguards and Bobby were together lowering the effigy. Rex kissed Cathy and released them both and put his hand on Jamar's shoulder and said, sounding kindly, "I'm sorry, friend. I have a temper. I'm working on controlling it." Liz saw Rex even smile a little as he added, "I have just been told what it is that you believe. It's wrong of me to interfere with that. Just please, with whatever you believe, read the Teacher's words, too."

Rex looked calm and cheerful as he started up the aisle with Jamar beside him. The priest held that check carefully in two fingers. He looked flummoxed. Rex was saying, "Let's go do this and make my Cathy happy. Just please don't tell our baby she's so evil that God can't forgive her without the murder of Jesus. She's two months old. Already she knows better."

What had begun with an impulsive invitation on the joyous afternoon of Milly's birth to celebrate her christening at Ted's home with just a few friends and a casual supper had grown by inches, and then by miles. Fifty guests was Jack's original limit. But, okay, black tie and a fancier dinner. Pictures. An orchestra. A singer. And, sure, mention the wedding if you like. Have a cake. And, fine, include dancing. Rex had insisted that his family ride together from the church, so Liz and Jack were alone in their car as they drove slowly through a curious crowd and up the circular drive of a house that announced that Ted had done well for himself. Uniformed security and local police had established a perimeter along the house's street frontage. Waiting by Ted's front door were four approved photographers, allowed within the security perimeter and already taking pictures.

Jack and Liz were American-married now. Her eternity ring was a wedding band. The ten-carat diamond she wore with it said only that her husband considered a big diamond to be a good investment, and not that she had become his property. He had sworn to her when she tried at the last minute to effect a different outcome that nothing whatsoever between them would change.

The plan had been for the christening to take place at three, and then the wedding at three-thirty, so even with a leisurely departure and even allowing for some traffic, they would be at Ted's house by four-thirty. Freshen up, then take Ted's formal pictures while guests arrived and were escorted to the tent behind the house. They would be comfortably ready to join their guests for cocktails at six. But what with all that confusion about the crucifix, and Rex's need now to negotiate what the priest was going to say because of what he had just learned about Catholic beliefs, they weren't through with even the christening until four-thirty. Then Jamar raised the lights in the sanctuary, and they all went down the aisle together to hold the wedding in front of the altar, innocent now of all barbarity, where the family could stand in a semi-circle amid the banked pots of daffodils and tulips and hyacinths that had been Jack's last-minute inspiration.

Liz was standing where Jamar had put her, breathing in the hyacinths and trying not to think, when she heard Jack say, "Please excuse us for a minute." He took Liz's hand and led her back up the aisle to the vestibule, where he stood looking at her. He cocked his head and smiled a little.

"I'm sorry. I didn't think you'd go through with it."

"Tell me."

"I don't know."

"Can't you see the irony here? The normal you would have found this funny."

"You mean, you really want to do this?"

"You mean, you don't?"

Liz was studying an abstract stained-glass window. How could she find a way to say this? There was a perfect equilibrium in their sort-of marriage now. What they were living felt precisely right. But Jack's wealth gave him an overwhelming ballast that made Liz worry that becoming American-married would destroy this lovely equity between them. She would be owned by him, just as everything else in their lives was owned by him. That wasn't what he wanted, was it? After too long a pause, she said, "We're already married. We got married where there's no such thing as money. I think I need that to be enough."

Jack stepped and took her into his arms. She couldn't rest her made-up cheek against his black satin lapel, so she stood rigidly a little away from him. That seemed to make him stiffen, too, as if he were reading from it more than what she meant. He rested his cheek against her hair. He said gently, "I want this, honey. Tell me what it will take to make you want it, too." She could feel his jaw moving as he added with a smile in his voice, "Here's something else the normal you would find funny. I'm used to buying what I want with money. To buy you will apparently take anti-money?"

Liz stepped back out of his arms and looked up at him. Oh, she could see the ironies. A whole lifetime of ironies. Of course she should be finding this funny. But she said, sounding grimmer than she meant to sound, "There's no way you can buy me. At one time you considered that a plus. Apparently now you just want this done." Her eyes were filling. She had been stupid to let it get this far, because whatever happened now was going to change their relationship and that was the one thing she was fighting to preserve.

After a pause during which she had to tip up her chin and she couldn't look at his face, he said, "I get it. I always thought you were kidding. What you're saying is you only want me if I'm poor. That's what you're saying?"

No, that wasn't what she was saying. But she was so upset with herself now that she couldn't say anything.

After a further brief pause, he took another of those cream-colored checks from an inside pocket. He turned it over and handed it to her. Then he took his fountain pen from his chest pocket and handed that to her as well. She took the check and pen reluctantly. He said, "Write a number on the back that seems comfortable to you. Everything I own above that number I'll give to Rex or put into Milly's foundation. I'll give up whatever is getting in your way."

Liz looked up at Jack, feeling slack with wonder. How could he possibly mean that? Was this another financial game to him, so when she wrote a number down he would have his checkmate? She realized that he had acted spontaneously and hadn't really thought this through when he added, "Remember, we've got a few decades to cover. It costs a lot to live well." Another brief pause. Then, "It would be good if we could take a few years to get it done. Otherwise, gift taxes will be horrendous."

She jumped and hugged him around his neck, carrying him backward a step. He lifted her in his arms and hugged her, then he set her down and kissed her. When he broke the kiss, she took a catch-up breath and said, "Okay," and nodded. She handed the pen and check back to him.

Father Jamar had insisted he couldn't marry them unless one of them was a Catholic. Fortunately, Jack was a nominal Catholic. So they stood hand-in-hand and recited their vows, and Jack put Liz's eternity ring back on her finger. She imagined he must be thinking, "That's for you, Milly," as their little family mobbed them in celebration. Even their bodyguards were smiling.

It was only after they had signed the license, and Rex and Cathy had signed as witnesses, and they all had hugged or shaken hands with Jamar while Peters was bringing their car to the door, and even after Jack had climbed inside, that Liz suffered an awful realization. As she slid onto the seat with an assist from Peters, she said to Jack, "Sweetheart? Wait. Wait a minute. You forgot the prenup." Peters closed the door. Jack opened his arms to Liz, and she slid over and snuggled in close to him. He tipped up her chin with a finger and kissed her, and then he began to build his kiss as the car started to move, and he felt for the button to raise the partition and pulled her nearly into his lap and kissed her with such purpose that she thought he might be planning an immediate consummation. She broke his kiss enough to say, "Wait! You forgot the prenup."

He looked at her then. He settled her in beside him, looking at her. He began to smile a little. He said, "Honey, have you ever read a prenuptial agreement?"

"No. But you need it? It protects you?"

"It would give you a predetermined amount upon divorce. At our stage, that's all it would do. I thought about it for five minutes. I couldn't imagine even showing you the language, never mind asking you to sign it." He paused, studying her face. "When I thought about it, I realized I wouldn't mind giving you half. I knew you wouldn't take it, anyway. And

apparently, as we just saw, I'd be willing to give you a lot more than half."
He paused thoughtfully, as if that realization were just dawning on him.
He added, "Ted insisted. I refused. And the way I feel now, my only regret
is we didn't do this years ago."

He drew her close and began to kiss her again, but the drive from the
church had been brief. They were already beginning to pass through the
crowd at the foot of Ted's driveway. Liz noticed that, broke their kiss, and
reached for her purse from the floor so she could hurriedly reapply lipstick.
Then she saw that Jack had a little lipstick on his cheek, so she pulled a
tissue and had him spit on it and cleaned him up as he sat looking out
through the tinted window. She said, "You look beautiful. I'll walk ahead
of you. It will just take a minute."

"We'll walk together, honey."

So she waited for him and took his hand. They both at the same time
saw this as funny, so by the time they reached Ted's door they were glancing
at one another and snickering.

⇥ 24 ⇤

Ted became increasingly flustered as photographers took pictures of endless combinations of people posed in his sunroom and in front of his living-room fireplace. As the time crept past six-thirty and Ted wanted still a few more pictures, Liz came to understand why this day was so important to him. Ted had built his whole social presence around the fact that he was Jack Richardson's right hand, yet for two decades Jack had done so little socially that not much public evidence of their relationship existed. This evening was not about just baby Milly. It was also Ted's proof to the people he wanted most to impress that everything he had been claiming about his relationship with Jack Richardson was true. And Liz was feeling so much fresh tenderness now toward all the world that she was happy to give him his proof.

More than a hundred and fifty people were waiting in an enormous tent, one end of which was attached to the house. When the pictures were done, Rex and Cathy and the baby were ushered into the tent to light music and soft applause. Jack took Liz's hand so they could follow Rex and Cathy, at which point the orchestra switched to a few quick bars of "Here Comes the Bride" before returning to whatever it had been playing. Liz glanced at Jack's face and caught the end of a wince. There was clapping and good-hearted laughter.

Liz hadn't known how Jack would take to being out among people again, but he returned to socializing as if it were a well-remembered tune. He knew some of the people there, others were money people who conversed with him easily, while others were people who simply wanted to meet and have a word with him. Liz, however, was finding that her now looking like a genuine post-post-post debutante didn't translate into her feeling like one. Among all these wealthy and successful people congregating around her husband and trying to converse with her as well, she was so unbearably shy that she slipped her hand from his and got out of the way. Without Jack beside her, she was relieved to find that she was no one. She got herself a gin and tonic and found a place beyond the groups of people from which she could covertly watch Jack's face. He was smiling, talking easily, laughing comfortably. She was so glad to see how much fun he was having that she soon realized that here she was standing all alone, grinning like a fool and running happy tears.

Jack came looking for Liz as people were being seated for dinner. But their seats were at the head table, and people kept coming by to speak with Jack, so soon Liz told him she wanted to go and sit with the kids. He looked at her, understood what she was feeling, kissed her a peck, and let her go. Cathy and the baby were cuddled in Rex's lap as they watched the party from their table across the room, so there was an empty seat beside them. Liz set down her plate and sat, feeling relieved.

Dennis and Bobby both had dates. Liz introduced herself to them, and she suggested to Rex that if he wanted to take the girls home in the limo that would be okay. He looked at her. She loved seeing the deep contentment in his face, the way his expression claimed as his own this woman and this child and this moment. He had been practicing shielding himself from energies that his mind found troubling, and Liz assumed that now the trick was complete. Rex said to her, "They have rides home. Let's not ruffle the old man's feathers."

A tiered white cake topped with roses stood in the center of the dance floor. Ted had known better than to ask Jack to cut a wedding cake, so the waiters were cutting it and serving it when Liz noticed that Ted was standing near the orchestra. Then he had a microphone in hand, and he was stepping partway across the dance floor, tapping the microphone and calling out, "Excuse me, everyone!"

A spotlight that Liz hadn't previously noticed found him, so he was wincing blindly.

As conversation in the tent subsided, Ted said, sounding happier than Liz had ever imagined he could sound in his life, "Thank you for being here to celebrate two great family events! Last year my daughter married the son of my best friend. How perfect is that?" There was brief applause. He added fussily, "The wedding was private. Sorry about that. But today we celebrate the christening of our first grandchild, Millicent Larkin Richardson. And we could not be happier!" Liz guessed that Rex and Cathy were supposed to show off the baby now, but Cathy was comfortable and Milly was sleeping. Then the spotlight found them, so Rex waved generally. Ted went on, squinting as the spotlight came back to him, "And today Jack and Elizabeth Richardson married for the second time." He was improbably grinning. "They were married twenty-five years ago on their private island, but it turns out that wasn't a legal marriage in the United States, so today the kids made it legal!"

As Ted finished speaking, the spotlight was moving to find a stocky young fellow in black tie, holding a microphone. Ted added, "They've allowed me to choose their wedding song. I've been Jack's friend for forty years. I know how he feels about his wife. Only one song fits. Jack and Liz, your wedding song."

The keyboard intro was starting, but good grief, Jack was across the room! He had anticipated what was happening, so as Liz was standing, he was reaching for her hand and he led her to the dance floor. It was then that Liz remembered that she hadn't danced even once since college. Jack held her in his arms, but loosely. He was moving. Waltzing was what she imagined he was doing, but she was stumbling. He drew her close then and held her against him and whispered, "Just follow me, honey. Don't think." That worked better.

They had increased the tempo of "Be My Love," a song that Liz thought she had heard long ago, but still it wasn't really a waltz. And the words were so intimate that they were embarrassing, full of a man's naked yearning for his woman. Was it possible that Jack really felt that way? And that Ted knew it? Liz was getting the hang of dancing now, and grinning and tearing up as she was realizing that her Jack, the husband of her soul, the rich and famous Jack Richardson had now for certain and forever chosen her from all the women on earth. Despite the spotlight on them, Liz was so lost in the perfection of this moment that she barely noticed Jack waltzing her past the singer twice to ask that he sing their song again.

By August, Free the People was turning into what Rex thought of as an actual business. Of course, he had no concept of what a business was supposed to be, and in fact the controlling and dominating attitude that seemed to be necessary to running a business was such anathema to him that he was trying to shield his mind from getting anywhere near it. But his father had been happy to let him name Bobby Ingersoll the president of his company, so Rex could just stand back and observe. And by August, Jack was joining them on many afternoons, even eventually wearing jeans, so Rex had the fun of watching two men he loved as they made his ideas a reality.

Rex's primary interest remained the protection and further development of his mind. Where he had been born, the unity of minds had been as essential to human life as breathing, so if you had told him there could be a place where human minds were numb to one another, he would have considered that notion ridiculous. It would have seemed to him impossible that people even could survive that way. But Dennis remained Rex's only successful experiment in the development of awareness in someone who had been born in this place. Cathy was so distracted by Milly and motherhood that she never got around to doing the exercises that Dennis and Rex were developing to try to strengthen people's minds; and Rex was coming to see, too, that something about their own relationship was getting in her way. Knowing how marriages worked in his home-place, he thought Cathy was too intensely focused on trying to effect her husband's happiness. How could she access her own deepest self if all that she was thinking about was him?

Where Rex had grown up, people understood that in order to perfect the marital union that was important to the universal unity of minds, they had to deeply access and understand and free their minds individually. And they had learned that an essential way for people to better access themselves was through intense cross-gender friendships. People needed deepfriends. No pair of spouses could expect to be everything to one another, and if they even attempted that, they would put a tremendous strain on the marriage. Rex himself had had two deepfriends when he lived in his people's world, and he was wishing now that he knew other women besides Cathy with whom he could simply be friends. Here he had Liz and Dennis. Perhaps Bobby. But it wasn't the same.

When it first occurred to Rex, late in the season of flowers budding, that Cathy's obsession with him was getting in her way, he tried one time to explain to her how finding another man to be her deepfriend might help her to better access herself. That turned out to be a mistake. She though Rex was saying he was bored with her. He wanted to have an "affair." He was proposing something she called an "open marriage." No matter what he said to her, for Cathy it was all about sex. Two days of her tears and his repeated assurances that she was the only woman he wanted had brought them back to speaking terms, and eventually back to being comfortable together; but there was a little rip in their relationship now that Rex couldn't see a way to mend. He wasn't going to try that again. So he was surprised when Dennis announced to him casually one day in the season of dry grass that Sissy, his extremely patient girlfriend who was going to college on a scholarship from Jack, had been playing with their mind-strengthening exercises, and she seemed to be developing her mind just as Dennis was developing his.

Rex's relationship with Dennis had become what felt like the rock at the center of his life. It was the only part of his daily experience in this benighted place that seemed even remotely reminiscent of home, where he had had one particular close friend he had similarly considered his brother. He felt at peace when he was with Dennis. There were no traps in their relationship, no misunderstandings, no stresses. Dennis was soft and thoughtful for a man, wise and deep more than sharp and bright, so Rex thought that in some ways each of them made half of one whole. Dennis had told Rex that since his mother's employer preferred to hire the relatives of staff, he had been assuming since he was a child that he would end up working with cars at Sea Haven.

And then had come what Dennis referred to as the "mind-thing." Rex had fretted initially that Dennis was so intently focused on trying to develop his mind just because he wanted to please the boss's son, but for Dennis it had gone beyond that now. After several months of concentrating on accessing his own desires from moment to moment, and giving himself such absolute freedom of mind that he accepted Rex's invitation to move into Sea Haven in order to free himself from driving laws, one glorious morning Dennis realized that he could feel a difference in the grass when he moved from shadow into sunlight. He seized on that, began to work with it, learned to concentrate without concentrating, and spent his every waking minute playing with the mind-thing. It was he who discovered that there were things he could do, little exercises that seemed to help, so perhaps it wasn't surprising that he was testing them on Sissy when he saw her several evenings a week.

Sissy still lived with her parents in Providence, Rhode Island, nearly an hour's drive from Sea Haven. She and Dennis had both grown up in old-fashioned ethnic families, and they hadn't wanted to distress their parents by doing something so radical as moving in together without the benefit of marriage. What they really wanted to do was get married, but because working with Rex seemed to require that Dennis live at Sea Haven, and Sissy's father was an ex-convict so Sissy couldn't live at Sea Haven, their being married wasn't currently possible. So Sissy would drive down from Providence and pick Dennis up at the gate to the staff parking lot two or three evenings each week, and generally they didn't go farther than a secluded spot in the woods beside the Sea Haven fence because even when he wasn't driving, seeing a traffic light now irritated Dennis.

Dennis had recently begun to tell Rex that working with his mind like this was what he wanted to do with his life. "But we can't, you know, do this for a living, right? Although I guess you can play forever, dude, but there's those of us that need a job." He thought Sissy might be a natural at this. "I think she's got a gift, anyway," Dennis said to Rex one day in the season of dry grass as they were looking along the fence for additional damaged trees. "She can even see ghosts? I bet she could help find these trees."

There had turned out to be no way to save the trees that had grown right on top of the wreckage of houses whose owners had been upset about moving. But once those trees were taken out and the remnants of the bulldozed homes were gone, the contractors doing this work could generally pull out whatever was entangled here and there in the roots of the surrounding trees. Rex was finding that once all of that was removed, over days those trees seemed to lose their feeling of emotional damage. But what with all the trees and house-debris being hauled away, all the logging roads that had to be cut, and all the trucks full of gravel and loam that were being brought in to fill the holes, the woodland to the east of the house was a mess. Jack was at first stunned to see the dramatic advance of so much damage, but then he conceived the notion that a park would be a great improvement over what had been just random re-growth. He brought out of retirement the landscape architect who had designed his formal gardens, and already there was a concept plan for an English-style park including gardens and fountains and copses of trees. Jack wanted it completed by next summer, when he planned to get baby Milly a pony.

Rex and Dennis had been at this work ever since the season of little leaves, coming out every several days and trying to mark enough trees to keep the workers busy for a few days more. They assumed that there was no house-debris left under the long lawn down to the sea, because they hadn't found any hotspots there. There seemed to be none in the narrower strip of woodland to the west of the house, and of course not all the families being bought out had left emotional pain in their possessions. But Rex had learned this morning that in the past three months the crews had removed more than forty trees, and there remained at least another ten acres or so of woodland to be surveyed. The process was tedious, but the wonder of being able to walk that path to the ocean without having to guard against pain in the plants seemed to Rex to make it worth the effort.

With their primary venue for afternoon walks now mostly a sloppy construction site, and with Jack spending many summer afternoons working in the Free the People office with the boys, Liz now had too much time on her hands. She had agreed informally to write her memoirs, and that gave a nominal shape to her days, but she wasn't going to write about Jack, so she imagined that whatever she wrote wasn't going to be worth anyone's time to read, anyway.

Even writing her memoirs, Liz had to write in third-person. She had learned long ago that trying to write in first-person was unbearable for her. When Jack had first briefly left his family on Atlantica more than two decades ago, Liz had still had hopes that it might be possible to separate him from his wealth altogether and free him to live a genuine life. In an effort to help him better see his choice, she had written a memoir of their life together since the day they met. The story was their own, so she had begun to write it in first-person and addressed to him in second-person. You and I. A letter. She had written it on paper scrounged from the Farm's office, with ballpoint pens until she could find no more pens, then in pencil until the sharpener broke, after which she had tried to use chicken-quills and a bottle of ink that had been meant for Jack's fountain pen. Liz was left-handed, so the ink kept smudging. In the end, she had gone back to writing with stubs of pencils that she sharpened with a wood-carving blade borrowed from the Morakan carvers.

After Liz had written maybe ten longhand pages, she thought she would give herself the fun of reading what she had written so far. Before she even got to the end, she had to crumple it up and start over. She couldn't write a letter to him about the way they would talk for hours every night on his yacht on the way to Atlantica, while she tried to ignore whatever he was doing to whichever tart he was cuddling. Perhaps she had understood even then that he was using his women as a defense against whatever he already was feeling for her, but still she couldn't write to him about it. She had to start over. Write it all in third-person. And she had to omit some of the worst things. Once, before Jack was used to the fact that Liz was working on the computers in his office on the yacht, she had come upon him sitting behind his desk with his back turned and gazing out the window-wall at the sea. She hadn't realized that someone was fellating him until it was too late for him not to know she had noticed.

Thinking about that long-ago letter to Jack inspired Liz to ditch her memoirs early one afternoon and call up a new Word page. On a lark, she began to write about the shock of her assuming that Ted's unexpected return to Atlantica after so many years had to mean that Jack was dead. She was writing about Jack and Rex now, everything that mattered to her, and compared with trying to write with chicken-quills on the backs of copies of letters, this was easy! She wasn't sure why she was writing this, but it gave her something to do. Or perhaps she was writing it for baby Milly, who was so often in Liz's suite now that Liz had her own playpen and her own changing table. Today Cathy had gone to lunch with two of her friends, so Milly was here babbling and working on her rolling-over trick while her grandmother watched. So then, should Liz ditch the sexual stuff, if the baby might ever one day read this? She had gone around that barn a hundred times while she was writing with nubbins of pencils by candle-light, but she always had decided that sex was no more personal than the other personal things she was discussing. If she couldn't write with fulsome honesty, there would be no point in her writing at all.

⫷ 25 ⫸

At what Liz pretended was Milly's suggestion, they soon headed over to check on whatever Daddy and Grandpa were up to today. As she walked in, just carrying Milly in her arms because the Free the People office also had a playpen, Liz could hear Bobby saying, "No! The whole trick is getting the parking right." She found Bobby with Jack and several others, standing together as they studied three sketches on easels. Bobby was adding, "You've got to make it easy or they won't come back. If it won't fit the site, we'll find a different site."

Jack said, "What about a pentagon? Keep the footprint tight. Put parking on the outside?"

Bobby said indulgently, grinning at Jack, "We've already established that someone who has only ever ridden in the back seat is not a parking expert."

"No, look," said Jack. He flipped a sheet on an easel in order to get a clean sheet of paper. He picked up a charcoal crayon from the easel's tray and began to sketch in broad strokes. "Store, service, lube and tires, restaurant around the outside. Gas and carwash over here. Or maybe over here. Used cars in back. They drive in from off the street on two sides." He drew a small box that Liz assumed was a gas station. "A kiddie park in the middle. Here. The stores face out, but to walk from store to store once

241

you're in, you go through the kiddie park." Then he said to Bobby, "Okay hotshot," and offered him the crayon.

Liz could tell from the tone of Jack's voice that he was enjoying whatever they were doing. He was wearing jeans and a polo shirt in a room full of chaos and productive mess, working with people half his age. Liz could feel herself beginning to smile. Then Bobby noticed her standing there. He stepped and took Milly from her arms, saying, "Give Uncle Bobby a hug. Tell Grandpa it's time he got his driver's license."

Jack noticed Milly, looked around, saw Liz and said, "Hi honey!"

"Where's Rex?" Liz said to Bobby as she took back Milly.

"He and the Denman are out finding loco-trees. Hey! Inspiration," Bobby said to Jack. "Motorcycles. Add two-wheel sales out back with the used cars." He clapped Jack on the back, but respectfully. "Brilliant, right?"

Jack was studying his drawing. It looked like an angry black mess to Liz. He said to the designer, "Can you read what I did here? Draw it up for me?" To Bobby he said, "Is it the same demographic?"

"We'll need to research it. I like your pentagon idea, though. It's got to be in the round that way, so everything is accessible from the outside."

Jack was studying his incomprehensible drawing that the designer had begun to try to replicate on another easel. He said, "We're going to need better real estate. Highway visibility. Frontage on two roads if we can get it."

"There go your returns, cuz," Bobby said.

"I don't mind. I'm banking the land. And you'll do more volume, so we'll make up the difference."

Rex walked in then, took Milly from Liz, lifted her so he could blow raspberries against her tummy to make her shriek, then settled her comfortably in his arms. The baby looked around at all of them with a pleased, bemused, here's-my-daddy expression. She had the same large, wide-set eyes that her father and grandfather had. And at six months old, her eyes were still blue.

Jack was giving pointers to the designer. Bobby was taking a cellphone call. Rex said to Liz, "I'd like a family conference upstairs. Do you have time?"

⸻ ✦ ⸻

The elevator and the door to the stairs were locked. Security staff checked them often. The second floor of the office building held millions of dollars worth of art, while the first floor was open to the public. They waited for someone to come with the elevator key, then rode upstairs and went into what had once been Jack's office. After that it had been Liz's office. At Jack's invitation, Liz had taken down the heavy representational paintings that he favored and hung just the Degas painting of three dancers from the library, a Cezanne still life, a Renoir child's portrait, a busy Monet garden. Jack looked around with interest at what had been his environment for so many years. He said to Liz, "Why am I suddenly thinking that the fact that I'm now living in jeans and working with people who feel free to tell me what they actually think is another of little Lizzie's gotchas?"

She went to him and slipped her arms around his neck and murmured, "What comes after checkmate?" and kissed him. He was developing her kissing impulse into an actual kiss, and she was taking it further, and then so was he, so Rex had to say it two or three times.

"Folks! Liz!"

They broke their kiss and turned to face Rex. Jack had his arm around Liz's shoulders; she had hers around his waist. Rex had set baby Milly sitting shakily on the carpet in a seldom-trod corner of the room with a bright-red stress-ball from the desk. He sat perched on the arm of one of the guest chairs, intermittently glancing at Milly but primarily looking at the two of them as he said, "In case there's a doubt in anyone's mind, I'm not angry. If I start to sound angry at some point in this discussion that we should have had long ago, it's because I'm angry with myself."

Jack went to sit in the desk chair. Liz turned a guest chair sideways and sat down, facing both of them.

"It's coming up on two years by your months, isn't it? Two years ago I gave up everything that mattered to me and a joyous life that made sense, and I came to a place that still makes no sense and is so full of unhappy people it breaks my heart every day. Dennis kept telling me I'd get comfortable with it. You've always assumed it was obviously better here," Rex said, looking at Jack. He added, "Don't worry. I can feel that I'm scaring you. And that's the point, isn't it? I can tell what you're feeling, but your mind is numb! Doesn't that show you all by itself that it's better where I came from than here? Don't be smug about having more stuff, Jack. It's all hrastinit. More is less. Boy, is that clear to me now." He stood up off the chair's arm. Milly watched him stand and destabilized herself, so he had to rush to catch her before she fell over backward. He put the stress ball into her hand again and started pacing. He said to Liz, "How old am I?"

"Your birth certificate says you're twenty-five."

"Is that an adult age here?"

"Yes."

"Then I'm a man. I'm going to start living like a man. I'll have my own house. I'll work at Free the People for as long as it interests me. I'll raise my children the way I want to raise them—And yes," he said to Liz, "we've got another on the way. They come a lot faster here."

"She stopped nursing early. Wow!"

"I'll learn to drive a car," Rex was saying to Jack. "I'll come and go as I like—"

"I wish that were possible."

"I don't need your money! I'll make my own way."

Jack half-shrugged. He said, sounding calmer than Liz was feeling, "You can change your name and move to Toledo. I'll give you as many lube shops and car washes as you can manage. But there'll never be a minute when your children are safe, son. Someone will figure out they're my grandchildren. All they have to do is grab one child, and immediately they're a billion dollars richer."

Rex looked at Liz, flummoxed.

She said to him, "You're right, sweetie. You've been a good sport. You deserve to have a freer life. But your father is famous for being rich, and there's nothing you can do to get away from that."

"So we'll go home."

"Cathy won't go."

Rex looked at Liz grimly. She winced to see the frustration in his face. He said, "How could you do this to me?"

Jack began to say helpfully, "We'll set up a foundation to protect Atlantica—" He stopped talking when Liz snapped him a glare.

Liz stood and put her arms around Rex. To her surprise, he hugged her. He said, "Fix it."

She stepped back as she was saying, "Okay. Tell us what you want."

"I want freedom! I've always got these idiots babysitting me. You don't make yourself live like that, Jack! Okay, I'll take a bodyguard with me, but I'm going to learn to drive a car. And the only way I'm staying here is if this place stops revolving around just you!"

Jack said, "Why don't you move to the west wing? I'll give you the second and third floors. We'll put in an elevator. It'll be like living in your own house."

Liz added, "We can put in a kitchen. You can eat with us or do your own meals. "

"I'm uncomfortable having you drive."

"Get used to it, pal."

Liz said, "Okay. One step at a time. Will you let us give you the second and third floors of the west wing? It will be all yours."

"No guards near me that I can see. And if I want to take a stroll on the beach, they leave me alone."

"Fine," said Jack.

"Sell the new limousine. Cathy's got your old one. I don't want one."

"Maybe I'll use it," Jack said with a glance at Liz.

"I want a car. Not a fancy car. Let Dennis pick it out. I want a car nobody will look at when I drive in to buy something at Free the People."

"Can it be armored?"

"No. If they want to kill me that badly, I'm sure there's a blissful village here, too."

Jack said, "We'll work through this. I've never had someone so important to me I couldn't protect, but I'll deal with it."

"One more thing. Dennis lives with us, Jack. Married." Jack looked at him. "He's getting married in the same place I got married. With Sissy's whole family there." Whatever Rex was reading from Jack's mind made him add angrily, "With her father there, too! Every fancy thing you don't want him to see goes away, and it never comes back. If it makes a difference between people it's for shit, Jack." Rex added, looking at Liz, "Sissy's father did stupid things when he was young. People here think it makes sense to lock people up and make them sad? How does that help anyone?" He said to Jack, "Dennis says her father is a good man. Who are you to hold a grudge against someone you've never even met?"

Dennis had seemed stunned when Rex told him the wedding could take place at Sea Haven whenever they liked. Was next weekend too soon? And by the way, the boss was contributing a three-carat diamond to make Sissy even happier. Rex was so eager to meet Sissy and test her mental powers that he couldn't sit down, but he was wandering the terrace on a sunny morning in the season of first harvest as he waited for her to arrive. All the while, he was reminding himself that he had to stop thinking of her as Sissy and remember that she had a real name, and it was Cecilia. Cecilia. She had been at Ted's party, but Rex had been so caught up with Cathy and the baby that he had realized only after it was over that he had never managed to say hello. And here they came down the path from the staff parking lot, where Dennis had gone to meet her. They were holding hands.

Dennis had told Rex that he and Cecilia had been very close since childhood. Rex and Gaprelagh, his forever love, had been emotionally close as children, so when they made their marital union they were able to attain a unity of minds in an ecstasy of such intense pleasure that Rex wasn't able to resurrect anything like it now, even in memory. He had trusted at first that the fact that the union physically felt the same here as there must mean that the emotional pleasure of it also would develop in time. But Cathy's mind was still numb, and from what Rex could see she was too distracted by the baby to even make an effort at developing her mental powers. So even now, so many seasons after their wedding, when they came together all they could manage was that brief physical connection, that bit of localized pleasure, that sense of warm closeness. How was it that people in this benighted place were willing to settle for so little in their lives, and especially in their marriages? But with Dennis and Cecilia both developing awareness, perhaps something like what Rex and Gaprelagh had had together might be possible for them as well.

Cecilia was as small as Cathy, not as pretty, but pretty enough. Her eyes were properly brown, and her hair was an amazing shade of yellow that seemed to have tones of green and blue in it. Rex smiled at her and bent and hugged her as he said, "You can't know how happy I am to finally meet you, Cecilia!"

Her mind had a soft and fluffy kind of feel, not so purely childlike as Cathy's mind, but lightly cheerful and without much aggression or fear that Rex could perceive. She felt by mind very much like the sort of woman who could make Dennis happy.

"Well, and wow, likewise!" she said to Rex, grinning up at him, squinting in the sunlight. "Denny told me stories, but this is quite the place you've got here. I could get used to this."

Behind her, Dennis was saying, "Let's go check on the trees, babydoll. I'm dying to see if you can do this."

"As am I," Rex said as they started across the lawn to the trail that would lead them into what was left of the woods.

From the time she arrived, Rex had been able to feel Sissy's mind scanning her surroundings, even though her active attention had been focused on him. Everyone back home did that automatically, but Rex realized now that unless Dennis was specifically looking for something, he didn't seem to be always mentally connecting with his environment this way.

"Where's all the guards, dude?" Dennis asked then.

"I told him I don't want to see them, so now they sneak around behind things. Can you believe he pays people to do nothing all day but watch me live my life?"

"Where's the bad trees?"

"Down a little farther, baby."

Then Sissy remarked, "Boy, it feels ishy here, doesn't it?"

Rex and Dennis glanced at one another. Rex said quietly to her, not wanting to break her concentration, "There are trees here in what feels like human emotional pain. Roam around. Dennis and I will step back. Don't try," he added as they were leaving her mind-space. She was venturing forth cheerfully, apparently still scanning, although Rex was too far away to feel that now.

Then in a few minutes, "Hey, this one?" they heard her call from a little distance. They glanced at one another and hurried down the trail. She was standing with both hands flat against a tree trunk, looking up.

Dennis grabbed her into a hug. Rex was smiling as his mind confirmed her discovery. Then he said, "How would you like a job?"

⇥ 26 ⇤

What they had been calling Free the People's "big reveal" had been
scheduled for a mid-November morning that was two years
almost to the day after Rex stepped off the Sea Haven launch
and began this adventure. The core of the Free the People team of former
Levigard employees was here, some seventy people. The first floor of
the office building was arranged with easels and display boards and big
monitors at the northern end of the room, with couches and chairs and a
banner above in the style and colors of the infant company's logo. Liz sat
with Cathy and a very busy Milly on the couch-of-honor at the front. But
where was Jack? Rex and Bobby were chatting in the open area that had
long been designated as an informal stage whenever meetings were held
here. They were waiting for everyone to arrive and settle down. Liz stood
and crossed their stage area and put a hand on Rex's arm. He stopped
talking and looked at her.

"Where's your father, sweetie?"

"He's not part of Free the People. He said he'll get the landlord's presentation when we're ready."

Liz felt blindsided. Now she didn't want to be here for two hours! She
and Jack had breakfasted together that morning, holding hands while
eating as was their habit, made easy by the fact that she was left-handed

and he was right-handed. When Liz had stood and kissed him and said cheerily "See you in a few!" he hadn't said he wasn't going to be here. He had seemed a bit subdued, she thought, and she realized as she thought about it further that he had been more quiet lately, a shaded version of himself, not abnormal, and probably natural for someone who was soon to turn sixty-four.

Growing old may be as difficult as growing up. After having lived for half a century in what feels like a state of equilibrium, we begin to experience changes in our bodies and minds that are as disconcerting and profound as the changes of adolescence. Jack had shared that insight with Liz one morning last week as he sat at his desk and she sat on his sofa, trying to write about their wedding and finding herself unable to describe how she had felt at that moment. It hadn't been so much the fact that now he actually was not only willing, but even eager to marry her. But moments before they were married, Jack had finally proven to Liz that she was more important to him than his money. Standing there beside him, holding his hand and breathing in those hyacinths, her mind had been so crammed with that brand-new amazement that now she couldn't remember actually taking vows.

As Liz was struggling to recall their wedding, Jack asked her whether she had noticed that his hair was thinning on top. Well, of course she had. His valet was creative, but Clay wasn't there on Wednesdays and Sundays and the trainee who worked on those days was less so. Anyway, by now you could see scalp-shine. But she wouldn't care if he were bald as an egg, so she told him it wasn't enough to notice. No hair-plugs, darling! He had said then that old age was turning out to be a depressing reversal of adolescence. She had chuckled companionably at his little insight, but perhaps he hadn't meant it to be funny.

Or perhaps, Liz thought, the fact that they had begun to do some social things like attending a Dartmouth fundraising dinner and a reception to benefit the Guggenheim, both on the same weekend, might be overwhelming him in some way. They even were planning a Christmas reception in the penthouse that had been all his idea. But if he were deciding now that he would rather live more privately after all, that was fine with Liz. She just wished that she had asked him earlier what was bothering him, and she was desperate to push this meeting past so she could get out of here and find him.

Those monitors were flickering to life, showing the Free the People logo. It was a play on the first words of the preamble to the Constitution, with "Free" in place of "We" in the same quill-style lettering, and with a red-white-and-blue ribbon twining. Rex stepped forward, smiling, to a trickle of applause and then a crescendo of it. He lifted both hands as he said "Thank you! Thanks! What a great day this is!" He was wearing a microphone clipped to his T-shirt. Liz thought he was beautiful in the bright diffuse light from all those windows, his blond hair glinting copper and his face strong and confident. With all the wrong things Liz ever had done, what felt to her like the accident of her having produced this magnificent man made her whole life right.

He was saying, "As of September, Free the People is a Delaware corporation that employs most of you. We're independent of Larkin, so thanks to all of you who've taken the risk of joining our start-up." There were a few chuckles at that, and some applause. No one believed that moving from one of the Richardson family's businesses to another could be anything but a move upward, and they knew that already plans were being made to roll out Rex's idea nationwide.

Rex said, "I'm Chairman of the Board of Free the People, but I expect you to treat me as part of the team. We're going to work in the only way I know how to work, which is each of us doing what we love. My cousin, though, is a real business guy. Here is Bobby Ingersoll, our president. It would be a good idea to clap for him!"

So then Bobby stepped forward, wearing his usual ironic little smile. Liz often had the sense when watching his face that Bobby found everything around him amusing in a way so complex that only he could perceive it. He was another beautiful young man, not as tall as Rex and with a slighter build and a more angular way of using his body. Bobby was so flexible that he had a habit of resting a foot on the seat or even on the arm of a chair, and then resting his elbow on his thigh, and sometimes then resting his chin on his hand, all while he kept on thinking and talking. Liz knew how much Jack was affected by Bobby when she noticed him now also occasionally resting a foot on something, and then an elbow or a forearm on his thigh. Bobby had a lighter, redder, curlier variant of Jack's mahogany hair. The freckles fading on his nose made her think of him as a business Huckleberry Finn.

Bobby began to say before the applause died down, "This is where the fun starts! We break ground next week on our pilot Free the People location. We're going to test-drive this baby and work out the bugs. Today I'll show you plans for the pilot in Holyoke, where Levigard bought a lube shop with a roughly square twenty-acre parcel with frontage on three streets. We've torn down everything that was there. Here is what's going up."

Bobby stepped aside, and all the monitors began showing brightly-colored flat and then gradually three-dimensional plans for five car-related businesses in a pentagon shape, with a park-like go-cart track in the center, with used-car sales to the rear and a combination gas station and car wash as part of the right-hand parking lot. This was the idea that Liz had seen Jack propose in August, now fleshed out as plans and being built before their eyes until there it was, complete, with cars using the restaurant drive-thru to the left and more cars driving around the pentagon, parking, exiting onto one of three roads. The mock-up camera seemed to pan down and circle the complex, so you could see that the store in front carried the full Free the People logo and the ribbon then rippled around the building, carrying red-white-and-blue signs in a quill-pen lettering style identifying the other services. Perhaps it was mostly the fact that these were animated drawings and meant to make it all look good, but Liz thought the result was amazing. Where was Jack? He had to see this!

Bobby was saying, "These are retail stores, open to the public, but people can choose to join as members. If they join, they'll receive discounts of ten percent on purchases, and they'll be eligible to share in the profits generated at that location. We'll need to pay off loans and build a cash reserve, but all our excess profits will go to our members. I'll show you numbers in a minute that suggest that five years after a location opens, the actual discounts for members who shop there with profit-sharing included should be at least twenty percent."

Liz was so enraptured by what the boys had put together that she was able to sit through presentations by leaders of each of the five store teams, then the leader of the team seeking new locations, and even the kid who was masterminding what he referred to as "go-karts as performance art." But when the numbers guys got started, she kissed Cathy and Milly, gave a small wave to Rex, and left unobtrusively.

———◆———

Jack generally spent his mornings managing Larkin and his other investments while Liz kept him company on his sofa. She found it hard to imagine that he had stayed in his sitting room rather than being at Rex's debut, but that was the only place she could think to look for him. So she hurried through the front door and up the east front staircase, and as she reached the top she saw Shrinky Chuck leaving Jack's suite. She thought Jack had fired his analyst before their combination christening and wedding six months ago. What was going on? Chuck startled when he saw Liz, then barely nodded and hurried past her down the stairs. She went to Jack's door, wondering. She assumed his door would be locked, but when it wasn't locked she ventured in.

As Liz reached the end of his suite corridor, she saw Jack sitting hunched on his sofa. She rushed and sat down beside him and slipped her arm around his waist and said, "You should have been there, darling. Your pentagon idea was a hit!"

Jack straightened then, staring at nothing. He rested the back of his right hand against his mouth and caught the middle finger in his teeth and bit it, hard. Liz was off the sofa and kneeling before him and pushing that hand away and taking his face into her hands. He looked at her.

"Darling, what's going on? Why was Chuck here?"

"I can't discuss it with you." He drew a breath, in and out. "I'm back in therapy."

"But what happened? Tell me."

"We've been talking by phone for the past few weeks. You weren't going to be here this morning, so I risked letting him come."

"Please tell me what's wrong." She combed Jack's hair above an ear with the fingers of one hand. He sat back on the sofa and put his arm around her, and she nestled in beside him.

"Chuck thinks she used me as a weapon against my father. 'If you go out tonight, I'll do bad things to Jackie.'"

"God," Liz murmured.

"This has blighted my whole life! I've got to get rid of it. Whatever it takes."

Jack drew Liz up into his lap and cuddled her with her head on his shoulder. She said, "Please tell me, darling, why was he here?"

"A couple of months ago I had this random creepy thought. That's how the memories come. It doesn't seem like a memory, but he coaxes it out.

I called him about it. I won't tell you details, but it turns out I was very young. And it was bad."

"I'm sorry, darling." Liz stroked his cheek, looking at him in close-focus. When he didn't say anything more, she said softly, "That was long ago. It doesn't matter now."

He blinked and said, "At least now I know why I've never liked intercourse! It's a wonder I wasn't put off sex altogether."

"That was long ago—"

"He says I have to hate her. I only think I love her because I'm still afraid of her. A grown man is afraid of a woman who's been dead for more than forty years?"

"He's wrong, darling. You can't hate her without hating yourself."

"No, apparently I can. She's guilty. I'm innocent. Until I understand the difference between guilt and innocence, I'm going to have this mess in my head."

"He's wrong, my love. Please don't hate her!"

"I've got to go back and finish this. I need you not to get in the way."

Liz struggled out of his lap and stood so she could think more clearly. She took a step and spun to face him and said, "Let me make my case first?"

One big foot came up to rest on the opposite knee.

"Make your case. Then I don't want to hear anything more from you about this. Agreed?"

"No. Sweetheart, he's trying to keep you dependent on him. What he should be doing is helping you get free of him! You've paid him a lot. Three visits a week, for . . . how long?"

"Doesn't matter."

"Okay. Fine. Well, and you're emotionally healthier now. Don't you think your mind is retrieving all this now because you're finally healthy enough to process it? You used to be emotionally damaged, darling.

Remember how we'd talk all night, and you'd be cuddling with someone? You couldn't just sit and talk—"

"As I recall, you rejected me. You were the one who didn't want a relationship."

Well, um, yes, that was true. Liz could see from his face that this was turning into a game for him.

"What about getting married? You couldn't have gotten married back then."

"I did get married. When you rejected me, I married Louise. You drove me to it." Then he added, "Hey, look what we've discovered. Milly's not the cause of my problems. You are!"

"Damn it, Jack, will you cut me some slack?"

"Fine. Listening."

"You know what? I don't believe a word of this! You and I did a lot of talking on Atlantica, and never did I hear anything else but your parents fought like cats in a bag, and your father was a rake, and your mother started having sex with you as a way to get back at him for cheating. Disgusting, sure, but you were thirteen years old and twice her size. You made a big point of that. Twice her size! She wasn't abusing a little kid. Never did I hear anything like that."

"No. Apparently I blocked it."

"And you always talked as if you really loved her. You understood her. You were wishing it never happened, but you always talked more as if the three of you were victims together. He's a Catholic so he can't use birth control and she mustn't have children, so waddayagonnado? So now it started when you were—what? How old was this one?"

"He thinks I was maybe four." Jack winced a little as he said it.

"Four? So she started sexually abusing you at four, and you blocked every single bit of it until the day when you were thirteen years old and she brought you into her bed? And that event you remember vividly? Does anything about this make sense to you?" Liz paced a little, thinking. She added, "And what does 'he coaxes it out' mean? If you don't remember it yourself, then how is it even a memory? Maybe it all comes from him! Have you thought of that?"

Jack slouched and dropped his head against the top of the sofa-back, looking at the ceiling. He said, "When I'm talking with Chuck, I feel damaged. He brings out that miserable little boy. Then I talk with you, and you make me feel normal. How do you do that? I was never normal before I met you."

"That's love. That's what love does."

He lifted his head and looked at her.

"The problem is, you make me feel normal, but I've still got that damaged boy inside. I need to know how it feels to have him gone."

"Once you forgive your mother, he won't have any reason to stay."

"Forgive her? Shrinky Chuck says—"

"I know another boy who was hurt by a parent he adored. Take away the ick factor with your mother, and you and Rex aren't that different. He could have nursed his bitterness against you forever, darling, but he told me later that forgiving you for leaving him and forgiving himself for pushing you away was what saved his sanity."

Jack looked abruptly sobered. Liz felt a bit rotten for having brought that up, but she felt as if she were fighting for Jack's sanity, too.

He said, "I need you to butt out of this. Chuck's going to come by twice a week. You're going to ignore him. And you're not going to try to get me to discuss this with you. Ever again."

⊰ 27 ⊱

Rex was so distracted by overseeing the removal of the last of the damaged trees and the build-out of his new home while at the same time he was taking driving lessons from Dennis and trying to keep his pregnant Cathy happy that when Bobby called one afternoon in the season of sleeping trees and asked him to step to the office for a meeting, Rex's response was, "Why don't you just make all the decisions? I don't know what I'm doing, anyway."

"You're going to like this, my friend. Get a move on over here!"

Rex had lately given in and begun to use a cellphone. He still found the fuzzy energy of a cellphone uncomfortable, but he was becoming ever better at shielding his personal energies against it. And with all the things he had going on now, he was away from Cathy enough during the day that she needed to be able to reach him. But he was finding out that the problem with having a cellphone was that now Bobby also was able to reach him.

The ground floor of the office building remained un-partitioned, although now there were discrete working-group areas. Bobby's area was in the middle of the room, with chairs, couches, a table, and his standing desk. People spoke softly to avoid bothering others, which meant that there was a hum of human noise when Rex entered that lifted his spirits. It felt like a workshop back home, but absent the random singing. When Rex got there, Bobby was standing with his foot on a chair and talking with three men seated at his table. Bobby was wearing some amazing shoes. They had a tall heel, two colors of leather, and what looked like sewn decorations on the sides.

"Where did you get those shoes?"

"Cowboy boots. Want some?" Then Bobby said to the visitors, "This is Rex Richardson. Rex, thanks for joining us. John and Sam and another John here are from the three auto dealerships near our Holyoke location. John Shelton from Honda came to me a couple of weeks ago with a proposition. I told him we'd talk if he could get the other two dealerships involved. Now, here they all are!"

Rex sat down at the table. It was covered in gaily-colored car brochures. He sat looking at all those beautiful pictures, wanting to pick them up and examine them, but realizing that would likely be wrong. He said to the group, "I'm planning to get a regular car. You know cars. What's the best regular car there is?"

They looked at one another. Rex knew from their pings of mental alarm that yet again he had said something inappropriate.

Bobby said smoothly, "Rex is looking to buy a car that's not showy and is fun to drive. Why don't each of you come up with your two best options and send them down here tomorrow so he can take his pick?"

"Sedan or sports car?" someone asked.

"Luxury, I assume?" said someone else.

"Regular. Your brother got a raise, but he's still on a budget. He needs a reliable family car. That's what Rex wants."

Again Rex felt confusion in their minds as they glanced at one another. Even after two years here, he still found it impossible to grasp all the nuances of human interaction that were needed in this benighted place. What had he done wrong? Why were they glancing at him with those little uneasy blips in their minds? The fact that even after two years here he still didn't know, and if he were told he likely wouldn't understand the explanation, made anger begin to rise as he thought about it. Where Rex had grown up, someone who was a little different was treated with special kindness, while here whenever Rex was outside the family, he confronted repeatedly the fact that he wasn't perfectly like everyone else.

The men were talking with Bobby as they glanced at Rex. Bobby was saying, "We thought we'd do the build-out from the northeast, but now we're being courted by Texas. They're aggressive! The governor has called me personally, and he sent me these boots." Bobby lifted his foot as he said in an aside to Rex, "He wants to send you a pair, too. Just tell me your size." He went on, "No decisions have been made, but the incentives are so good that we'll probably keep our demo facility in Holyoke and start the build-out in Texas—"

Rex didn't like being so close to the aggressively timid mind-energies of these men, he had no idea why they were here, and something much more important to him had been interrupted back in the house. He said to the man nearest him, "Do you want something?"

"Ah—what?" the man glanced nervously at Bobby.

"Because if you want something, you can have it." Rex was starting to stand as he said to Bobby, "I agree."

Bobby said, giving Rex a sharp look, "We're talking about comparison new-car shopping—"

"Good. I agree. Do it." Rex nodded at the men at the table and clapped Bobby on the back and got himself out of there.

———— • ————

Rex and Dennis had been waiting for Jack to come over and discuss proposed revisions to their apartments under construction in the west wing when Rex had received that call from Bobby. Now, as Rex came back through the front door he encountered his parents coming down the east staircase. He fell into step beside Jack, saying, "Did you know we're starting the build-out from Texas? What's Texas?"

"Bobby mentioned it. God, what a mess!" Jack stopped at the foot of the west staircase. Everything you could see for the length of the west first-floor corridor was wrapped or dust-sheeted. The floor was a taped-down canvas runner. Workmen and security staff came and went, including on the canvas-covered staircase.

Rex said, "Sorry. I guess it looks bad, but we love what this is turning out to be. Cathy is thrilled."

"Well, good," Jack said flatly as he and Liz started up the stairs, hand in hand. "I feel personally violated, but at least she's happy."

"Would it help if the workmen pulled back on the first floor as far as the elevator? They can come and go that way?"

Rex had wanted his new home to have an independent entrance, so the architects had turned what had been the ballroom's entrance and cloak-room midway on the west wing's first floor into a vestibule and the base of an elevator shaft.

Jack briefly stopped mid-staircase and looked around. He said in response to Rex's suggestion, "That would help."

The second floor had been mostly demolished as they turned bedroom spaces into living spaces and installed a kitchen. Jack hurried them right up the next staircase. The third floor hadn't yet been much affected by construction activity, and seeing that seemed to make Jack more comfortable. He led Liz on a little tour, going into bedroom suites to poke around and look out windows. Rex and Dennis trailed along.

"Wow, spectacular views up here," Liz said at one point. "Maybe we should move to the third floor on our wing?"

"It's funny seeing all this again. I haven't been up here since the house was built. I don't know what possessed me to want all these bedrooms."

Liz said at once, "Probably orgies." Then she remembered that Rex and Dennis were there behind them. She said over her shoulder, "Sorry for that mental picture!"

When Dennis showed Jack the big windowless closet beside the third-floor library door, Jack said, "All I can think is they wanted the staircase to curve." He added to Liz, "We used local architects. They had trouble dealing with this scale." Then he said to Rex, "Do whatever you want with it."

As they were poking around in the adjacent bedroom, puzzling out how the spaces could be merged, Rex said to Liz, "Did Cathy tell you we're having a boy? They can know that here."

"That's wonderful! Have you thought of a name?"

"She says I named the last one, so she gets to name this one. I just said, 'Not Rex.'" He glanced at his father. "She's due March twentieth. Milly's birthday is March eighteenth." He added to Liz as they started back down the stairs, "Now we have to have two nurseries and two baby-nurses? Back home, another baby means the mother spends more time in the childhouse for awhile. I've told Bobby I want to use 'hrastinit' in our advertising. 'No more hrastinit. Shop here!' Maybe if your people had a word to use, they'd find it easier to get it out of their lives."

———◆———

"Tell me again, why am I paying you a million dollars a year?" Jack asked after an hour of companionable silence.

"I'm your love-slave," Liz said distractedly. She was typing, trying to finish a thought.

"Have you been reading these emails from Public Relations?"

"They're to you. I'm just copied." Then she looked at him and said, "So I'm only getting a million dollars now? Damn. I knew it was a mistake to get married."

"Read the one they sent this morning."

Liz had read enough of the emails they had been receiving since last summer to know their gist. It was a year now almost to the day since Liz had finished that final lube-shop deal, which meant there were no more briefcase walks for photographers. There had been a gap in publicity before Ted's party at the end of May, but the press on that had been wonderful: that Jack had emerged from twenty years of almost no publicity at all to let himself be photographed and modestly interviewed on such a highly personal day, both the christening of his first grandchild and the renewal of his wedding vows, had made the country fall in love with him as it had fallen in love with Liz a year earlier. But then . . . nothing.

Liz opened the email they had received that morning.

Sir, we are getting questions about whether the Mrs. is still president of Larkin.

We tell them she is. She has been working on her son's new company. Announcements soon. There are rumors your marriage is in trouble, and that is why she isn't out there.

Advise you counter that.

"Does it occur to people we might have a life?"

"Now read this one. It's from my head tax attorney."

Jack—Disc yest. Raise prof. Book pub ideal. Prop token & close thru 02 lmk

"It's written in Lithuanian. What does it mean?"

"We're having issues with the IRS. I hold my assets outside the country to protect them from confiscation, not to dodge taxes, so I pay U.S. taxes on everything they could possibly find. But now they're actually auditing me for '99. They never audit people at my level, but they're doing three this year. All big Democratic donors. I have four of the best tax attorneys in the country in my exclusive employ, so they won't find anything, but that's not the point.

It's an intimidation game. They want to make an example of us." He paused, then added, "They're accusing us of hiding income offshore. They've actually mentioned the F-word. Fraud," he added when she looked startled.

Fraud? Liz swallowed and murmured, "But, um, you do have secret money offshore?"

"I do. They'll never find it, but those trading accounts are worth more than seven billion dollars at this point. You and I are the only two people who know that," he added with a pointed look at her.

"But what if they do find it, darling? You won't go to jail, will you?"

"No. And now I wish I'd never brought it up. I don't want you worrying about it." He added, sounding thoughtful, "My father began moving assets offshore in the sixties. He told me I wasn't going to be a U.S. citizen all my life, and this is exactly what he predicted. He said the federal government was going to get so bloated and corrupt it was going to start cannibalizing the most successful. I thought he was—crazy isn't the word, but alarmist. How can they be this stupid? I pay hundreds of millions of dollars in federal taxes, and I could so easily move elsewhere and the U.S. gets nothing. If I were forty, with what I know now, I'd be gone by the end of the year. And they know that, so we're dealing. But what I wanted you to see is that Tax feels the way Public Relations does. We've got to establish and maintain a public profile." He sighed and added, "So they want us to do the *Strange Dogs* interview for *Forbes* after all. That list of the most influential books of the eighties? Apparently now it's coming out this December. Accounting thinks we've created more like ten million jobs worldwide since the sixties, so they're trying to prove that and do a press release. They think the feds will back off if I'm seen as likable and not reclusive. It's ridiculous. I'm thinking now about just turning the whole mess into Benjamins and papering the house with it."

Liz faked a little smile while she swallowed and tried to un-knot her stomach.

"How can I help, darling?"

"Put your suits back on. Time to earn your keep."

———◆———

Cathy went into labor during Milly's first birthday party. They had their midday dessert in the informal sitting room, where Milly could blow out the candle on her cake set at her height on the coffee table and toddle around babbling while the cake was shared. She was the sort of year-old baby who couldn't be made to sit without screaming; she had to be on her feet all the time. Laughing at her antics made one loving family of all of them, including Ted and Linda, and even including Dennis and Sissy and Bobby and his new girlfriend, Lara. Linda was sitting beside Cathy, who was vastly pregnant. They were whispering together.

Liz and Cathy had not become close. Cathy seemed to Liz to be too soft and tentative, perhaps overplaying the stereotypes of her gender, and occasionally trying too hard to be cute. A woman can detect that in another woman, although apparently men are oblivious to it. And Cathy seemed to revel in the trappings of wealth, while Liz had always hated Jack's wealth as her rival for his very soul. Cathy would invite friends over, enjoying the fact that they had to be cleared by security beforehand, and she would show them the wonders of this house as if they were her own. Cathy had appropriated Jack's previous limousine as her personal car, so now she had Clark as her personal chauffeur. The car was eight years old, true, but it had been so little used that it was effectively new. And meanwhile, Rex had a new blue Honda Acura that he was practicing driving around the staff parking lot with Dennis, clowning and faking imminent crashes while security staff guarded the perimeter.

The plain fact was that Liz thought Cathy wasn't good enough for Rex. Each time she saw Cathy manipulate him into doing something she wanted, Liz could work herself into paroxysms of impotent outrage made worse by the fact that she couldn't talk about it, and there was nothing she could do about it. To be frank, his marriage was none of her business. To be perfectly frank, she knew that no woman alive could be good enough for Rex. To be even more frank than she was willing to allow herself to be most of the time, Rex's marriage had been all Liz's doing, and Cathy really wasn't the best-choice wife for him. She was a moth, and he was a tiger. Well, true, Liz had originally seen her own relationship with Jack that way, but she had struggled mightily to be his equal. Cathy, on the other hand, seemed to see Rex as just part of a kind of wealth-set that she had magically fallen into and now owned by right. Liz had engineered this marriage, and now Rex was stuck with Cathy for life because he never would divorce her, nor would he even cheat on her. So all Liz could hope at this point was that Cathy would be able to make him happy.

Cathy wasn't going to do a fully Atlantican birth this time. The walking and the birthing stool were fine, and she would try to do it again without drugs, but she was not again going to wear Atlantican clothing that she thought was smelly and unclean, and she certainly was not willing to give birth ever again in front of spectators. Liz could see now that Cathy seemed uncomfortable. She caught Linda's eye, and Linda nodded. So then Liz went out to let Carlson know that it was time to call the doctor and arrange for the precautionary ambulance. When she came back, Rex was hunched on his heels beside his wife's loveseat, murmuring to her. Linda had her arm around Cathy's shoulders.

The best part of the deal that Liz had made in choosing Cathy for Rex was that now he had Linda in his life. Linda was in every way the opposite of Ted, calm and strong and dignified and beautiful. Rex had early on explained to Liz that Linda had a lovely mind-feel, almost on a par with someone from his home-place, and by now the two seemed to share an easy closeness. Linda had come from wealth and she was socially graceful, so Liz was especially glad that now Rex had someone in his life who could guide him in a world in which Liz was sure that she would always feel clueless.

Soon the family dispersed for what Liz assumed would be a long while. Bobby and Lara went back to Free the People, Dennis and Sissy went out to look for the last few damaged trees, Jack and Ted went off to what Liz assumed would be Jack's sitting room, and Rex and Linda went to the infirmary with Cathy. So Liz and her little buddy, Milly, wandered around the first floor until the baby would be cranky enough to nap.

Liz found a satisfying symmetry in leading baby Milly into the drawing room and showing her the original Milly's vermeil clocks and Faberge eggs. Liz would carry her to the doorway because none of the distances in this house accommodated toddler-sized steps, and Milly would know where she was going and squirm to get down before they arrived at the double doors from the hallway into the drawing room. Liz would set her down. Milly would toddle in happily, babbling, and head right for the fireplace. All the clocks and eggs were above her reach, but Liz would choose one and help Milly up onto the beautiful Louis XIV settee, and there she would help those little hands explore the wonder of so much glitter, so much to see and touch.

Jack's therapy seemed to be helping him. Liz rigorously avoided seeing Chuck, but she was watching Jack's moods. He seemed a little happier. What Liz didn't know was whether that meant that Chuck was persuading Jack to learn to hate his mother, so she didn't know whether seeing him perhaps feeling better was good news or bad news.

Living here, Liz was developing a sense of kinship with the original Milly. They had in common the fact that, alone among all the women of the world, they had loved and been loved by the man Liz saw as the sun and moon and all the stars together. And Liz used to listen by the hour as Jack talked about his weird teenage relationship with his mother. His own attitude had consistently been that she had been wronged by her rake of a husband, and sometimes he even had seemed to feel that in retrospect he was glad to have been there for her. He never seemed to blame her. Liz had come to realize, listening to Jack, that somewhere in his latter teens he seemed to have fallen in love with Milly, no longer even seeing her as his mother, but coming to love her as a man loves a woman. The intensity of his love for Milly had seemed genuine to Liz as she listened to him talk, as at one time it had seemed genuine to him. Milly had been both his mother and his lover, his first love, and perhaps even the love of his life.

So Liz didn't know what to make of this revelation that Jack had been abused in early childhood, but she saw it as a potential trap. Jack had seemed to her to feel oddly personally responsible for his teenage affair with his mother. While knowing he should end it, he hadn't managed to end it, so it continued until Milly died when he was twenty. Jack seemed to feel some guilt for having fallen in love and kept it going, and guilt surrounding her death as well. So Liz was coming to worry now that if he managed to learn to hate Milly, inevitably he would start hating himself.

Liz was deep in writing in her sitting room when her cellphone rang at a quarter to seven that evening. The baby had been born, the whole family was in the infirmary, and Jack had thought Liz was working with Bobby. But then Bobby and Lara wandered over for dinner, and it turned out that no one had seen Liz all afternoon.

When Liz arrived at the infirmary door, she found a party underway. Jonathan James Richardson III had been cleaned up and dressed, and everyone was sharing beluga caviar on Sea Haven toast and drinking a couple of bottles of Clos du Mesnil '95. The Atlantican custom of holding each new baby in grandparental order had broken down with this second child, to the point where his new baby-nurse was holding Jonathan when Liz walked in. Linda took him into her arms when she spotted Liz and brought him to the door, smiling kindly, and Liz accepted him with care.

The baby was tightly bundled in a receiving blanket and hospital cap, and there was again that small round sleeping face that Liz had seen in the circle of her arm long ago. He looked like his father. Like his father's father. Then Jack was there, and she was looking up at him with the baby between them. She felt overwhelmed by so much unexpected joy that she was grinning and brimming tears. As he always did, Jack knew what she was feeling. He helped Linda take the baby back. Then he took Liz into his arms and held her and rocked her a little and murmured to her, "Thank you, honey. For everything. For my life."

⫷ 28 ⫸

Rex hated limousines. Had he been an ordinary rich man's son, Liz would have seen his attitude as nothing more than false-egalitarian brattiness; but having lived for so long where Rex grew up, she understood that his real objection to wealth was the way it wrecked the unity of minds that he saw as essential to complete human life. His being willing to join Liz and Dennis in the silver car that morning in April and go out cheerfully for a photo op was the product of a lot of talking.

Liz had been back in harness for the past two months. Back with the stylist, the personal trainer, the people for makeup and hair and nails, the body-coaching, the talks with her publicist. Public Relations wanted badly to put Rex into harness, too, to the point where people had driven up from New York twice to meet with him. Jack joined the first of those meetings, which went badly. Liz and Bobby joined the second, which went better. Bobby explained to Rex how useful his being the face of Free the People would be; and Liz pointed out that when we lay down our life for our friends, we don't balk at riding in limousines.

In view of Free the People's expansion plans, Rex's new stylist had created a Texas look for him that featured cowboy boots with designer jeans and a yoked tweed jacket. Rex flat balked at wearing or even carrying a Stetson, however. He had never seen a hat, and he thought the whole idea of balancing something on your head was ridiculous.

Jason had long since left Larkin, and Liz didn't want to hire another kid just to carry her empty briefcase, so now Dennis was a bagman for both Rex and Liz. This morning was the first of three planned local jaunts before they headed to Texas in June. They would be touring the Holyoke Free the People facility under construction, which none of them had yet seen. Bobby had let them know that now he thought they might need fifty acres per location instead of the thirty they had thought would be enough because the parking lots in Holyoke looked cramped, and he thought the scale of the stores felt tight. These matters of size had been worked out with consultants when this demo facility was designed, but now Bobby was reconsidering. So a stated reason for their visit today was to let Rex and Liz check the feel for themselves.

Rex was gazing out the car's window, not talking. Dennis wasn't talking, either, and Liz thought he looked flushed and uncomfortable where he sat on the right-side jump seat. Jack had his cars built with rear-facing jump seats for ease of holding meetings, but the sight of people riding backward that way made Liz feel vaguely nauseous. Come to think of it, now Dennis looked as if he might be carsick. But he also looked gorgeous. Dennis and Sissy had had a running battle about his hair, which he thought should be shorter but she liked longer and she wouldn't let anybody else but her cut it, so for as long as Liz had known him, Dennis's hair had been a mess. Now he had a professional cut, small sideburns, a little beard-shadow, and a custom-tailored suit. With his black hair and olive skin and fine Italian features, he looked like a heart-throb movie star. Liz said to encourage him, "You look great, Dennis."

"Don't talk to him," Rex said under his breath. "He's nervous. I'm holding him."

Liz looked from face to face quickly. She couldn't see or feel anything. She murmured to Rex, "Do you have that much of it left, sweetie?"

"Yes. Talk later."

For reasons that Liz couldn't fathom, there were seven or eight photographers taking pictures of the car as it arrived. Her impulse always was to be amazed that anyone would want a picture of her badly enough to show up. The bodyguards and security people had preceded them unobtrusively, so Peters was able to drive up at once to what was going to be the facility's front door. Liz stood out first, smiling and looking around at a messier and less finished construction site than she had been anticipating. The gigantic pentagon building was framed and boarded, but the interior walls were still open. There was electrical and plumbing work going on.

Liz wore a black Armani pantsuit, so she and Rex and Dennis were in different but harmonious styles, she thought. Rex's hair had been styled longer in accordance with his Texas look, and it was curling and wind-mussed. He had his arm around Dennis's shoulders now, animatedly talking with him as they came back across the big central area where the go-cart track was going to be. The light was right, and three photographers were rushing in to get a shot of Rex. Liz could see that wasn't bothering him, which made her think he might be a natural at this. As they reached Liz, Rex said cheerfully, "I don't know what Bobby's talking about with the size thing. It looks enormous, don't you think? But it's his vision. What's the harm in making the stores bigger?"

"That makes the go-cart track bigger, too! This is cool, Mrs. R.!"

When they were inside the unfinished building and probably out of earshot, Liz said to Dennis, "Are you feeling better now?"

"Yeah. Sorry. They've been teaching me to be a bodyguard, you know? And I was just realizing there's two of you but one of me. But nobody hardly ever attacks you?"

"That's what was bothering you?"

272

"Can't let anything happen to you, Mrs. R.! And my buddy Rex, here. Who do I save first?"

———— • ————

Jack had an email social life with several billionaire friends with whom he could share extreme-wealth shop-talk. In December, one of them had chanced to send a blast email offering his new Gulfstream G550 for sale. Jack's international presidents had been asking him to buy a long-range corporate jet, and now Free the People was moving to Texas, so Jack had done some research and made the deal.

Liz had flown nine round trips as she finished Jack's lube-shop deals, always in commercial first class with Jason beside her and two bodyguards a row or two behind. She had gotten used to flying, and she even had enjoyed those trips; she never had thought she was afraid to fly. But now she and the boys were in a narrow cylinder roaring down a runway and into the sky, and it occurred to her that she might be a bit phobic.

Rex had his nose pressed to the window beside him. He called, "Look, Liz, we're not going up. The ground is falling down!"

"I'll pass. Thanks, baby."

"Looking down feels seasick. How can you do it, dude?"

"Of all the hrastinit things these people do, this is the most fun!" Then Rex looked at Dennis and said, "You're feeling really bad. Are you okay?"

"I think I'm getting morning sickness. That's a negative of this mind-thing. I pick up whatever Sis is feeling."

They were behind Liz, but her seat was made to swivel. She turned it part way and locked it as she said to Dennis, "You know, that might be the cutest thing I've ever heard. Are you going to get labor pains, too?"

"He will. I did. Not as bad as the women get them, though."

"Thanks. That cheers me up a lot." Then Dennis added, talking to Rex, "Been meaning to tell you, we drove up to see Clarence. I told him you want to hire him but your dad would have to check him out. He said don't bother. Too bad. You're right about the good feel of his mind."

"Who's Clarence?" Liz asked mildly.

"He's the guy who taught Rex to paint that day we didn't have security. Rex wants to hire him to paint our apartments. He's got a nice mind-feel so we can experiment with him, but he's got an arrest record. And I guess that whole experience with us and the way the police showed up kind of traumatized him."

"Keep his address. When we move out, we'll hire him."

"Sweetie, what?" Liz sputtered.

But they had their own apartments. Weren't they all set?

"No worries, Mrs. R." Dennis gave Rex a pointed glance.

"I'm getting nothing done living in that house!" Rex said grimly to Liz. "You said it before we even left home, remember? We've got to fix the bigger world so it won't swamp our little world. I can see that now. You were right. So, why am I wasting my time with Free the People? Let Bobby have it. Let me do what I was born to do. I tried saying that to Jack. I just upset him. You tell him!"

"But, why do you have to move out?" Liz was surprised to hear a tremor in her voice.

"We've got to figure out a way to help people everywhere develop their minds. Our home won't be safe until we do that, and you know it! One world. One sielrah. Everyone's a part of it. We've got to experiment on a really big scale. And with people like Clarence. Real people!"

All Liz could think was, *Don't do this to your dad. Let him have his peace.* And she could see from Rex's face that he was picking up enough of her emotions to pretty much read that thought.

"You've lived where human life works. How can this not matter to you?" Then he sputtered, "I'm your son! My happiness should be at least as important to you as his!"

Liz almost blurted, "You're my son, sure, but he's the husband of my soul." But she realized now might not be a good time to say that.

Dennis said hurriedly, "Don't worry, Mrs. R. We're just talking."

———•———

It was a great day when Rex passed his driving test. He had taken lessons only from Dennis as they horsed around in the staff parking lot, but Rex was so enraptured with driving that whatever Dennis had taught him had been enough. When he bought his Acura, Rex also bought an Accord to carry his inevitable bodyguards. Rex and Dennis chose four more body-guards whose mind-energies they thought they could stand, so there always would be two on duty whenever they wanted to hit the road. By early July, there was a caravan of two normal cars going out the front gates of Sea Haven many afternoons as Rex continued his explorations.

Rex had come to think that a lot of what was interfering with the development of people's minds here might be all the electrical, television, cellphone and other physical energies that this lifestyle seemed to require. As his mind-room was taking shape at the top of the third-floor staircase, Rex tried to find someone who knew how to shield the room from physical energies. Eventually a contractor remarked that they might line the room with metal mesh and ground it, making it into a Faraday Cage. With no other options, Rex directed that his mind-room be constructed as a Faraday Cage. It turned out to be surprisingly large, something like fifteen by twenty feet, and it was lined with copper mesh and sound-deadening padding and covered with carpeting on every surface. They furnished it with piles of big round cushions. Liz took to calling it the "big kids' playpen."

For Rex, though, it was serious business. Adding Sissy had strength-ened their mind-connection, which helped to confirm Rex's hunch that the number of minds together was important. Still, they seemed to be working too hard at it. Where Rex had come from, that sielrah connection with other people had been a constant, whether waking or sleeping. Here, though, Rex was feeling a real connection with the others only when at least some part of his conscious mind was attuned to enforcing it. Dennis had the same problem, but Sissy seemed to be in it naturally. She had told Rex she was psychic, so he had looked up the dictionary definition of the word. It was related to mind-power, true, but Rex could see one crucial difference: while psychic powers like Sissy's seemed to be individual and under human control, the power of the sielrah was instead something like an aggregate of human minds. No person could control it. Indeed, its strength was greatest when everyone yielded to it.

Thinking about that difference made Rex decide to teach his friends the power of yielding. Where Rex had grown up, to submit to the sielrah had been a source of daily miracles. When there was a crisis, when someone needed healing, whenever anything important went wrong, people would sit cross-legged on the ground and surrender with their minds, going deep into what felt like an intensely pleasurable void. It seemed to work best if they formed a circle, but whenever someone was suddenly hurt, people would drop and yield right where they were.

The power of Atlantican yielding didn't always bring about a miracle. People had come to understand that what it did was to better ensure an outcome that was in accordance with the sielrah; and, surprisingly often, that was a miracle. Jack's first heart attack had happened on Atlantica when he was only thirty-eight. So much was he loved that half the island had felt his crisis as it was happening and gone into the void in an instant, and from his childhood Rex had heard his mother say that his father could not have survived otherwise.

One morning in the season of flowering fields, Rex and Dennis and Sissy sat cross-legged in the bluish light from the mind-room's mesh-screened windows. They were wearing Atlantican woolens and beginning what had become their early-morning ritual, relaxed, eyes closed, encouraging and enjoying the flow of mind-energy among them. Once they had it well established, they could maintain it while Rex experimented with distance, with electronic interference, with introducing other minds to the mix. Rex opened his eyes and looked at those two deeply peaceful faces. He said quietly, "I want to teach you about the greatest power there is. Stay in it. Just listen."

He paused then, thinking. No one in Rex's home-place talked about gods except as the beloved relics of old superstitions. People there understood that mind-energy is the only reality, but Rex had learned that Americans found comfort in seeing mind-energy as a being separate from themselves. To talk with Americans about spiritual matters, you had to talk in terms of God. Even the Teacher spoke in terms of God to people who were not developed enough to understand the Teacher's words when he said that the kingdom of God was within them. Rex was trying now to think quickly how he might make these truths seem sensible to Americans.

He said, "What your people call God is the only power, and it loves us infinitely. Our problem is that we think we know what's good for us. We don't. God does. And when we wish for an outcome, we set the power of our individual minds against the power of God, or what my people call the sielrah, the unity of all minds. So to wish, to pray, to hope for some outcome is to say to the infinite and only power that we, with our little understanding, know better. We don't. So when something goes wrong, when someone is hurt, our first instinct must be not to fight, but to yield. We get ourselves out of the way. To do this isn't easy. It's hard. When your own child is hurt, every instinct you have is to heal that child if it costs your life. But you can't heal your child. So, what do you do? You yield. You get out of the way of the only perfect power.

"Our word for how to work with the sielrah would translate as something like 'dynamic yielding'. You feel your mind becoming loose. It becomes like an unraveling garment. You slip below awareness and into what my people call the void, into a pleasure like nothing else I've experienced. You can stay there forever, until eventually of course your body has needs and that pulls you out of it. The whole key to doing this is not trying! It's holding in your mind the certainty that God's will is perfect, and the only impediment to God's will is you. It's that intensely-felt need to yield that makes yielding possible."

So, now what? In Rex's home-place they would say to the children something like what he had just said, talking not in terms of God, but instead in terms of the intense mind-energy grid that even little children there could feel and could access. Then they would teach the children to play mental games to help them learn how to yield. One of the first children's games had been what Rex and his friends had called the stepping-backward game.

"Here is an exercise children do in my home-place. Imagine that someone you love is hurt. Know what the hurt is. You're desperate to help, but there's nothing you can do. So, as upset as you are, you step back. Then another step. Back away in your mind, while still knowing that your loved one is suffering. If you can imagine it intensely enough, when you've stepped back far enough you'll see a beautiful being appear and bend over your loved one and heal him. Don't try to imagine the angel. Just imagine the suffering, and the angel appears. Although some of my friends never saw the angel, they still learned to do dynamic yielding. I think it's the stepping-back and not the reward of seeing the angel that's important. Just concentrate on knowing there is nothing you can do, so you get as far out of God's way as you can."

⊰ **29** ⊱

Meeting Rex Richardson

New York—*One of the world's most elusive figures has long been Jack Richardson, an investor and financier whose net worth is estimated by* Forbes *to be about $20 billion. After achieving celebrity status in the sixties and seventies, Richardson spent the eighties and nineties declining all interview requests. Then in 2002, his office announced that he had long been secretly married, his marriage had produced a son, and his family had been living on a remote island in order to give that son a normal childhood. Now back in civilization, Jack's son, Rex, 26, is being groomed to take over a worldwide financial empire that includes real estate, closely-held businesses, and considerable cash, but little in the way of publicly-traded securities and no eponymous businesses or buildings.*

In person, Rex looks like a mid-twenties version of his father. He seems naturally at ease and almost aggressively friendly. In conversation, he reveals the extent to which he grew up without an awareness of his family's position and his own future role. But after almost three years in civilization, this man who insists that he never heard of automobiles, television, or even money until he was 23 seems to have adjusted well.

While the Richardsons have steadfastly refused to reveal the location of their private island, it is generally believed to be in the South Atlantic, where a number of spent volcanoes peek above the ocean's surface. One of these mostly un-named islands has long had private naval protection. The family's press office refuses to confirm or deny whether that might be their island home.

Rex talks about his island with affection. Even now that he has found himself to be a member of one of the world's wealthiest families, he says that he would move back "in a heartbeat" to live among natives whose culture he insists is more advanced than our own. When asked how that can be possible, he claims that these natives have for hundreds of years had a stable way of living rooted in personal freedom and spiritual union which allows them to live in harmony with one another without laws, without government, without religions, and even without a recognizable social structure.

He says, "All people are connected by mind. Where I grew up, everyone knows that, and they've learned to use their combined mind-energy in powerful ways. Do you want to end wars? Do you want people to support and trust one another? You can't have that kind of human unity until people understand what they really are!"

Rex Richardson is a young man who is going to make a difference. It will be interesting to watch his progress.

———◆———

After flying to Austin and meeting with members of the Texas Economic Development Council, then closing on their fifty acres in Dripping Springs and touring parcels in Georgetown and Bastrop and Kyle, Liz felt entitled to take a break. She still was working with her trainer and eating what Jack referred to as her "fighting weight diet," but it was summertime. She had the joy of two grandchildren. Rex had his driver's license, so he and Dennis were playing most afternoons. The only member of their little family still working hard was Bobby, but he didn't live in this house. For those who lived here, it was a lazy summer.

When Liz first took off her suits after Austin, planning to go back to work in September in the lead-up to the Holyoke Free the People opening, Jack and Liz resumed their habit of taking walks each afternoon. Work was underway on Jack's park. It wasn't going to be finished until next spring, which was fine, since realistically Milly wasn't old enough to ride a pony, anyway. But what with the bridle trails, the formal gardens, the stonework, the fountains, and the planting of ornamental trees, there was something new to see there every day.

So they would begin their walks by meandering down through the park, then sit for awhile and enjoy the ocean view and the salt smells and the rhythm of the surf, after which they might go as far as the west fence before they headed back up to the terrace. Or sometimes they went to see what was going on in the Free the People office. Or they visited the greenhouse. Or one day they went as far as the garage up near the helipad, where they checked out the new dark-blue limousine that had been ordered for Rex as a gift before Jack knew the sort of man he had fathered. Now that Rex had rejected it, Jack was thinking he might use it himself; but Liz thought she should be the one to use it, which gave them the chance to creatively play-argue.

By late July, Jack was losing interest in taking those daily walks. It happened gradually, so one week he excused himself on one day, and the next he might beg off on walking twice, but by the middle of August he was generally going back to his suite every day after lunch. Liz turned fifty-eight on the fourteenth of August. Jack remembered her birthday with a diamond-and-emerald bracelet dropped into her lap that morning as she tried to write about their trip to Texas. There was a lot to say about the meetings, the way Rex had liked the freer feel of the people and his astonishment at seeing longhorn cattle. But writing it down made it look more boring than it had felt when they were living it, so eventually she deleted most of what she had written.

Rex and Dennis and two of their bodyguards had set off on a road trip that morning. When Liz went to the west wing after lunch to visit with Cathy and Sissy and the children, she learned that Rex had just called Cathy from a restaurant in Worcester, Massachusetts. They had intended to make it all the way to Boston, but in view of the fact that it had begun to rain, they thought they might start back after lunch. Eventually Liz headed back toward her suite, thinking about taking a bubble bath. But Jack had been so quiet all morning, and it was her birthday, for heaven's sake! She didn't want to have to worry about him sitting there brooding all afternoon.

Since the two young families had moved to the west wing, Jack and Liz were alone on the east bedroom floor, which meant that Jack wasn't locking his suite door anymore. Liz was able to go right in. She found him sitting at his desk, working on his computer. As she emerged from his suite hallway, he looked at her over his glasses and said, "Hi, honey. Did you forget something?"

"I forgot to ask what's bothering you."

"We're not talking about it, remember?"

"This is all Shrinky Chuck? Then I hate to tell you, baby, it ain't working." She went to stand behind him and hugged him from behind and kissed the back of his head. He took off his glasses and pushed away from his desk and rocked back and accepted her into his lap. Liz was used now to the fact that his chair was strong enough to hold them both, but she still worried about its stability. It seemed okay. She sighed and settled in comfortably. She said, "I'm going to take a nap here now. You just go on about your business."

"You don't read newspapers, do you?"

"No. It's always the same news. I used to think I had to read newsmagazines or the world would come to an end, but—"

"No TV news?"

"No TV. You know that."

He kissed the bridge of her nose, what he could comfortably reach, and settled her head against his shoulder and his cheek against her head. He said, "You promised not to talk about it. You're breaking our deal."

"Have you ever tried not thinking about not thinking about an elephant?"

"I know. I'm being unreasonable. Of course you're curious."

She said, still cuddling, "I'm fifty-eight now. You'll soon turn sixty-five. Each day is so precious, darling. We don't know how many more we have, but here's one less today. Another one less tomorrow."

"That's depressing. Thanks."

"It's not depressing now. But it will be."

Liz sat up then, being careful about stability, and looked at his face. His eyes slid under his lashes, and he was looking at her. She said, "I think you're going to regret one day that you decided so young to give up on sex just because some shrink with a need to make a living gave you issues about it. There. Sorry. I had to say it." She struggled out of his lap. "I'm sorry, darling!" she called over her shoulder as she headed for the hallway. "Sorry. Enjoy your issues. Carry on."

He said, "Wait, honey." He stood up from his chair. She rushed back to hug him. He put his arms around her, then after a moment he said above her head, "If you'd been reading newspapers or watching TV news, you'd know that Chuck's having legal problems. It's been big news. I kept thinking you'd mention it."

"Doesn't surprise me. I'm sorry, though. I know he's your friend."

"He's been accused of giving patients false memories of childhood sexual abuse."

Liz drew back slowly and looked up at Jack's face as she caught the import of what he was saying. Then she pulled out of his arms. She stomped a little circle as she ranted, "I knew it! I knew it! The whole thing was a lie! She didn't start when you were little. It was all a lie!"

He was standing there looking at her.

"Your first memories were right all along! Doesn't that make you feel better, darling? She was only dumb and sad, but she wasn't awful! Now you don't have to hate her after all!"

He sat down again in his desk chair, watching Liz.

"Now you decide what your memories are. It's up to you! Life is just the story you tell yourself, anyway. So now you can make up your own story! Your mother did the best she could with an awful situation, and she made a wonderful life for her son. Why can't that be your memory now?"

He was still watching her, his face unreadable.

"I know you're getting older, darling, but you have a wife who craves your body, and today we've got a whole afternoon. You've got a happy new history now. So, go for it!" He was standing. She was backing away, smiling playfully. "I remember you said once that bad money drives out good money. Well, good sex drives out bad sex. Fancy that!" He was advancing on her. She ducked behind his sofa. "You're depressed? Endorphins are great for depression. And guess where you get endorphins? From sex! Are you seeing a pattern here?" He smiled at that, watching her closely, heading for one end of the sofa as she dodged back and forth and tried to run out from the other end. He reached and grabbed her easily. He pulled her into his arms while she play-fought him, and he kissed her with purpose. His hands were moving. Liz was astonished to find that unexpectedly she had gotten him this far.

"Sir!" Carlson was calling as he hurried down the corridor into Jack's sitting room. "Oh! I'm so sorry, sir. You need to take this phone call."

Carlson offered Jack a portable house phone. Clay, Jack's valet, was right behind him. Carlson said to Liz, "I'm sorry, madam."

"What's going on? Is something wrong?"

What Jack was saying into the phone didn't make sense. Then he said sternly, "This is Jack Richardson. Do you know the name? Then ask if someone else does." He muttered to Liz, "I'm too famous until I want to be famous." He interrupted himself to say, "Hello. I'm Jack Richardson. That boy is my son. I don't care! Get the jaws of life in there and shut down the highway. I'll pay for everything." He paused, then said, "I want him taken to Mass General. I don't care if he's dead. Get pen and paper. You've got a blank check."

Liz looked at Carlson quickly. "It's Rex? He's dead?" How could Jack be sounding so calm? He was finishing his phone conversation by sharing what Liz knew was the American phone number of his team in the Caymans.

Jack turned off the phone and handed it to Carlson, looking calm and thoughtful. He paused to write something quickly on the notepad on his desk. Then he said to Clay, "No plans for the next few days? I want you to put on civilian clothes and find Dennis's parents. Have them pack for overnight and bring them here. Use Cathy's car and driver. Tell them their son has been in a crash. Stay with them. Keep your phone on. Can you do that for me?" He said to Carlson, "I'll need the silver car in half an hour. Tell Peters we'll be overnight."

"Security, sir?"

"Six, I guess. Six."

As they hurried out, Jack looked at Liz and said, "Rex lost control of his car in the rain. He hit a tree sideways. Dennis is trapped in the car. He said 'crushed'. We'll say 'trapped'. He said 'Dead'. We'll say 'Close call'. I cannot think what Rex's life will be like if he's killed Dennis." Jack drew a long breath and said, "So he's going to Mass General. Time for a miracle."

Rex generally called Dennis "little buddy." The man was maybe five-foot-ten, three inches shorter than Liz and more than half a foot shorter than Rex. Liz and Jack thought of him as "little Dennis," Rex's shadow, the Pepper to Rex's Salt, mild and calm and sweet and always and endlessly right there with Rex, so you seldom saw one without the other. Dennis was shy around Rex's parents, but Liz had overheard him a few times talking with her son, and she had come to think that Dennis might even be the leader in their relationship, that Rex listened to him and trusted him and that little Dennis kept Rex calm and focused.

Rex needed that. He had taken up drumming on Atlantica when he was small, and with Jack's encouragement he had stuck with it, eventually becoming the leader of a team of what were said to be the best drummers in their world. Rex's closest friends had been his fellow drummers, and one of them had been much like Dennis, always mild and calm and centered and able to talk Rex down when he needed it. Rex was upset less often nowadays, but he still needed a Dennis beside him. Liz thought that Dennis knew Rex better now than anybody else really knew him, including his parents, and especially his wife. Oh my God. Liz's eyes were filling. They had taken that boy entirely for granted, but he was so much more to them now than staff.

Jack saw the look on Liz's face, and he stepped and took her into his arms. She said softly, "Is Rex okay?"

"They think he is. The tree hit Dennis's door. The cop said Rex may have a head injury because he's unconscious, but his vitals are good. I choose to believe he's fine." Jack added, "It gives you some perspective, doesn't it? Here I am, wasting another day because somebody filled my head with crap, and now all of a sudden that sweet kid who's about to be a father for the first time is dead."

"He's dead? But—?"

"The cop I was talking with said they just pronounced him dead. They need to move the car. It's a traffic hazard."

"Oh lord! How will Rex survive? And what about Sissy?"

"Just tell her he's been hurt, honey." Jack paused, then added crisply, "When I asked him how they were sure he was dead, the cop had no good answer. I told him Dennis is my son, and he'd better be alive when he gets to Mass General so get the hell busy and get him out of that car."

Liz was quietly running tears. Apparently Jack felt the way she did, that without their noticing it, little Dennis had become a central part of their family. She murmured, "I wish I realized before how much I love him." Her breath caught. "I don't think I ever said it."

Jack tipped up her chin with his finger and looked at her face and said, "You've got to hold it together, honey." He swiped at a tear with his thumb as he said, "You're going to have to be strong for their wives. Can you do that for me?"

Well, um, when he put it that way, then yes, she could. Liz nodded once. He stroked her head against his chest and hugged her.

"I sent Clay off, so now I've got to pack my own things. I should be doing that."

"I should be going to tell the wives."

"Tell them the boys will be okay. Don't upset them. Not yet."

"But I don't feel like going over there."

"I don't feel like packing."

Liz looked up at Jack and said, "As long as we don't move, none of it happened. Everything is fine." She added, "You're really sure Rex is okay?"

"He has to be. The alternative is unthinkable."

"Will you please keep calling, so I know what's going on?"

"Of course. I'm leaving you the new car, honey. Peters will call someone in to be ready in case you need to use it."

"Where are they taking Rex?"

"Some hospital in Worcester. I've written it down."

⪦ 30 ⪧

Liz spent the next several hours on the couch in Cathy's family room on the second floor of the west wing. From her first sight of those two wives' faces, she had understood that this was not about her, so then telling the wives had been easy since the words were so flat and the possibilities so unimaginable. "Rex lost control of his car in the rain. He's in the hospital, but they think he's fine. Dennis was hurt a little worse, so they took him to Boston. I'll take you there, sweetie, but he's in surgery now. Let's stay comfortable and go in the morning."

Liz had made up the surgery bit, but if Dennis were alive he was going to need surgery. She felt so oddly composed at this point that her calmness seemed to reassure the wives, who sat in side chairs with the children in their laps. Even Milly sensed the somber mood, so she sat in her Aunt Sissy's lap and stared at Liz with her father's beautiful wide-set eyes. When she had a play-urge, it was only to slip down and stand with her head resting against Sissy and peek-a-boo a little with Liz, not smiling, before she clambered into Sissy's lap again.

Three cellphones lay side-by-side on the coffee table. When Liz had first told them what had happened, each wife's instinct had been to call her husband's phone. Then they felt foolish about doing that. They even joked a little. Most of their conversation involved attempts to talk about something else, but then one or the other wife would ask Liz a question.

"Was Denny conscious, did they say?" Sissy wanted to know.

"Mr. R. said neither was conscious. But that's normal."

"Why are they in different hospitals?" came from Cathy.

"There was one nearby, so they took Rex there. They thought Dennis might need fancier treatment, so they took him to the best hospital there is."

Men in white jumpsuits brought them dinner trays at seven. Liz was annoyed that Jack still hadn't called, but she wasn't going to call him, and neither of the wives suggested that she call him. Cathy's phone rang. She left the room with it and soon came back, saying, "That was my mother."

Then eventually Liz's cellphone rang. It was after nine o'clock.

"Jack?"

"Dennis is alive."

"Wow! Thank God! Thank God! How's Rex?"

"They can't figure out why he's unconscious. Cat-scan and MRI were fine. They thought briefly he might have a tear in his aorta. They prepped him for surgery. What a nightmare! But they've ruled that out. He's—"

Sissy was looking fixedly at Liz's face.

"How's Dennis?"

"They won't tell me. I've got a friend on the board, and all he can tell me is they've got him in surgery. Clay is taking his parents to Boston, but Sissy is his next of kin. Take her to Boston, honey. They won't talk to anyone but her. That's the law now."

Then there was a muffled clamor behind him. Jack said, "I'll call you back," and hung up.

"Well!" Liz said brightly to those two expectant faces. "Mr. R. says they're both doing fine. He wants you and me to go to Boston, honey. We'd better do that. I'll stay right with you."

Cathy said, "I'll stay with the children. Rex has his dad."

"Good. Thank you." Liz kissed the top of Cathy's head as she passed her chair, heading for the intercom. She asked Carlson's night assistant to send up housemaids to pack bags for her and for Sissy.

Then Liz's phone rang again. When she answered it, Jack said, sounding shaky, "Rex just stood up out of a coma and headed for the bathroom, pulling tubes out of his arm. He went in, came out, told the nurse she was hrastinit and leave him alone, and then he—Do you remember what they did on Atlantica? He went down cross-legged on the floor and did the circle-trance. I'm looking at him right—Don't touch him! They're trying—Leave him alone! Got to go, honey," he said, and hung up.

Liz said, "Oh God," aloud. Then she saw the looks on the wives' faces.

"I'm sorry. Everyone's fine. It's just—sit here with me for a minute. The maids will pack our things. Sit down, sweetie. When I lived on Atlantica a long time ago, someone got knifed in the chest. They were sure he was going to die, but people sat down cross-legged in circles and went into trance. They saved his life. Then they saved Mr. R.'s life, too. That seems to be why Rex has been unconscious. He's doing the circle-trance for Dennis."

Sissy said quietly, "It's not a trance. Rex was teaching us. It doesn't save people. It gets us out of God's way."

"Then you know more than I do, sweetie!"

Sissy was looking at the ceiling, blinking. Liz realized that neither of the wives had yet cried. She started to say, "It's okay, sweetie—"

"No! Please. Mrs. R., please tell everyone who knows about this not to hope or pray for Denny. Or no, Rex said if we have to pray, it should be just to thank the Holy Spirit for doing its will in the world." She drew a long breath, in and out. She said, "God must want Denny to be okay. We just have to get out of the way and let it happen."

As Sissy was speaking, Liz's phone rang again. She said, "Hi sweetheart. How's Rex doing?"

"He's got a blanket around him. Honey, go over to my desk. There's a false bottom on the second drawer on the left. Hit it in back, and it opens. Take two checks, then put it back the way it was."

He paused, talking with someone in the room. Liz heard only, "He has a medical condition." Then Jack was back. "I've ordered a private suite for Dennis. They can do intensive care in the suite. Mass General wants a check tomorrow, and those accounts should contain at least a million dollars so don't leave checks lying around. Someone will meet you at his suite first thing tomorrow to set you up to sign. Be sure you bring your ID."

"I don't have an ID."

"Okay. My passport should be with the checks. Bring that. Whoever comes will have to call me and I'll okay you. And let's get you a passport, honey."

What with helping Cathy and the babies settle in, correcting the housemaids' packing errors, family phone calls, confusion about finding an acceptable chauffeur on a Saturday night when neither backup driver was available, and then the long drive to Boston, they didn't make it to Dennis's suite until it was nearly five o'clock in the morning. He still wasn't out of surgery. Liz was talking about trying to find a place where they could nap, but then they entered the suite to find Dennis's parents sitting tight together on a couch in the anteroom, holding all four hands. Clay sat on the edge of an armchair facing them. Liz and Sissy rushed to sit on either side of them. Clay gave Liz a helpless look.

Dennis's mother had always looked to Liz like a little old lady, even to the gray hair up in a bun. Liz had never met Dennis's dad, but he turned out to be short and plump and sporting a scanty tweed-colored crewcut. His suit was too small. His collar was so tight that against his neck it made a muffin-top. Sissy had been telling Liz in the car how cute they were, how devoted they were to their late-in-life son, and how anxious they were for their coming grandchild. Liz hugged Dennis's mom around her shoulders and whispered to her that Dennis would be fine. Just then the suite's double doors opened, and through the anteroom rolled a hospital bed being pushed by three serious-faced men wearing green scrubs. The person in the bed could have been Dennis. But he was swathed so thickly in white, with all four limbs encased in plaster and held in suspension, with his head wrapped and with tubes everywhere, that what the bed held was really anyone's guess. They all stood. Dennis's parents looked at him, looked at one another, then sat down slowly. Liz rushed to hug Sissy, who said just, "Stay with me."

Liz was saying, "Of course, sweetie," when a slight and weary-looking woman in green scrubs approached them and said, "Who's Cecilia Silvestri?"

Sissy insisted that Liz stay with her, but the doctor wanted no one else to overhear. She sat with them at a tiny table in the hallway and told them that Dennis had many broken bones. He had internal injuries and bleeding, caused primarily by the fact that he had fractured some ribs. He seemed by cat-scan to have no injury to his head and spinal column beyond a small bleed at the base of his skull that might have been caused by whiplash. She said to Sissy, "I know he looks bad right now. Are you expecting? When are you due, dear?"

"December Second."

"Congratulations. Bad timing for the kidderoo, but great for you. Your husband's not out of the woods, dear. That's a lot of trauma for one guy to take. But he's young and fit. I'm not supposed to say anything positive, but between you and me I think he'll be walking into that delivery room on his own. No guarantees, you understand. But he looks to me like one lucky guy."

As the doctor was speaking, Liz's cellphone rang. She stood and stepped away, saying, "Hi sweetheart! Dennis is going to be fine."

"Rex stood up twenty minutes ago. He's discharged himself. They tried to keep him, so now this whole country is hrastinit. We're about to head for Boston."

"No! Don't bring him here. He can't see Dennis like this. Send him home, darling. Tell him Cathy needs him."

———— • ————

Jack didn't arrive at Mass General until they were all taking seats around Dennis's bed, having just shared a cheerful luncheon in the anteroom. Dennis was groggily awake. Attendants had taken his arms off elevation and lowered his legs to make him more comfortable. They were lowering his bed so Sissy could hold his hand without having to strain, and she was talking to him. Smiling. Liz was just sitting down, enjoying watching them begin to interact, when she felt a rough tap on her shoulder. There was Jack, beckoning to her. He looked so upset as she joined him in the anteroom that she said under her breath, "I know he looks bad, but he's going to be fine!"

He muttered, "I know." He closed the doors behind Liz carefully, so as not to disturb the others. Then he said to her, sounding furious, sounding bitter, beginning to pace the room as he spoke, "I've just spent the morning talking about what happened here. They pronounced him dead, Liz. Dead! A nice kid with everything to live for, and apparently with injuries not hard to fix. He was written off because they couldn't be bothered to pry him out of the car and shut down the road for a medflight."

"But he's fine, darling!"

"I found out who the responding police were. On my way here, I stopped to thank them. The sergeant at the desk told me they had to shut down two interstates to use the jaws of life and land the medflight. And it was raining. It was a big shopping weekend. He was really crushed in there. God, don't ever see those pictures! They couldn't hear anything through a stethoscope. The wrist they could reach didn't have a pulse. And he looked dead. The fool at the desk wanted me to know that. So they pronounced him dead. They wanted to move the car so it wasn't a distraction when people started driving home from the malls."

"He's okay, darling. Please don't—!"

"So then I talked to the ER downstairs. Honey, people so badly hurt go into shock. Sometimes you can't find a pulse. One of the doctors who saw Dennis said he was no more than half an hour away from dying of shock and blood loss. He told me they seldom see them transported in that condition. Nobody bothers if they're so bad off that just the process of removal will finish them off, so they leave them in the car. If they're not dead now, they soon will be." He was pacing. Not thoughtfully. Quickly. A tiger in a zoo, in a hurry to go nowhere.

"It's okay! Please, sweetheart!"

"Liz, what is wrong with you? It's not okay! Closing two highways on a big shopping weekend? Why the hell does that even matter? Damn it, you're the one who's supposed to say a human life is more important. I'm the one who's supposed to say selling pencils matters."

"Yes, but—"

"They should have been thrilled to shut down every goddamn road in the state on the chance they might save that boy's life!"

Liz glanced at the door to Dennis's room. "Please, darling, don't upset—"

"And what if the kid in the car doesn't have someone who can sign a check? If she hadn't randomly started working for me thirty years ago, that mother wouldn't be at a bedside today. She'd be making funeral arrangements."

Liz thought of pointing out the fact that if his mother hadn't come to work for Jack, Dennis likely wouldn't have been hurt in the first place. But Jack was on a roll.

"How often does this happen? How many get caught in this calculation where other things matter more than people?"

Liz said softly, "You sound like Rex. He'd be so proud of you."

"Well, he's right. He's right. On Atlantica it's clean." Jack stopped pacing. He added, "I always thought the word 'hrastinit' meant those people out there were lazy. They couldn't be bothered to make the effort. But now I'm starting to think when we make our lives more complicated, we distract ourselves from what's important. Any culture that can make a calculation where things like selling pencils and how much trouble it is to shut down a road in the rain even factor in when we're talking about a human life is a dead culture." He looked at Liz. He said, "Do you know what the hrastinit noun-pieces mean?"

"Well, '-it' makes it plural. The 'hras- ' part is probably a contraction of two words that mean something like joy and lack. That's what I always thought. But a lot of the language doesn't directly translate." She added, "I guess I thought the way you did. They're trying to avoid complicating their lives because they are extremely into fun. But you're right. It may be deeper than that."

"God, Liz, what if they're aware but they just can't communicate? What's in the mind of someone dying in a car when the people around him think he's already dead?"

"Please, darling, stop now. Come see Dennis. Come see his mother! She was all over me, thanking me, but I didn't do anything."

"I don't want her thanking me. I don't want anything but the peace of knowing nothing like that can ever happen again."

⇥ 31 ⇤

Rex was in Boston seeing Dennis on Monday morning. There was nothing Liz could do to prevent that, and no way to smuggle herself along, so she had to rely on Sissy to help Rex deal with the shock of seeing Dennis's condition and knowing his own part in having produced it. "No worries, Mrs. R.!" Sissy said when they talked by phone on Monday afternoon. "I don't think he, like, thinks it's his fault. You know? Now he thinks he needs a stronger car. They're joking about that, but Denny can't laugh because it hurts too much."

As Liz thought about it, she realized that another peculiarity of the Atlantican mindset was that they seemed to have no concept of guilt. She couldn't recall that there even was an Atlantican word for guilt. Or words for sin or shame, for that matter. This confounded her, as she considered it. But it seemed to go back to the overriding importance they gave to their ability to work with the sielrah, for which individual autonomy was essential. It was something else that she planned to ask Rex about, once he was home again and less distracted. By now, she had a list.

Jack was in Boston for most of the week after Dennis was hurt, in touch by phone but not saying much. "It's business, honey. We'll talk when I get back." Sissy and Rex were in Boston, too, so Liz spent that week theoretically helping Cathy with the children. But Jonnie had his own baby-nurse, and Cathy liked having Milly to herself so much that she was giving Milly's nurse most afternoons off. What Liz mainly did therefore was just sit around and wait to be needed, nestled cozily in a corner of Cathy's sofa with her laptop. She was reading through and editing her magnum opus.

Was it dumb to begin this on Atlantica? The contrast of cultures was so extreme! She was adding more details about Atlantica as she went, trying to point up how different it was. From where she now sat, in a normal room in what could have been a normal house, she couldn't imagine how living on Atlantica ever would appeal to an American. But she had loved it there! Had never wanted to leave. How could she convey the daily joy of being there to a reader who could have no concept of it?

And how could she describe the man she loved? Jack was so many contrasts, deeply kind and deeply self-obsessed. Often feeling burdened by the details of his wealth, but still so dependent on knowing it had no practical limit that he had a habit of handing out blank checks for trivial reasons. His attitude toward sex had seemed unusual to Liz when they first met, although at the time she had a history of no father and one previous relationship, so she assumed that whatever she was learning about Jack was just another basic set of facts about men. He kept women as pets because he could. Made sense. Now, though, she thought it was plain strange for him to be in a loving marriage and deciding to give up sex altogether. And how was it that, after he felt overpublicized and embarrassingly famous in his thirties, he could withdraw and be almost a recluse for decades; and then, when his seclusion no longer felt practical, he could end it so easily and resume a social life? Liz thought that at the core of Jack's contradictions might be his obsessive need to avoid unpleasantness. He seemed inordinately fearful when it came to small things, but still somehow fearless in the face of big ones.

And what about his relationship with Liz? She could see now that from the moment they met, they had connected profoundly and forever. How often does that happen to people? In retrospect, their improbably falling in love had seemed to Jack to be an adventure. He was thirty-six, and amused to find himself in love for the first time in his life. For Liz, though, falling in love with Jack Richardson had felt like a frightening loss of control. For a long time she had fought hard against it. In some ways she was still fighting it. Their personalities meshed so perfectly that perhaps she could explain their love at first sight, but how could she describe these feelings?

By Friday, Liz had rewritten about half of whatever this thing was. What had been fun on Tuesday and felt serious on Wednesday was feeling by Friday like a long-term sentence. Who was ever going to read this, anyway? Cathy decided to nap with Milly because Rex was on his way home at last, and she wanted to be fresh for him. So then Liz went back to her own suite, dismissed Dolly an hour early so she could go home to her boys, and drew her own bubble bath. She hadn't heard from Jack all day.

There was an enormous half-sunken tub in the center of Liz's gold-and-crystal bathroom. Soon after moving in, she had conceived a habit of taking a bubble bath late most afternoons so she could feel relaxed and refreshed at dinner. She was dozing a little in the tub when she lazily opened her eyes and saw Jack standing in her bathroom doorway. He was leaning on the doorjamb, his head canted a little, looking amused. But the way he was dressed amazed her! He looked like Bobby, in jeans and a white dress shirt open at the neck and a cowboy belt with a fancy buckle. Where the heck had he been? She was pretty good at reading his face, and she could see that he had come home full of himself. She stirred and said, "Hi darling! Were you selling something or buying something? How come you ditched your suit?"

"I think this is the new me. I'm trying it out."

She said, "Oh lord," and stood out of the bubbles and grabbed the long terry-cloth robe she would have put on after showering. She went to him and stood on tiptoe and tried to put her arms around his neck and kiss him. He seemed to be inches taller.

"What—?"

"Cowboy boots."

"Sweetie, you don't need cowboy boots!"

He was following her through her bedroom and into her sitting room, saying, "Bobby brought them to me yesterday. He told Perry's office I still wasn't sold, so they sent up both the boots and this belt. Look at the buckle! A bucking horse? Did you ever think I'd wear something like this? The three of us went bar-hopping last night. Bobby told people we were Texans in town to buy the Red Sox. Didn't sit well at all!"

Liz was dropping curled onto her sofa. She simultaneously laughed and gasped, "You? Bar-hopping?"

He was standing there, giving her his amused-at-little-Lizzie look.

"You couldn't have been there, but I wish you'd been there. I've spent the week getting to know our son." He went and dropped onto the other end of the sofa and pulled off his boots with difficulty as he added, "They're a little small. And you're right, I don't need another inch. But being a Texan in Boston, and especially not being me, was amazingly freeing. You don't realize how the burden of being yourself every minute starts to weigh on you."

"Nobody recognized you?"

"I'm not as famous as I used to be. And drinking beer in public wearing jeans and this belt is something the old me never would have done." He laid his arm along the sofa back. He turned a little to face Liz comfortably, and one foot came up to rest on the opposite knee. He had returned with an air of cheery omnipotence, so far above having vanquished whatever had been on the table to be vanquished that he had no need even to gloat about it.

"Rex has such an amazing mind! He sees everything from an angle you didn't know was there. You point out this boulder in your brain. He flits in and lands on it like a butterfly, and it's gone. I've been carrying such enormous guilt about the fact that when he started standing up to me, I abandoned him there. It was about you and me primarily. I wasn't going to make you leave. But it was also the fact he was so precious to me, but he was such a handful! I didn't know how to deal with him, and I had one shot. So I let you deal with him. By Wednesday, I was able to tell him how sorry I was about having abandoned him. And he told me letting him grow up there was the best thing I could have done for him. How wise I was to give him that freedom. How hard he knew it must have been for me, now that he's got children of his own. He sees the worst thing I've ever done in my life as a big gift to him!"

"And it was," Liz said softly.

"We talked about money, too. I've been good at making money, but now it's at the point where what Jude used to call the money-machine runs better if I have nothing to do with it. I didn't feel guilty about being so rich when I was working. But now I see what *Forbes* thinks I'm worth each year, and I know there's more that they can't see, and I'm starting to take a little-Lizzie view of it. Or maybe now it's more a Rex view. It's ridiculous! It makes me different. And not in a good way. So I say that to Rex. And he says, 'Since you see it that way now, it's not a difference anymore. Now it's more like a talent. Everyone's got something to contribute. That's what you've got.' Poof! Butterfly lands. Gone."

Liz was smiling, mostly to herself.

"So then he asked me what single thing I most wished I could fix for other people. I had this nightmare of what almost happened to Dennis on my mind, so I told him about that. He said, 'Find people who've had someone they loved die that way, and now they'll never know if they could have been saved. Don't let them try to blame other people. Instead, get them to figure out how to use your money to fix it forever.' Okay! Done. I've already got people on it."

"How's Dennis?"

"They say he's getting better. Sissy's with him constantly. But he couldn't take all of us for more than a few minutes at a time, so Rex and I had time to talk. We started with trivialities. By Thursday he was rummaging deep in my soul and finding good things. Where did all that come from?" Jack added, "I haven't taken one business call from Tuesday morning on. I assume the money-machine survived."

Liz glanced at the little clock on her desk and noticed that it was after six. She stood, saying, "Nearly time for dinner. I'll get dressed."

"They're sending it up to us."

"I've lived in this house for almost three years. It's like camp, or maybe prison. You show up for meals!"

"I've been doing room service for the past four days."

"Oh. Well, that'll be a nice change. I'll get dressed, anyway. When is it coming?"

"Don't get dressed."

She turned and looked at him. He patted the cushion beside him. She went back and sat down, close to him now. He was feeling so full of being Jack, with that same air of mastery about him that he would have when he returned from a penthouse closing. She sometimes had the sense when he was feeling this way that his face was giving off too much light for her to look at him directly.

"We went back to talking about me after Bobby left this morning. I told Rex how I paid that fool shrink at least a million dollars, and all he did was rearrange things in my head. Pull stuff out of corners and drawers and make a mess, and make me think he was bringing order to the mess. What Rex seems able to do is make the mess disappear without pulling it out first. How does he do that? He said the core problem is Americans live in our heads. We believe life is about thinking. But it isn't. Life is feeling. It's spiritual. The head-stuff blocks the spiritual stuff, and that's why our culture is so dead. His word. How's that for a whole new perspective?"

"That's my boy," Liz murmured. She was feeling so titillated by the fact that Jack had asked her to sit close to him in just a robe that she was squirming a little. She shuddered through her shoulders to try to get rid of that.

"At lunch he asked me whether I had any more messes he could make go away for me. Of course, the biggest pile of mess I had was something I'd never mentioned."

"You told him?" Liz met Jack's eyes.

"Honey, by then there was nothing I couldn't tell him."

"What did he say?" Liz was looking away now.

"He said it's tragic we think of sex as something related to our bodies. He said sex is spiritual. Spiritual! If we'd started with that on Tuesday, I would have thought he was off the wall."

Liz met Jack's eyes again. She said softly, "Did he help you?"

"I don't know. He gave me a new way of thinking about it, though. He talked about it in terms of the sielrah and the unity of all things and how marital sex is integral to that. Who knew?"

"Did you tell him about Milly?"

"I started with Milly. It was odd, you know, he had a sister named Milly and now he has a daughter named Milly, and it's only now he's finding out the original Milly had an affair with her son? But that didn't seem to faze him. He said if people had a spiritual connection with one another here, that kind of thing could never happen. He said being connected to spirit is the ultimate pleasure. People here don't have it, so we go after physical pleasures as a substitute.

"We talked about it all the way home. You're always saying I've got to forgive her? He thinks I've forgiven both my parents. He said the problem is I can't forgive myself. I loved them both, honey. I admired my father more than I can tell you. And the three of us were living this awful triangle! Rex said, 'You keep telling me how bad you feel about it, but you never put any blame on them. Don't you find that odd? Dad, I think you took whatever fault was in it on yourself so you could see them as innocent. So now you've just got to forgive yourself!' He calls me 'Dad' now, apparently."

"Did he tell you how to fix it?"

"I didn't ask him how to fix it. He was on to talking about Atlantica, anyway. He said they try to keep the kids from knowing anything about sex. Then when they get married, their Solagh—that little old lady with no teeth—she tells them being married makes it possible for them to connect with their people more deeply, so go for it. That's the sum total of their sex education. Since they're so young, you'd think they'd be randy, but he said the urge there feels more like an urge to connect with your wife as deeply as you can. By the time they get around to what we call sex, they're so connected on a spiritual level that he said the spiritual part of orgasm is extraordinary. The physical part is just nice."

Two men in white knocked, then entered with trays of covered dishes and set them on the little table where Liz generally stacked and sorted things. They began to remove the covers, but Jack thanked and dismissed them. As he and Liz were uncovering and removing plates and bowls so they could put the trays aside, he said, "I didn't ask him for advice, but he gave me some. I don't know how much I want to take, but I'm thinking about it. Let's try it. Tonight we get naked and read the Teacher on forgiveness." He glanced at Liz and added, "The getting-naked part was my idea."

Dennis came home two days after Labor Day, nearly three weeks after he was injured. He was stable and out of danger now, so all he needed was a lot of tending while his body mended. Mass General had wanted to discharge him to an affiliated care facility, but that idea didn't sit well with Jack. He wanted Dennis's parents to be able to visit him easily, he wanted pregnant Sissy close to home, and he wanted Rex to stop his frequent highway trips in his brand-new Hummer. So the conference room in the west wing was converted to a hospital room staffed by private-duty nurses. With the home gym next door, they were set for Dennis to transition into rehab when the time came.

Rex understood that his father's third reason for wanting Dennis here was his big one. To be frank, seeing how injured it was possible for someone to become while riding in a car, Rex's enthusiasm for driving was not what it had been. Liz phoned him at the Free the People office as the ambulance came through the gates, so he and Bobby went out to join Jack and Liz and watch it come down the driveway.

Whenever Rex was with his father now, he would be trying to decide whether perhaps their conversations in Boston might have helped him. Jack's mind had always seemed to Rex, despite its expansive, gentle feel, to be weighed down, somehow. Softly sad. So, was he happier? At least Jack seemed to be happier with Liz. While once he would have stood just holding her hand, now today he was drawing her to stand in front of him and holding her with his arms around her and kissing her hair.

Sissy was out of the ambulance as soon as the back doors opened, moving carefully and with two EMT's supporting her because she was visibly pregnant. Then out came the stretcher, with Dennis propped to half-sitting and looking around. Jack and Liz were approaching him, but Rex knew how Jack could overwhelm his friend, so he sidled in and touched his father's arm so he would step back. Then Rex began to walk beside the stretcher. Sissy was on Dennis's other side. They each had a hand on an arm-cast, holding Dennis's attention as he was wheeled through the front door and down the west hallway. Sissy was saying to him chattily, "Milly's talking more now! We're teaching her the alphabet. At a year and a half! She messes it up, but she says it so cute. I'm glad we're having a girl, aren't you?"

Rex hadn't known that their baby was a girl. It never would have occurred to him before coming here that anyone would care about a baby's gender. He said to Dennis as they entered the former conference room, "This is all set up for you, little bud. Look! Do you want to be right at the window? Do you like the view? Or too much light?"

The ambulance attendants were about to move Dennis to his hospital bed, but now Rex wasn't sure about the setup.

With his head free of bandages and with his color back, Dennis looked more like himself. He glanced up at Rex, then out the window, then at Sissy, and said, "I'm putting your family to so much trouble. Sorry, dude. You're sure your dad doesn't mind?"

"This is all his idea. Over here or over there?"

Hospital-grade connections showed that Dennis's bed was meant to be placed with its head against the west wall, and Dennis told Rex that gave him enough of a view. It left room toward the window wall for a couch and chairs, and room toward the door for a dining table, and plenty of space for the enormous TV that had been installed on the eastern wall of the room. Rex was showing Dennis which button would summon a nurse, which would summon service staff, and which were the controls for his TV. Dennis looked solemn now.

Sissy said, "Are you okay, baby? Does something hurt?"

Dennis said with a sidelong smirk at Rex, "I'm going to get used to living like this. Hey, bud? When I need it, would you mind doing that tree-trick again for me?"

⪦ 32 ⪧

During the summer months Free the People grew to occupy the whole office building. All the art from upstairs was back in the house. The office furniture was gone as well, and replaced by conference rooms with whiteboards and audiovisual equipment and collapsible tables with collapsible chairs. The open lower level was thick with groups of people working, some very young and sporting backpacks and others as old as late thirties, with laptop bags and leather folders. The effect from Liz's perspective was one of intensely focused chaos.

One afternoon late in September the president of Larkin International was meeting with the president and the chairman of the board of Free the People in one of the smaller conference rooms upstairs to review the Holyoke punch list, to approve some last-minute advertising changes, and to begin to discuss what Bobby saw as a fairly radical change in direction.

"We can go ahead with our original plan and build out the country on our own dime," he was telling Liz and Rex as he stood with his left cowboy boot on a chair, his left forearm on his thigh for balance, and his right hand quickly sorting through a pile of papers on the table. "Can't find it now. There's one particular email. This pretty reasonably capitalized investor bought our seven HappyLubes in New Jersey, but that's not enough for him. He's been up to see the Holyoke demo, and he loves the Free the People idea. He wants to know why we can't franchise that, too."

"What does that do for us?" Liz asked.

"For one thing, franchising would put other people's funds at risk next to ours. Putting so much of one guy's money into an idea that has not, frankly, ever been tried seems too risky to me. What may be just as important, though, is that offering franchise opportunities will get you a million worker-bees scurrying around to find suitable sites in every state. We're seeing in Texas what a job it is to vet sites when our people are the only boots on the ground—" He glanced at his foot and raised it for admiration as he added, "—Even if they're nice boots. Back of the envelope, if we do it right, we could be open in every state in as little as five to seven years if we franchise, versus maybe fifteen for doing it all ourselves. That lets us make the most of national advertising. It lets us better own the concept, too. If we build out slowly and it's working well, we're going to get copycats."

Liz said, "Why not do it, then? Looks like a no-brainer."

"Larkin's never done franchising. Mr. Control-Man wants to own it all. If Levigard hadn't fallen into having to do HappyWash and HappyLube, I don't think I'd be so eager to suggest franchising, but we've got some in-house expertise now. I think from my perspective—"

At that moment Jack walked in. Realizing a meeting was going on, he took a quick step backward.

"Sorry! I was looking for Liz. Sorry, honey—"

"Please join us, sir! Good timing."

Whenever he was talking business with Jack, Bobby always called him "sir." Otherwise, he seemed to call him whatever first came to mind.

"Sit down. Do you have time, sir?"

Jack sat down next to Liz and covertly took her hand beneath the tabletop. But with him added, the room felt too small.

"Sir, we're thinking about making some adjustments to the Free the

People business plan. How would you like to reduce your own outlay, reduce your risk, and get a better return on your investment?"

"I'm open."

"Done! Now, how can we help you?"

Jack tossed onto the table in front of Liz what looked like a faxed copy of a newspaper article featuring a picture of palm trees. He said to Rex, "I'm sorry, son. More fall-out from the *Forbes* profile."

It seemed to Liz that in recent weeks Larkin's tax team had taken over their lives. They were in negotiations with the IRS, apparently confident, but still warning Jack that there wouldn't be much sympathy for a rich guy if this thing blew up. Jack wasn't telling Liz what was going on, but he had spent some recent afternoons working in his sitting room and suggested that she not be there. At the tax team's insistence, Jack and Liz had been interviewed for the December issue of *Forbes* that was going to name *Strange Dogs and Their Masters* one of the "Ten Books That Made the Eighties the Eighties." When he had come to Sea Haven to interview Liz and Jack, the *Forbes* reporter also had done a quick interview of Rex for the August issue. The idea had been to build upon the family's good publicity over the past two years and further humanize them in the public eye. But the law of unintended consequences had been in full operation with Rex's interview, and had given the family a brand-new worry.

Rex said, sounding tense, "What is it now?"

Liz said, reading, "Ugh. Someone's saying it's illegal to claim islands in the open ocean. They're going to the U.N."

Jack said quickly, "We're preparing a case for the World Court. We've increased the level of offshore security. I'll spend whatever it takes, son. Don't worry about it."

"I've had six invitations to speak, believe it or not. Speak? Make people listen to me? I said I'm going to the family reunion so I can't do the one on Memorial Day weekend, but the others—"

"No! Tell them to stop forwarding that stuff. Or I will. The last thing we need is more controversy!"

Bobby said to Jack, "My father's on my back, bro. If you say yes to the family reunion early enough, he can dangle you in front of people."

"Wow, that sounds appealing."

"We've been talking for years about doing a Saturday banquet at Monticello. I told him Free the People would half-sponsor it, so now he's made the reservation." Bobby was still trying to find that one email among his papers. He looked at Jack and added, "You didn't know you trace to Thomas Jefferson twice, did you?"

"Jefferson? No. She never told me anything."

"We like to joke that's why we've got so much red hair and height in the family. Here it is. Read this email, Rex."

Jack and Liz continued to take most meals in the formal dining room, but the rest of the family dined with Dennis. Liz soon began to try to make it to Dennis's room in time for dessert, so then Jack was generally skipping dessert and sending her off to be with the family while he headed upstairs early. He was on a mission, although exactly what his mission was, Liz couldn't tell in much detail. One evening late in September Liz made her usual family visit for dessert, then kissed cheeks and snuggled children goodnight and went upstairs to her sitting room. As had been true every evening since Rex had counseled his father in mid-August, Liz found Jack sitting on her sofa with his feet on her coffee table and his glasses halfway down his nose, reading the Bible. She walked in and flopped into one of her side chairs, looking at him until he looked at her. She said, "Darling, you know, I love how much time we're spending together now, but, um, didn't you used to have your own couch in your own suite?"

He looked at her over his glasses and said, "I've just had three possible responses flit through my head, any one of which would have given us the chance to spend the evening fighting. Or I can just say what I guess I'm about to say. Yes, honey, I did formerly have a different couch in a different room." He went back to reading.

Liz kicked off each of her shoes, trying for height while trying not to hit anything.

"Okay, second attempt. I want to be supportive, but I'm not sure what I'm supporting. If you'd tell me, maybe I could do a better job of it."

"You're supporting the un-messing of my mind."

"And that's helping?"

"Rex's insight that the only one I blame is myself was exactly right. I'm amazed I didn't see it before. Rex tells me if I read all the Gospel red letters ten times, I'll find that I've forgiven myself. All that garbage in my head will be gone."

"Is it helping?"

"This is read number six. The jury's still out."

Liz sighed. She didn't want to interfere with his reading if it was helping him, but because he was reading in her suite, she knew what was going to happen next, and she wanted to get him talking about it well before it actually started so she wouldn't seem to be protesting it.

Most evenings, after he had read the Teacher for awhile, Jack would propose that they do something together. They might cuddle and talk and neck all evening. They might lie naked on her bed and take turns stroking and admiring one another's bodies. One night he proposed strip-poker, but it gave Liz the giggles so they didn't get past the third round before they were helpless with laughter. On a couple of evenings she came back to her suite to find him reading in the buff, and of course then he wanted her naked, too, and sitting naked all evening while each tried to ignore the fact that the other was naked made Liz feel ridiculous.

Actually, she found all of this too strange to be very sexually stimulating.

Sometimes it felt rather cozy and sweet, but all of it was so unlike him that she had thought at first that he was just following some suggestions from Rex. The fact that it had gone on for a month without progressing in any direction was what was making her feel the need to get him to talk about it.

"Darling? Are you about through with reading?"

"Soon. I want to finish John."

"Don't all the Gospels say the same things? I haven't read them in awhile."

"Three are similar. John is a little different."

"Um, well, now—"

"Did you take your bubble bath today?"

"No time. I was working all afternoon."

"Let's take one together. I've never had a bubble bath."

So then Liz could think of nothing else to say.

Her tub was big enough for several people. She could anchor herself by laying her head on a waterproof pillow that she had suction-cupped at one end of it and let her body float beneath the bubbles. She thought it was the absolute release of tension and stress that came from floating like an astronaut in warm space that was most therapeutic about her bubble baths, and the lovely rose aroma and the bubbles just perfected the experience.

Liz had drawn their bath and undressed and put on her terry-cloth robe against the air-conditioned chill, but Jack still hadn't joined her. She went back through her bedroom to see what was keeping him, only to find that he had put down his Bible and picked up a report.

"Ready, darling!" she said cheerily.

"Foundation."

"Is something wrong?"

"I asked them to find situations where funding citizen activists might help solve problems, and here they've just given me fifty pages of no. That's not what foundations do. Milly's foundation just gives away whatever is the minimum to whichever public charities I check on the list they send me each November. I insist they at least make sure all the charities they list meet certain standards. But, come on. American Heart Association? American Cancer Society? PBS? At this point, they're just phoning it in!"

"Oh. Well, you know, bubble baths are good for that. Come on, darling, I need to go to bed early. Spending a whole afternoon with Bobby Ingersoll is exhausting."

Jack put down his report and followed Liz, saying, "He's quite a kid, isn't he? Don't you wonder if there are more like him? Maybe we should go to that reunion after all."

"I thought we already were going? You're just teasing him?"

As soon as they reached the tub, Liz was unbuttoning and removing Jack's shirt and pulling off his T-shirt and unbuckling his belt. She paused when she realized he was watching her face, wearing a bemused expression. When she looked up at him, he said, "I think what I love most about you is things like this. You know I'm being a jerk not to tell you what this is about, but you never say it. Go ahead. You can say it."

She gave him a shy smile. Never in all their years together had she thought for a moment that he was a jerk. Until there was something he wanted to tell her, the truth was she really didn't want to know. He unzipped his own fly, and he finished undressing and took her hand and stepped into the tub.

"Warm enough? Too warm? You can have the pillow!"

"Don't fuss, honey. It's perfect."

He lay down in the bubbles with his head on her pillow, and she cuddled in close under his arm. His feet touched the foot of the tub, but barely.

After a moment, he said, "It wasn't just casual sex that Chuck put me off. As soon as he convinced me she had abused me when I was so young, it was as if a switch flicked in my head." He paused. He was playing with the bubbles a little with his feet. "Clarice thought all I needed was Viagra. I tried Viagra. It didn't help my head." His hand was exploring the curve of Liz's waist, softly stroking her skin. He went on, "Rex thinks all I need to do is forgive myself, but what I really need is to get my sex drive back. I think I'm back to knowing she started when I was thirteen and all that other crap came from Chuck, but still it's hard to forget. I'm trying to replace it with you."

Liz murmured, "Is this helping?"

"It's making me feel closer to you. I appreciate so much the role you've played in my life! There I was, so young and already at the top of the mountain. Little Lizzie walks in and sticks a pin in my bubble. Not a big pin. Just, 'Hi there, you're rich and famous and full of it.' I never noticed how full of it I was until you pointed it out to me." He glanced down at her, lying with her head on his shoulder. When their eyes met, he smiled a little. "I know from seeing other people's relationships that it's hard to find someone who'd love you just as much if you had nothing and were no one. You make me feel as if you'd love me, regardless. It's taken me nearly thirty years to fully understand what a gift that is."

Liz had several responses pass through her mind, affirmations and extensions. None was adequate. She lifted herself in the water enough to kiss his cheek, then settled back in cozily beside him.

He said, "Yes, I think it's working. I'm afraid to even say that. But when the Teacher bludgeons you over the head through four Gospels times six that you're loved and forgiven, little child, don't make it hard when it's easy, it does start to sink in."

The warm, soapy water and lying full-length, skin against skin, his hand stroking her waist, and then on top of that his affirmation of love, all were making Liz feel titillated as nothing else had done in awhile. She said, "So, um, we're allowed to be affectionate?"

"Of course."

313

"Good. Okay. Here goes." She moved up to hover over him and began to stroke and softly kiss his chest above the waterline. His chest hair was wet, his skin smelled like roses, and she was feeling so much need to take this further that she was running a foot up and down his leg without realizing it. She was moving a little. And then more.

He murmured, "Just affection, honey."

She said, still kissing his chest, "Don't worry. We won't, you know, do anything."

He laughed a brief, taut laugh and said, "That's the new pink ribbons, right? The bathwater is now the oil?"

"Oh no! No. I'll stop. Do you want me to stop?"

When he didn't answer her, she settled in beside him again. She tried to keep her body still. Then after a pause, he murmured, "I don't think I want you to stop."

Liz couldn't let this be another mind-game. Pink ribbons and oil. Costumes and blindfolds and props. Jack had a highly suggestible mind, so every new idea worked wonderfully on him. But now, just perhaps, they might be moving past the need for new ideas. She lifted up and began to kiss him tenderly as she stroked his chest and belly above and below the waterline, slowly and softly, thinking about the way his skin felt, the way his mouth felt on hers, and then the pleasure of burying her face in bubbles and the scent of roses as she kissed his neck and shoulder and chest and then swiped the soap away as she went back to kissing him on his face and then again on his lips. She was concentrating on her own tactile joy in appreciating his body, so it surprised her to realize that his breathing had changed. He was lying with his eyes closed and his face sweetly blank, accepting, not responding, but still being affected by what she was doing. So then her legs were appreciating his legs, and the skin of her breasts and belly and thighs had the joy of appreciating the way his skin felt, but all just softly and without any purpose other than the tactile pleasure of it. And, behind that, her fresh awareness that this husband of her soul did love her. Go figure.

He was beginning to respond, but also gently. He was kissing her face, he was stroking her skin, but not close to anything significant. It affected her, though, to have him active, so she couldn't help feeling a purpose to it now. She resisted the feeling. This couldn't be about sex. But he was moving with her more and more, his hands on her body were feeling stronger, and he was kissing her now the way he used to kiss her, as if the kiss itself were a sexual act. So then she couldn't keep from moving, she was hearing his breathing growing harsher, she couldn't keep from whimpering, she wanted to have him inside her, please Jack! But always before at about this point he would shift from mutual arousal to bringing her to orgasm a couple of times before he let her help him come as well. But please, Jack, not this time!

Then his big hands lifted her at her waist and placed her astride him and he was deep inside her, just that easily. Her eyes opened at the surprise of that, then slipped shut, holding the thrill of what Atlanticans called the union. Not two people anymore. Again, one. She was weighing him down against the floor of the tub so she would be doing most of the moving, and none of this could be about sex, it had to be about loving connection, so she moved that way at first, slowly and deeply. Being so in control, she found that with just little shifts she could immensely increase her own pleasure. She went deeper and deeper into concentrating on building the pleasure of it without letting it get past the tipping point. Why had she never known about this? Why didn't everyone do it this way? The intensity was moving beyond exquisite, but yet she was so in control that she was managing to hold off the ending, and still it built. She opened her eyes and found that Jack was deep into it, too, from the tension in his face, but perhaps also fighting it. She whispered, "I think you're all better."

Then she needed to move faster and deeper and more and more and faster and faster, and then her orgasm caught her and she couldn't get her legs together enough so she fell into his arms as she tried to hold it. She could hear that orgasm was happening for him, too. They lay connected for what seemed to Liz to be a long time, with her tight in his arms. But eventually he wasn't inside her anymore, and he lifted her and placed her beside him and cuddled her close and kissed the top of her head. She said, "Was that simultaneous? Do we get a prize? Does Guinness have a category?"

⊰ 33 ⊱

Dennis's bones were mending so well that he began rehab before the end of September. His old casts were off, his legs were in removable walking casts now, and his arms had slings available for when they ached. He had rehab sessions scheduled at ten in the morning and again at three in the afternoon, and most of the family would show up for one or the other session, encouraging Dennis and visiting with one another. On an afternoon four days before the late-October opening of the Free the People demo facility, Liz went down to Dennis's afternoon rehab session, looking for Rex. It seemed to her that in recent weeks Rex had lost interest altogether in his business. Now he was never even there! Liz wasn't sure what he was doing with his time, and when she asked him about it, he simply said, "It's a project. Not ready to talk about it yet."

She asked Jack if he knew what was going on. He would just say, "Rex has some amazing ideas. You're going to be so proud of him, honey!"

So he was working on something else? But now here it was, such a critical time that Bobby and the core of his team were putting in long hours, and Rex hadn't come to the Free the People office even once this week. Liz thought someone from the family should be offering support, so she had spent part of each afternoon there. She wanted Rex to try to make it in tomorrow, which was why she was looking for him today.

Cathy and Sissy were in the gym with the children, sitting and chatting while Dennis practiced walking with two canes. The fact that he had broken both arms made it more difficult for him to learn to walk again using a treadmill or a walker. With platform-based canes, though, he could use each arm independently. Watching his painful early rehab sessions had been so unbearable for Liz that she could be there for just a few minutes at a time, no matter how he kept saying that having company was a welcome distraction. Now, though, he didn't seem to be in pain, and he was making progress every day. This afternoon he was scurrying back and forth in an effort to amuse Milly, who stood gravely beside her mother's knee and watched him. He would come by, stop and bend and whisper or grin or say "Boo!" and then hurry on past while Milly leaned away, eyes wide, and clung more tightly to Cathy's knee. Perhaps at this point she only half-remembered her Uncle Dennis. Her confusion had everyone smiling.

"Where's Rex, sweetie?" Liz said to Cathy.

"He's with Mr. R., I think."

So after watching Dennis for a bit and then waving to him, Liz headed down past the library and up the east staircase. She found Rex standing by the fireplace in Jack's sitting room, while Jack sat on his sofa with one foot on the opposite knee and both arms casually laid along the sofa's back. Liz realized as soon as she emerged from the suite's hallway into afternoon sunlight that she was interrupting something.

"I'm sorry! Not a good time?"

"Come in, honey."

Jack held out his arms to Liz, she folded onto the sofa next to him, and he began to kiss her the way he was kissing her lately, never mind that Rex was standing right there. Their bubble-bath breakthrough seemed to have gotten him past whatever squeamishness he had been feeling. Liz assumed that perhaps Chuck had made him see sex so negatively that he hadn't wanted to sully their relationship with it, or perhaps Liz really had become his attempt at redoing his relationship with Milly, or—sure—maybe what he had needed all along was just to forgive himself. She didn't know what had been going on in his head, but whatever it was, he seemed to have conquered it. He had belatedly discovered sex from a mostly male point of view, so now Liz was basically living in his suite. They were taking frequent bubble baths.

"Dad!"

Jack broke the kiss and looked over at Rex as if he had forgotten he was there. Liz was embarrassed. Jack seemed not to be. He started to say, "If you can't get enough of your wife when you're my—!"

"This is important to me!"

Liz was rearranging herself, giving Jack a little pointed glare, settling appropriately into the curve of his arm with her feet drawn up beside her. She said to Rex, "What's going on, baby? Are you okay?"

Rex was giving them what Liz thought of as his fierce look. When he was deep into thinking about something, even as a child he would have an arresting intensity about his face and demeanor. It looked like anger, but it wasn't anger, although if you got in his way now he could get very angry. He said to Liz, "Why does nobody else even care? The more I learn about this place, the more wrecked I can see it is. But nobody cares? It's like living in your own privy!"

"What—?"

Jack said, "He wants to fix the entire world immediately—"

"It would be fine if people were happy! Sure, be screwed up. Have fun. Enjoy. But everybody here is so miserable! You can't feel them the way I can, so you have no idea how bad it is. Carlson! You've got no idea because he's so good at hiding it, but his wife walked out on him three weeks ago. People do that here?"

"How did you—?"

"I can feel people's emotions, remember? I could feel how upset he was, so I rang for him and asked him to bring up a couple of beers. He's a really decent guy. But everyone I've seen here is in pain! You build all these controls on people's minds, all the governments and religions and rules, and for what? Nobody's happier. All the garbage your people load on themselves only makes all the bad things worse!"

Jack said to Liz, "So we're fixing it."

"All I can think to do is get rid of all the things dividing people. We know at home there's a powerful urge to unite our minds, and I have to believe that's true here, too. They just need to get rid of all the divisions between people so they can even notice they have the urge to unite their minds. Dennis says race and religion. Dad says politics. Politics! There's another whole area of completely futile ridiculous nonsense that apparently your people have thought up because they needed additional reasons to be unhappy!"

Liz said, "Wow."

"You think I can't do it, don't you? I can't do it alone, but what I can do is help people understand they've got choices. No one has to live this way."

Jack added, "And I've got my talent to contribute. Rex tells me he wants whatever money I would be leaving him to be devoted to his clean-up-the-world project. I've told him that means he's got a blank check." Jack sighed and added, "Suddenly all those zeros are looking more appealing to him."

"Sweetie, what you're doing is really important. But, you know, this is a big week next door. Won't you go over tomorrow and give them some moral support?"

"Bobby calls me. He says you're spending time with them? How does it look to you?"

"Bobby's in his element! I had no idea opening a store was so much work. But I guess it's really five stores, right?"

"He says none of us can go to the opening, but he plans to go."

"We're too famous. He's afraid we'll be recognized. He says this is just a demo, so we can fine-tune Dripping Springs and get ready to franchise. But he's excited about it. You can tell! Come in tomorrow, sweetie. Let them see you care."

Rex sighed and said, "He's happier without me there. Dad and I have the same problem. Wherever we show up, we deform the air around us."

———————◆———————

Strange Dogs and Their Masters

Jack Richardson *as told to* Elizabeth Lyons *beneath a tree*

Reclusive billionaire Jack Richardson hasn't sat for an interview since the seventies, so when this reporter was assigned a brief interview with him and his wife at their oceanfront estate, I experienced some sleepless nights. But I needn't have worried. Their home is spectacular and carefully guarded, but I stopped rubbernecking as soon as the door was opened by Elizabeth Richardson herself. She ushered me into a cozily-furnished family room where her husband sat on an overstuffed sofa with his laptop. She offered me a comfortable armchair and settled in close to him with her legs tucked up. He finished typing something, put his arm around her, and greeted me pleasantly. In person, Jack Richardson is a mild and genial man.

Strange Dogs and Their Masters *has the only odd title among* Forbes's Ten Books That Made the Eighties the Eighties. *Where did the title come from?*

Mrs. Richardson said, with a glance at her husband, "We were newly married. He was teaching me what he did for work. He said he bought these strange dogs where all the heads were at odds with one another, and then he had to get control of both the dogs and their masters. That stuck in my mind."

Her husband added, "It made us laugh. A publisher friend was after me to write a book, and I was living on our island so I had the time. We thought we were writing something so ridiculous they'd never print it."

Strange Dogs *has been translated into fourteen languages. It has sold almost four million copies in English alone, it is on the reading lists of many MBA programs, and since its publication in 1981 it has never been out of print. How would its authors sum up their book and its appeal? Richardson said, "It's all Liz. I think in sound bites, but she thinks in jokes. And she sees things from a more poignant angle than most people do. She made it gritty-funny."*

"It's really all Jack," his wife insisted. "I re-read it for this interview. It's the wisest book I've ever read, and not just about business, but about people. He says businesses are really just people, anyway. It's all him! I just made his sentences longer."

Again they smiled at one another.

Mrs. Richardson didn't use her married name in authoring Strange Dogs *because when they wrote it her husband was hiding the fact that he was married. As he explained it to me, "She had led a sheltered life. Taking me on was enough by itself. She couldn't also cope with the fame and complexities of the life I was leading. And we wanted to raise our son out of the spotlight."*

Was the book really written under a tree? Here the Richardsons glanced at one another. She said, "There's a kind of tree on our island that grows like an umbrella, with the branches starting high up and spreading wide. There's one very big umbrella tree on a hill with a spectacular ocean view. We wrote some of it under that tree."

Have they thought about writing a sequel? Here their faces turned more solemn. He said, "They say we've all got one book in us. That's our one."

She said, "We're too busy now. He worked hard for so many years while I lived away, raising our son. Now making one another happy is our full-time job."

On a cold but sunny morning about the first of December, five months after their interview was conducted and a week after they first read the article together, wincing and giggling, Jack sat at his desk while Liz sat on his sofa and he forwarded to her three emails. The first was actually the third email from Public Relations in as many days, each more agitated than the last, so this one was nearly hyperventilating.

> *Sir, now we have nearly 100 interview requests. Will you do TV together? Oprah, Leno and SNL! That's a hat trick! Strongly urge you capitalize on this. We can select and suggest. Pls let us hear from you!*

At about the same time, he also received a cryptic message from his head tax attorney.

> *Jack—Grt Forbes. Do Times WSJ Peopl asap?*

The third email, from the friend who had sold Jack his Gulfstream, had him chuckling a little as he sent it to Liz.

> *Hey, loved the interview. I kept wanting to suggest you get a room.*

⊰ 34 ⊱

People were talking as they came through the doorway. But then each would realize this was one big room, and Rex Richardson was sitting there alone, so an odd silence fell. Nobody seated was talking. It was such a brilliant January day, with the light greatly magnified by new snow, that Rex was wishing they had thought about installing shades on all those windows. Too late now. At least it wasn't snowing! Too much snow might have meant they couldn't make this announcement on this important day.

Right now, today, in only minutes, Rex would be beginning an effort that he knew was going to take the rest of his life. He intended to protect his home-place forever by bringing to all the people of the earth the kind of core-deep joy that was possible only when all human minds were united. Now it began! And it seemed to Rex that he had found a cause that was worth his life.

Using the Free the People facility at Sea Haven for Rex's announcement had been Jack's idea. Rex had wondered about using the Levigard building, but Jack had said that wasn't personal enough. Apparently it felt symbolic to him that this day would be the first time he was opening his home office to the world. They had credentialed eighty-five reporters and cordoned off a press section at the front of the room, including an open area to each side

---

for still and video cameras. Rex had insisted on leaving room at the back for people already working on this project, but no members of the family were here. Seeing Dennis or Jack or Cathy or Liz would have made Rex feel that he was playing to them, so his father had agreed that he should do this alone.

Rex stood off his stool a little early, as the last few reporters were being seated. It felt so good to be doing something! Looking around, smiling at individual faces and getting a few smiles in response, Rex said, "Welcome, everyone! Thank you for being here. I'm Rex Richardson. My father is Jack Richardson. Today is his sixty-fifth birthday. And today we're making an announcement that makes him very happy. Happy Birthday, Dad!"

There was a little ripple of applause, but not much. They were waiting for Rex's announcement. There had been rumors.

"I didn't enter what you think of as the modern world until three years ago. You're used to it. I'm not used to it. I can see that it's broken. I want to help you fix it." Rex was relaxing a bit, feeling buoyed by the thrill of this day. He said, "My father and grandfather have made a lot of money, and money has uses. We intend to use what they've built to end human suffering all over the world. We want to help you build a future in which everyone is free and happy and the world is united in love and peace. We have a big dream! And we have to start somewhere.

"An American hero had his own dream. Nineteen-sixty-three was the hundred-year anniversary of the Emancipation Proclamation that ended American slavery, and that was the year when Martin Luther King told the world his dream was that someday his children would be judged not by the color of their skin but by the content of their character. He was murdered for daring to have that dream. And more than forty years later, his dream still is nowhere.

"My father's childhood friend had a dream, too. His ancestors imported slaves. He wanted to do what he could to fix that, and he died trying to

325

make his dream a reality. So today, in memory of those two heroes and in celebration of my father's sixty-fifth birthday, we announce an initial gift of five billion dollars to the new Steven S. Symington Foundation."

There were murmurs then. That was quite a few zeros.

"We're going to complete Steve Symington's work in a way that we think will help to heal the separations between people in this country, so at last Dr. King's dream can come true. We can't unite this country when people's minds here are so separated. And until the United States is united, we can't even begin to unite the world! So we're announcing today that everyone born between 1990 and 2020 who had an ancestor held in slavery in the United States will receive the best education our money can buy, from kindergarten through graduate school. Steve's foundation will pay for everything, including clothing, tutors, and a car when they need it. Our goal is to give them the same advantages they would have if their parents were rich."

There was a buzzing in the room now. Rex kept going.

"Five billion dollars is not enough. This new foundation is a public charity, and we hope as many people as possible will join us in effecting this healing. That likely still won't be enough. After my grandmother died in 1960, my grandfather established a foundation in her name. We announce today that the more than forty billion dollars in the Millicent Larkin Richardson Foundation and its affiliated trusts will be repurposed to help make this dream happen."

More buzzing. That was a lot more zeros.

"Because we're trying to effect a healing, we won't fund courses that make a separation between people. No religion. No politics. No government. No gender or racial or ethnic studies. No lawyers. Our students can study those things. We just won't fund them.

"We've established a genealogy project. Now we're asking that every parent of a child who might have an ancestor who was held in slavery give us an application, and we'll do the work of proving eligibility. And we're asking today that every successful American consider becoming a mentor to one of our students. These children won't dream what you call the American Dream unless they know someone who has lived it.

"No descendant of our students will be eligible. Once we've educated the parents, we're sure they will be able to provide for their children. And to help them do that, Levigard Holdings, which is one of our companies, will be offering lifetime assistance to any of our students who want to go into business for themselves.

"Our goal is a big one. By 2063, which will be the bicentennial of the Emancipation Proclamation, we want every descendant of American slavery to be independent and empowered. And my personal goal is an absolute end to all the separations between people in this country!

"I'm not planning to take questions now. If you want to interview me, call the Larkin International publicity people. Now let's work together and build a glorious future!"

Rex made a quick bow. He had meant to say more. He couldn't remember it now, though, and the applause went on for so long, with people standing, with whistling and stomping, that he thought that perhaps he had said enough.

The public response to Rex's announcement was not universally favorable. Some people thought there had to be a catch. Liz was astonished and indignant to read some of the irritating things that were being written, but when she complained about it to Jack, he just said patiently, "Why are you surprised? Rich people can't have good intentions, honey, or how did we get to be so rich?"

Liz found especially distressing the fact that some of the most vocal critics of Steve's foundation were civil rights leaders. How was that even possible? One particularly outrageous op-ed in *The New York Times* attacked Steve Symington personally, saying that he was trying to force modern black children back onto the plantations where his ancestors had put their ancestors, and if his foundation really wanted to pay reparations, it should give the money outright and not tell people how to spend it.

Breakfast at Sea Haven was bleak on the morning in March when that op-ed appeared. Nowadays Liz and Jack routinely shared breakfast in his suite, since the children breakfasted in their apartments and beginning the day with eighteen empty chairs felt strange. Jack read the op-ed first, then he folded the paper to display it and passed it to Liz without comment. Since he had said nothing, she also said nothing, but she read it with a rising sense of horror and rage and then tossed it to the floor. She glanced often at Jack's face as he went on with his eating, looking calm and thoughtful. Liz wasn't calm. She was especially outraged to note that the op-ed writer had altogether disregarded the fact that Steve Symington had spent his life trying to help people he thought were descended from slaves, had died in that effort at the age of thirty-three, and had been dead for more than thirty years.

As he was sipping the last of his coffee, Jack said, "What we think doesn't matter. I've been asking myself what Steve would do."

"Do you even know what Steve would do?"

"Unfortunately, yes. Yes, I do."

"And . . .?" she said, when he hesitated, still looking thoughtful.

"Unfortunately, Steve would throw a party and invite every damn self-important racist S-O-B to come here and meet him and vent to him. That's what he'd do."

"Here?"

"Here."

So after having been Jack's intensely private home for more than thirty years, on a Saturday afternoon in July of 2005, Sea Haven opened its gates to fifty-four people flown in from twenty-three states, all put up for the weekend in local hotels and transported back and forth by limousine. Every invited couple had a member who had criticized Steve's foundation, and to everyone's surprise, all the invitees accepted. A chamber orchestra in the library played show tunes. People wandered through elegant public rooms and enjoyed an open bar on the terrace. The only public room off-limits to guests was the drawing room, but its doors were open and blocked by rose-colored ribbons. A man in a white jumpsuit stood at each entrance to explain that the furniture in that room was antique, and too fragile to be used.

Rex refused to attend the reception, and Dennis and the wives respected his wishes. Rex had been so outraged by that op-ed that his position now was that since the family's motives were pure, every critic of Steve's foundation must have a malicious personal agenda. But Liz kept wishing that Rex and the others were there. For more than four hours that afternoon, the house was full of a happy buzz of conversation and considerable soft laughter as old friends caught up with one another and Liz and Jack circulated, welcoming guests and listening. Liz was surprised to find that no one she talked with objected to the Symington Foundation's mission. Even the author of that awful op-ed apologized without apologizing, saying that now that he had seen Steve Symington and heard his story directly from Jack, he could support Steve's foundation. He intended to say so.

There was a large oil portrait of Steve in the library, painted expressly for this day, framed in gold and garlanded with white roses. Jack had taken snapshots during Steve's last visit home. And the portrait based on those photos was such that when it was delivered and set on an easel a few days before the reception, Jack stood for a long time looking at it, holding Liz's hand, smiling, frowning, running a few tears.

Liz had long imagined Steve Symington as a burly, outdoors kind of guy. But it turned out that Steve had been slight of build and only barely five-foot-eleven, with thinning sandy hair and firm, straightforward, hazel-green eyes that had been painted to meet the eyes of the observer. Steve's face in the portrait was at once unremarkable and arresting: Liz thought it was the eyes that struck you. Looking at those eyes, she could imagine that this otherwise ordinary-looking man could have had the grit to live the life he had chosen. Steve had one surviving brother, now in his seventies. Freddie and Barbara Symington spent most of the party standing beside that portrait, chatting about Steve and answering people's questions.

Jack had framed this reception as a social event, so pictures soon appeared on society pages in most of the country's major cities. All of them were captioned with a few words about the Symington Foundation and showed a local couple or two smiling beside their inordinately tall hosts.

Liz had told a number of guests that she thought of this project as a personal tribute to Dr. Martin Luther King. She never mentioned the fact that since she had moved to Atlantica less than eight years after Dr. King's death, and then had lived there for twenty-five years, her knowledge of recent American history was close to nonexistent; so Dr. King's assassination and the riots that followed it still loomed enormously in her mind. Nevertheless, her comment was repeated in so many newspapers over the next few weeks that the Symington Foundation soon adopted "Making the Dream Real For Children" as its slogan. All in all, Steve's party had turned out to be in every way a triumph.

But still, this whole project was Rex's primarily, and he found a number of things upsetting. He was troubled by the public focus on how much money the Symington scholars were going to make. There was speculation that their increased spending would eventually create a more robust economy, but that was so much not the point for him! He was trying to do away with divisions between people, so the last thing he was hoping to do was produce even more divisive money. And Rex was outraged that Jack was allowing the Symington Foundation to refer to these scholarships as slavery reparations, when neither this family nor Steve had had anything to do with slavery. But Jack insisted to Rex that his long-dead friend would have wanted to call this project reparations. And from his first sight of that portrait in the library, it had seemed to Jack that Steve had to be in charge.

Liz soon came to think that his opening Sea Haven to what he had expected would be hostile strangers represented a turning point for Jack. That reception, how-ever much it had been deeply resented and dreaded beforehand, had turned out to be a love-filled celebration of Steve's work still being carried on even three decades after his death. Seeing that, Jack seemed to relax into what Liz knew would be the next phase of their lives. He told her that while it had been fun to make the money, it was turning out to be even more fun to find creative ways to spend it.

<hr/>

Rex showed up in Jack's sitting room one morning toward the end of July. Jack and I had been talking about a honeymoon ever since we were American-married, although neither of us really wanted to travel. What we enjoyed was coming up with unusual potential destinations and play-arguing about them, with always the chance that one of them might click. It was a testament to the fundamental un-seriousness of these discussions that we were still referring to this hypothetical trip as a honeymoon more than two years after our wedding.

The one place I wanted to go was Atlantica. My nieces and their children were there. Jude and Teralagh and so many people I loved and still thought about were there, and except for Jude, I never had said goodbye. I hadn't expected when we left that we never would be in touch again, but Rex was insisting that there be no communication with Atlantica what-soever. Gaprelagh believed that Rex and I were dead, and Rex refused to saddle her with the burden of knowing that against every custom and con-vention of their world, she had remarried while her husband was alive.

Jack seemed not to want to go back, anyway. His attitude toward Atlantica was so complex that for years it hadn't seemed prudent to remind him that he was spending more than a hundred million dollars a year protecting the place where little Milly died. But he was still dealing with the fallout from Rex's interview of the previous year, so now Atlantica was much on his mind. Even if Rex stayed dead, I could turn up alive. We would figure it out. What the heck.

"Why don't we take our honeymoon trip to Atlantica, darling?"

"Outdoor plumbing! That's romantic." He was busy with his emails.

"Well, okay, maybe not a honeymoon. But let's go back sometime, can we?"

"They think you're dead, honey."

"It'll be a miracle!"

"We can't go back until it's safe. They're turning boats away every day now. The State Department may take it over as what they're calling a private protectorate, but we'll need an Act of Congress. We're working on it. We can't go back until—"

Jack stopped talking when Rex appeared in the doorway, looking crestfallen. He came in and dropped onto the sofa beside me and leaned automatically to accept my cheek-kiss, my beautiful, dutiful little boy who is bent on singlehandedly fixing the world. He said to Jack, "Forty-two thousand applicants. Shouldn't there be a lot more, when we're covering fifteen years of births?"

"There will be."

"We've got to start somewhere, sweetie!"

"The problem is, they think it's about slavery. Or money. They have no idea what's possible for them. You've lived where human life works, Mom. Why don't you write a book?"

"She's already written a book." Jack was looking at me, beginning to smile, daring me to show our son those pages I had written on Atlantica a quarter-century before.

"I've written two, actually." Which was news to Jack.

As Ted's yacht was being readied for us on our last Atlantican after-noon, I left Rex with Jude and walked out to Morakan and fetched that wool-wrapped bundle of papers from beneath the table in our house. I left everything else the same, so when people came to clean out the house they would believe my death had been accidental. I began my errand with the thought that I didn't want anyone to find what I had written, but once I had that bundle in hand it felt precious to me. It had been on a shelf in my closet since I moved into Sea Haven. So that afternoon I emailed to Rex in manageable chunks an early version of the book that you are reading now, and I dug out those scraps of paper that I had written for Jack so long ago. The pages weren't in order anymore, and some of them were so faded that their pencil marks were nearly illegible. Jack and I were up that night until past two o'clock in the morning, just figuring out what went where.

It took me two weeks of work and considerable eyestrain to get the first book transcribed. Then Rex surprised me with his own version of this book, including pieces he had written to fill in what he saw as gaps. I didn't email the manuscripts to Jack until a Saturday in September when we had no plans, so I could be there while he was reading.

I soon realized that I needn't have worried. He loved reliving from my point of view the end of what he refers to as his "full of it" phase, even chuckling at things that I thought were not in the very least bit funny. He was far enough away in time that all the things I had thought might upset him didn't faze him. Indeed, the only thing that seemed to bother him in either book was my description of a library in which one wall was all glass.

Jack's actual library has a window-wall on the first floor, but the upper two floors are climate- and humidity- and light-controlled to protect a book collection worth millions of dollars. As a result, that enormous room seems to have just a very tall vault of a ceiling, but unless the walkway lights are on you have little sense of how vast is the void above your head. I wrote this book for my own amusement, so I made the library's glass wall three stories tall to thoroughly let in the light.

Jack was astonished to come across this detail.

"Do you know what that would do to the books? You make me look like a fool for building it that way!"

Eventually we compromised. I wrote that the glass is of a kind that he insists does not exist, and he agreed to let me keep my metaphor for the Atlantican fusion of mind and spirit.

———— • ————

I believe I owe you a postscript here. We finished writing these books years ago! And for me, just writing and polishing them was enough to let me put a bow around the past. They are too personal. I never wanted to publish them, and I find it embarrassing now to re-read them. I'm appalled to see how stubborn my need was for so many years to avoid attempting the joy that always had been possible for me. Don't do that in your life. Trust yourself to grow.

I am still reluctant to go public with our lives, but Rex is becoming ever more determined to single-handedly fix the world, and he thinks our story can help you better understand how much more is possible for you. He is busy now assembling all the Atlantican children's stories we can remember so he can tell the history of the place that he still considers his true home. I wish him well. For my part, all I want to do is spend every minute of the rest of my life enjoying the husband of my soul.

Once Rex manages to persuade his father to allow publication, he is talking about putting our books on the Internet. If you have found them, please know that while we have had to change a few details, in every important way these words are true.

⊸ The End ⊷

⊰ About the Author ⊱

Roberta Grimes is a business attorney who majored in religion at Smith College and then spent decades studying nearly 200 years of abundant and consistent communications from the dead. What she has learned from these communicators about human nature and the nature of reality deeply informs her thinking.

A lifelong writer, Roberta published two novels in the early nineties before work and family intervened. *My Thomas* (Doubleday, 1993 BOMC QPB) is a well-researched account of Thomas Jefferson's beautiful marriage. *Almost Perfect* (Berkley, 1992) is a 1980's coming-of-age novel, later retitled *Rich and Famous*. Both were reissued by Wheatmark in 2014.

Roberta began thinking about the Letters From Love Series in the seventies, when she wrote a first draft of *Letter from Freedom*. Although that story comes first in time, each novel in the series is independent and they can be read in any order. Over the next ten years, four more novels will complete this half-millennium saga.

Roberta blogs and answers questions at robertagrimes.com.

THE LETTERS FROM LOVE SERIES

LETTER FROM WONDER
Preview

⚔ 1 ⚔

The swelling stress that Rex always felt as he waited for these gates to open was eased a bit by his fresh awareness that he would not be living here much longer. All the complexities of his eagerness to see Cathy and their children after a week away, his need to deal with his parents' issues, and the plain shock of this real estate would generally produce in him a feeling that mixed eager butterflies with nauseous dread.

And this car! Rex hated limousines. Before he began what had become half a decade of commuting to Texas, Rex had happily driven himself around Connecticut in an off-the-lot Hummer. Now, though, all his local trips were back and forth to the airport in Cathy's limousine, which was seven years old but so lightly used that its cherry-wood and dark-blue leather interior still looked and smelled brand-new. Cathy had fallen into this car when the conversion company that Rex thought of as his father's limo-pusher had convinced Jack that mere armor-plating was insufficient in these uncertain times, and he had to have a car that was vacuum-sealed against a possible chemical attack. The new one was cranberry red with an ivory interior. Rex could not imagine what Jack had been thinking. So now the gorgeous stainless-steel model that had been Jack's first million-dollar car was being used to transport Rex's children.

In Texas, Rex drove an F-250 crew cab that he had bought lightly used at the Free the People facility ten miles from his east Texas ranch. He hated riding in limousines, the boredom and the lack of control and the fact that his family's cars were the only stretch Bentleys he ever saw on the highway. He kept the partition down because Clark was a friend, but Rex's father forbade conversations while chauffeurs were driving family members, so if Rex said anything, Clark would bring the car to a stop before answering him. On some of these rides he used to text with Cathy, and he routinely texted "I luv u" to let her know he had landed, but lately she was too busy with the baby even to check her phone.

Just as Rex was having that thought, his cellphone rang. Bobby Ingersoll was Rex's cousin, and he had obligingly taken Rex's place in learning to manage a forty-billion-dollar financial empire. In recent years Bobby had become what amounted to Rex's dutiful and indulgent older brother.

"Be there in a minute," Rex said into his phone.

"Thought you should know you're in the shitter again. Not that you care. Papa's new bag is – "

"Tell him I'm sorry, but I got a great story for him out of it. Just coming through the gates now."

""We've gotta lower the axe, twinkles. Your punishment is you're getting your own plane. I'm ordering it as we speak. Any preference as to trim colors? Shit. Says here it doesn't qualify for Amazon Prime."

Bobby had lately begun calling Rex some variant of "twinkletoes." Rex had no interest in knowing why. The three of them spent their weekday mornings working in Jack's sitting room, so Bobby was playing this for Rex's parents. Rex could envision Jack's face, grim with his resolve to maintain his anger until Rex could get there and be chewed out, but now smiling a little at Bobby's joke. Liz sitting on the sofa, smiling with Jack, wanting him to go easy on their son but always siding with her husband.

Rex knew that his mother loved him and loved his children, but what mattered most to her was his father. And it had occurred to him two weeks ago as Liz blew out her sixty-four candles that Jack would be turning seventy-one in January. Atlanticans interacted so easily with their dead that death seemed not to matter there, but in this benighted place death was an ending. Rex had realized as he watched his parents, alone even in the midst of family, smiling covertly at one another as they enjoyed their private world, that he ought to start teaching his mother how to converse with the dead, just in case.

Rex said to Bobby now, "Tell him I'm fine and I'll be there in three." Then he added under his breath for what was probably the millionth time, "Thanks, bro. Put it on my tab." Rex and his father loved one another, but each found the other so inexplicable that adding Bobby between them as a translator had immensely improved their relationship.

Beyond those wrought-iron gates was the whole expansive vista of Sea Haven, with the house at the end of its long driveway. That house was five hundred feet from end to end and three and a half stories tall, so massive that it blocked the ocean view that dimly sparkled beyond the edge of its roof.

This property was two hundred acres in size, with a quarter of a mile of frontage on Long Island Sound. It had recently been appraised for gift purposes at two hundred and twenty-one million dollars. The family was being advised to buy up at least another hundred acres and demolish all the buildings, including all of Sea Haven, the thirty thousand square feet of main house and office, the staff buildings, the garage, the greenhouse, and the pony stable. Once it was fully permitted as an exclusive golf and boating resort, three hundred acres of land in this spot could be worth as much as half a billion dollars.

Rex had lived until he was twenty-three on a private island in the South Atlantic because his billionaire father had wanted him to have a carefree childhood. So until he was grown, Rex had been so completely isolated from American life that he had come to the States nine years ago with no notion of time, no understanding of money, not even any concept of ownership. He had come from a place where people lived in absolute freedom of mind, and in such fundamental spiritual unity that the society on that tiny island had been joyously stable for four hundred years. Atlantica was twenty miles from end to end and eight miles wide at its widest point. Rex was reluctantly coming to see that it was the only place on earth where there were truly happy people.

The accident of his having been born to a reclusive billionaire and a woman intimidated by her husband's wealth had bought Rex the gift of spending the first twenty-three years of his life in what he saw as perfection. But then, nine years ago, New York had suffered a terrorist attack on the World Trade Center towers. Atlantica had long been well-protected by a mercenary navy, and for a couple of decades that had been enough to make Rex's father feel safe when he was there. But Jack was becoming more security-conscious, and that terrorist attack had been his wake-up call. So Rex and his mother had joined Jack here, and Rex had suffered the shock of learning that Atlantica was not the entire world. Soon thereafter had come his realization that unless he could elevate all the people on earth to the Atlanticans' level of mental development, the home that he loved could not long survive. So that was when Rex had embarked upon this urgent quest to fix the world while somehow maintaining who he was, which was a daily battle even nine years later.

The Labor Day weekend was only beginning, but already gardeners in dark-green jumpsuits were ripping out the multicolored floral borders along both sides of the driveway and planting thousands of yellow chrysanthemums. Rex's father loved yellow chrysanthemums.

There were always between fifty and a hundred people working at Sea Haven, day and night, not including the staff of Free the People, which was Rex's auto services company that his father had hoped would inspire him to become a next-generation business mogul. Rex wanted to give Free the People to Bobby. So far, Jack was nixing that idea.

Half of those on staff here were security, wearing brown jumpsuits as they patrolled the woods at both sides of the estate or piloted seven white cabin cruisers. Rex traveled with security, too. Their plain black Cadillac peeled off to the right as soon as it cleared the gates, since the security break-room was attached to the garage. Rex didn't need bodyguards here because the whole estate was double-fenced, with ten-foot-high black wrought iron to the inside and chain link topped with razor wire to the outside. Toward the ocean the estate was open, but those white boats were always patrolling. Jack had gradually come to feel that the patrol boats were not enough, however, so a set of motion detectors had lately been installed along the whole beach frontage, and now they had to be disabled whenever Rex's children wanted to swim.

In front of the house's main portico there was a circular formal garden. This house was so vastly oversized that its front door and the fountain that was centered in the garden seemed to be only nicely proportioned until your car entered the driveway loop. Then you realized that the dark-green raised-panel door and the fountain were enormous. The door measured twelve feet tall by six feet wide, and the graceful marble maiden who was most of the fountain had to be fifteen feet tall. She was a Grecian lady who was awkwardly draped: one breast and one leg to the waist were bare. She was gesturing with palm upraised toward the children's riding park while her classical face seemed to be deep in a thoughtful conversation. Her left hand held an urn that had tipped while her attention was diverted, so water was endlessly spilling out. It didn't seem to Rex to be much of a fountain, but it was an eighteenth-century French masterpiece so fragile that the cost to move it was going to be more than a million dollars.

Rex's family had its own apartment and its own entrance. Normally Clark would proceed around the circle and open Rex's door by the walk that led to his family's elevator lobby. By the time they were rounding the fountain, Rex would be suppressing a grin, almost already feeling Cathy in his arms as Clark opened his car door. Now, though, Rex was sulkily texting, "Dad but home asap" to his wife.

This house's front door was so heavily armored that it weighed more than a ton. It had to be moved hydraulically, and the lever that did that was on the inside. Over time, Rex had become so irritated about having to ring the doorbell of what was theoretically his own home that whenever he was planning to use the front door, Clark would phone the house as their car passed the gates. He must have overheard Rex on the phone. As Rex glanced at it, the front door was opening.

———◆———

Rex had meant to bound up the east staircase and jolly his father out of his annoyance so he could hurry over to be with his family, but even before he was through the door he could hear the Silvestris drumming in the ballroom. And they were doing an appalling job. Without thinking, Rex began to stride briskly, and then he half-ran down the west first-floor hallway.

On Atlantica, drumming nicely filled every entertainment niche. It was major league baseball, movies and rock music, symphonies and television and Broadway plays: in that tiny world it was an obsession, and those who could do it well were stars. Jack listened only to classical music, but he had come to love Atlantican drumming. The fact that seven drummers could play together pieces as complex and engaging as a symphony had fascinated him. That they did it by melding their minds intrigued him. He had encouraged his son to learn to be a drummer, and by the time Rex abruptly left that world he had become the leader of what was said to be the best team of Atlantican drummers in memory.

"You're thinking, little bud! Stop thinking!" Rex called as he rounded the corner through the ballroom doorway, grabbed up his gloves from the table by the door, and hopped up onto his own drum's platform.

Atlantican drumming was work. Dennis and Sissy were red-faced and sweating; Sissy's hair lay in strands against her cheeks. They both stopped drumming in mid-stroke and grinned at Rex.

"Show us how, buddy," Dennis called to him indulgently.

But these were such crappy drums! On Atlantica, drums were five or six feet tall. They were slow-burned out of hardwood logs that were typically three feet across. Their ponyskin leathers were precisely stretched and cured: just making the drum-skins was an art. These little two-foot-thick pine logs had been burned out with a blowtorch, and commercially-tanned horsehide was not Atlantican ponyskin. No attempt had been made to tune these drums, which meant that playing real music was impossible. Rex pulled on his gloves. He couldn't drum without gloves now because back home he had developed the appropriate calluses, so here when his hands and body just automatically did what they always had done, he found drumming painful.

The gold-leafed walls and ceiling of this ballroom had been padded to muffle sounds and to protect the murals so Rex's children could play in here, but still Rex knew that his parents would hear him drumming. Cathy, above them, would hear him, too. He could really drum, while Dennis and Sissy made noise. Cathy would patiently understand, but Jack was going to see Rex's need to spend a few minutes with his friends as an irritating show of disrespect. However, this was important to Rex. He had only lately realized that one of the best mind-strengthening exercises that existed in all the earth was the deep connection among minds that was essential to Atlantican drumming.

Rex tried a quick finger-trill. One problem with horsehide was that it couldn't hold its tension like Atlantican ponyskin, and this skin already needed tightening. He played a quick range, knuckles and palms and heels.

It would have to do. The drums that they were building in Texas using California redwood logs and ponyskins that Rex was preparing himself were going to be whole worlds better than these.

He said, "Okay. Sis, you were leading, right? Now I'm leading." He paused. "I'm thinking a tune." He paused again. "Can you feel it? Sis?"

Sissy had developed considerably more Atlantican mind-sensitivity than her husband. While sometimes Dennis was able to drum, he had trouble sufficiently quieting his thoughts.

Sissy's eyes were closed. Her face was tranquil. She was five-foot-three at best, a pert little woman with fake-blond hair, but the higher platform on her middle drum made her almost as tall as Rex. Dennis was five-foot-ten, so his drum had a lower platform than hers; Rex was six-foot-five, so his drum had the least platform height of all. Before Rex had taken up drumming back home, drummers had stood on whatever tables or benches were near whichever drums they happened to be playing at the moment. Rex had figured out what was the precise relationship between the top of the drum and the drummer's waist that produced the most effective sound, so now nearly all Atlantican drums had platforms tailored to the heights of their drummers. Rex was pleased that he had left them that gift.

Sissy was starting to smile. She said, "Go."

Atlantican drumming required such arm-strength that very few women were drummers back home, and Atlantican women were tall and lean and robust from living outdoor lives. That this little mite of an American woman could drum at all was amazing to Rex. That she had developed sufficient mind-sensitivity to yield her body to him was astounding.

He began. It was just a little easy tune of the sort they used to play while people were eating supper, before they moved on to the complex and glorious dancing drum-work that had been Rex's bliss. At home he had been able to play seven pairs of hands at once, but even playing two pairs was thrilling. He began to grin as he heard her hands doing what his mind was directing them to do, even despite the crappiness of these drums.

"Can you feel it, little bud?" Rex called to Dennis.

Rex had been a drum-leader for so long that he was used to keeping the tune going while a part of his mind let him speak to one drummer. Dennis was tentatively starting in, but he was doing it himself; he was a full beat behind. "Don't think! Feel!" Rex called to Dennis as he spotted Carlson in the doorway.

Jack's butler was a good friend of Rex's who had spent many hours drinking beers and telling stories and opining about life at Rex's kitchen table. Like Clark, he became a different man when on duty, and now there he stood in the ballroom doorway in his black-tie uniform, looking solemn. Rex sighed as he stepped back off his drum. He went to grab Dennis into a hug, touched Sissy's arm as he came back past her, called over his shoulder to Dennis, "Don't think!" and followed Carlson out the door.

CPSIA information can be obtained at www.ICGtesting.com
Printed in the USA
BVOW05s1342220315
392677BV00001B/5/P

9 781627 870542